Praise for John Marks's *Fangland*

"[John] Marks melds the go-for-the-jugular world of TV news, keen knowledge of the Eastern bloc (the scenes in Romania are to die for) and a much-beloved tale for a nifty and engaging flourish that provides a crisp twenty-first-century take on an old favorite. With teeth."

—*The Baltimore Sun*

"*Fangland* is the rare real thing: a novel about a monster that evokes all the sadness, brutality and hideous glamour of human depravity. It's about the abyss, and the big hole in lower Manhattan, and the strange, dark, funny stuff in each of us. It'll grab you and not let go until it's done with you."

—Audrey Niffenegger, author of *The Time Traveler's Wife*

"In this remarkable book, Marks has brought the epistolary novel into the twenty-first century. Just as Bram Stoker fabricated dozens of diary entries, articles, letters and other documents to give *Dracula* an air of authenticity in 1897, Marks has created a vast array of journals and e-mails and used the cast and setting of *The Hour*, a thinly disguised *60 Minutes* television newsmagazine, to give *Fangland* a forceful presence in the present day. . . . Don't expect your garden variety vampire novel here. *Fangland* is a shocking, original and literary masterwork."

—*Rocky Mountain News*

"*Fangland* is a novel that will keep you up late: It's sad and terrifying and darkly funny." —*BookPage*

"An unforgettable reimagining of *Dracula* for the twenty-first century. It takes a rare talent to make a seductive, perhaps even murderous female protagonist into a symbol of a strong modern woman, but John Marks has done just that. Ambitious, career-minded, yet vulnerable, Evangeline Harker is the anchor to an equally ambitious and powerful novel."

—Mitch Cullin, author of *Tideland* and *A Slight Trick of the Mind*

PENGUIN BOOKS

FANGLAND

John Marks is a critically acclaimed author and former *60 Minutes* producer. His fiction includes *The Wall*, named a Notable Book of 1998 by the *New York Times*, and *War Torn*, named one of the best novels of 2003 by *Publishers Weekly*. His most recent book is *Reasons to Believe: One Man's Journey Among the Evangelicals and the Faith He Left Behind*. He lives with his family in Massachusetts.

FANG LAND

John Marks

PENGUIN BOOKS

PENGUIN BOOKS

Published by the Penguin Group
Penguin Group (USA) Inc., 375 Hudson Street, New York, New York 10014, U.S.A.
Penguin Group (Canada), 90 Eglinton Avenue East, Suite 700, Toronto,
Ontario, Canada M4P 2Y3 (a division of Pearson Penguin Canada Inc.)
Penguin Books Ltd, 80 Strand, London WC2R 0RL, England
Penguin Ireland, 25 St Stephen's Green, Dublin 2, Ireland (a division of Penguin Books Ltd)
Penguin Group (Australia), 250 Camberwell Road, Camberwell,
Victoria 3124, Australia (a division of Pearson Australia Group Pty Ltd)
Penguin Books India Pvt Ltd, 11 Community Centre,
Panchsheel Park, New Delhi – 110 017, India
Penguin Group (NZ), 67 Apollo Drive, Rosedale, North Shore 0632,
New Zealand (a division of Pearson New Zealand Ltd)
Penguin Books (South Africa) (Pty) Ltd, 24 Sturdee Avenue,
Rosebank, Johannesburg 2196, South Africa

Penguin Books Ltd, Registered Offices:
80 Strand, London WC2R 0RL, England

First published in the United States of America by The Penguin Press,
a member of Penguin Group (USA) Inc. 2007
Published in Penguin Books 2008

1 3 5 7 9 10 8 6 4 2

Excerpt from *The Odyssey* by Homer, translated by Robert Fagles. Copyright © Robert Fagles,
1996. Used by permission of Viking Penguin, a member of Penguin Group (USA) Inc.

PUBLISHER'S NOTE
This is a work of fiction. Names, characters, places, and incidents are either the product
of the author's imagination or are used fictitiously, and any resemblance to actual persons,
living or dead, business establishments, events, or locales is entirely coincidental.

ISBN 978-1-59420-117-2 (hc.)
ISBN 978-0-14-311253-2 (pbk.)
CIP data available

Printed in the United States of America
Designed by Stephanie Huntwork

To Trevor

Contents

And once my vows and prayers had invoked the nations of the dead,
I took the victims, over the trench I cut their throats
And the dark blood flowed in—and up out of Erebus they came,
Flocking toward me now, the ghosts of the dead and gone . . .
Brides and unwed youths and old men who had suffered much
And girls with their tender hearts freshly scarred by sorrow
And great armies of battle dead, stabbed by bronze spears,
Men of war still wrapped in bloody armor—thousands
Swarming around the trench from every side—
Unearthly cries—blanching terror gripped me!
I ordered the men at once to flay the sheep
That lay before us, killed by my ruthless blade,
And burn them both, and then say prayers to the gods,
To the almighty god of death and dread Persephone.

◆ HOMER, *The Odyssey*

To Whom It May Concern:

First, as happy prelude to an otherwise grim prospect, thanks are in order. I know that I speak for everyone on the committee when I say that my gratitude to Ed Saxby knows no bounds. His unshakable confidence took Omni Corp through the most difficult period in my forty years in broadcast journalism. While most news divisions no longer exist in the form that they did, we have managed to survive the crash of the old model that, God bless it, gave so many of us our vacation homes, our summers in France and our kids' educations. At some cost, we have survived. Ed's shrewd reimagining of first principles, and his uncanny business sense, allied to a vision for our future in an era when the concept of "news" no longer corresponds to traditional definitions, allowed us to endure as one competitor after another folded in the face of financial pressures, legal entanglements, and, in the case of our great rival, to near inexplicable management errors. I would say that Ed is to be congratulated, but that seems small beer. He deserves a tribute, and so the following document, generated in the spirit of the 9-11 Commission Report on the Terrorist Attacks of September 11, 2001, as he requested, is dedicated to him.

. . .

My methodology is simple enough. While I worked in the inquisitive and nonpartisan spirit of the 9-11 Commission Report, I chose an alternative narrative strategy. That report runs in a single line, and is, in a very real sense, an heir to the great novels of realism of the nineteenth century, a Tolstoyan account of calamity. This realism is based on a surplus of documents and images that give grainy detail to the most obscure corners of the story. I had no such luxury. While there are documents in our case—quite disturbing ones—and while, in some respects, I found those documents adequate to the chronicling of these events, on the whole, the gaps in our knowledge are quite profound. It made much more sense for me to quilt this story, if you will, using swatches of clear, available information, which flavor the larger circumstances with a sense of reality; snatches of the e-mails and journals, bits of transcript and relevant memoranda. In the interests of full disclosure, I must confess that I also used my personal knowledge of personalities and places. For a period in the 1980s, I was employed as a producer at *The Hour,* where I came to know many of the people who later became involved in the debacle, and, more to the point, perhaps, I had a business relationship with Ms. Evangeline Harker, whom I employed for a year as a personal assistant before Austen Trotta hired her away to be an associate producer at *The Hour.* The available documents and these personal relationships form the basis of my interpretation of events.

In the end, you must draw your own conclusions about the success of this enterprise. But before you read this document for yourselves, and I suggest that you do, right away, I must deeply and honestly apologize for making one last decision without going through the usual channels of consultation and discussion. And I'm more than sorry that this document must be accompanied by the news of that decision. Ed, in particular, deserves better. But after a long season of horror and sorrow, I simply became exhausted. I think you will see that I've concluded matters in such a way that no disrepute falls upon Omni. Please do not approach my family with either help or inquiry. All their earthly cares have been addressed.

Yours Truly,
James O'Malley,
Senior Vice President for Business Affairs,
Omni News & Entertainment Network

BO OK

The Change Agent

One

How to begin this account? I must be quick and arbitrary. On the eve of my departure for the east of Europe, Robert proposed. We marry in early summer of next year. The church will be Saint Ignatius Loyola, the reception will be at Wave Hill. As soon as I get home, we must launch the long campaign to make sure that the event comes off in a civilized manner. Neither family must end up feeling alienated, defeated or enraged. We do have a numbers issue. With a maximum occupancy of one hundred fifty people at the reception, I have already begun hostile negotiations over the guest list, operating on a principle inherited from my mother that those who are not married may not bring guests to weddings. No ring, no bring, as she says.

Discussions about music, food and vows must be had. Robert wants jazz standards, I prefer a honky-tonk band from Austin. Here is one of those moments when my Texas upbringing seems a clear nuisance, even an embarrassment, to him. Most of the time, he takes quite the opposite approach, using my relatively exotic heritage as a daughter of oil to great effect at dinner parties. Food, of course, will be a source of contention. As a much-lauded *patissier* in one of the city's finer kitchens, he has tabled discussion of wedding cake specifics and exercises kitchen despotism when I try to broach the subject. He's ruled out smoked meat of any kind, despite my express wish to have brisket and ribs shipped up from my favorite central Texas BBQ shrine for the rehearsal dinner. Even now, four thousand miles from New York City, my mind reels with the number of swords that will have to be crossed between now and next June. His family, the most secular Jews I have ever known, have suddenly become outraged by the prospect of a church wedding, while my family, completely lacking in faith, whisper of the conversion option. But in light of my present circumstances, I should dwell on the good; it's all extremely good. It's lovely, in fact.

Robert took me by surprise. We'd gone to Sammy's Roumanian, where we had our first date, and he asked the keyboardist to play "San Antonio Rose" on behalf of his Texan lady friend. The keyboardist made a spirited attempt. We ate a greasy bowl of chopped liver and had those pan-fried steaks with the long bones jutting out, so the meat resembles an axe. It was a generally happy meal, though we did have a moment of tension over a box of gifts that he had recently brought me from Amsterdam. Let's just say that it was a batch of bed wear the likes of which I have never seen and would never have chosen myself, including one contraption made of a material more typically associated with horseback riding. I voiced some slight though playful surprise at this sudden development, at which Robert became sullen and said that he would send the entire Amsterdam batch back across the Atlantic by air mail, forget he'd ever done it: the whole thing was a horrible mistake. I felt bad. The subject was dropped.

Over egg creams, he asked me if I was anxious about Romania. I told him that I had had an unsettling nightmare involving a Price Waterhouse report about Transylvania. In my dream, I scanned line after line, and every line was the same, "MISSING REPORTED IN ALL MAJOR CITIES." He suggested that I might be giving too much credence to national stereotypes, and I replied that I hadn't a clue what stereotype might correspond to Romania. As if in response, he pulled out a small, light blue box.

I knew, but could it be true? I opened in suspense. The ring flashed, a pear-cut diamond set in 24-karat white gold. I gave my answer. Sammy whispered into his microphone, "One Goy, One Hebe, One Love." Everyone clapped. I cried. Robert had a car waiting, and we went back to my apartment, where I packed a few things, including the least offensive of the Amsterdam batch, and then on to the Maritime

Hotel. He knows me. I like nothing better than to wrap my newly showered self in a terrycloth robe, open a mini-bar bottle of Grey Goose and watch a Hollywood action movie on pay television. After three years on the meager salary of an associate producer at *The Hour,* that is my idea of sweet sin.

The following Monday, seventy-two hours later, I flew to Romania. I didn't sleep on the plane, thanks to turbulence. I had an unusual number of inventory problems, I later found. Out of a pack of five legal pads, half had vanished en route. But who would steal legal pads from luggage? All but one of my ballpoints had run dry. I shook the pens, scrawled them across every available surface, and got nothing but ghost marks. The Internet connection in the Bucharest hotel worked, but the modem in the company laptop wouldn't boot. I didn't bring enough tampons. I should have brought my own toilet paper.

My ring is a solace, but it should have stayed in America. Shadowy types haunted the lobby of the hotel, the airport. Before customs, I turned the engagement band upside down, so the stone couldn't be seen, but the customs officer studied my finger, as if I had tried to deceive him. After that, I slipped the ring into my front pants pocket. Robert begged me to leave it home, but I didn't listen. It's not something that I like to admit, but I could not bear to be parted from my ring. I can't help myself. Robert would be surprised to hear this sort of talk. He assumes, because I grew up with wealth, that the ring has less power to impress, but that couldn't be further from the truth. This gem signified that I now belong to something larger than myself, to a community of two, and when I think about that, everything else recedes, and I see back through the generations, to distant people contained in my blood, to the Venetians and Dubliners on my mother's side, to my father's complicated heritage, in particular. Two separate branches of his family line fought against each other in the last uprising of native Americans on U.S. soil, Creek Indians related to his grandmother battled a party of U.S. marshals, one of them kin to his grandfather. And yet, decades later, here they all are in one family, in one person, and I see that reconciliation in my ring, and think about what old and bloody, now-resolved family secrets of his own Robert will bring into mine, and of the children to come, and of how their children may one day look back at our very ordinary lives. Robert might be concerned for me if he heard these private thoughts, so I haven't shared them. As my father says, it's wise to keep your own counsel on the deep matters of life.

Two

How to describe my first impressions of Romania? That's my job, in fact: to gain first impressions. As an associate producer for the most successful news show in American television history, I find stories suitable for broadcast, and I vet those stories for substance and entertainment value. One of my colleagues calls me a soft news samurai. I use my judgment as a knife to separate the potential piece from the passing fancy. A story may very well be true, but if it cannot be told well on camera, the truth hardly matters. In this case, I had been asked to meet a gentleman by the name of Ion Torgu, a Romanian believed to be a major figure in Eastern European organized crime. It was a three-pronged assignment. Confirm his identity. Assess his claims. Judge his appeal. It mattered profoundly whether or not he spoke English. Like the American people, my show abhors subtitles.

I had to think ahead. If the story gained traction, we'd be back soon with crews. I had to scout out locations—we'd need establishing shots of Romania, images that could be used to illustrate points about the culture, the economy, politics, the past. As the fug of a bad flight wore off, I studied the view out the car window. At first, the road could have been anywhere in eastern Europe—familiar brands from the world of international commerce, Coca-Cola, Cadbury, Samsung, decks of capitalist cards fanned across developing tracts of ex-Communist land, rooted in the beds of construction sites that looked freshly cleared, newly bulldozed. A horse and wagon pulled in front of a Coca-Cola sign, a vision of a laughing, bikini'd girl raising a bottle above a bearded man with reins in his hand, regarding the traffic with distinct unease. A key shot, I thought, contrasting old and new Romania. I shorthanded it in my notebook.

It was ten or so in the morning, and the September air churned with exhaust. The driver rolled his window down and lit a cigarette. The airport road gave way to a boulevard running through dense clusters of lime and linden trees through which I glimpsed yellow walls encircling old villas. I saw a cupola with shattered windows, a line of fat black birds breaking from the roof. A graffiti swastika crept bug-armed up a wall. A woman beat a rug against a curb, and our fender almost caught her. She cursed the driver, he cursed back. The boulevard fed into a traffic circle beneath a version of the Arc de Triomphe in Paris; it was three times as big as the original, like a mutant mushroom spawned in the heat. A pack of haggard dogs roved in the shade of the stone. I shorthanded another note—the animals usable as an image of social deterioration. Every idea required its picture. Say cow, see cow. Through the trees ahead, golden metal glimmered, the gilded curves of Orthodox church domes, and we headed into a more charming district of furbelowed windows and mansard roofs. Romania had once been considered the Paris of the east, and there were expensive boutiques, and beautiful women entered them. My all-male camera crew would appreciate the opportunity, and I would get surplus documentation of long legs and high breasts. Before long, these visions of loveliness dissolved in construction dust behind us, and we crossed the concrete banks of a river and turned into a warren of dictator-built tenements. We drove through one section, rounding a corner past a wide circle of bare concrete, and I received a shock. I sat up in my seat. At first, I thought that the jet lag played a trick on my eyes.

The thing looked like a mirage, or like the kind of object that gets distorted in a rearview mirror. It was the dictator's old palace, unfinished at the time of his death, a gigantic marble rectangle seated on a glob of earth. It seemed too vast to be practicable. I couldn't guess how many rooms. I scribbled an instruction to my future crew. The size of the palace wouldn't be possible to convey from below. You'd have to get up high. You'd have to hire a goddamn helicopter. It was now the seat of the democratically elected Romanian government, but the structure itself, four-sided, each side as deep and long as every other side, dwarfed the idea of parliaments and parties and prime ministers. At the end of the road in front of the palace, the car pulled across a traffic circle and into the curved driveway of a much smaller building, which was nevertheless massive. I would be staying across the street from the palace.

"Your accommodations," my otherwise silent driver explained to me, seeing some alarm in my eyes. "It was Defense Ministry before."

Gold-braided and crimson-uniformed ushers took my bags and led me into a marble lobby that might have been the interior of the world's largest mausoleum. The ceiling vaulted four stories, upheld by columns the size of cottages. Beyond the columns were two spiral staircases of marble, leading like water slides to second and third stories where piano music tinkled and presumed guests whispered. A small army of panicked retainers moved around the lobby floor, pushing and pulling at people and things, while others were more watchful, dressed in dark suits, holding walkie-talkies to their lips, pressing headsets to their ears. Before I reached the front desk, a slinking young woman in a slitted red gown held up a tray of glass flutes, my complimentary orange juice or champagne. It was not yet noon, but I took champagne. I lifted the flute in a toast.

She was young, maybe a teenager. Men in the lobby followed her with their eyes; they took me in as well. I'm a long woman, reasonably curvy. A boyfriend once attempted a compliment by telling me I had an earth mother's body, but I resented the notion, suggesting as it did hippie chicks who go braless in tie-dye T-shirt dresses. I'm no earth mother, but the body works, if I do say so. I have dark curly hair that I blow straight every morning, so most people don't even know it kinks. I have dark brown eyes, which my mother used to compare to chocolate drops, longish eyelashes, and a serious upper lip, which I used to be self-conscious about. Everyone tells me that I should try for a position as an on-air correspondent. The camera loves me, I'm told. But I don't trust cameras. I don't like the steady gaze of anything, man or machine.

The girl in the gown stared at me with eyes of sorrow. I handed the empty flute glass back to her. Thank God, I thought, I would not stay long in that place.

I slept through the day, and in the evening, called my superior, the producer William Lockyear, to confirm my arrival. I confessed to Lockyear that I was on edge. He met my words with a length of amused silence and then said, "Try a month in Iraq. Then we'll talk."

I should say something about this man, William Lockyear, my boss. He behaves like overthrown royalty, and I'm his one remaining subject, the servant wench who can never quite work up the nerve to confront him. He considers me a feckless little rich girl, killing time before marriage and babies.

I rebelled, foolishly. "Would you like me to find a story for you in Iraq, Bill? Shall we meet in Baghdad?"

"Will you still have a job when you get back to New York? These are difficult questions."

I cast the blame elsewhere. "Stim's got me paranoid."

I was referring to my friend and production associate Stimson Beevers who had been jealous of my trip. Stim scolded me before I left. He told me that I was thin-skinned, and that my negative feelings about Lockyear reflected burnout, and he's half right: professional burnout mixed with a euphoria related to my engagement. I had fought to get out of this assignment.

On the morning of my departure, the Monday after Robert proposed, I broke my marriage plans to Lockyear. I explained to him that I now had to make wedding arrangements, extensive ones, and suggested very delicately that he might like to fly to Romania in my place. After congratulations, he told me that my wedding plans had nothing whatsoever to do with our professional relationship, that it was unwise for me to ask him to do my job, and there were plenty of unencumbered young people in the office who would be more than happy to fly to Romania on his behalf. I came close to quitting. My two confidantes, Stim and my dear friend Ian, counseled reason. Ian reminded me that this was vintage Lockyear, and I shouldn't take it so personally. Stim told me that a story set in Romania would be an opportunity to steep myself in the one-hundred-year history of the vampire genre in movies. That made me laugh. Stim stews in movies. He thinks that morality is loving Sam Peckinpah and eating salted edamame. He doesn't grasp death beyond celluloid. He thinks that no real difference exists between the actual country of Romania and vampire movies set in Romania. I call him the Over-Stim.

"Wait a minute." Lockyear cupped the phone with his hand. Obviously, someone had just walked into the room. I heard a muffled commotion. Lockyear got back on the line. "Another of your little friends, the boy wonder, Ian. I told him everything, and he has advice about listening to Stimson Beevers."

I was glad to hear Ian's voice.

"Hey there, Line."

"Help me, Ian."

"Stim is a complete dick. You'll be fine."

"Really?"

"Really. And another thing. It's Romania. They're horny, and they know how to party. Think positive. Let this be your last wild fling before you end up with the fry cook. Gotta go."

Lockyear got back on the line. "Find the criminal, dear."

I couldn't sleep. I rose long before sunrise, pulled up a chair, and stared out my window, across the road, at the palace. There were no lights that I could see, but the walls glowed as if they contained phosphorous. Dawn came, and a thousand pink-eyed windows stared back at me. I could no longer bear to be by myself in that room. I dressed in my navy blue slacks, crisp white blouse and workaday heels, and went to find the car rental business, which belonged to the hotel. That evening, I had an appointment in the Transylvanian town of Brasov with a man by the name of Olestru, my contact to the criminal overlord. I wanted to leave plenty of time for the drive.

The car rental place, down in the shadows beneath one of the spiral staircases, didn't open till ten. I took an elevator back up one floor to the business center, where I e-mailed Lockyear and reassured him of my competence. No one in New York would be up for another eight hours or so, so no point in calling; I was tempted to wake Robert, but such a call would leave an impression of fragility and neediness. The sooner I got out of Bucharest, and on to the real work, the better.

I went for breakfast in a stretch of the second floor unpleasantly packed with an international business crowd, Germans in tangerine and mauve suits, laughing too loud, Japanese conferring in whispers over spreadsheets, an all-male gathering—except for a lone, ponytailed woman whom I noticed instantly. She could only be American. Her blond hair was tied back by a daisy yellow scrunchy. She wore a pink oxford cloth shirt and sandals. I could see her unpolished toes from the hostess podium. She looked about my age, right around thirty. I could have gone to high school with the woman.

She noticed me, too; or rather, she noticed the ring. She stared at the diamond as if it had whispered into her ear. My new best friend, I told myself.

Three

Clementine Spence hailed from Muskogee, Oklahoma, about two hours north of the Texas border. She went by the name Clemmie. When she was three, the family moved to the Permian Basin, where her father worked at a crane and rigging company. When she was fifteen, he changed professions, from crane and rigging to automotive insurance, and moved the family to Sweetwater, Texas.

Her accent was west Texas, her clothes Dallas or Houston: Those pink button-down oxford cloth shirts hang like signature local fruit in the racks north of the Woodall Rogers Freeway and south of the LBJ. Her face, when it turned in my direction, had a fresh-scoured glow. It appeared that she'd ironed her khaki pants. When I approached her, she regarded me with eyes of faint blue, a bit red around the edges, as if she'd been rubbing them. She didn't appear to be a businesswoman, didn't have that pointed sense of organization. She wasn't wearing a jacket to match her pants. She didn't quite fit the mold of a tourist either, though the map and the book on her table suggested otherwise.

The woman amounted to a sedative, easing my anxiety about being in Romania by myself. The same feeling of deep loneliness had gripped me once before, on a scouting expedition for a story about the shanty-towns of São Paulo, a case of thundering nerves. But Lockyear was right. There could be no excuse for such petty fear, not when journalists were getting kidnapped in the Arabian desert. It was sheer inexperience. And yet I couldn't shake the misgivings. That Price Waterhouse dream about missing persons still unsettled me, a nightmare enhanced by the otherwordliness of my surroundings. And I had reservations about my contact in Romania. On my arrival at the hotel, I had expected to receive a warm greeting of some kind to confirm our appointment in the lobby of the Aro Hotel, Brasov, 7 P.M., Friday evening, September 13. That would have been enough. But there had been no greeting, no human salutation at all. I didn't know whether Olestru was a man or a woman. Given the shady milieu, I assumed that he was a man, but I knew nothing for sure.

Clemmie Spence dispersed these shadows like a ray of Texas sun. I felt instantly comfortable. I told her my name, my hometown, and what my father did, and she decoded me immediately. "You're an Azalea girl." Azalea is a wealthy suburb of Dallas, and many people in Texas have a low opinion of it. She might have had those feelings, too, for all I knew, but didn't say so. She didn't mention my origins again, and I liked her for it. I liked her, in general.

Ian would shake his head. "Lord, how you Southern girls flock together," he'd say, though technically he's wrong about that. I don't bond with Southern women, generally. Texas is not the South, except for one scrawny piece of East Texas. I don't even like to be associated with Southerners, with their façade of effusive gentility, their peach cobbler and fried chicken, their dogs and fish, their genealogies going back to the first five hundred families in some state that is less than two hundred years old. Texas is a border state, and people in border states shun such sentimentality.

Clemmie and I talked about football and colleges. It turned out that both of us had been cheerleaders at the same stadium in 1990 when her high school and Azalea played each other in the state semifinals. Her team won, but neither of us could recall the score, or any details of the game.

"I remember that you guys had a marching band dressed in kilts," she said, laughing. "And didn't someone dance on a drum?"

"You had to remember. We were the Azalea Highlanders. The drum belonged to someone's clan." I didn't know why my team had been called the Highlanders. It seemed a very long time ago.

We picked up the rental car at ten, a BMW with tinted windows. I told her it was expense account, and she laughed and said that she had a whole new appreciation for corporate America. She was headed for the city of Brasov, too, on a trip to visit friends. I could drop her on my way. It was my rental, so I took the wheel, but we agreed that Clemmie would drive part of the way.

She had the shiniest hair. It glistened in the light that flashed off the windows of grubby apartment buildings. Her ponytail shook with her laughter, and her daisy bright scrunchy bounced like a bow at the back of her head. She had a small cute nose and a round chin. Boys would have liked her in high school. It was both a comfort and an oddity to be sitting in that car with this woman, so far from the places where we grew up, talking about the things that we had both experienced. I hadn't talked with anyone about things like barbecue, football, Austin music and South Padre beach in ages.

We left the northern edge of Bucharest behind, and the countryside commenced, flat green fields stretching away to the north, littered with more construction sites, brand-new billboards, shiny red umbrellas in front of a dozen shiny red cafés. The traffic gleamed with fabulous new German, Swedish and Japanese cars, and the gas stations, built just for them, seemingly yesterday, rippled with purple flags and shimmered with fresh plates of glass, behind which bulged great rows of potato chip bags and western European chocolates on high metal racks. What a sight it is to see a country behaving as if it is brand-new. Everything is disorganized, scattered around the landscape, just like boxes and packing paper. Or that's what it felt like to me—some brand-new clothing store just opened in the Village, with electrical work still being done in back, hammers pounding, drills spinning, while an overworked, excitable sales force tries a little too hard to move the goods from the shelves. Fifteen years before, Romania had lost its dictator, and ever since, it had been trying to be a capitalist democracy. Clemmie and I agreed that it seemed to be getting there.

I told her that I'd lived in New York for ten years, and the conversation turned more serious. She asked me if I had been there on the day, and I knew what she meant. Sooner or later, when I meet strangers and tell them where I live, the subject always comes up. Most of the time, I just shrug. But that moment in the sun, on the road, put me at ease.

"My building was right there. Next to the towers."

"You poor thing."

"There were people who, who had a much worse day." I hated talking about it under the best of circumstances.

"What—um—did you see? If I can ask?"

The old emotions surged up. "Everything." I couldn't say much more in answer to that question.

She changed the subject. "You live right in the city?"

"Brooklyn."

"I knew it."

"What gave me away? Please don't tell me I have a Brooklyn accent."

"Something about the look," she replied. "Sorta dark."

Compared to her, I guess, but I didn't know quite how to take that. She didn't mean it badly, I'm sure, but it sounded vaguely insulting; the *look*. On the other hand, Robert would have been pleased. Before me, he dated troubled girls, and he always wanted me to be a little edgier than I was. Hence, the Amsterdam batch.

"I have a dark look?"

"Intense, I mean. You look like I imagine a Brooklyn woman to be. White woman, anyway. Not Texan at all anymore. Do you like it there?"

"Love it."

"Really? I always thought that it would be so hard to live in New York City."

"Can be." On my salary, sheer hell, but why tell her that? "Where do you live now?"

"Gosh." She seemed to have trouble with the answer. "Around."

"Around what?"

She grinned, but I could tell she was hesitant to actually say. That intrigued me more.

"Well?"

"Beijing. Kashmir. Lake Malawi."

"Get out."

"For real."

Beijing attracted everyone with a passport, but Kashmir and Lake Malawi would have been at the absolute bottom of my list of guesses. They would not have made my top one thousand.

"No kidding?"

"Honest to goodness."

"Wow. What's that like? To live in those places, I mean?"

Clemmie Spence didn't look in the least like a woman who lived outside the comfort zone of the so-called developed world. Most of the time, you can see that geography in a person, a trace of rawness around the eyes, a mannerism, an affectation, like those women who come back from a year in France wearing scarves around their necks and smoking Gitanes. There are other signs, too, world-weariness, or a kind of confidence, or a cynicism. But she had none of those. She had no hardness at all, no trace of the wanderer. For a moment, I doubted that she could be telling the truth. But why would she lie? In almost every detail, she looked like a woman who had spent her entire life in the plush of north Dallas. She peered out her window in silence.

"I loved Kashmir," she said. "That I can tell you. Most beautiful place I've ever been. Till they destroyed it."

We hit a four-lane highway, and the driving became easy. Off the road, tilled fields stretched away into hot distances. When we cracked the windows, September air filled our lungs, ripe and sweet. Fruit stands glowed with melons, peaches, peppers and tomatoes. They hummed with bees. We stopped for a sack of wet peaches and changed seats. Clemmie drove with urgent focus. She changed lanes frequently and honked the slowpokes out of the way. We got swept up in a fleet of petroleum trucks, a dozen, at least, and they carried us forward as if aboard a silver jet. When we came to our first major city, a place called Ploesti, the trucks detoured down a bypass, their drivers waving at us, leaning on their horns. The breeze in Ploesti began to reek of petroleum.

The cheeriness of a small provincial city gave way to steel and grime and flattened mud. Refineries rose like immense car wrecks on the horizon. Pure white clouds unfurled from smokestacks. On the side of the road, billboards still advertised in bright colors; women in tight red dresses sipped bright blue cocktails. But they labored against a growing ugliness. After a while, we hit a detour and had to get off the highway. The signs led us into a cul de sac, and the map didn't help. We were lost, and the suburbs gave nothing away, offered neither landmarks nor exits, but they weren't endless either. We ended up in the heart of the oil complex, holding our noses, overshadowed by blackened pipelines, forced to backtrack by rusting, gaping freight cars that blocked our way. Outside, as the sun moved west, shadows darted through the bars of a giant's scorched chemistry set. Men clattered down iron rails. Flames jetted from holes, orange and blue fires, a colony of genies. We rounded one corner and found an extended family—Gypsies, by the look: three women, one man, and a pack of children—who had made shelter in a shuttered, one-story building, a former restaurant, perhaps. The children skipped barefoot through pools of rank water. The women sorted through trash. Dressed in a coat and tie, the man sat in a chair and watched everything with milk-white eyes. The women approached us and begged. I gave money and wished for my camera crew. When such things happen, you have to be there to catch them. It sounds callous, but you cannot stage this kind of misery. It has to appear before your eyes, unchoreographed, and then you can film it.

Before long, we found our way. Ploesti vanished behind us. The land rolled forward again in a wide, shimmering wave. There were fewer billboards. We hit a plateau, and saw silver rivers in the far distance, and achingly blue mountains beyond stretches of wild forest. The road rose into a valley and went to two lanes. Before long, moving at high speed, we came up behind the petroleum trucks again, and our pace slowed. It was just past midday.

"Ploesti," Clemmie said. "Depressing."

"You must have seen much worse in Africa."

"It's true, but still. Some places just have that feel. You know?"

"Like what?"

"Like they've become the latrine of the species. Like all of our shit ended up on top of someone else's life."

It was an exaggeration, and I didn't care for it much. None of my

shit had ended up in Ploesti. There was a long silence in the car. I tried
to bridge it. "I hardly think this is our fault. A decade of violent fascism.
Fifty years of Communism, a megalomaniac dictator, and now raw-
toothed capitalism, God help them."

"Yes, God help them. We have to put our faith there. That's what I
try to remind myself."

Clemmie had misunderstood me. I noticed the silver chain hanging
around her neck and wondered, for the first time, if a cross dangled at
the end of it.

"I didn't mean it like that," I said. "I'm not religious."

"Neither am I," she said. "I hate religion." She paused a moment.
"But I love God." We drove a while longer in silence. "Do you mind if
we switch again? My feet are itching."

We stopped at a roadside restaurant and bought potato chips and
Coke. We took the sack of peaches and made a lunch in the shade of
a voluminous rose bush beside a smelly pond. Clemmie paid. After
lunch, we walked around the pond, disturbing frogs. Dark green blots
sprang into the murk. On the road again, I took the wheel, and she
rolled up her sleeves and started to knead the balls of flesh beneath her
toes.

"You said you were a journalist?"

I had. "Yes, ma'am."

She slipped off a shoe. "Who do you write for?"

This always happened. People automatically assume if you're a
journalist, you must work in print. "It's television. I'm a producer."

"Cool."

This was often an uncomfortable moment. I never wanted to sound
like a name-dropper. "For a show called *The Hour*."

She gave a grin. "A show called *The Hour*. I've heard of a show called
The Hour. Everyone's heard of a show called *The Hour*." Clemmie raised
an eyebrow. "I better watch what I say."

"You don't appear to have a problem watching what you say."

She laughed. "Can you tell me what you're working on here?"

I never talk about my stories with outsiders. That's Lockyear's first
rule of producing, and he gets it from our correspondent, Austen

Trotta, so I adhere to it. She let go of her left foot and put the sandal back on. She turned to the right foot, crossed it over the left and flicked off the sandal. "I bet I know."

Her tone had an innocuous ring, but I felt a slight shiver of disquiet. *Hour* producers have to be paranoid. It's the nature of the job. I reflected on the fact that I had approached Clemmie in the breakfast room; it had been my idea to offer a ride. But how convenient that she came from Texas, that she happened to be going my way. And then I recalled what she said about my being from New York. She'd known somehow. My intensity had given me away, she said.

I played it very light. "Want to guess?"

She went along, finishing the massage on her left foot. "Would it have anything to do with an amusement park?"

Lockyear would have told me not to answer that question. I was flustered, but I held my feelings in check. Our criminal overlord had been mentioned here and there as a major backer of a proposed theme park related to a famous character from the movies. She might have read it in the news.

"Nope," I said. "What do you do for a living?"

Rather than answer, she opened her purse, picked out a plastic bottle, and popped the cap. She squirted a dab of lotion onto her right hand. Then she rubbed it between the toes on her left foot. The purse remained open, and I could see inside a small black-jacketed book with onionskin pages.

"Sorry about this. I know it's disgusting, but I did a lot of walking around Bucharest yesterday," she explained.

"Is that a Bible?" I asked her.

She gave a nod. I let it go for a moment. Stuck behind the convoy of petroleum trucks, we could only move so fast, and the change in the landscape began to impress itself on me. Bluffs rose on either side of us, heavy with thicket and gorse, new development giving way to old settlement, wooden houses bunched together in rickety confusion, an onion-domed church topped by a cross. A military cemetery appeared on a hill, lines of regimented crosses the color of milk dwindling into the darkness beneath cedars.

"Is there some religious dimension to your work?"

Clemmie gave an ambiguous nod.

I had a hunch about something. "Are you married?"

She let go of the toes of her left foot and replaced the shoe. "Used to be."

"Children?"

"No."

She took off the right sandal and started the same procedure. The sound of the lotion squishing into the skin annoyed me. It took on the soft quality of an evasion.

"You?" she asked.

"Engaged."

"Congratulations."

She let go of her foot, and the sound of the lotion ceased. Clemmie put her shoe back on and stared over the dash at the road. I shifted my concentration to the road. In the space of a few minutes, the country-side had changed again—and so had the atmosphere in the car. A new frostiness suffused everything. We were up high now, with valleys opening below to left and right, as the road climbed toward the mountains. Towns hung over us on the sides of hills and gathered at angles below us. A small herd of horses moved across open meadow. In our two lanes of highway, trucks careened right at us, passing each other with blind contempt for the traffic in the oncoming lane. Every ten minutes, another eighteen-wheeler roared right at me, honking, and I had to swerve out of the way. Red blotches appeared on the backs of my hands. The wind boiled in Clemmie's bright hair. Above the road, the sun shone. We climbed out of valleys and had momentary visions of remote green country before plunging down again. The trucks sent gusts of wind rippling through pine branches. We'd made good time. By five P.M., I guessed, we'd be in Brasov.

"I get the feeling I said something wrong," Clemmie said.

I kept my eyes on the road. "Are you sure I didn't?"

"On the contrary. I thank God that we met. Truly. I thank Him."

"Come on."

"There are no coincidences, Evangeline."

My heart started to beat more quickly. She could have been a specter from my past, a daughter of Jesus in the Azalea High School cafeteria, her happy eyes blazing, hot with the fire of a final truth. If you could know what I know, her eyes said, your eyes would blaze, too. I had never believed in that final truth, though I played along during senior year, when I was a cheerleader, because my boyfriend of the time had joined the Fellowship of Christian Athletes and told me that he would only have sexual relations with me if we were both in Christ. So I joined the team and gave a quarterback head, neither of which made me very proud.

Clementine Spence turned her full gaze on me. "I can tell you're upset." My silence only encouraged her. "But I think that you're getting upset for no reason."

I shook my head. "I'm not upset at all."

"Just tell me. How did I offend you?"

I weighed my options. We had two more hours in the car, at least. We could have a confrontation, and those two hours would be ugly, or I could back off and wait her out. If I didn't rise to the bait, she'd probably be quiet.

"I'm a terrible bitch when I want to be," I said. "And you've made me suspicious of your motives. Sorry." I decided to test her personal discretion. "Was he a missionary, too?"

"Who?"

"Your husband."

Clemmie ran a hand across her eyes. "We hated that word."

"Really?"

"We called ourselves change agents." Clemmie rummaged in her rucksack and found tissues, which she applied to her face. She sneezed into the well-worn bundle. "Actually, my husband called us change agents. It's borrowed from management theory."

Her tears seemed real enough. The air smelled like rain. Cliffs of stone rose on either side of us, and cloudbanks rolled through the heights. We had come to the edge of Transylvania.

Four

Traffic had stopped. Clemmie pointed out that the petroleum trucks hadn't moved in several minutes. We rolled down our windows and heard birdsong against a tense silence. The drivers of the trucks had turned off their engines. Farther up, one or two men had crawled out of their cabs. The sun sank into the western range, and the shadows of the day deepened beside barns. Dried ears of corn swayed from eaves of whitewashed cottages. Clemmie took off her shoes again and put her bare feet up on the dashboard. The sweet smell of her lotion scented the car. The mountain pass was only a kilometer above us, but all forward motion had stopped. There was nothing to do but wait and wonder.

"Tell me something," Clemmie said. "Do you believe in the kind of stuff related to this place where we're headed?"

I was punchy already, and the question sent a new shock of irritation through me. "What in the world are you talking about?"

"I'll take that as a no."

She seemed to know about my work. She knew that it concerned the amusement park, and she knew that the amusement park concerned the usual stereotypes about Transylvania. But there was one more step to make, and she hadn't made it yet. And as long as she didn't, I wouldn't either.

"A friend of mine calls our place of work Fangland," I said.

"Yikes."

"Exactly. People are not nice in Fangland, to say the least. They are crazy. They are ambitious. They shout. They criticize and rebuke. They rise, at best, to a kind of low decency. But as far as I know, none of them are real bloodsuckers."

"You know that for sure?"

"Not for sure. But then, I don't believe in that sort of thing."

"That was my question."

"Are you telling me that you do believe in such things? In, in vampires?"

She seemed to consider my question as if it were a judgment, which it was.

"My problem," she said, "is that I can't rule them out."

It crossed my mind that she might have been sent by members of a crime syndicate opposed to the construction of the amusement park. But this seemed like a Stimson Beevers scenario, and I considered myself above that sort of conspiratorial thinking. The sun kept sinking.

"Change agent," I said. "It's an interesting term. What precisely does it mean?"

She sighed. "Precisely? I don't know. Someone or something who creeps inside a reality and makes it different. Basically. The term has always put me off a little bit, too. But Jeff believed it, heart and soul. A change agent. To him, it sounded heroic, like James Bond."

"I suppose a vampire would be a sort of change agent. Right?"

She smiled at me. "For the opposing team. Yes."

"And tell me again what's wrong with the word *missionary*?"

"A bad image. White picket fences in jungles, and 'Nearer My God to Thee' morning, noon and night. Forced conversions of the dark-skinned. No one wants that, least of all those of us who have given our lives to the effort. We want Jesus to come to people in their own culture, on their terms, not ours."

It was a convincing answer, but I realized that, on top of everything else, I was growing tired. She must be, too. She became quiet. Clouds passed overhead. Drops of water pattered the dashboard. "Do you mind if I smoke?" Clemmie asked.

Wasn't the body the temple of the Lord? I indicated that I didn't mind. She plucked a smoke from her bag and lit it. She caught me looking sideways at her.

"Nothing in the Good Book about these, I assure you. Want one?"

I gave her a guilty smile. I hadn't smoked in years. Robert considered the habit unladylike. But I wouldn't be kissing him for another week, at least, and by that time, the flavor of smoke would be out of my mouth.

Clemmie lit one with her cigarette and handed it to me. "We planted churches."

"You planted what?"

"In the Himalayan range north of Srinagar in Kashmir. We were trying to bring Muslims to a faith understanding of Christ. We didn't want Christians, mind you. We wanted followers of Jesus. Muslim followers of Jesus. But it didn't work out so well."

She put a hand over her eyes again. My cigarette tasted delicious. "My husband." She took a drag. "He lost it." I must have looked perplexed. "His faith, I mean. He was disabused, is how he put it to me. He left me."

At first, concentrating on my cigarette, I didn't register that last comment . But a few seconds passed, and the meaning of the words sank in. "Oh, God. Your husband left you? In Kashmir? That's awful. When?"

"A year ago. No. Two years now."

Her earlier sympathy for the September 11 attacks came back to me, and I felt like a fraud for feeling that anything bad had ever happened to me. "I'm so sorry, Clemmie." She stared ahead. She didn't seem to have much to add on the subject. "Is that what you're doing here now? In Romania? Church planting?"

She sniffed and looked up, gazing at me with her soft blue eyes. "No. It's not my gift. I'm much better one on one."

I didn't inquire further, fearing the hard sell. On one side of the valley, rain fell. On the other, dusky red sun filled the cleft between the mountains. The disc itself had turned bright gold. The rain glittered and flashed. Clemmie leaned her head out of the passenger side.

"Hey," she said. "Something's going on."

We got out of the car, and it was a relief. The sky drizzled, but I didn't mind getting wet. A truck driver saw our cigarettes and bummed a smoke. Clemmie fished in her purse and pried out another for herself.

"What's happening?" I asked. She repeated the question to the truck driver in French. He shrugged. He didn't appear to know French. We waited. It was a low elevation, but cliffs loomed on either side, and there were dark green shards of conifer beneath the razoring peaks. On a summit to the west, I saw a cross, blackened against the sun. I pointed. Clemmie blew smoke through her lips and nodded.

"These mountains were once a fortress," she said. "They guarded against Islam."

She lowered her cigarette and gazed with a sudden intensity up the road. "Listen," she said.

There came a noise of movement, a crowd on the march. She walked into the middle of the road to get a better view. Ahead, a few hundred feet up the slope, a procession moved on foot. They had taken over the highway. Clemmie became rigid at my elbow. She tossed away her cigarette, bowed her head and put her hands together.

At the head of the procession walked a priest in a light brown robe. His head was bowed, too, and he spoke words in a language I didn't understand. Another sound emerged, a clop of horse hooves, a heavy knock on the cracked asphalt of the road. The procession moved toward us. Clemmie continued to pray. Her lips didn't move. I couldn't hear words. How out of place we both looked, dark blue business suit and crisp pink shirt, out of place and out of time. But at least she had a connection to the scene. Her faith joined her with the other people who crossed themselves as the horses neared. I should have done so, too. I should have bowed my head, exactly like her. But I broke my own deep rule of foreign travel: when in doubt, in someone else's land, do what the locals do. The priest came within a few paces, and I saw the point of the exercise. Behind him reared two grayish horses with limp white manes. Behind the horses, pulled by them, rolled the wooden wheels of a wagon, a low-riding vehicle with mottled brown timbers on either side. High atop the wagon, on a bed of aromatic hay, rode a coffin roughly the shade of Clemmie's oxford cloth shirt and about half the size of an adult human being. This was the funeral procession of a child. It stopped right beside us.

"Look away," my companion whispered.

Five

A sign came up in the headlights, Brasov, thirty-five kilometers. I had lost any sense of the relationship between kilometers and miles; thirty-five kilometers should have been about twenty miles, but it doubled in my mind. Seventy miles to Brasov, I thought. I couldn't shake the sense of a wild, impending disorder in things, unleashed by the sight of the coffin on the wagon.

"What do you think happened to that child?" I asked, knowing it was a ridiculous question. How could she possibly know?

Clemmie seemed untroubled. She sat beneath a halo of cigarette smoke, as before us rose one more piece of Transylvania, one more pine-crowned earthwork. "God knows," she said.

The hour of my appointment with N. Olestru had passed, and with it, I feared, my chance to land this story. I tend to be punctual in my social dealings, but at work, I'm fanatical about it. We at *The Hour* deal constantly with strangers who suspect of us of malign intent. We fight this prejudice as a matter of course, and in that battle, first impressions make the difference. For me, victory begins with a polite and professional phone call, followed up by e-mails or faxes, and is then supported by every single tiny detail that lays the groundwork for an initial meeting and can only be guaranteed when I appear five to ten minutes early, dressed impeccably and with the same demeanor of unruffled politeness with which I initiated contact. Anything less, and my chances of success are cut in half.

I doubted very much whether N. Olestru could have a high opinion of me. I would be lucky if he would trust me enough to continue any serious dialogue about a story involving his employer. I expected a few apologetic bromides—he had waited for an hour, and couldn't meet me again for several months—a vague promise to do so, and then silence. I was livid with myself.

Lockyear had wanted me to call after the meeting, but I could no longer even think about that. I would have to lie to him. I couldn't tell him the truth, that I had hit bad traffic and missed the appointment. I would call him in the morning and tell him that no one had shown up. He'd berate me. He'd speak quickly and talk low. He'd remind me that we could not afford another debacle, that his rodeo clown story had put his job in a state of high vulnerability. Or maybe I wouldn't call him at all. Or I would call him as soon as I got to the hotel and tell him that no one had turned up and ask his advice. I could call Stim, but it was afternoon now, and Stim would be playing hooky either at the Anthology or the Film Forum, pretending to be on a search for archival tape while he caught a film.

Clemmie coughed, and the noise startled me. For a few seconds, it was as if she hadn't existed. The passenger seat might have been empty. The ponytail was now gone, the scrunchy, too, and her hair hung straight.

Another truck appeared in front of me, a wheezing, creaking old wreck loaded with wet timber. The ends of logs swung at my hood. I slammed on the brakes and felt the engine of the rental car shake. I had a frightening thought that the motor would stop, and I wouldn't be able to get it started again.

Clemmie jerked up in her seat. "You're too close to the truck."

"I'm trying to get around it."

The two lanes of the road were narrow, and there was no shoulder. If I swerved right, I'd hit a pine tree. If I tried to pass on the left, to get around the truck, I'd have no room to dodge an oncoming car. I honked at the truck to put on the gas. The grade became steeper, winding toward an unseen summit. We slowed to a near standstill.

Two dogs came out of nowhere. At first, they were blurs of whiteness, but they turned into fanged mammals. One hit Clemmie's window with a splat, its tongue exploding with saliva on the pane. Another leaped onto the hood of the car. I popped a gear, shifted into reverse, and mashed the accelerator, shooting us backward, hurling the dog on the hood onto the pavement. We gained speed going downhill, and I was losing control. I shifted gears out of reverse. The other dog stayed with us, springing beside the window. Clemmie reached into her purse and pulled out what could only be a can of Mace. She rolled down the window a crack and sprayed the dog, which went yelping and reeling off the road. I got into gear and roared back up the hill. We caught up to the truck again, crossing the lane behind the straining timbers, heading for the oncoming lane to attempt a pass. But I saw a light and didn't like my chances and pulled back into my lane just as another truck came roaring around the curve. As I moved into the lane, my wheels hit something that sounded unpleasantly like a dog.

I looked at Clemmie in the glow of the dashboard.

"Amen, sister," she said.

The other dog receded into the gloom of my rearview. The truck turned onto a woodland road and was gone. The solitude of the night came over us, though my heart pounded in my chest, and sounded loud enough to disturb the forest. Clemmie didn't seem to notice. We came to a break in the trees, and away to the east, we saw the rise of the moon.

"Want to hear a story that I haven't told another living soul?" Clemmie asked.

She lit her fourth or fifth cigarette of the night. I asked her for one, too.

Clemmie touched the butt of a cold cigarette to her burning one. "You know I told you I was a relief worker in Malawi. In sub-Saharan Africa?"

"Yeah."

"I ran an immunization program in the bush. Do you know anything about Malawi?" she asked.

I shook my head.

"One of the poorest countries in the world. High infant mortality rate. Lots of local superstition. One of those latrines I mentioned."

I couldn't believe that I was actually driving at night in the mountains of Transylvania with a superstitious Texan missionary. Not even the jaded denizens of *The Hour* would believe it.

"There was a string of villages on the shore of Lake Malawi, mostly fishermen, about a thousand people in a fifty-mile radius. It was my job to vaccinate all children under the age of five for measles and polio. Jeff, my ex, was my team leader then, and part of his tent-making function . . ."

"You lost me there."

"Tent-making, you mean?" I nodded. "It's your cover. You know, the way spies have a cover when they infiltrate a country where they may not be wanted? We do, too. It's a job or an assignment to convince the local authorities you're not just there to win souls for Jesus."

"But you are, aren't you? There to win souls?"

She shrugged. "Some of us just want to help, believe it or not. We call it tent-making. My job was to inoculate in those places where the government immunization plan was underfunded, which was everywhere. But Jeff had work all over the region and left me in charge with a local doctor and a nurse."

She spoke in a matter-of-fact way.

"It was easy work. The villagers believed in the program and had no suspicions of us until the end, when everything had gone wrong. I can't remember exactly which day it started." Her words trailed off. "It was a Wednesday, I know, because the mail boat came from Lilongwe."

For a minute, her eyes closed, and I thought that she had gone to sleep.

"Clemmie," I said. She opened her eyes. "Lilongwe."

"Yes, yes. I know. I'm just collecting my thoughts. It's exhausting to think about, really. You have to think about our situation. There were about twelve villages along that particular piece of the shore, about one hundred folks per village, kids, old-timers, families. Once every two weeks, I would hit each village, spending a night, two nights, before heading on. These were house calls, basically, and the system worked. People stayed healthy and gave God the credit, which was great. Every time I showed up, the kids would come shrieking out to greet me, and for a woman without kids, you can imagine the thrill, a woman who wanted kids, I mean, but didn't have any of her own, it was like inheriting a whole bunch at once."

Her hands trembled as she squashed her cigarette into the side of the lotion bottle.

"Before the local doctor vanished, he told me that the only real bad deal around were the AIDS victims, and they weren't our problem. Lilongwe hospitals took them. Most of our folks weren't actually sick. No one had a fever. So when they started to drop out of sight, it didn't make much sense. The children had their immunizations. And before them, so had the adults." A quiver came into her voice. "But I knew that already. I was the one who brought in the medicine. I watched the nurse immunize those children."

I watched the road, bathed in moonlight. Clemmie's voice trailed away. I would be married in June. We had already booked a pavilion at Wave Hill. There was so much to do. I should be making phone calls from Romania. I should be setting appointments with the priest at Saint Ignatius Loyola. I should call Robert and apologize for making him feel bad about the Amsterdam package. When he gave me the pink box, he said, "In case you ever feel like lap dancing." This line had been in my mind when I opened the present, and it had somehow provoked me. But I looked back now and thought how silly that was. I would call Robert from the hotel in Brasov and promise him that lap dance.

"It seems to have happened all at once. I started out on a Monday, making my rounds, and it just unfolded. One village after another. I would go to the elder, and the story would be the same. The kids had all gone. By the time I reached the last village, I was beside myself." Her voice quavered. "Terrified. Like eight years old and lying in my bed, staring at the closet. Like that. You see?" She turned to look at me. I didn't see, didn't want to see, but I nodded. If I don't acknowledge her, I thought, she'll get even more upset. "The last two inhabitants of one place, a man and woman, told me that their children had gone into the jungle. At night, a group of white men had appeared on the shores and walked right through the middle of town and trailing behind them, every last one of the kids."

It sounded suspicious to me. "Did they describe these white men?"

Clemmie's voice lowered. "Ghosts. That's the term they used. I called them white men."

Her response didn't reassure me. Who said ghosts had to be white? But I was intrigued. "Then what happened?"

"After the kids went the grandparents, the old folks, and together, they had all walked by night along the old paths into the jungle, and they had disappeared. These two people told me that the ghosts would come for me, too. I heard it again and again. The few survivors in every village would pinch my pale skin and shake their heads, meaning, this won't protect you none."

Clemmie could be responsible, I told myself. That was a real possibility.

"I have often thought since that those ghosts must have been a species of vampire," she said. "People there believe in vampires."

The air seemed to go out of the car.

"No."

"They never came for me, but by my last visit, at the end of my last circuit down the shore, there was no one left to help. In those villages, there were no people anymore. Not a soul remained. No one came to the water purification facility at the well. No kids played. So I packed my rucksack and walked into the jungle after them. Jeff found me in a hotel in Lilongwe, but I could never tell him how I got there. I never told him anything, and till the day he walked out, he thought our villages had been attacked by guerrillas. Tell the truth, he blamed me for not being more . . . more present of mind, I think he said."

I tried hard to think the best of the situation. Maybe it had been guerrillas. Or maybe she had murdered those people by accident and could not face it. Her immunization program killed the children. Or perhaps some disease got them anyway, and she blamed herself. Probably, they had been sick already, and the medicine came too late. This sounded right to me. She was telling the story of her failure in an attempt to expiate it. Clemmie folded her arms around her body. She was shivering. I felt a terrible, unwanted intimacy.

"We need some rest," I said.

Her head jumped as the car hit a bump in the road, and for an instant, her hair shone like silver in a ray of moonlight. We didn't speak again for the rest of the drive.

Six

We reached the hotel near ten. I decided not to attempt to make contact with anyone that night. Near delirious from the drive, I would only make things worse. Instead, after a good night's sleep, I would wait to hear from N. Olestru and try to make apologies. Clemmie and I lingered in the lobby, trying to say good-bye. I invited her to have a quick dinner, but she declined. She seemed to regard the hotel with anxiety and wrinkled her nose as if she smelled something rank.

I was of two minds about Clemmie. I wanted her to leave. She exhausted and unnerved me. I would be happy if I never saw her again. But I had become attached to the woman. A bond had been formed against my will. I was engaged, she had been abandoned by her husband. And I experienced pity. She seemed a lost soul. I offered dinner again, but she told me that she had "associates" in town. The word had a ludicrous ring. Associates. I couldn't resist a smartass remark. "Change agent convention?"

She smiled wanly. "Nothing so grand."

When we first arrived, she'd made a phone call. Afterward, she told me that plans had been made for her retrieval. She didn't tell me where she was headed, and I didn't press. She could keep her strange secrets. She had pulled a pale blue V-neck sweater over her pink oxford cloth shirt and brushed her hair back once again into a ponytail and fixed it with the daisy yellow scrunchy. She'd doused her face with cold water.

"You sure you don't want to have at least a drink or something?" I asked. "My appointment has been cancelled. We could try the local wine. I know you drink."

"I do." She hesitated.

"On me," I insisted.

She glanced through the doors of the hotel, as if she saw a familiar face in the dark. "It would be too much of an imposition," she said, "and besides, you're just being nice. I know how it works with you Azalea girls. Your central nervous systems are wired for politeness. You can't help yourselves."

"That's bitchy."

"Then I take it back."

The desk clerk peered up at us. An ashen young bellhop appeared and hauled my bags away. Neither of us moved. From the outside, the hotel exhibited a gray concrete and glass face, a true 1970s Communist block. But inside, an effort had been made to give the place the feel of a hunting lodge, with thick timbers in the ceilings, deer heads mounted on walls and a thick red-and-gold carpet on the floor. The dim lighting suggested a fire in a stone hearth. Electricity flickered on and off, a bulb here, a bulb there, winking behind lampshades of orange and yellow. A few guests traveled between the desk and the doors to a dark bar identified by a sign as SOMA.

"Look," Clemmie said. "I have to be honest with you."

She put down her bag and her coat and put her arms around my shoulders in a hug. The move startled me. I flinched, but she held on.

"You're on the brink, Evangeline, of your true life. And if it's not too late, I pray you will open your eyes."

That finished it for me. I was sick of the condescension and the games. I pushed her away.

"Who are you, anyway? What are you up to?"

"You know that."

"I goddamn well don't! Who are you working for? What is your real name?"

She tried to back away, but it was my turn to grab her. I took her by the arms.

"Tell me who you're working for. Are you with another network?"

Other people noticed. I glanced at the desk and saw a clerk speaking with two girls who had emerged from the back. I saw someone else near the entrance to the lobby. At first, he was so still, I thought that it was an object, not a person. His eyes faced the night. But he heard the commotion and turned.

"Let go," Clemmie said.

I refused. Out of the corner of my eye, I watched the advance of the man who'd caught my eye. He was coming toward us. Clemmie couldn't see him, but she seemed to sense his approach.

"Evangeline?" She clutched my arms and put her lips to my ears. "What you're in the middle of?" She waited for the words to sink in before she continued. "It isn't ever going to be on television."

The stranger, showing no sense of discretion, addressed us at that awkward moment. "Madam Harker?"

He spoke my name, but had a particular interest in Clemmie, it seemed to me. Clemmie noticed, too. She stared at the man, who, at first glance, was exquisitely hideous. We disengaged. I had the stark sense that this person bore a direct relationship to the words she had just spoken in my ear. I was sure Clemmie knew him.

"Mr. Olestru?" I asked. He gave no indication of owning that name.

Clemmie backed away from me, still staring at the man. She headed through the glass doors into the Transylvanian night, the bright daisy scrunchy glimmering out of sight.

The man, who turned out to be quite short, stretched a huge palm toward me. I stared at the hand for a long moment. The last look in Clemmie's eyes, that odd sense of knowing, came back to me. Someone like this man had led the children into Lake Malawi. That had been in her mind. The thought made me almost dizzy.

He cleared his throat and raised his hand in the direction of the bar. "Shall we?"

Seven

He was small without giving the impression of smallness. If anything, he radiated a kind of fullness. His head was part of it; his body culminated in a large, pale skull that was crowned, at its apex, in a blondish-white twirl of hair. He had hard, thick eyebrows matching soft, thick lips, which curled back in a voluptuous smile to reveal the saddest set of teeth I have ever seen. Of course, I had monsters in the back of my mind, thanks to Clemmie, and maybe that's why I paid such close attention. But these teeth weren't sharp at all. They were round, like pegs, and shone dark blue, as if they had rotted in his grayish gums, rotted but refused to abdicate. His eyes were blackish brown, with pupils that had no defined edges, and they gazed at me with a measuring stillness. They were red-rimmed with exhaustion, and I had a notion that he was a man who drank too much coffee and had too much on his mind to ever get a decent night's doze, though he wasn't exactly sleepy in his manner. I might have described him as theatrical, except for the absence of any trace of theater in his gestures. He smiled as he shook my hand.

I tried again. "Mr. N. Olestru?"

He shook his head, a hint of embarrassment and irritation on his face. He gave a dry chuckle that did not indicate amusement. "My dear Olestru is lost in the mountains with a Norwegian photographer. Sadly."

"I see." At once, my concerns about losing the story gave way to a combative sense of entitlement. No one had said anything to me about a Norwegian. Our understanding had been that *The Hour* alone would be granted access to Ion Torgu. The possibility of other interested parties had never entered the discussions.

We headed slowly for the entrance to the bar. "I guess there are worse fates."

Another dry chuckle came out his mouth. He seemed to take something in my facial expression amiss. "It's nicotine, dear."

"Excuse me?"

"My teeth. It's a nicotine stain."

"Oh no . . . I'm so sorry. I didn't even notice."

"Of course you did. You're a journalist, aren't you? You were staring, weren't you? Miss Evangeline Harker."

The man stopped and gave a slight bow, and I hoped to God that I hadn't, in those few seconds, added insult to injury, humiliating him by staring at his teeth after arriving so late. At first glance, other than the general oddness of his head and its features, he seemed normal enough, but as he rose from his bow, I noticed other little details that puzzled me. He wore a white suit with a dark blue shirt open at the throat, an outfit more appropriate for a Caribbean stroll than an autumn evening in the mountains. If I had to say, I'd guess that he wore a size too small. The hems of his pants revealed half an inch of blue sock. His blue shirt cuffs stuck out from his jacket, and the great pink ham hocks of his hands stuck out from wrists that cleared the cuffs. His shoes had not been polished in a while. These surfaces had an aftertaste of modest poverty, as if he had lived a long time without the ability to improve his wardrobe, but I also had the impression of steel reinforcement, the kind provided by a certain amount of financial security. His appraising look didn't suggest vulnerability. He put his hands by his sides. He seemed to be waiting for some sign.

"I'm at your disposal," I said.

"Wonderful." The lips curled back. Their sinuosity was unsettling. We resumed our walk to the bar. "I want to have the longest conversation with you. I want to share a conversation. Is that correct, in English? Share a conversation?"

"Close enough. May I ask you a question?"

"Which?"

"Your name?"

"Torgu." I think my mouth opened wide, and he saw my surprise, and he gave a slight wince, as if his own fame mortified him. But I couldn't hide my shock. Torgu, Ion Torgu, was a mythical figure. Senior FBI officials had told me that he might not exist at all, that he might be nothing more than a coded identity for a consortium of Romanian criminal organizations. In the very first e-mail exchange, N. Olestru had cast doubt on the prospect of actually meeting the man himself, the Torgu. He described his *chef* as a creature who shied from the public eye as a wild animal shied away from civilization. Yet here he was, Torgu himself. Or so this short, odd man maintained.

He assayed me with narrowed eyes. "You are puzzled?"

"I'm honored."

This remark gave him obvious pleasure. I had a moment's scruple about saying such a thing to a crime lord, but reminded myself that I had a job to do, and certain tools to do it, among which had to be counted flattery.

He led me through the entrance to the hotel bar, empty save for the bartender and a waitress. They studied Torgu, but he ignored them. He pulled a seat for me at a table as far away from the bar as possible.

"What will you like to drink?" he asked, placing all ten fingers on the tabletop in front of me. His fingernails had the same dark tint as his teeth.

"Mineral water will be fine."

"Have liquor."

I had to laugh. "If you insist."

"Hungarian wine may be acceptable?"

I gestured that it would be. My notebook and pens had gone upstairs with the rest of my luggage. He strode to the bar and ordered a bottle of red.

"Your trip took longer than expected," he said upon his return. He sat across from me. I opened my mouth to apologize, but he waved away the impulse. "It's not your fault. Romania does not yet have a national highway system, I am unhappy to say."

It was too warm in the bar. I felt a languor ease into my limbs. I wanted to lie down. When I get like that, and it's a rarity, I'm talkative, though I didn't want to be. Alcohol almost never helps.

"We were delayed by a funeral procession," I told him, for no particular reason.

"We?"

"My traveling companion and me."

His eyes narrowed again, and his lips closed in a scowl.

"That woman, you mean." His head tilted in the direction of the lobby. "May I ask? Who is she?" His eyes searched mine.

"If I may inquire about this unexpected Norwegian."

His scowl deepened, and I thought he might give a canine snarl. The expression frightened me a little, coming as it did from a man with a legendary reputation for cruelty.

"Honestly, Mr. Torgu, I had the impression that you knew her."

"She's no one that I know," he said. "But I will find out."

This sounded like an unpleasant promise, so I decided to tell him what I knew. "She hitched a ride with me, and at first, I thought that was her only interest. But later, I did have the feeling that she was here for a particular reason. She seemed to know something about my story. Has anyone else contacted you about an interview? Any other American network television show? I would appreciate your honesty."

It was clear that the notion of other American television programs competing for his attention hadn't occurred to him before now, and it evidently delighted him. He put the tips of his fingers together and came close to a smile. He popped a small black square of what looked like nicotine gum into his mouth. "We shall see," he said, giving another dry chuckle. "Everything will be known."

The bottle of Hungarian red arrived and was uncorked with an alacrity that had motive. Wine swirled into the glasses.

"Now tell me about the reason for your adventure into my part of the world, please. I am very curious."

I was glad for the change of subject, though my pitch had not been intended for the man himself. It had been tailored to the vanished Olestru, who had passed Torgu's concerns on to me. "For one, my sources at Justice won't believe me when I tell them that I actually met you. That's one reason to be here. To prove you exist."

"If I exist. Yes. Very good.".

"Uh, yes," I said, little disarmed. "Let's presume, for the sake of argument, that you do."

He sniffed at the wine. Did he have any idea of his celebrity in the world of law enforcement? Even if we never shot a second of tape, I would have to tell the boys at the FBI about my encounter, just to make them jealous. When Lockyear's source in the Bureau gave me the address of a bedraggled Romanian language Web site that had not been updated in three years, he said that this was the only known place where verifiable information on Torgu had been posted publicly. He said that one N. Olestru allegedly maintained the site, which contained an e-mail address that seemed outdated. FBI e-mails came back unread. Romanian law enforcement showed no curiosity about the matter. Somehow, my e-mail had gone through. Six months later, long after I'd given up, I received the digital invitation from N. Olestru to come to Brasov. It was very strange, in light of everything, that he hadn't made the meeting.

Torgu's face glowed with pleasure. Color came into his pale cheeks. "Tell me. What do the law enforcement communities say exactly?"

"Let's see. They say you were a political prisoner under the old regime."

His brow creased, rows of shadow in a wide brow. "Very true."

"That you are a Romanian nationalist."

He shook a finger. "This is not accurate. I am not even Romanian. But we'll get back to it. What else?"

"That you run the human and drug smuggling networks west of Moscow and east of Munich. That you run guns, too. That whoever wants to buy enriched plutonium in this part of the world has to deal with you. That you also happen to be one of the most successful legitimate businessmen in Romania, with total assets in the hundreds of millions."

It felt a little funny to be telling these things to him, like reading him back his own biography, but his eyes compelled the truth. If I deemphasized the enriched plutonium aspect, he would have sensed the concealment. I wanted to tell him everything. Of course, and this is all too common, I wanted him to like and trust me, though I knew already that I neither liked nor trusted him.

"And that's the tale you want to tell. Merely that I am successful at what I do?"

"More or less. Is it all true?"

He put his hands up defensively. "My goodness. That's the most important question. Perhaps we should put it off. I don't deny anything. I don't confirm anything. Isn't that the right way to talk for American criminals?"

I shrugged and drew a breath and had another sip of the wine. I was glad for it now. The liquor in my blood put me at ease. It gave me confidence. It was a nice red. I could suddenly imagine doing a superior lap dance for Robert, maybe on our honeymoon.

"You are a representative of a very mysterious class of people, Mr. Torgu. We know about the Russian oligarchs, for instance. We have seen them interviewed, and read the books about them. We know about organized crime figures in the United States, the John Gottis, and so on, ad nauseum. But what do we really know about organized crime in Eastern Europe? Not much. And in these days after September 11, there are rumors that Islamic terrorist groups may be using crime figures like you to buy weapons and raise money . . ."

Torgu's fist slammed down on the table, and his dark teeth were bared.

"Liar!" he roared.

I kept my cool. I put down the wineglass. One anticipates emotion in these exchanges. I try never to take it personally. People who talk to our cameras often have compelling reasons to do so. Some face indictment. Some already sit behind bars. Some have been accused by neighbors and friends of the most horrendous acts of mayhem and murder, and if they agree to do our show, they mean to defend themselves. Torgu would be no different. His government had tried without success to prosecute him. The FBI informed me that extradition attempts had been made by the United States, to no avail. So it didn't surprise me that Torgu reacted badly to the laundry list of his crimes, and I didn't budge. I didn't blink. It's a piece of the negotiation. We coax, cajole, seduce and even bludgeon people into agreement. We fend off rage and suspicion. We circumvent indifference. I've used every imaginable tactic, short of selling my body. It is no small thing to appear on camera in front of millions of people. It is a risk for our subjects to allow the lights to bathe them, to give their faces and bodies to the lenses. I don't blame them for struggling against us. Some are more eager, of course. They fly toward *The Hour* like wasps to sugar. But I have seen every kind of reaction. I have had people tell me that they would shoot themselves before they would appear on *The Hour*. I have had threats against my life. People have called me a whore and a villain. They have told me that I am saving the country. They have told me that God will bless me. This man had begun our relationship with a whopper. We had not even begun to discuss an appearance, and he had called me a liar. And I hadn't even lied. I waited for him to explain himself.

"I know the true angel of your show, madame," he said, his ire dying down. I saw with disgust that his nicotine gum had fallen into his wineglass.

"Angle, you mean."

"No I do not mean angle." He raised a hornlike fingernail. "I mean, my dear, the Angel of Destruction."

His lips sucked back from his teeth in contempt. He shook his head. He pushed back from the table as if about to rise.

"I could mention the name of a certain fiend," he said, his head trembling, as if a shiver had gone through him. "A certain well-known, financially lucrative gentleman in a black cape."

"Are you referring to the amusement park?"

"Ha!"

I felt an odd sensation of hilarity in my body. At any moment, I might begin to laugh, and if I did, it would never stop. It would be like hiccups. My skin goose-pimpled. This man in front of me slapped his hands together. He chuckled at some private inner joke, scooted his chair back to the table and took a sip from his wineglass. I began to suspect that this might not be Ion Torgu at all, that this man was in fact a mentally unhinged opportunist who had lured me to Transylvania in an effort to extort money. Perhaps he mistakenly thought that we would pay for an interview with a major criminal.

"I must tell you that this kind of outburst does not fill me with confidence. How do I know that you are, in fact, Ion Torgu? Do you have identification?"

He gave me a dripping, blue-toothed smile. He winked and sipped. "I haven't had identification since they released me from the camps in the mountains."

Another problem unanticipated by Lockyear, I thought. How in the world would we ever verify that this man was who he claimed to be? Without proof of his identity, we could not possibly move forward. For all we knew, we would be filming an interview with a retired civil servant, or a lunatic, or both. We couldn't verify his nationality either. By his looks, this man could be a Hungarian, a Russian, a German, a Serb; there was no telling.

"Now that you have raised the subject, let's talk about that amusement park. I've read newspapers speculating that you are the lead investor in that project, and if so, that's of interest to us. Vlad the Impaler is a Romanian national hero and has nothing to do with Dracula . . ."

His lips contorted in another scowl. "I urge you not to repeat that name."

I took Romanian money out of my purse. He must not be allowed to pay for the wine. I would have to call Lockyear and apprise him of the situation. It was a doubtful interview. Even if this person before me turned out to be Torgu, the interviewee would be nothing but a royal pain in the ass to us. This much seemed clear.

"I'm tired," I told him. "I'd like to pay for the wine, and then I will go to my room and speak with my people in New York. We can talk in the morning."

Torgu appeared to realize that he had overstepped the boundaries of my tolerance. He changed his tone.

"But I want to bring you to Poiana Brasov this very minute."

I marveled at the man's audacity. "Out of the question!"

"If you pass up this chance, I cannot promise there will be another."

My hands were in my pockets, and my ring slipped onto a finger, as if seeking human warmth. If it were only a magic ring, I thought, and I could disappear. If only I could rub its surface and make Robert materialize and whisk this goblin into the night. Robert would make sly jokes about the scuzziness of the hotel. He would promise me a stay at the Four Seasons when we got back. We could have a glass of his favorite scotch together and play crazy eights. But that was fantasy, and I had to deal with reality right then and there.

I knew it would be a grave mistake to lose the interview without first consulting Lockyear. But I also knew what my boss would say about this man. Lockyear would hate him. Lockyear attributed moral qualities to surface attributes, and he would be unforgiving of a man with rotting, nicotine-stained choppers. I imagined the future of this story. Our correspondent, Austen Trotta, would be disgusted by the mere presence of such a person, but he might gamely try to make a story out of him. The first screening of the story for the executive producer, the chimerical Bob Rogers, would be a disaster. Torgu would be despised as a character. I could hear the criticism. We can't show this guy on American television. Look at his goddamn teeth. Look at his hair. He's a freak. I wouldn't put this guy on *The Hour* if you held a gun to my head. What the hell were you thinking? And Lockyear would blame me. He would blame me for those teeth, and he would blame me for dragging him to Romania, and he would blame me for the bad screening. Resolve built within. I would not go to Poiana Brasov. I would get up from the chair and call Lockyear and tell him that we were off.

"Let me understand," Torgu said. "You have the power to activate or obstruct this process of television?"

"I don't follow."

"I mean to say"—he paused, as if collecting his thoughts—"I mean to ask whether you have sole empowerment from your place of work to give me this chance to appear before your so-great audience on your so-great show. You have so much power in your possession, Miss Harker?"

I had never heard it put quite that way. But he was right. In this matter, I did have the power. I absolutely did. That power might not gener-

ate a real income, but it conferred on me a certain leverage over potential interview subjects. If I gave Lockyear the thumbs-down, Lockyear
would never in a million years come to Romania and meet Torgu for
himself. He would never risk placing Austen Trotta in an interview situation with a subject to whom I had refused my blessing.

This man was clever. He appealed to my vanity. I saw right through
it, but succumbed nonetheless.

"It has to be tonight?"

He gazed long at me. "I am desperate to cooperate, but it must be
on my terms. You see, my dear, I am a hunted man."

The words had a pitiable quality. "Under one condition," I told him.

"Name this condition."

"Before I go, you tell me exactly what I want to know. No fiddle
faddle."

He nodded his acceptance. "No fiddle faddle."

"First. If you are who you say you are, you must prove it."

He nodded. "There are some records of land title at my domicile.
Will those suffice?"

"We'll see. You also said that you weren't exactly a Romanian nationalist. What did you mean?"

"I meant, my dear, that I am not even Romanian, so that I can hardly
be called a Romanian nationalist."

"What are you then? What's your nationality?"

He gave another of those wasteland chuckles. "Oh my, that's a long
answer."

"Something please. I need something."

He cleared his throat. "Racially, I am nothing specific. If you have to
know, I carry the blood of those people who migrated out of Central
Asia through the Caucusus and into Europe. I am Scythian and Khazar,
Ossetian and Georgian, Moldavian and Mongol."

I confessed I was skeptical about such a hazy pedigree.

"What can I do? The two hundred languages of the Caucusus bab-
ble all night inside of me. The Byzantines still fight the Pechenegs. The
Bulgars wage perpetual war against Novgorod. I am a road, by itself,
upon which all of the people have traveled. It's the sad fact. Would it

were so that I could be a Romanian nationalist. That would be easy enough. Wear Green. Murder some Hungarians. Maybe a Jew."

He slapped his hands together. "That is my answer."

"But your name is Romanian," I insisted.

"My name?" He threw up his hands in despair. "Perhaps we should abandon this project, after all."

I found that I had to believe him. Or rather, I wanted to. He might be insane, and he was certainly difficult, but he might also be who he said. Whatever, I prided myself on being as tenacious as my father: If there was a story here, it would be mine.

We struck a deal. It would take about an hour to drive to Poiana Brasov, and Torgu said that we should leave immediately. He said that I must call New York and tell my people that negotiations were under way. No promises had been made, but there was room for an agreement. The discussions could take a certain amount of time and would have to be conducted in a secret, undisclosed location in the Transylvanian Alps. It would not be possible for them to communicate with me until those negotiations had concluded.

Torgu owned the hotel in Poiana Brasov, and he had explained that he would supply me with a room of sufficient luxuriousness to compensate me for the lateness of the hour. There would also be a delicious hot meal waiting for me, he said, the best meal to be had in the entire country of Romania. He excused himself to go to the toilet, and I went to my room to retrieve my things and make the call. I left the message verbatim on Lockyear's voice mail and made to leave the room. As I turned the key, I realized that the phone was ringing; by the time I got to it, the caller had hung up. I had taken too much wine, and my mind grew fuzzy and dim in the stuffiness of that place. I shouldn't have agreed to his terms. I thought of Clemmie and her African demons. I stumbled around in the dark of my room for a moment. I couldn't find the light. I placed my hands on the cold surface of a mirror and recoiled. The phone started ringing again, but I ignored it. I would call Lockyear again as soon as I had something to say to him.

I discovered that my things were not in my room. In a moment of panic, I ripped the sheets off the bed. Everything had gone wrong.

I called the desk clerk in the lobby, and he informed me that my belongings had already been transferred from my room to a car that waited outside. Downstairs, as I passed his station, the clerk called out, "Your friend left something for you."

"Mr. Torgu?"

"The lady."

He placed an envelope in my palm. It was from Clemmie. I tore it open and found a tiny metal cross on a necklace. It was her cross. She had some nerve. She had been fishing for my soul all along. She was one of those people who judges, who believes in the purity of her soul. But diamond ring trumps cross, I say. Human love beats divine love. Human love means skin, and I am skin. I am of this world. My kingdom is here. This was the alcohol talking, I told myself, but so be it; she pissed me off. The desk clerk watched me with expectation. His eyes were big with worry. He wanted a tip. I plucked the necklace from the envelope and hung it around my neck. I left five American dollars for the clerk. Robert would have called that overgenerous. But I am an overgenerous woman, and I hope that fact is remembered.

Eight

The road snaked through dark, hilly country. Torgu never spoke. I glanced a few times at his face in the green dashboard lights, and it struck me as fragile and pitiful. The car was an old Porsche with leather interior, but still. He shouldn't have to drive himself along such difficult, lightless ways. He should have a driver. Why didn't he? Should this be a warning sign that the man was something other than a major criminal? For the moment, I had nothing to lose in believing him, and I pondered the options.

I knew he would be a difficult man to coax into an interview. We would have to haggle over everything, and such negotiations took time. Suppose he assented to the interview. Then we'd have to talk about his face. Could we show his face or would he insist on a profile shot? Would he have to be blurred all together until he was no longer visible? Or would he remain a dark shadow, a black outline against a blaze of white light? Anonymity might be a deal-breaker for Lockyear. Would people watch an entire segment about a man they couldn't see with their own eyes? But if we could get him to sit down full face in a lengthy and comprehensive interview, we might unearth an entire hidden history in this part of the world. That is, if he really talked. He might clam up and say nothing. He might use the entire interview to deny any involvement with crime. He might try to make himself look like a political martyr and nothing else. But it might be worth the gamble. This was my professional judgment.

Eventually, we came to a town, a kind of ski resort, lights twinkling in a few establishments, and I thought that I saw a few large houses scattered along a lane of alpine-style hotels. It was off-season, though, and the activity in these lodgings ended on the lower floors. There could be few guests. Still, I hoped he would pull into a driveway.

"Poiana Brasov," he murmured, noticing my interest. "That's the name of this place."

"I recall. Your hotel is here."

"Not here. Farther up. This was the dictator's resort. I like to drive through and reflect on the violence of his overthrow."

"If they have a phone," I said. "I wouldn't mind calling my fiancé."

"Surely they have phones," he replied, "but we are late, and our dinner has already been prepared."

On our way out of town, not far from the entrance of the final hotel on the main strip, he slowed the car to a halt. My hopes soared. I took my purse in hand. He leaned his head out the window and spat loudly into the road. He rolled up his window and drove on. He saw my disappointment, which may have looked like panic. I recalled the phone that had been ringing in my hotel room as I closed the door, the phone I had decided not to answer. As my mother would say, we all make our choices.

"Surely you have noticed that I am not a pretty old gentleman. This monster here was to blame for that. He made my life hell, and I make a small justice of my own by always stopping on the way through his town."

How can one ever argue with a concentration camp survivor? We came to the end of the cement lane, struck a swath of dirt road and plunged down. He drove too fast in this inappropriate vehicle. Clods of earth and rock flew up. Going downhill, he applied speed. The pines loomed over us. How ridiculous had been my fear in the car with Clemmie. We'd seen a coffin. So what? That was nothing.

After a time, the road improved, and the moonlight showed landmarks. We passed through a rolling meadow of grass, where I saw a small graveyard, a low thicket of pale crosses. Beyond that, we passed a small stone church and what appeared to be the remains of a farming village. But there were no lights. I thought I saw the black shapes of cows. Torgu watched me as we passed through this island of civilization.

At last, he began to slow down. He pulled into a black space that must have been a parking spot, though I could see no buildings. The headlights flicked off before I could get a good look around. He opened the car door and got out with surprising agility, and I was alone for an instant. The passenger door swung open, and his hand reached for my valise.

"Please."

"I don't care for this situation."

Dogs or some other animal began to bark and yelp in the distance.

"I will go ahead of you and light the way," he said. He snatched the valise. "You'll be reassured. In any case, the hotel will seem preferable to the wolves in these forests."

I got out of the car and strode after him, leaving the door open. A light in the car gave faint illumination. But I was striding toward a hole of pine in the night. I could smell the trees. I had smelled them ever since our arrival in Brasov, down the mountain, but they had been a pleasing distant scent, like the aroma of salt air when you are still miles from the beach. Up here, left to themselves, the trees made a suffocating mass. The sap burst from the cracks in the bark and flowed to the earth. The needles had fallen in great drifts, and an oozy moisture lay beneath. This closeness of vegetation in still, animal rank, as if the pines were tall nude humans at attention, ate at my nerves.

But it was more than the trees, really. I have to be honest. People, alone in dark woods, will get scared. It can happen to anyone. There was a difference in this place. Right in the middle of the trees, also invisible at first, stood an object made by human hands, a big structure that emitted its own smell, one that tipped the scent of pine into something funereal. That's the only way I can describe it. This scent came from the combination of the building and the trees. They were all one thing. For a few seconds, I couldn't see my hands, my legs. I felt my skin and almost jumped, because I felt that my skin stood next to me. When a tree branch scraped my arm, I experienced a searing pain and cried out.

Torgu did not light the way. He'd raced ahead and was gone. I would be murdered here, I thought. This is how those people feel, the ones who are led to a place in anticipation of a settlement or mercy and who then hear the crack of a twig behind them, and we see the look of terrified loneliness in their eyes before the gun sounds and the screen goes dark. Is this what people mean when they talk about facing your own mortality?

Under other circumstances, I might have run for a tree and tried to climb. But I didn't climb. I didn't trust the trees any more than I trusted Torgu. I stopped, I crouched, I hugged myself. You find that when you have no choice, matters become clear. It's a lovely feeling, in a way. All those decisions that face you at other times, they just melt away, and you do what existence has handed you. I had felt this way on the night that Robert proposed. That had been another instance of total clarity, though so different. I wanted to cry then and there, when he offered the ring, and I did. I wanted to cry in the forest, too, but didn't. If tears fall from my eyes, I thought, then I will never leave this place. That was the self-imposed test, and I passed. I willed the tears to remain in my eyes.

The lights came on. They erupted in yellow, as if torches had been lit, and I saw that I crouched at the edge of a covered driveway, a portico reeking of mildew, cut logs and gasoline. The logs had been stacked inside the columns, a wall of firewood. The smell of fuel came from what looked like a generator within a concrete hut just to my left. The portico curved back to the right, to an entrance. The lamps hung in squares on the eaves of the portico, right where the columns reached the roof, and they continued up to the doors, which were made of beveled glass and gave a murky reflection. I turned around and looked back at the forest and the car. The Porsche could not be seen.

"A last corner of the Urwald, the ancient European forest. Do you like it?" Torgu had ended up behind me somehow.

I was honest. "No."

"We agree then."

"It doesn't feel like any forest I've ever been in. Do you live here?"

He grimaced. "I habitate."

He seemed to have become more fragile, even less healthy. He seemed to have shrunk.

"If you have seen my days in this life, you will know why I prefer the company of humans to vegetables. People have a stunning life and afterlife. Their deaths are even more interesting than their lives. But a tree . . ." He paused and looked up in disdain. "It does this and this and this until it falls, and is shat upon by small forest creatures. Are you hungry?"

I realized I was famished. I felt suddenly safe and at the same time stupid for having my fit. That's how I thought of it, at that moment. I had had a fit, like a seizure. There would be a call to a therapist as soon as I got back to New York. There would be a new physical regimen: yoga, hearty food, jogging in the park.

Now, of course, I can't explain or try to excuse this ignorance. For someone like Stim, perhaps, there may have been obvious warning signs. He knows the movies. He's read the book a dozen times. He can quote lines. But I had never been a fan, never had any interest in that sort of thing, and certainly never expected to encounter similar plot lines in my own life. Furthermore, even when I knew that I would be coming to Transylvania and had enough cultural conditioning to get the allusion, even when Stim told me to read the book and see a few of the movies, I barely paid attention. I started the book and tossed it away, for the same reason that I dropped those books about elves and goblins. I was never a Narnia girl, never a Hobbit chick. I am a realist. I am a believer in the things that you can touch. I have always preferred well-built men and clothes made by geniuses and food made by pros and the stuff money can buy. Maybe that makes me shallow, but it's simply true, and I have never felt the need to apologize. I reason, and still do, that most people are like me. Most of us, even if we're poor, even if we're religious, even if we subscribe to the strangest creeds, nevertheless want the cream in this life. We want to feel the softness of the bed, not the edge of the blade. And when we have children, as I will someday soon, I hope, we want them to lie in the softness that we ourselves have cultivated. No matter how odd, no matter how criminal, I reasoned, Torgu must feel the same.

As I entered the glass doors, I conducted a silly test based upon my one reliable bit of idiot arcana. I searched for a mirror and found one immediately. It covered one wall of the lobby. I froze in horror. Torgu was clearly visible. Unfortunately, so was I. Nothing in that hotel could have been as shocking as the sight of my own visage. It made me want to cry. I hadn't bathed, and I hadn't brushed my hair, which had begun to curl up in the damp, and my mascara had run, and there were pine needles on my clothes, and my blouse was untucked. Torgu, on the other hand, conveyed an eccentric elegance in his reflection. I became furious at myself for my self-neglect, and at Stim for suggesting ludicrous possibilities. I resolved to become professional again. I took the engagement ring from my pocket and put it on my finger. Resolutions welled up. Torgu would grant me the interview, and our segment would get an Emmy, and even Lockyear would be forced to sing my praises at the awards show dinner table.

Nine

I cleaned up well, changing clothes quickly in the lobby bathroom, scrubbing my face and reapplying rouges. Nothing could be done about the hair, except to tie it back. We had a surprisingly fine dinner, roast chicken with mamaliga, a kind of polenta, and a salad of tomato, cucumber, onion and sheep's cheese. Torgu opened a bottle of wine from his own cellar, this one French, very old and no doubt conspicuously grand, a 1963 Chateau Margaux, and my confidence grew. This man had begun, at last, to behave like the powerful and successful leader of an organized crime syndicate. I noticed, of course, the lack of staff, but figured that the lateness of our arrival, and Torgu's need for absolute privacy in our conversation, had made their appearance unnecessary. The help had cooked the meal and gone to bed.

In a bit of welcome flirtation, he complimented me on Clemmie's crucifix. It was a piece of junk antique, I thought, but he seemed pleased by it, so I let him have a closer look. He became a little emotional.

"Such a tale of human suffering encompassed by this emblem. Are you aware?"

"Like the Spanish Inquisition? Or the Crusades, you mean?"

He sighed. "I mean the total sum of horrible pain and gruesome atrocity visited upon believers and nonbelievers alike in the shadow of this simple pictogram."

I didn't for the life of me know what he was really getting at. "Religions have cruel histories, you mean."

He paused a moment, seeming just as perplexed by my words as I was by his. "Truly, you don't see? The persecutions of the Roman Emperor Julian alone, his assault on the early Christians, would fill the Danubian estuary with blood. Fifteen centuries later, the Thirty Years' War would fill a sea. It is moving beyond words."

A typically bizarre comment from this man, I thought, but worth recalling for the purposes of a possible interview question. Did these musings indicate guilt over his own murders? Or was I being too melodramatic?

After the first course of salad, he asked if I would like to see his art collection and I jumped at the chance. Both Trotta and Lockyear had specifically mentioned the importance for our segment of visible displays of wealth, and Austen had even singled out the possibility of a collection of dubiously acquired masterpieces.

"Bring your gustation," he said. He pointed at my wine. I didn't correct his English.

I followed him out of the empty restaurant through the lobby and down a corridor to a door on the left. He entered first. As soon as I stepped across the threshold, I smelled something off, like the odor of trash left in the sun too long. He lit a series of candles on the walls. As the flames came up, one by one, I had the unsettling feeling of being in a graveyard that had become a junkyard. The odor intensified and seemed to be coming from the objects. The gallery extended farther than I had expected. Between our position and the walls rose a pair of long rectangular stone daises, elevated a few feet off the ground by squat granite columns. On top of the daises bristled a collection of detritus.

"Here lies my strength in old age," he said, "the only objects in the world that I truly cherish. I go nowhere without taking a few of them along."

"Quite a collection," I replied, not knowing what else to say.

"Yes. You may burn the rest of my possessions. You may burn the earth and poison the waters, for all I care."

His reference to burning was certainly apt. Many of the objects, it seemed to me, had been burned, or had survived fire, at any rate. There were pieces of blackened concrete stone that might have been corner-stones of buildings; segments of crosses and icons, also burned; tablets inscribed with various alphabets—Arabic, Chinese, Hebrew, Latin, Cyrillic, Egyptian hieroglyphic, Anglo-Saxon and Finno-Ugric, fragments of German and French, what must have been Romanian and Hungarian, a bric-a-brac of the world's cemeteries and ruins, it seemed to me. There were shards of pots, appendages from statues, broken plates, bent cut-lery, slabs of tomb and what might have been the leftovers of mummies, bundles of rag and pale stick. Not everything was old. I saw a melted en-gine block, of all things, and a piece of a wall writhing with electrical cir-cuitry and inscribed with Slavic words. There was a collection of defaced plastic dolls, and I glimpsed more recent items, too, but didn't have the stomach to investigate. In truth, I was repulsed and disappointed. This wasn't exactly the kind of art collection Austen Trotta had in mind, and I wondered whether it would even read on camera. Would people see anything onscreen but a pile of horrific old crap? I became nauseated by the growing reek, a smell reminiscent of gas leaks. I had to get out.

He saw my discomfiture and began to blow out the candles. His eyes glistened. "I call it my avenue of eternal peace, the remains of every obliterated place that I have ever visited."

We returned to the dinner table. I gulped my wine. He watched with some curiosity.

"It's an, an arresting sight," I said. "Very disturbing, in fact."

"Indeed?" He passed a hand across his eyes. "I find it all unbearably poignant. I find it more devastating than the sublime poetry of the Per-sians, more piercing than the words of Shakespeare. This is the true substance of our world, is it not? This brokenness."

"I prefer the more straightforward kind of beauty," I said. "But I'm not so sophisticated as you, I think." I made an unfortunate remark then. "You must crave some form of horror in your surrounding."

He blinked in surprise. "In fact, I despise it. Where do you see horror?"

The question stumped me. It hadn't occurred to him, perhaps, that his tastes ran to the morbid. But then, that word would be meaningless to a man whose entire life seemed to be dedicated to an appreciation, a near incomprehensible appreciation, of the most hideous side of the species. But he quickly softened. He could see my earnest attempt to grapple with the meaning of his beloved objets d'art, and it flattered him. In truth, I was playing a bit of the ingénue. I had seen my share of grotesque displays in the art galleries in SoHo. Ugliness was one of several expensive, voguish, downtown aesthetics, as tried and true as portraiture. But Torgu's menagerie did feel a little different. It didn't suggest a preoccupation with art, for one. It felt a lot more committed than that.

"Horror," he said. "It's in the eye of the beholder, of course. But I see. I do. Yet we disagree only on the surface. To you, horror must be a harbinger of fear. For me, it is pure sorrow. Horror is truth, to me, and truth is beauty. So we have the same impulse, manifest in different ways."

I disagreed, but changed the subject. "You seem very much alone with your collection up here. Do you ever tire of the solitude?"

"Oh, this place was not always so cut off as it seems now. I don't mean the hotel, which is quite recent. But the place itself. The ground was once a crossroads. It straddled the great lines of communication between the eastern and western worlds. Remember, two world wars have been fought through here. I have seen more bodies thrown into caves than you can possibly imagine."

Was this a confession already? Or was he just a helplessly gross old fellow? I could have pursued the comment, but didn't want to make him suspicious of my intentions. For one, it could be a test. He might want to gauge my level of interest in his bloodier crimes. But also, I reasoned, if he was willing to offer such morsels without prompting at such an early stage, then it shouldn't be difficult to tease them out in greater detail later.

"Tell me about your family," I said.

"I have no children."

"Parents?"

He groaned a little, as if finding memory a strain. 'They came from the steppe. My father was what later came to be called a kulak, a well-to-do farmer, though, for all his wealth, he received a disgraceful burial."

"Mind if I take notes?"

The first glint of hostility returned to his eyes. "About my parents? This interview is likely to be much more interesting than you currently imagine."

I held off on the notes. I cut into the chicken. "Can you tell me, anyway, what you mean when you say your father received a disgraceful burial?"

He pointed at the curve of the chicken breast on my plate with the tip of his own knife. "That's the best bit, I find." He cut a slice from his own portion. "There was no money. Like so many of the dead in this part of the world, my father was dishonored, and he took revenge. He is still taking it, in point of fact."

Just as I can pose a question without words, through an expressive look or the most ethereal exhalation, I also display shock or surprise or disbelief more eloquently with my silence. Kill the mime, Robert tells me when I give him a stern look. It's one of his favorite witticisms. I hadn't meant to be dismissive, but Torgu took offense. I hadn't killed the mime in time.

"It's quite rude, Ms. Harker, to hold the beliefs of others in contempt."

"But—I don't . . ."

"Not to mention dangerous."

He drank the wine. He cut another slice from a breast of chicken, and his dark teeth bit into the flesh. "I made the funeral arrangements myself, under the shadow of debts that we had not foreseen. My mother had spent everything, you see. So I buried my father without the proper means. He was gone, she argued, and would want the best for his heirs. We buried him without his horse. She would not allow me even that."

Mom sounded sensible. I couldn't imagine that anyone had buried a corpse with a horse in a thousand years. "But, just so I understand. You said that he took revenge? After his death?"

The wine dripped from his chin. He trembled. "Beyond any doubt."

I thought of Clemmie Spence. She would have had no problem with this conversation.

"How did you know your father wanted revenge? If he was dead?"

Torgu put down the knife and fork. He wiped his old hands on a napkin.

"Myself, dear."

"How do you mean?"

He put down the napkin. "Look at me. Really. I am a testament to the man's endless rage."

I could sense his sorrow in the room, a wave of it, palpable as heat. There was every chance—it was a probability—that he would never re-peat what he had just told me in front of a camera. But it worried me that he might. And then what would we do? Wouldn't we be obligated to show our viewers? In theory, stories about the improper burial of his father would turn a routine tale about a crime lord into something far more mysterious. But in reality, if this was meant to be a story about organized crime, then such macabre tales would be off-putting. People would recoil in confusion. It wasn't good, in television, for too many things to occur at once on the screen. But perhaps Torgu wanted me to know his background for personal reasons.

"But wasn't it your mother's fault?"

"Indeed. She is the source of all unhappiness."

Before I could follow up, find out more about this woman, he changed the subject. "When will you be married?"

I preened, showing the ring. "Next summer."

"Congratulations. Is this man your age?"

"He's a bit older."

"Is he vital?"

I couldn't resist a laugh.

"You could say that."

He smiled his first genuinely kind smile. "Rich?"

"He will inherit nicely."

Torgu gave an approving dip of his head.

"Then you've conquered the first dragon of this life."

I wondered what the second and third dragons might be. "Are you married, Mr. Torgu?"

He shook his head.

"Never?"

He attended again to his meal, chewed for a while in silence, drank some more wine. My question provoked another awkward response, like the one about family. This was worse, in fact. As the seconds ticked by, he seemed to experience a panic of mortification. That's the only way I can put it. He looked up at me with a blush on his pallid cheeks. There was no hotel staff. We were alone in a dining room that looked over floodlit trees stretching away from the portico. Nothing moved in the forest.

He said, "I was informed long ago that certain states would be injurious to my health."

The words came painfully, as if he had wrestled with telling a lie. Once out, they lingered there, and he seemed to regret them, peering at me in a kind of defensive hush. I didn't understand his comment, but his mortification seemed to deepen. An air of apology hung over us, horribly out of context. If you've ever been in bed with a man who has suddenly, inexplicably, found himself unable to perform, you'll have some idea. I couldn't look away from him, nor he from me, and if I'm honest, a weird erotic charge lay in that silence. He wanted to tell me a deep secret, and it terrified me.

I stammered out a question, at last. "An illness?"

He drank again and cleared his throat. He shook his head and looked into the empty spaces beyond our table. "No more of an illness than life itself."

"Ah." His answer had the ring of finality. He wouldn't address the subject further. All of my alarm bells should have gone off, and some did, but they were the wrong ones. Torgu must not say such things to Austen in the interview, I thought. If he mentions this malady, whatever it happened to be, then he will become instantly ridiculous, and if he's ridiculous, he will have no credibility at all. He will not be credible when he claims to be the head of organized crime in Eastern Europe. He will not be credible when he talks about his concentration camp experience. I couldn't yet bear the thought that I would have to make that same judgment long before Austen would, that this interview was dead in the water before a single camera clicked on. My employers would be gravely disappointed. I rationalized Torgu's comment. He probably suffered from a routine sexual malfunction, an impotence, perhaps, magnified by his pride and solitude into a much more severe condition. And yet it was such an odd thing to admit, such a uselessly revealing, totally embarrassing tidbit that I figured it must be sincere. I wanted confirmation of my suspicion.

"That's just unfortunate," I finally managed. "By certain states, you mean—"

He turned his eyes on me with a new energy of defiance, but with a hint of something else as well; a pained spark, I thought. "I don't wish to discuss it now or ever again. I will ask that you forget the matter. I don't know why I answered at all. You're unpleasantly compelling, at times."

What else could I say? He looked at me with steady eyes and waited for the next question. Despairing, I relented. "Do you have any help up here? Someone must have made this excellent dinner."

He thanked me for the compliment and gave me his second kind smile. I was relieved. "The Vourkulakis brothers run this hotel."

"It's a working hotel?"

Torgu shrugged, as if he didn't quite get the drift of the question.

"It sounds like a Greek name. Vourkulakis."

This caused him to smile. "Very good. It is indeed Greek. They are low-born Greek, I should say. They mixed with Turks long ago and are not of the high-born variety. In this country, high-born Greeks ran the government for over a century. Phanariots, the people here called them. They were rich aristocrats of the Ottoman Empire. But the Vourkulakis brothers are dirty little islanders. They come from Santorini. Do you know it?"

"Oh my God, I do know it. It's where Robert wants to go on our honeymoon. Is it beautiful there? We're also thinking about Vietnam. But I'm partially Greek, on my mother's side, so we'll probably do the Aegean."

Torgu seemed displeased. He paused and his lips gave a funny tremble. "Judging by the Vourkulakis brothers, it is no place for romance." He wiped his mouth with a napkin. His high forehead wrinkled. "This is the thing that I will say about the Vourkulakis brothers. If you see a beautiful young man with dark hair coming toward you down the corridors of this building, you must stay clear of him. Avoid his company . . . the brothers are ill . . . they are ill in a way that the entire Greek civilization, pardon me, is ill, with an inability to look away from certain things that others avoid at all costs."

I tried to pretend that we were talking about the same thing. "Greek men are known to be very forward. . . ."

"Yes. That's it exactly. The Vourkulakis brothers are very forward. But they are not allowed on the upper three floors, and they know this, so as long as you keep to those floors, you will have nothing to fear."

He stood. "Forgive me," he said. "It's late, and I'm exhausted. If you're finished, I will show you to your floor."

"My own floor. Goodness."

There was no coffee, no dessert. We stood. I thanked him for the meal again, and he bowed as if I were a princess.

Ten

He hoisted my valise and led me past the room containing the broken artifacts of his collection. I almost tripped down a set of three steps and caught my balance right in front of a contraption that appeared to be a working elevator. I had never seen anything like it before. Instead of a single car that opened when you pressed a button, this elevator had no doors and two cars, and the cars were constantly moving. On the left, the cars rose up. On the right, they came down. They moved at a steady pace, soundlessly, and you had to jump on as soon as a car became level with the floor or your chance passed. It was a little unnerving, and I hesitated. He shoved me on, and we took off. He called this thing a paternoster and proudly told me that the hotel had been designed and constructed by East German engineers before global safety norms interfered.

"Cripples cannot manage," Torgu said with contempt. "They lack even the minimum of nimbleness."

Our car rose quickly, and, because it had no doors, I glimpsed snatches of the forbidden floors, the levels where the Vourkulakis brothers evidently ranged. The light from the paternoster lit the corridors for an instant, and they looked like the corridors of any other cheap hotel, except gloomier, and on one or two levels, doors hung open, as if chambermaids had been cleaning, though there were no carts, no pails and mops, nothing else to suggest that kind of work. The smell of rot had got into those spaces. The mildew had sewn itself into the fabric, and another odor, too, of decay, the presence of dead vermin within the walls, had infiltrated. The higher we got, the colder I became. I didn't ask him if the upper three floors had heat or light. After the dinner, I had come to trust his immediate plans for me. The meal had been exquisite. He had been mostly pleasant. He needed something from me, it was clear. He needed the camera. Until he got it, he would treat me well.

"Almost there," he muttered. "These are the worst floors, these last before the penthouse. Disgraceful."

I saw what he meant. My head rose from the level of the floor, and I caught a whiff of scorched plastic and wood. There had been a fire. The light of the paternoster revealed blackened walls. The contraption seemed to slow a fraction or two, and I felt a charge in my nerves. I thought I saw movement, a wisp of something, like the tail of a large animal, or it could have been a hand, waving at the edge of my sight. It seemed to come from the maw of a room without a door. It couldn't have been more than twenty yards away, but the light of the pasternoster didn't shine brightly enough to pull it from the shadows.

"Did you see that?"

A cluck came out of Torgu, as if to shush me. The last of the burned floors receded.

"Please off." He shoved me lightly out of the paternoster. "We enjoy stairs from here."

The floor beneath my feet felt solid. The odor of mildew and fire had gone. I considered the possibility that this addition had been built after the conflagration, on top of it, like a new city constructed upon an ancient one. Torgu sprang up the steps ahead of me, surprising me with his sudden agility. He placed his hand on the knob of a door and glanced back.

"I will survey," he told me. "The maid service can be sporadic."

He opened the door and peeked inside. Warm yellow light spilled on the stairs.

"Lovely," he said, and he whisked me, with my valise, through the entrance. I expected to walk into a corridor, but the floor stretched away in a single wide expanse, like a showroom, divided by pieces of heavy furniture, sideboards, a grand piano, couches, divans, a number of beds. A series of richly piled and brocaded Oriental carpets covered the ground. They were hand-woven silk, one could see at a glance. Candle fires flickered here and there. Lamps were attached to thick extension cords, snaking along the carpets to hidden wall sockets. I could see a bar, heavy with colored bottles of whiskey, vodka and liqueurs, and several armoires, a vanity with a wide, round mirror and art nouveau filigree. The pieces might have belonged to Torgu personally, but they didn't seem to reflect any particular taste, except for ransacking antique shops. I heard the hum of space heaters, also attached to extension cords, and saw their orange glow, like little fires. I asked myself whether there would be enough electricity to power my blow dryer and knew the answer. There wouldn't be. The fiendish frizz would come back to my hair.

On all sides, on the walls, shone reflections of the candles, lamps and furniture, a glittering surface, almost like water. "It's beautiful, Mr. Torgu."

He nodded. "There are rules in this place, Ms. Harker. You already know one."

"Steer clear of the Greeks." I saluted him, eyes drooping.

"Yes. And that means you have no business on the floors between here and the ground. Yes?"

"Agreed."

"I'm a businessman with errands around the province and won't be back till late this next evening. We'll have dinner again, and, if you like, you can bring your camera this time."

I corrected his misunderstanding. "Not so fast. That's not how we work. Cameras come on the next visit."

His mouth curled down in dismay. "But a screen test is surely in order?"

"We're not making a Hollywood movie, Mr. Torgu."

He turned away. His vanity seemed wounded. "Never mind. I will come for you in the late evening for another meal."

I wanted to fall back on the bed. It had been a horrendous day. But I stood there, yawning, waiting for him to leave. He glanced back, and I received an impression, very quick, of sexual interest. I recalled his un-named malady and wondered if it had been nothing more than a mis-guided attempt at seduction, an old man's wayward notion of what might turn on an American woman. It seemed an absurd speculation, and the impression did not linger. On the contrary, that last glance at me seemed to chase him out of the room. But at the door, Torgu stopped, placed his hand on the frame and looked back once more.

"A last word."

I crossed my arms, straightened my posture, and attended to this parting admonition with effort.

"The door is locked for a reason. When I'm ready for you, I will come and get you. I have the only key."

That was his final bizarre revelation. I was too tired to object. As soon as he vanished, I dialed Robert's number on my phone. The cell searched for service, flickered into connection once or twice, but the number never rang. I hit the buttons a dozen times or more, without luck. I shook the knob of my door and called out Torgu's name, but no one answered, neither the man himself nor his theoretically malignant Greeks. I went back to the bed, dialed several more times and fell asleep with the phone in my hand.

Eleven

When I woke the next morning, coffee steamed in a pot beside a basket of breads and a jar of honey. Sun blazed in my eyes, and I saw that the walls were nothing but plate glass windows, pane after pane, on every side of the room. I walked the perimeter, nibbling on bread and honey, looking in every direction at a grand vista of pine-topped mountains, south, east and west, as far as the eye could roam. Northward lay the flat plain of Transylvania. On that side of the range, unlike the southern flank, which rose gradually out of the flatlands, the mountains shot straight from the floor of the valley to thousands of feet. They reminded me of frozen waves, curling up off the beach, arrested at their crest. I perched on one crest, like a hawk on a peak, gazing into level distances. The valleys themselves must be very high, the land of Transylvania itself one enormous, flat-hearted mountain.

After exploring, I tried my cell phone again. I pounded on the door. I slept.

My second dinner with Torgu began in silence. I was furious. A camera, not like the ones used by our crews, an older thing, much bulkier, stood beside the table like a manservant. At an adjacent table, I noticed a primitive soundboard. Mobster arrogance, I thought.

The meal didn't help, pork chops on top of corn meal mush, an unpleasant sight, wet sand seeping up through gristly rock. My professional agitation grew as we dined, as the stillness pressed. I didn't like to be railroaded. He had no business introducing the tech hardware, any more than I had a right to advise him on where to open his next casino. Moreover, I objected to being locked in a room, however profound his need for security. It had occurred to me that he suspected my credentials and feared that I might mean him some harm, in which case it made a twisted sense for him to lock me up. But it didn't reconcile me to the situation.

More than anything, I wanted cell phone service. If I could talk to Robert, or anyone, I would be fine. Finally, I spoke up.

"Tomorrow, could you please drive me to someplace where I could get a decent cellular signal, please? I need to call home." I tossed out a quick lie. "My father is in the hospital for surgery. Was."

He grunted in dubious sympathy. "But we had an agreement that we would be in secret negotiations until both sides were satisfied."

"I'm talking about a personal call, Mr. Torgu."

His eyes smoldered with some resentment. He wiped his lips with a napkin. "But your loved ones might contact your professional colleagues and give away some information that would be detrimental to my well-being, no?"

"I doubt it. Can you please be reasonable?"

He changed tack. "I know nothing about these new technologies."

I looked at the technological miracle of the camera and back at him. He dissected his chop. He chewed. I pointed at the camera. "Does that, by any chance, belong to you?"

He banged his utensils down onto the table. He sighed, resting his eyes on me with a sort of finality, as if he had reached a conclusion of some kind. "That is the work of Olestru. He informs me that it functions. I thought it would help in your work."

Olestru, I thought, who had disappeared with some Norwegian journalist, who had lured me into this mess in the first place, who probably didn't exist. I placed my napkin on the table beside my plate. "I would like to have a chat with him."

Torgu regarded me with a growing coolness. "He is not available."

"Of course he's not available!" I blurted. "He's not fucking real!"

Immediately, I regretted the outburst, not for his sake, but for my own. I could feel myself slipping into desperation.

"He is most certainly real. He gave me what I wanted. As soon as I asked." He clapped his hands together, and I jumped in my chair. My blood began to beat loudly in my ears. "This camera."

"It's, it's obsolete," I stammered.

"Swords are obsolete," he replied. "They work."

Was that a threat? I didn't ask. I clenched my hands in my lap and looked him right in the eyes.

"I feel that I should be honest, Mr. Torgu. You're not an appropriate subject for my show."

He gave a horridly unfriendly smile. "May I ask the reason?"

I could feel my cheeks coloring. The tendons in my arms and chest tightened. Slowly but surely, my hair had fallen across my face. I brushed curls from my eyes. I sipped wine to tamp down the growing agitation. There were several options from here, some of them extremely female. I know colleagues who will cry, as a last resort, in order to get their way. I know one woman, a print journalist, who baked a plate of cookies for an entire group of women, East German kindergarten teachers, and then burst into tears on purpose when the cookies didn't work. She got access to their files. Others use cleavage or aggressive flirtation or emotional blackmail. I tend to get mean.

"Our show has been running for three decades, Mr. Torgu. We have a sixth sense about our stories—what will work, what won't."

He mocked me. "Three decades. My, my. So very long."

He went back to his meal. His enormous hands clutched silverware that might have been tailor-made for him, a triple-tined fork and big serrated carving knife adapted to his needs. Silverware is the wrong word. The metal had a dark, somewhat rusted hue. The knife, in particular, looked ancient. I had never seen a table utensil like it, never seen a human being use such a thing at a meal. Unable to avert my gaze, I followed the flow of ingestion, from the blade to the fork to the fingers wrapped around them like vines. Torgu swallowed, and I thought, watching him, that he looked slightly younger than he had before, his forehead less wrinkled, his silver hair streaked with lines of black. But his teeth, which hadn't seemed so black by the end of the previous night, now glittered as if repainted with a fresh coat of darkness.

I forced down my alarm. I would have to be a bitch. I would interrogate the hell out of him. "You call yourself a businessman. What business, exactly, did you do today?"

He didn't answer.

"Where were you born?"

He continued in silence, eating and eating.

"How long were you incarcerated by the government?"

"Forty years."

This struck me as a lie; at best, an exaggeration. He looked too young, and besides, if he'd been in prison so long, how had he found time to become a head of a sprawling criminal enterprise? Unless, of course, that was an even bigger lie.

"Describe your work for me. Do you sell weapons? Do you steal oil tankers? Do you launder money for terrorists? Are you working, in fact, for governments in the region as an enforcer?"

Beyond him, the ocher lights flooded the woods. I thought that I could see the front bumper of his Porsche, a hump of glinting metal between columns of pine. How long would it take me to get there? Was it locked? And where were the keys? He gave me a look that made me realize my error in coming here. This man would never give me an answer that I could use on television. "Before I go," I snapped, "will you, at least, admit to me that you are engaged in criminal activity?"

"Breaking the law. Yes?" I shook my head. His coyness added insult to injury. He repeated himself. "Please, Miss Harker. A criminal is someone who breaks the law. We may agree on that point?"

I refused to play along, and his mood swung like an axe. His words took on a tone of personal grievance. "Yes. I have broken the law. But what do you call a person who breaks a promise?"

My purse lay on the floor next to a leg of my chair. I reached for the strap without lowering my body, but my fingers couldn't make it. I answered him. "A liar."

"And he who breaks a neck?"

"If it's his own, a dumbass." I feigned a sneeze, doubled over, grabbed my purse and dropped it in my lap. "Someone else, a murderer."

"Dumbass." He liked this. He gave me one of his most unsavory grins, teeth ashine. "And what do you call someone who breaks time?"

I glanced left, noting the exact placement of the lobby entrance. I placed my napkin over my dinner knife, thinking to put it in my purse. "I know what you call someone who breaks wind."

"Please, Miss Harker."

"I don't follow."

His throat gave a rattle that might have been a chuckle. His left hand fell on the handle of his own dinner knife.

"Doesn't a television producer break time? Into very small pieces? Are you not a criminal, too? Of a different sort?"

"You're not funny at all," I said.

He persisted with this mad attempt at humor. "But wouldn't you say that breaking time is a far greater crime than breaking law? After all, laws vary from culture to culture. But time is everywhere the same."

"You're wasting mine."

"Thank you, my dear. Yes, exactly. And I will trust a devoted criminal like yourself to conduct this interview far more than I would an upright citizen. More wine?"

A sham of civility had returned to our conversation. He busied himself with uncorking another bottle.

"You have convinced me, Ms. Harker. I have decided to do the interview. What do you think of that?"

It was as if the previous conversation had never occurred, as if I had not told him that we were done.

He filled our glasses once more. "We talk first about location. Where will we hold this interview? I propose New York City. *Chez vous.*"

I was too stunned at the absurdity of the idea to play along. "You must be joking."

He was not. Even under normal circumstances, I would have rejected the notion, but I would have been more diplomatic. I would have explained the near impossibility of getting someone like him, a wanted criminal, an American visa. I would have sketched out the lack of adequate security. I would have underlined the thematic importance to our segment of keeping the head of organized crime in Eastern Europe in his own domain. Finally, I might have relented and said that we could talk further about the possibility. But there was no point.

He didn't give me a chance to list the objections. He didn't care. "I will handle most of the arrangements," he continued, "but you must do two things for me. You must sign your name to my visa application."

"Out of the question."

From the chair to his right, he produced a large square envelope stuffed with papers. He fished around in the paperwork, looking for something in particular. I saw the American seal on a consular document. "We must settle on dates, and I am impatient to get to America before the year is out . . ."

Wordlessly, I watched, and I understood. He wanted me to help him to leave Romania and get to the United States. I had been duped. Once I had signed the papers, he would no longer need me, and then what? He placed papers on the table: airline tickets, typed itineraries, a passport.

"I demand to be taken immediately back to Brasov," I said.

"Of course, I will require you to stay here with me until I go, as an adviser." He took a postcard from the envelope, a banal and badly taken photograph of a green mountain. "I will need your e-mail address, password and account number, naturally, so that correspondence can be established between my place of business and your operation. And please, at last, send this postcard to your workplace, and this one"—he plucked another from the envelope, which contained endless depths— "to your beloved."

He intended me some harm. "I will do nothing of the sort. You drive me down from this mountain, sir."

"Perhaps one of the Vourkulakis brothers can do it," he said. I darted a glance toward the paternoster, and he saw it. "They have driving permits, I believe."

Everything shifted at that instant. One reality became another. In life, that's how it happens. Terrible and wonderful change reaches us at the end of its long journey out of an unimaginable distance. We realize in a single moment that a new state of affairs has been building itself around us, rising like a new house over our heads—suddenly, the walls connect to the roof, and you are there: the sky has vanished. I leaned forward, placed both of my hands on the table, nauseated.

"I am going to turn on the recording devices now," he said. He came to my side of the table and placed the postcards beside the flatware. "You give me your information now."

I looked at my fingers on the table. I fixed my gaze on the diamond on my left ring finger, and the true hardness, the terrible nature, of a diamond struck me at that moment. It had shot up in fire through the softer earth; it had cooled into my destiny. And my destiny was here.

Torgu loomed over my chair, smelling of wine, pork and more distant things: a sour stench of dirty clothing, the long-doused fire on the upper floors, and something even farther away, more final, an odor of rot that I imagined came from destroying other humans. I wouldn't sign the papers or write the postcards. But I gave the e-mail information. I didn't know how he would use it, but the question struck me as a secondary concern. With a pencil and a piece of paper from inside his coat, Torgu scribbled down the details.

He turned his attention to the camera. He puttered around the equipment, pulling off the lens cap, replacing it, running his hands up and down the legs of the tripod, frisking the machine, as if its legs contained clues. It dawned on me that he didn't have the slightest clue what he was doing. He had summoned me to Transylvania, in part, for this expertise and was probably pondering how he could coerce me into giving a hand. Little did he know.

"Let me help," I said.

He weighed my offer, gazing at me, and I sensed a mingling of interest and anxiety. His eyes burned bright between narrowed lids. He must know that I would do anything to buy time and his favor. "If you please," he said.

Like most associate producers, I didn't know a goddamn thing about cameras. We leave that to the crews. But I knew more than he did. "Why don't you tell me exactly what you want to accomplish."

"I merely wish to address the camera," he said. Then he hesitated, a deception forming visibly on his face.

"And?"

He explained that he wanted to face the camera directly and speak for approximately an hour. He would like to sit in a chair that he selected. The chair would be pushed against the wall. Once I had set up the equipment and turned on the camera, he would like me to sit next to him.

"You want me in the shot?"

"No."

I agreed to everything. His eyes regarded me with calculation, but he seemed relieved to defer to my professional judgment.

"Sit," I said, "and I'll check the lighting and sound."

He returned to the dinner table and took the knife. He glanced at me, and I looked down through the viewfinder of the camera, as if I hadn't seen. I put my hands around the base of the tripod and gave the camera a quick hoist, moving it to the left a bit, positioning the frame for a better image. The equipment wasn't so heavy. Torgu pulled his chair to the wall and sat.

I left the camera and went to the soundboard, retrieving my purse along the way, laying it beside the piece of audio equipment. I checked beneath the table. The soundboard was attached to an extension cord that ran from the floor to a nearby wall socket. I flicked every switch on the board, and a series of green lights came on.

"Are you miked?" I asked. "For sound?"

Torgu looked at me in perplexity. He really didn't know shit about it.

"Microphone? No? Maybe it's on the camera."

I went back to the camera and lifted it again, moved it slightly closer to the man, checking for audio. I found it. A button said so.

"There's sound here," I told him, "but if we have a mike, you'll have insurance, in case the audio on the camera finks out on us."

Jesus, I thought. I sound like the real deal. I went back to the soundboard. I saw plugs for mikes.

"There is further gadgetry," Torgu offered. "Over there."

He gestured toward a chair pushed against another table. I kept one eye on him and went to look. On the seat of a chair sat a gray metal case, of the kind favored by television crews from one end of the earth to the other. I saw a name and address inscribed in black ink on one corner of the lid: Andras something from a street in Oslo. I pressed a couple of buttons, the bolts shot, and the case opened. Inside were microphones of various sizes, a line of cable, a spare battery pack, condoms, bags of peanuts and cigarettes. Glancing back, I snatched a bag of peanuts, shoved it down the front of my pants. I took the line of cable and the smallest mike, plugged the mike into the board and ran it to the foot of Torgu's chair. Beneath the chair, slightly hidden by his feet, I noticed something that hadn't been there before, a bucket like the kind you find in hotels used for ice machines, except I hadn't seen an ice machine in his hotel. Sticking out of the bucket, I saw the wooden handle of his dinner knife. I looked up at him.

"I will clear the rest of the table later," he said.

I returned to the soundboard, plugging one end of the cable into it, connecting the other to the camera, blood slamming in my head. I asked Torgu to say something. He uttered a few unintelligible words, something with a lot of vowels. I couldn't find the audio monitor, but it didn't matter.

More words hissed out of his mouth, and I gave him a thumbs-up. "Perfect," I said.

"May we begin, please?"

I put up my hands. "Give me two to get the camera into position. I want this to work for you."

He seemed impatient. One hand dangled below the seat of his chair and fiddled with the handle of the knife in the bucket, rattling the blade around. I took a deep breath. I hoisted the tripod again, moved it slightly closer to him. I knelt and peered into the viewfinder. I could see the chair and the bucket but no sign of the man. I concluded that there must already be a tape in the camera, and I was looking at a previously shot image, a test picture, perhaps. I didn't have time to check, and it didn't matter.

"One more thing," I said.

Torgu squinted. He let go of the knife and crossed his arms.

"I need you to hold up something white, like a cloth or a piece of paper," I said, improvising a piece of TV set business that I had seen but never really understood, "so I can get a white count and make sure, make sure the camera is in sync with the lighting in the room. Can you do that?"

I thought I heard Torgu grumble a refusal, but he stood up, went to a table, and took a napkin.

"Will this do?"

"Bingo."

"Now what?"

"Sit down and hold it up."

He did as I instructed, but it wasn't enough.

"Unfold it all the way, Mr. Torgu, and hold it over your face."

He sighed. "May I ask why?"

"Because that's where the camera lens will be focused, and if the lighting is wrong, no one will see you."

He hesitated, I could see. He wanted to say something, but he thought better of it. He raised the napkin over his eyes and stretched it taut.

"So?" he asked.

"Right there," I said. I unplugged the line of cable that connected the camera to the soundboard. I folded the three legs of the tripod into a single stand. I picked the camera up by the feet of the tripod. I said a technical countdown in my head, a calming mantra, *three, two, one.*

"You're about right," I said.

I swung the tripod stand. I swung it like a club and struck his head. Equipment crashed against skull, but I didn't wait to see. I let go of the tripod, grabbed my purse off the table and dashed for the lobby of the hotel. My foot caught in the cable that had connected the camera to the soundboard, and I went rolling, but I gathered myself back up and hurtled for the exit. I didn't care what might be outside. I reached the glass doors of the hotel. I grabbed the handles, knowing that they must be locked. They opened, and I stumbled back in shock. Cold mountain air hit me, the delirium of pine and night. I ran down the steps, along the hall made by the hotel portico, reaching the ocher-lit maze of trees. The generator coughed in its hut beside me. I had no plan. There wasn't time. I thought of the village and the church in the meadow. There had been a light under the door of the church. The road couldn't be more than a hundred yards ahead. Something rustled in the bushes behind me. A log fell off the woodpile. I glimpsed a pale, terrified face, my own in a pane of glass. The generator coughed. Lights went out, and darkness burst. I sprang forward, and my knees struck bark. I staggered back, sinking to the ground. Ahead, in the night, yellow eyes winked. The howls of animals furled out like a wind. I saw stars up high, and I wished that I had been one of those housewives in suburban New Jersey who never did anything in this world except make a home for a wealthy commuting businessman and his well-protected children.

Twelve

Robert, my love, there isn't much time. This will be my last communication, unless by some chance I survive. If I don't, I pray someone finds these notes and can make heads or tails of my remarkable trip. I have tried to report everything as it happened, in great detail, so there can be no doubt about my veracity. I have to hurry or the sun will go down, and I will have to deal with this menace in the dark.

I don't even know why I am still here. I should be dead by now, but for Torgu's one weakness. He has some plan in New York, that's clear. He is a form of terrorist; but his terror is strange. It's like a virus, and I have it. He gave it to me. It's most apparent when I lie still and close my eyes. He has put something terrible inside of me.

But let me try to piece this together. I woke the day after my attempted escape in a bed on my floor. Someone, probably Torgu, had left me the usual breakfast, and I consumed half of the bread and all of the coffee. In an odd show of solicitude for a woman who had assaulted him, he had placed my purse on the nightstand beside the table. I looked inside. My wallet with passport and money remained, the useless cell phone, too. Why? But it didn't matter.

As far as I could tell, my person had not been violated. I was still dressed in my clothes from the night before. I discovered the bag of peanuts from the camera case. I dropped the peanuts into my purse for later consumption and went to my valise. To my deep chagrin, I had worn everything—in some cases, more than once. Even in extremis,

I'm a bit anal on this subject. I hate to wear dirty underwear more than almost anything. It makes me feel unclean, depressed. Dirty underwear feels like the first step in a process that, once started, cannot be stopped. I dug through clothes, looking for the least-worn pair of underthings, a thrice-worn black brassiere and a pair of pink polyester panties, popping threads on a side seam, a hideous combo, but the best of the dregs.

I slipped on sweats and a warm sweater, stuffed a few odds and ends, including a crust of bread and Clemmie's crucifix, into the purse, and tried the door. It was locked, as I expected, but for a moment, I panicked and pounded it. I yelled. Then I pounded again and realized that it was made of flimsy material and might be knocked down with a dose of the same adrenaline that had allowed me to swing the camera.

That hadn't worked out so well. I made a search of the rest of the floor. The bar laden with alcohol caught my eye. I was sorely tempted by a bottle of Jameson. If all else failed, I could sit on a fine Ottoman rug and nurse my despair with spirits. But I wasn't so far gone. My bark-skinned knees stung, and I grasped that my life wasn't worth a damn, but a giddiness filled my heart; I had discovered for the first time the true nature of things. I knew that I might be dead soon, and I knew that I didn't want to die and would fight to survive. I uncapped the bottle of Jameson. It had been there a while, but smelled all right. It must have belonged to another of Torgu's guests, I thought, and I toasted that lost person in my mind.

Through the glass windows of the penthouse the sun blew a silver radiance. Carrying the bottle, I walked a line along the edges of the room, looking down through the windows at the pine forests. I knew when I had reached the northern exposure because the pine-thick mountains fell away and I saw the flatlands of Transylvania, a gray-green haze.

Only one corner of the floor had no windows, and I had never bothered to explore it. Now I did. An hour had passed before I came across a brand-new, unplugged ice machine. So there you are, I thought, recalling the ice bucket from the night before. Something else about the appliance caught my eye. It seemed out of place in that menagerie of antiques. The thing had a scoop, like all of its cousins, but I was sure that the interior had never seen a single dropped cube of ice. You could take a whiff and grasp the absence of moisture. It was stainless, unsullied steel.

When I tried to plug it in, I found the fire exit to the lower floors.

How shall I describe aromas only hinted at by the most primordial of summer camp latrines? Behind the ice machine, a stairwell led down into a darkness smelling of fire and excrement and abattoir. This was how Torgu moved back and forth between my room and the lower floors, bringing my breakfast without making a sound. This was how he could spy on his guests without being detected. The ice machine covered the entrance perfectly.

Under any other circumstance, I would have pushed the machine back against the wall and stacked furniture against it to hold the stench at bay. But I saw my chance. This was an escape route. The alternative, to try to smash down the locked door, would only alert those below to my intentions.

I said an atheist's prayer. I asked merely for courage. I dug Clemmie's crucifix out of my purse and hung it around my neck. The ice machine didn't weigh much, and I pushed it out of the way. I wanted the upper room's natural light to shine down into the stairwell. At the very least, in the beginning, I would be able to see my way.

I knelt at the threshold of the exit, taking a moment to get my bearings. I thought about the layout of the hotel as I had seen it from the paternoster, and about my precise location in the building. I was on the top floor, at its far eastern end. At the far western end lay the locked door and the paternoster, which was the fastest way to the ground. Beneath me, I surmised, would be another floor like those I had glimpsed, long corridors flanked by a series of rooms. So, I reasoned, if I could climb down to the next floor and gain access to the central corridor, I could simply walk to the paternoster and take it down. This plan assumed many things—that through this exit behind the ice machine, I could gain access to the next floor; that, once on the floor, I could reach the corridor; and that once at the end of the corridor, I would find the paternoster working.

I peered down the stairwell. Steps went to the next landing. I saw flaking cement walls, and beyond that, the shadows. I hoisted the purse onto my shoulder. There were no Greek brothers. They were Torgu's invention. Otherwise, I would have seen them. Yet I lingered at the top of the stairwell. I had seen a pale hand on my first trip up the paternoster, or thought I had. I crept down a couple of steps and looked over the railing into the depths of the stairwell. I searched for any sign of life, but there was nothing. Water dripped. Wind groaned against the walls of the hotel, swirling like a river of noise. I thought I heard the tinkle of glass. The sleep of reason produces monsters, but now my reason had come awake: even if there were two Greek brothers around the place, they were no more than hirelings who made food and did odd jobs.

I forced myself down the stairs, one step at a time. The sunlight stopped at the first landing. I crossed the line of illumination and immediately stepped back. Beyond was pitch black. The stairwell seemed to plunge out of sight, a sheer drop, like the place off shore where the gradual descent of land yawns suddenly to bottomless ocean. I stuck my hand into the darkness. I lowered it onto a railing. What if I put my foot wrong and fell? What if the stairwell had burned up and the steps simply gave way to an abyss? Far down lay the source of the great stench. I could smell it. The odor came out of the lower regions, as if sewage ran free or fresh graves lay open.

I looked over my shoulder at the light on the flight of stairs. It would fade soon enough. I fought my pitiful nerves. I gripped the rail with my right hand, held the purse strap over my shoulder and poked my head down, as if entering the tunnel of some giant animal. Once out of the light, my eyes began to adjust. I waited, giving them time. Below lay a series of flights of steps, one landing after another. I would merely walk down one flight and try the door. If it wouldn't open, I would take a deep breath, and go down another flight, try that door. They couldn't all be locked.

I didn't hurry. Holding the rail, as if blind and moving only by touch, I walked down the flight and came with a hush to the next landing. I saw the faint outline of a rectangle; the door to the next floor. The noise of wind persisted, but I couldn't hear another sound. I stood before the door and put my ear against the surface, listening for anything human. Nothing stirred on the other side. I stepped back and put my hand on the knob, a round ball of cheap brass.

The knob came away in my hand. The door began to topple forward, its hinges clattering to the ground in pieces. The door fell to the floor with an echoing bang. I froze, leaning forward, feeling a draft of mildewed air from the corridor beyond the threshold. The echo of the door's bang had gone down through the bones of the edifice. I waited, veins thumping in my head.

I crossed the threshold and felt something soft and yielding beneath the soles of my shoes. Moldy carpet, I hoped. I heard it squish as I moved. The floorboards creaked beneath the substance, but the noise did not reverberate. The structure seemed solid.

I passed door after closed door and wondered what might lie behind them. Now I could make out a sound, a kind of mechanical hum. I stopped. Was it imagination? I couldn't make out the distance; it might have been fifty yards ahead, a hundred, even more. I started to move again. A door swung open, and I almost let out a shriek, clapping a hand over my mouth just in time. My heart babbled in my chest. You scared the shit out of me, I wanted to tell the door. It swung with a slam back into the jamb. The wind had done it. Goddamn you old hotel, I thought, and began to run. Tears streamed from my eyes. Ahead, I could make out the end of the corridor.

The paternoster made the hum. On the right, cars went up. On the left, they went down. I hung back a moment, half expecting Torgu to rise from the depths or descend from above. Nothing but nerves, I told myself. I would be in the lobby in seconds. Still I lingered there, watching the revolutions, thinking to myself, why should it be so easy? More cars passed, up and down. Surely Torgu must have reckoned with the possibility of my escape. Surely he had foreseen that I might find a way to the paternoster. On the other hand, I reasoned, he was an extremely odd and unpredictable man who had fallen for an obvious trick the night before.

Maybe he's dead, I thought, with a sudden rush of hope. Perhaps I had killed him. But it seemed unlikely. Someone had carried me upstairs; someone had made my breakfast. I had to assume that he was alive. But he might be on one of his "business trips." Or he might not care at all if I escaped from the hotel; it might relieve him of the burden of having to kill me himself. Even if I did get out of the hotel, I wouldn't know how to get back to civilization. I would be lost in the woods, prey to wolves and whatever else; the Vourkulakis. I glanced back the way I had come. The door behind me still swung in a breeze, and there were other noises, creakings and rustlings. And what about the lower floors? The open cars of the paternoster descended, one by one. If I went down this way, the Greek brothers would see me coming, legs first. There would be no hiding place. Time was running out.

I jumped into the next car and felt the machine tremble just a little, as if the paternoster had actually perceived the additional burden. I settled against the back of the compartment and lowered myself into a squat. I readied myself for an attack. I passed one, two, three scorched floors. Something shuddered in the depths, and my head bumped against the back of the car. I threw my hands down to prevent a fall. The paternoster jolted to a stop. The bulb in the ceiling flickered out. I crouched in silence for a long time, straining to hear any sound of human activity, hearing nothing but the sound of my own pulse in my head. My car had stopped between floors. At my feet lay a foot-high space, a glimpse of the lower floor. It was exceedingly dark down there, and I couldn't bring myself to look. Upward felt safer. I stood and peeked out the top at a stretch of moldy carpet strewn with bits of masonry and trash. A swell of claustrophobia came over me. My head could just about fit through the crack. I crouched down and gazed again into the dark space at my feet.

It might be mechanical failure. Such things happened in old buildings. A fuse might have blown somewhere.

Faintly, I thought I heard something, a cross between a human moan and groaning wind. But it was nothing. I was still alone. I had no choice. I would have to lower myself through the crack at my feet and climb out, slithering like a snake onto the next floor. I peered down at the next floor. It looked empty enough. The crack would be just big enough for my body. First, I poked my shoes through, then my calves, knees and waist. I arched my back and slipped down, my hands on the ceiling of the lower floor. I landed with a plop on the carpet and had a ludicrous sensation of freedom, a flashing instant of euphoria. I would live! Peering down the corridor, into one more blind alley of closed doors and mildew, I experienced a long shudder.

I looked back at the paternoster. On the right, a car had been headed to the upper floors. On the left, at my feet, another car had been headed down. Too bad I couldn't make myself into a satellite feed, I thought, staring down into the black crevice that would lead to the floor below; too bad I couldn't transmit my body from a location in one part of the planet to a location on another part of the planet with the press of a button. The technology of my work could not help me now.

I didn't trust the ascending side of the paternoster. If the machine came back on, and it might, I would be headed up. I focused on the descending side. The crack between the top of the lower paternoster car and the carpet at my feet was small, the same size as the crack on the floor above, but I put my head inside and looked down. My body would fit. I put my feet through first and slithered down, my sweats bunching around my thighs. My purse got caught in the crevice, and when I jerked it, the contents spilled, causing a racket. I crouched once more, getting panicky, gathering up my things, my notes, the bag of peanuts, the crust of bread.

I willed myself forward. My thoughts turned off, and a rhythm of deep effort took over. I kept going down the paternoster, climbing from car to car like a child going down the rungs of a jungle gym. I covered three floors in about five minutes. I was proud of myself. I would be filthy from this slithering, and the vision of myself covered in the ash and slime of an ex-Commie hotel actually made me laugh and gave me courage. Floor by floor, I descended. My feet kicked out, then my body. I no longer bothered to look down each corridor. I didn't care.

I still heard the moaning. It had become loud and sounded more human, like someone in pain. But it was wind. It had to be. I reached another floor, brushed aside a mass of tar paper and other burned matter, and dropped down. I landed and went stiff. A dread whispered over me. The moaning came from the floor below, and it spoke a language, Romanian or maybe a Scandinavian tongue. Wind didn't speak a language. I remembered the Norwegian. I knelt in the corridor and bowed my head. It could be a man or a woman. They had got mixed up in some deal or relationship with Torgu, and it was none of my business. I wanted to live. They would probably die.

I considered my next move. It would have to be quick, more like a fish than a snake. As much as humanly possible, I would have to bypass the next floor all together. Go down into the crevice, hit the floor of the paternoster, spill out, don't look, don't linger, spill down into the next crevice and down again. I peered through the crack.

The man was naked as an infant, spattered chest to genitals in his own blood. Someone had tried to cut his throat. He saw me, snatched my arm and jerked me out of the paternoster. He fell upon me.

Thirteen

He wouldn't let go. He fell face forward on my knees, as if seeking protection there. He was a horrible sight, his skin pale and cold and hairy, almost blue in the darkness, streaked black from violence. I felt a fleeting terror. What if he was one of the movie creatures? When he lifted his head again, would I see sharp teeth and red, dead eyes? Would he bite? But, of course, the true import of this man was far, far worse than that, and in a moment, I saw it. If I didn't escape, I would end up like him.

"Let go of me," I whispered.

"You speak English, thank Gott, oh thank Gott, thank Gott!"

Over and over, this sentence came at me until I quieted him again. "Be still."

He sat up now and put his hands over his crotch. His eyeballs bulged white and round from his forehead. His blond hair flurried off his skull. A beard was coming on.

"You are Norwegian?" I asked. He nodded. I recalled the name and address in the metal case. "You are Andras? From Oslo?"

"Yes," he gasped. "For television. And you?"

"Me, too. American."

"Yes, yes," he whispered, ecstatic, "I hear it in your voice. Thank Gott you came. They dragged me here and tried to put a knife to me, but I fought like the fucking Siberian tiger, and they retreated. Cowards."

I put a hand across his mouth and shook my head.

"Vourkulakis," I said. "Are they real then?"

A line of absolute horror connected me to him, as if we breathed with the same lungs, stared with the same eyes. "Oh yes," he said. "Quite real."

"You help me," I said. "I help you. And we get out alive. Okay?"

He was nodding and glancing over his shoulder back down the corridor. "Then we put these fuckers away for good and ever," he said, again too loudly.

I helped him up, looking his body up and down with a clinical detachment. I had to think logistics. This was a big man. He must weigh more than two hundred pounds. I didn't honestly see how he would fit through the narrow crevices made by the paternoster cars. He was weak from blood loss. He shivered with more than cold. I wished that I could give him something to cover himself, but there was nothing at hand, and we had no time.

I showed him how to negotiate the paternoster, and we began our descent. Don't think I'm a saint. He had to go second. If he got stuck in the paternoster, as he might, weighing a good seventy to eighty pounds more than me, I refused to suffer the consequences.

I had remembered four or five scorched floors, but as we made our way, I counted seven, eight, nine, ten. Most of the hotel had been incinerated. Maybe that's why Torgu wanted to come to America. His home had been destroyed, and he wanted to make a new start. It couldn't be easy to find or build a new hotel to meet his standards. So like many an immigrant before him, he would go to New York City. With his criminal millions, if they existed, he would buy one of those little boutique hotels that were going up south of the meatpacking district. Austen Trotta had once said to me, "Just remember, there's always a real estate story."

Andras grunted in the stall above me, as if he were defecating. He took too long. I would move faster without him, no doubt.

My watch had long ago stopped, and I could only guess the time. It would be well past lunch, as late as three, which gave me a few more good hours of light—another hour to reach the bottom, and two to reach the church in the deserted village. When we left the hotel, I would sprint, and Andras would have to keep up as best he could. Once in the lobby, my obligation would be at an end.

I moved faster and faster, leaving him behind. I'm like a scout, I told myself, clearing the way. Every so often, I would stop and listen for his grunts. I reached what I guessed to be the sixth floor, and the burnt smell began to fade. I stopped and listened. Andras's breath, loud and stressed, an undercurrent to the grunting, had dwindled back into the utter stillness of the rest of the hotel. I waited. However slowly he moved, he seldom stayed out of my sight for more than thirty seconds. I crouched in the bottom of the stall between what I took to be the fifth and sixth levels. He had stopped completely. You have to go, I told myself. Every sorry SOB for himself, as my dad would say.

I made my decision. He was gone. I stuck my legs through the crevice into the fifth floor. As I did, the lights in the paternoster popped on. The thing shuddered into motion and started to rise. At the last moment, before the intersection of level and stall could crush my legs, I jerked myself back into the car. Before I had time to think, the paternoster reached the sixth floor.

Andras charged, gurgling, blood flying from his mouth, flailing at me. He had six arms. That's what I saw first, writhing arms, like serpents in ancient statues, around his neck, around his torso, his legs. They had him. They were pulling him back into the darkness. Someone had a knife, and it glittered. I sprang out of the car and caught one of his hands. We held tight for a moment, and I saw in him the entire struggling life of an itinerant newsman, saw the beauty and courage and foolishness in it, that life now trapped in blind shock and outrage in this horrible place. The serpent arms squeezed, Andras roared, our hands flew apart, and he went flying backward down the hall until a door slammed, and the noise of struggle abated. I froze for what felt like a long time, my hand extended, still warm from his touch. The paternoster revolved behind me. The shadows ahead quivered. The carpet stank. My purse had vanished below. Behind the door in the darkness, I could hear the whisper of amusement. I could hear a pulse of ferocious breath. Behind these doors lived all the horrors. I put my other hand up, warding off whatever came.

I ran forward into the dark, crying his name, "Andras!"

A door flew open, and I saw them, right in front of me, two men with shining eyes, long dark hair and sharp grins, the Vourkulakis. They moved together and swiftly, like panthers. One had a knife, its blade agleam.

"You," they said in unison, as if they had been waiting for me since my birth.

Fourteen

Life flashed before my eyes, but not as I had expected. In fact, it didn't flash as a camera does. It swelled. My father's voice told me *never start a weekend with less than a hundred dollars in your pocket*. My great-grandmother showed me the grave of a young Indian boy, buried beneath the gate to her tiny house. I ate birthday cake. A tan girl in a red one-piece dived off a board into a pool at the Dallas Country Club. I danced in white gloves at Cotillion. My mother cried at her mother's funeral. Robert tried to kiss me on our first date. Austen Trotta told me that I should be on camera. I heard an explosion on high. Robert proposed. Clemmie Spence whispered, *Africa*.

I had memories. I was real. This was real. The Vourkulakis were like a tar pool I'd seen in Los Angeles, a black, steaming surface in which things sank without trace.

"Where is he?" I asked.

I don't believe they spoke much English. I don't think it mattered. Their arms came around me. One pair circled my neck. The other engulfed my legs. I twisted and scratched, but I was a bone in the mouth of a wolf. I was choking. The arms carried me into the room across the hall from the one containing Andras. The Vourkulakis had the flat eyes of sharks, barely visible in the mass of hair. They crouched as they moved. Their tongues licked at strange words. They dropped me on the floor and scrambled out, across the corridor and into the other room, where the door remained open. My door slammed shut.

I listened for the sound of a key, turning a lock, but it never came. This room hadn't burned. It had decayed, like a body. I heard a shout in the hall. Something new was happening. Could Andras be alive? Could he possibly be? I heard the thump of a heavy object, the rustling of blankets. Any moment, I expected my door to swing open.

I knew when sunset came. The shadows in the room deepened to black, and the noise resumed next door, but this time, it had a different quality. Voices communed in a hushed, almost respectful manner. I believed then that another had arrived on the corridor. The conversation ebbed and flowed, and I heard the sound of heavy-booted feet leaving the room and entering the corridor. I braced myself. But the footsteps passed me by, and I could swear they headed for the paternoster and away. I waited. It wasn't hard. I couldn't move.

It must have been another hour before I finally ventured to the door and cracked it, looking down the corridor in the direction of the paternoster. At first, I experienced relief. The wind made its usual groan. I cracked the door a little more. The hinges didn't creak. I prepared to run. I pushed the door back another inch or so, listening. On the other side, out of view, lay the room where they had taken Andras. I had no idea whether the door to that room would still be open. I didn't want it to be. I dreaded to see. Distantly, I heard a rhythmic noise and thought that it must be a generator on a floor below. I looked again down the hall, and the paternoster bulbs shone intermittently only a short distance away. This was it. This was the chance. I thought again of Andras, of the feel of his hand slipping out of mine. I would look inside his room. I would be damn quick. If he could walk at all, I would try to help. If not, I would have to leave him. The wind groaned hard, banging at doors up and down the corridor. Right across from me, on the other side of the hall, the door to his room banged. I pressed myself back against my own door and heard that same rhythmic noise, louder now, like the teeth of a saw running through wood. It was a human being. He was alive, probably beyond help. Still concealed behind the door to my room, I bent into a crouch. I concentrated. With the tips of my fingers, I pushed my door back until I could just see into the foyer of the room across the hall, but no farther. I took hold of the edge of my door, and I put my head around. I saw several things at once in the dimness. At first, I couldn't be sure if any of it was real.

On the floor, with his hands hanging into a bucket, sat the man I had known as Ion Torgu. At first I thought he was vomiting. His eyes were turned up in his head. His lips trembled, and fevered whispers came out. I looked back at the bucket. The ice bucket, I thought, from dinner. His knife had been in it. I looked back at his face. The lower half of his face, from his nostrils to his chin, dripped with a dark wet substance, and I could hear garbled words, like place names, though it might have been my imagination, something like: *"Nitra, Rumbala, Cajamarca, Gomorrha, Balaklava, Nadorna, Planitsa, Ashdod . . ."* His hands moved on the rim of the bucket. His eyeballs turned up and shone bright, the brightest objects in that room. His legs splayed on either side of the bucket. I could see the sole of one boot. The lower half of his body didn't move. His hands jerked suddenly from the bucket to the floor, where they lay on the carpet, knuckles down, palms upturned, fingers twitching. Someone had hit him, I thought. I had hit him. Had I made him like this? His body had a plastic quality, as if he had been an object rather than a man, but his chest heaved, and the rhythmic sound, the sawing, turned out to be the emanation of his breath. The stream of his whispered words came across the hall with a strange effect. I began to hear them inside my own head, as if I were thinking them as he spoke them, even before they came out of his mouth, as they formed in his brain, *"Thessalonika, Treblinka, Golgotha, Solferino, Lepanto, Kalawao, Kukush . . ."*

I put a foot into the corridor, thinking he might be unconscious, when his body moved with another abrupt jerk. His head fell forward over the bucket. His hands rose from the carpet, found their way to the rim and sank inside. His mouth gaped, and his hands came up, cupped. The lower half of his face sank into them, and the dark liquid spilled through the fingers. I heard the drip of moisture into moisture, drops splashing. His breath came in gasps, and his lips moved against his palms. His eyeballs shone like stars. I began to understand. I saw beyond him. My legs buckled, and I fell to my knees. Behind his back, on the bed, lay a bare foot, and I knew. Torgu drank the man's blood from

the ice bucket. He drank Andras. I couldn't move. I listened in a horrified rapture as Torgu drank and spoke, as his black lips recited the place
names in my mind, as I recited with him, and I began to understand for
the first time that every man and woman who had ever been forced to
strip and stand before their own mass grave, every girl ever slaughtered
before her parents' eyes, every village ever annihilated, every name ever
extinguished for all time on the whim of a butcher, every single little
massacred citizen in every little place I had never heard of since the
dawn of time, had actually existed. My screams could not drown out
the words of that song.

Fifteen

I awoke in the bed on the penthouse floor, the light of the wild stars fading from the sky. I didn't know how long I had been there, and the thought crossed my mind that days had passed. Instantly, as I sat up, I realized that the room was different. It didn't have the stuffy feeling of the past. I saw why. A few yards away, the door to the upper floor lay open.

I lay on top of the covers, blank for a moment, before I remembered what I'd seen. A feeling tore through my chest. I had never in my life wailed until that moment. I put my hands on my face, and a sound wrenched itself from me. I wailed for my mother and father. I wailed for Robert. I wailed for Andras. I got off the bed and saw my bare feet: someone had taken my shoes. I came to the mirror on the vanity and saw my contorted features, my black hair frizzed out in ferocious revolt, my tears running everywhere, my eyes a mess of wet crimson shock. The top two buttons of my sweater had gone missing, and I could see splashes of dried blood on me. I tore off the sweater, my favorite, and stood there. It was a vision of myself that I could not have imagined. It was me on the verge of death. Next to the vanity sat the bar. I picked up a bottle of Amaro, a liqueur that I had discovered on that trip to Italy, when Robert swept me off my feet. You drink it with a twist of lemon. I hurled it across the room at a window, but my arm was weak. The bottle smacked a sideboard and tumbled along the straight line of a Persian carpet.

I noticed the bottle of Jameson. I'd had a lot before. Now I grabbed it, uncapped it, and gulped down the rest. I collapsed backward onto the silkiest of Persian carpets and guzzled. I wailed some more. The denseness of the fabric felt good under my back. I caressed the threads with one hand. I fought against total loss of consciousness. I thought of Clementine Spence and her cross, planted the bottle on the carpet, got up, riffled through my purse till I found the crucifix and hung it around my neck. I lay flat on the carpet. I emptied the rest of the whiskey into my mouth and rolled the bottle across the carpet at the open door.

Torgu's foot stopped it. Torgu came through the door and kicked the bottle away. The thing is here, I thought. The thing called Torgu was not filmable. It was not natural or even supernatural. In no way could it be seen as human. At best, it was a carrier of an unknown plague. At worst, it defied description, a substance risen from an immeasurable dark dream, my own personal omega.

Torgu stepped into the door, and the gaze of his eyes took in the cross around my neck. The lips glittered from long drinks. They moved on the mouth. The blood ran down the chin in strings, splotching the shirt, the same one worn on the night of our meeting. The mouth uttered its recitation of names, cut free of will or meaning. I put hands over my ears, but it was no use. The words had got inside me; they crawled in my heart like worms, and the thing knew it. The black teeth gleamed in a slobbered scowl. At first, the hands weren't visible, but it took a step forward, and there was one, the fingers trailing threads of godawfulness. The eyes didn't blink. The whites bulged big with egg vitality, the pupils knotted tight. The lower jaw thrust out, and Torgu walked to the foot of my bed, where, it seemed, I was expected to be. I didn't move from my place on the Persian. The Norwegian had been naked and unshaven before sacrifice. I was in my bra and sweats.

My arms were weak at my side. I tried to remove myself from what lay ahead. I imagined myself as an image of Persian womanhood woven into the intricacies of the carpet. I heard a strand of harem music in my head, cymbal pops and snaking strings, a strain from a stupid old movie about exotic Araby. I lay diagonal across the rug. I watched the movement of his silhouette. Torgu walked around the side of my body, to my head, till I looked at his face upside down, looked into his eyes, I should say, because Torgu would not release me from his gaze. One hand took my hair, and the other lifted the reddened, throat-cutting knife, and I didn't even think to cry out. But Torgu didn't strike yet. For an instant, I thought, I hoped, it might be Clementine's cross.

In the eyes, right there on top of me, I imagined I saw a dawning realization. A mutual revelation passed between us, though in my drink-dimmed state, I couldn't quite grasp it.

"Who are you?" I asked.

The answer bubbled out in blood. "An old man."

"What do you want?"

"What do I want?" Torgu seemed to gain in stature. The eyes shone. "I want to be on your television program. Alas."

"What's going to happen to me?" I whispered.

Torgu raised the blade. "That will be clear."

The words welled over his lips and dripped onto me. Under his gaze, I lost my will to question.

"But first," Torgu continued, "I require an invitation. We have discussed New York."

I must have looked confused. Torgu gazed into me, I gazed back. Why hadn't he put the knife to my throat? The alcohol clouded my mind. I closed my eyes for two seconds. When I opened them again, his attention had shifted to my upper body, where the cold air coming through the open door had made my nipples erect and my tumble to the carpet had pulled the sweats partway down my left hip. Another wail formed in my guts, this one of humiliation, but before it could come, another thought formed, a revelation dawning. He spoke again, as if to preempt the chain of my reasoning.

"I require that you extend to me a personal invitation, Evangeline."

It was the first time that he had ever used my given name; the effect was almost tender. Again, I felt the assault on my will. His eyes pressed mine as if he lay right on top of me. His free hand gripped my hair more tightly, insisting. I heard in my brain the whispered words from before, an echo of more remote echoes, out of time and space. I wanted to give permission. I wanted to tell him to come into my country, to come onto my show, to come into my body. Annihilate me. I would call it a form of sexual desire, but it was, in truth, the desire to be let out of my misery. I couldn't take another moment of my own terror.

I shut my eyes again and held them closed and said good-bye to myself. My limbs lost their capacity for sensation. I wanted death to come. But I heard him gasp, like a man who had been holding up a weight for too long. My head thumped back, and when I opened my eyes in surprise, he was blinking, as if smitten by too much sunlight, and retreating around the end of my body. The cross, I thought, goddamn finally worked. But he didn't leave. He turned at my feet and stood there, knife at his side, blinking. In those few seconds, as I watched this incomprehensible retreat, my bewilderment became knowledge. The revelation burst upon my senses. It wasn't the cross at all. I recalled the delicate condition of his health, the fragility of his body in relation to a certain, unspecified "state," and my thoughts crackled down the length of my torso, burning away the lassitude of mortality.

What I'm about to say is very difficult for me. I know what it means, or what it might mean for my future, for my relations with other people, for my life with my husband. But I am trying to give a strict account of what I saw so that others may have valuable knowledge when their time comes, as it will and must. Some will say that I was raised in a home without religious faith, and this proved decisive. Others will say that I was a postmodern girl unleashed in the era when it mattered little or not at all that an unmarried female slept with men and more, performed without shame a variety of sexual acts that a previous generation of women kept as their deepest secret. But I tell you now that I have always been a more than conventional example of a typical woman of my era, sexually experienced, yes, but only up to the usual specifications, very discreet and extremely modest, never one given to flights of imaginative fancy, a person with a minimal number of partners, a monogamist and a pragmatist and even a prude of sorts. I say all of this because, in that instant of decision, I knew my survival depended on a momentary repudiation of each and every one of these instincts.

Torgu trembled, beholding my body as if it were a lava bed. I was shaking, and I could barely move, but I inched the engagement ring off my finger and tossed the frail circle right into his face, so that he staggered back, snarling, lashing out with the blade. I could not bear to look. The dripping lips and terrible, mesmerist eyes threatened my resolve. I made a decision. Still on my back, I rolled over so that he could take me from behind; it was a terrible gamble, an awful gamble, but it was the last possibility. He hissed. I lifted myself partway off the floor, sank my thumbs into the waistband, and inched the sweats down to my knees. The crucifix swung at my neck, and the liqueur coursed through me. Listen to the song in your hips, I whispered to myself, please it God, please it God, a syncopated incantation. I gathered the strength in my fists, clenched them with fury, and began to sway. It was an act of faith, in a sense, faith not in the divine above, but the divine below, in my power over this evil. If I was wrong, then I would be raped before my murder, but I consoled myself with the thought that no one would ever know.

The devil burned, in that bizarre penthouse, with its endless reaches of silken filigree, its hints of kitsch harems, in the coming light of a Transylvanian morning. A growl simmered out of my chest, and I reached for a shoulder and flicked away one black strap of the bra and then the other. I perspired alcohol. I kept my eyes on the intertwined figures of the rug, on the deep blue, the pressed gold, the acanthus green, so that Torgu couldn't catch my eye. I expected him any minute to drop the knife and climb on top of me, I expected the animal to drive inside, but nothing happened. I am right, I thought wildly, hoping more than believing. I have discovered him. I slowed, became perfectly still except for the panting of my lungs, and rolled over to look at him, to see what I had done. It was an awe-inspiring spectacle, and I must admit, the sight changed me forever.

He had collapsed to his knees. The knife had become a crutch upon which he leaned. There was a tremendous shiver. Torgu tried to indicate with his free hand that I must quit, a pathetic stab at rekindling my fear, but his authority had gone. I sat up, I put my arms behind me, hands splayed on the floor, and I braced myself. I stood. As I did, my hair fell across my face, hiding my eyes from him. Clementine's cross glittered in the coming of the day.

Now for the kill, I said to myself, ignoring the last inner sanctities. My bra had come undone and hung from an elbow. I stood near nude and crucified above the creature, an inch or two from its gasping mouth. I no longer had to move much. Its eyes turned up in terrified witness. Torgu was boiling inside, but he could no longer look away, and I sensed with bloodthirsty resolve that I now had the capacity to wipe him from the face of the earth. It was a moment of pure knowledge. There he kneeled with his violence in his hand, and there I stood with my hot human skin, and it was suddenly, abundantly clear that the knife fears skin more than anything else on this earth, that it is subject to skin in all its bloody dreams, that its only recourse is to cut the nightmare apart, hack apart the vines in the endless forest of desire. I planted my legs a few inches apart and slipped one hand down. The slow final gyrations had their effect on him and on me. My fingers found their reception. A nightmare of fire and desolation bit into the mind of the monster. It was combusting, incinerating. The names of destroyed places washed over its lips in a desperate, frayed steam, coming apart into incoherent syllables. My mind flew across the Persian carpet in memory of a long-dead formula for fending off evil. I thought of faraway lives, of the women throughout time who had had to undulate their way out of murder and worse. It was a grand tradition, and its subtle powers flowed into my hips and breasts, as if the saints of desire had come alive in the room. And with those revelations came another, unbearable, that I might own the power Torgu possessed, that the drinking of human blood might hold lavish benefit, that the violence on his lips might flow down my breasts and belly and bring a song far greater than the one I heard. The thought vanished as quickly as it came. Feeling a dangerous but absolute confidence, I slipped my thumbs into the waist of my cheap pink panties and stepped out. In a last gesture of contempt, I balled the undergarment and thrust it into his mouth, a true act of hypnosis so complete that the creature's hands couldn't even muster the strength to peel the feral garment from its maw. The fever in the struggle mounted. The terror mounted. The thing staggered backward, and the explosion came on slowly now, I wouldn't stop it. I arched my back, offering myself up like the sacrificed Norwegian. I allowed the pure pleasure of the exercise to overcome my senses. The knife dropped from the fingers of the beast. Its mouth belched forth a horror of blood. At last, with ferocity, it wrenched the undergarment from its teeth. The polyester material stuck to its fingers, a final roar of frustration as the creature tried to rip the garment apart. I hissed its name, like the great Whore of Babylon, again and again, *Torgu, Torgu, Torgu*, raising myself in the air so that he could see every bit of me. I closed my eyes; I thought the room might be on fire. I heard another gasp, my own or his, I don't know, the hurried bursts of footsteps down stairs, a scuttle of a kind that sickened me, calling to mind the skitter and scatter of insects abruptly startled by light. I opened my eyes again, and he was gone.

I did not have time to be disgusted with myself. I didn't gloat. I didn't hesitate. I dressed again in most of the armor of my victory, the bra and sweats, in case Torgu came at me again. I left the panties and the engagement ring on the floor, but I snatched the knife. I will follow the monster down into the depths of the hotel. I will climb out of this lair and run with all my last strength to the chapel in the meadow in the empty valley, where someone, surely, will give me shelter. And if those doors are closed against me, I will run low to the ground, kill anything that tries to stop me, until I come back to human habitation. I will fight with skin, bone and sex to survive.

BO OK

The Whispers
in the Corridors

Sixteen

E—They tell me you're involved in some kind of super-secret negotiation with that criminal, but I don't believe it. Something's wrong. Their faces say so. You should have sent me an update by now. You should have sent a dispatch or two about his bad breath and clumsy sexual advances. But since you haven't responded to an e-mail of mine in a week, I feel the cold chill of disaster. Or maybe it's our own disaster that drives my fear. Someone has to tell you the news. Maybe the shock will shake you loose from wherever you're hiding.

Do you remember that last day before you left for Romania, when Ian came by your office to visit?

Picture that small, lovely, civilized moment in your mind, if you can. You and I were eating Asian chicken salad from two different delis, Munchies and Jamals, debating which made the best lime-sesame dressing. I was working up my nerve to say a significant word or two to you about our friendship when Ian walked in, slammed the door behind him and said, with uncharacteristic spleen, "It's official. I hate this fucking place." We tried to hide our amusement, because he was obviously in a state of genuine dismay. He looked good, you may recall. He always did. He had the visible exhaustion of a young man raising small children, but he also had that Cape Cod ruddiness from sailing and running on the beach and swimming in the sea, especially pronounced in his late summer incarnation. Ian dressed well, too—you set great store by such things—but on this day, he'd advanced on his usual clothes horsiness by dressing in a suit he'd ordered from that custom tailor shop at Rockefeller Center. In his crazy way, he must have thought bespoke attire would help him make his case as a producer with his correspondent, Skipper Blant, but Blant, predictably, had taken one look and called him a "strutting fashion buffoon," as if Blant didn't suffer from the most egregious bouts of buffoonery himself. But Ian's dismay that afternoon had nothing to do with inseams. Do you remember the rant? I can hear it this very moment in my head.

"So I'm here till three o'clock last night." He'd stolen my complimentary brownie and plopped himself on your blue sofa. "Never mind the fact I've got a two-year-old at home. Never mind my three-year-old cries all night and asks for Daddy. Never mind my wife fears for my health and wants me to walk and get a job with normal hours. Never mind all that minor detail. I was here."

"Of course you were here," you echoed, by way of moral support.

"I do cherish your call and response, Evangeline." Before eating my brownie, he took off his suit coat, a woolen job far too heavy for late August; he'd wanted to show it off before the season began, I'm sure, give it a dry run, garner a few compliments, fine-tune the whole effect. He was ranting about the latest outrages in his campaign to become a full-time producer for Blant, a hell's errand if ever there was one. "So I get this awesome character, a Harvard-educated black man who also happens to be a white-collar con artist worth Christ knows how much from selling bullshit stock tips to thousands of average American seniors, who lose their retirement savings, dude hasn't even talked to the *Times* yet." In the halls of our show, when someone lays out a story idea, I have felt it only polite to ooh and ahh with anticipation, whether I actually feel the story to be a good one, and you, Evangeline, share that conviction, but this one actually sounded good, so we oohed and ahhed with genuine enthusiasm, and he could tell and continued. "We nail the interview. Blant does a brilliant job, though I hate to say so. He brags about the story to Bob Rogers, and Rogers gets wet and says he wants it to be the lead story on the first show of the season, so, of course, I'm ball and jackin' it. I write a great script. I knock it out of the park. Like I said, I leave this office at three in the morning, three this very morning, my friends, and I get back in this office, which I have come to despise with all my being, at eight this morning." He waits for us to wince or gasp, which we do. "You see where I'm going. Leave at three, up at six with kids, in at eight. Anxiety, annoyance and fear for my health are on my wife's face yet again."

"We get it, Ian," you rush to say, full of the usual sympathy. You and Ian's wife are friends, and I have one of those bizarre moments when it becomes absolutely clear that you have a life outside of this office, one that doesn't include me.

He continues. "Blant doesn't show his face till noon."

"Of course he doesn't, Ian," you say, because we all know Blant's habits.

"I show a whore's restraint. It's noon, but I behave as if it's eight in the morning, you know, to spare him the embarrassment. 'How's it going, Skipper?' He ignores the question. He doesn't call me into his office. He doesn't ask to see the script. It's one. It's one-thirty. He's in there playing a video game."

I can't suppress a chuckle of shock in memory. I'd never seen Ian so red in the face. His crest of perfectly brushed, thick-sprayed hair sat like an island of granite in the storm.

"Finally, I grab my balls. I muster it up. I go in. He asks me if I have the script, as if I overslept and have just come to work, like him. I hand over the script. There is nothing objectionable. It is perfect. It is a cross between Flannery O'Connor and Murrow. He reads it in five seconds, looks up at me and says, Great, except it's racist."

"He did not," you said, not mentioning a word of your own troubles.

"You know me, Line. You know this is utter shit. I was in shock, I told him the best man at my wedding was my African American college roommate, and I asked him how it was racist, how it was possibly fucking racist, except for the fact that the main character happened to be black and a criminal, and he says, it's all in the presentation, and if you can't see it, it only confirms my suspicion."

"Oh my God," we both said in unison.

"But wait. That's nothing. About five minutes ago, he calls me back into the office and says he's tried to rewrite the script, a bald-faced lie, because I've seen him through the glass playing video games and trading stocks, but my version is so compromised by my clear bigotry that he's considering taking me off the story all together. I'm speechless. Finally, he tells me, before turning back to the video game clearly visible on his computer monitor, 'I've told you, Ian. You're good at getting the interviews, but anyone can do that. It's the writing. You can't write for television, and the show can't afford amateurs.'"

Ian's head drooped, he put a hand to his forehead and he said, "And the worst of it is, now I have a fever, and I'm probably going to have to go home and go to bed. This is it, man. I'm telling you. I am done."

I told him he could have my brownie, which he'd eaten a few seconds into the rant, and he grinned and said, "I'll getcha back."

Then he noticed your furrowed brow. "Oh no," he said. "I haven't asked about your situation. What happened?"

"Never mind, Ian," you said. "It's nothing compared to you. He's making me go to Romania. That's all."

"The dick."

"Doesn't help to say so."

"Evangeline. The Thin Blue Line. When will you ever learn? You have to fight the power."

You had too much on your mind to humor him. You were scared. You were furious. You were also excited about your engagement. We never got that chance to talk about my subject, but, despite my personal disappointment, I recall the last words Ian said to you before he picked up his coat and walked out.

"I do wish you'd be a little less complacent on your own behalf. Just a little. Then you'd understand where I'm coming from."

And you said, "I do understand, Ian. I just don't care as much."

He pointed at you, but looked right at me. "Isn't she adorable?" He swung around and walked back to your desk. "You remember how you once told me what an honor it was to be able to work at *The Hour*? You care more than I do. But you have no spine, Line. You're content to be someone else's soldier. That way, you never have to face the final responsibility."

That hurt look came into your eyes. You blushed a little in anger.

"But you know what? You'll probably come back with the story of the year, and your correspondent will love you. Meanwhile, I'm getting to produce my own stories, and I've led the show, what, seven times, and my correspondent holds me in base contempt. With that, I go to my bed."

He reached across the desk, took your hand and kissed its knuckles, almost courtly. "Sweet Line. Be very careful. We'll fete you on your return."

"No you won't," you sniffed. "But I hope you make Skipper Blant beg before it's over." Those were your last words to him, unless I am much mistaken.

We buried Ian this week. It was some kind of virus. I only saw him once more, on the street, and he was ailing, but it seemed more like the onset of a mild flu. We got the news by e-mail three days ago, a single paragraph about medical circumstances. He went into the hospital on Friday with headaches, was released on Sunday, went back again on Tuesday and passed away on Thursday. The news came from Skipper Blant himself, or as I like to think of him, the Koala, who has never shown the slightest recognition of my individual person—but who endeared himself to me by calling me "You." This morning, in the hall, he stopped and said, "You knew Ian well." We hugged. He seemed distraught, even though I got the feeling that he never liked our friend much. But you never know the truth about these things, do you?

It should be possible for you to check e-mail in Transylvania—tech support assures me that it should be. If so, you'll probably get this news late at night, and it will be worse for you than for any of us, because you are alone, because you knew Ian better than most of us, because he was your crusader. I'm so sorry, E. I'm sorry that it happened, and I'm sorry that you're alone to hear it. But you understand, if you're around, that I had to let you know.

How could it possibly happen? Something invaded his spinal fluid. Something terrible and unknowable invaded his spinal fluid and would not retreat. The body can be an avenue for spiritual warfare, and that's how I must see this development, as another lost battle in a long defeat of anything decent in the human spirit here at *The Hour*. It was a natural death, they tell us. I suppose I have to believe it.

Last week, after you left, I was crossing 96th Street, and I bumped into Ian. He was dressed in his usual finery, a light Armani or Hugo Boss. The bespoke suit had been shelved. His hair didn't move in the wind. His chin seemed halfway across the street. I can't recall what we said to one another. It couldn't have been much. Labor Day was coming. Maybe he asked about my plans, maybe I did the same. I can tell you this. He didn't mention tape. He didn't ask me for an update on phone calls. He didn't want to know if I had just been to archives or planned to go. He was a decent guy, who treated me like a human being, that's what I remember about that encounter. I will miss him. He loved you.

Anyway, I don't know exactly what got Ian, but I'm suspicious now of the very air we breathe. You know what he thought of this place, and I concur. We work in the heart of terror. Those outside have no idea what I mean, but you do. Terror, on its surface, cuts hard and sharp as a knife, but at its heart, it swells and rolls like a sea. It isn't fixed into permanent shapes or symbols or even shadows. It's liquid, and we ingest it, and it ingests us. The threat has deepened ever since we moved back into this building, which we should never have done. Some offices relocated to New Jersey, for God's sake, but not Bob Rogers. Talk about vanity. He had to move us back down here just to show we had balls as big as the *Wall Street Journal.* Now I can't sleep anymore.

I believe Ian died a natural death. One could never make an argument on that score, but sometimes I have these intimations. I can't help feeling that Ian was just too good at his job, in his life, in this world, so they disappeared him. He rose too fast. He was too well-loved. What kind of virus takes a young man in his early thirties and obliterates his existence in a matter of days? If I know you, E, you are staring at the screen with those deep brown eyes, and you are whispering a prayer to a god in whom you do not believe. You're not crying. You're too much the actress to let yourself fall apart in some grubby little Eastern European Internet café. You'll wait till you get back to your hotel room, and you'll hurl yourself onto your mattress, and you'll tear at that deep black hair on your head because you can't begin to accept the fact of this tragedy.

Before you do that, however, I'm asking you to do one thing. Respond to this e-mail.

I repeat: Respond to this e-mail.

People are beginning to whisper that there is some kind of trouble with you, too, that there is some kind of curse on us; first Ian, now you, and who's next, that sort of thing. You were only supposed to go to Transylvania for five days. I know. I booked your travel. I went through the fine details. I got you the upgrade from business class. I got you that fine hotel near the Parliament and even found you a place to stay in Brasov, as you requested. That wasn't easy. You budgeted one round-trip flight to Budapest without a crew, and five days, long enough for you to get to Romania, take a rental car up to Transylvania, meet your man and get back home. You obsess over the nickels and dimes. You dislike dirty places. There is no way that you would overstay in post-Communist Transylvania.

I am in the darkness where you are concerned. I feel like a medieval clerk in some great ancient castle keep, and a wolfish wind just blew out my candle.

E, I have to say this or I never will, it's what I wanted to discuss that last day, your shining brown eyes, your dark hair falling down your face, down your sweet-smelling cinnamon neck, down to your shoulders with just a trace of curl, onto mine as you bent over me to ask for the latest update on some insignificance pouched from London, your V-neck sweaters and blouses, worn against the advice of the greatest of the correspondents, the Prince of Darkness, swooping down to reveal a single red freckle on the swell of your right breast, your pale skin in January, your olive sheen in August, these things have given me my sanity on the twentieth floor of this building. A sound man once told me that you come from Venetian stock, on your mother's side, and the Venetian women were descended from the glorious princesses of Byzantium, the most renowned beauties of the Dark Ages. In your blue-and-white-striped blouse, scoop-necked, you come to me out of the shadows between the cantina and the lobby, like one of those women in Romanesque mosaics, placing your hands on my heart, whispering in my ears like the gusts of treated air along the dim corridors of this corrupted place, and I know that whatever got Ian will never touch me.

But what if something has happened to you, E? That I couldn't bear.

That would kill me. I have your e-mail address, and I can send this note now, revealing everything, that I am lost in you, that I've been so for three years, ever since we first exchanged confidences just one week before the planes hit the buildings next door, before that horrible time, under the watchful eyes of the Totems and their legions, who all wanted you but never had you, those dark gods who rule this place where the ceilings are crucifixes, the soup is strange, the walls of the halls reach out with clammy hands, and the air is cold like the skin of the dead, a walled camp of videotape, topped with razor wire, manned by invisible machine guns, daring me to deviate for even a second, when I relieve myself in the bathroom, when I bow and scrape to the librarians in archives or go to the cantina for a peach Snapple and a bowl of that diabolically awful split pea. Just by sending this e-mail, I risk obliteration. That's how much you mean to me, E. Please come back. I'm sorry about Ian. I'm in shock. My only comfort is that, statistically speaking, the odds that we would lose an associate producer and a producer in the same week are staggering. Please be all right. Please answer. Yours, The Over-Stim

Seventeen

E—Forgive me for that last crazy e-mail. Grief, poor wages and a run of bad summer movies have made me insane. But I feel more myself today. And I have the latest intelligence.

William Lockyear, Esquire, your lovely boss, just moved in for the kill.

"Stimson," he said in an uncivilized voice. "You know we have a screening tomorrow."

I nodded, but didn't turn around.

"You're still upset, I gather," Lockyear said. "Is it Ian?"

"Yes."

"And Evangeline, I presume."

He pronounces your name wrong. E-vang-e-Lynn. I try to tell him that it's LINE. Like Line dancing, but he never gets it. "Evange-*line*'s going to be fine. She's going to get your story."

As I write, it's ten A.M., light rising off the Hudson River, same kind of weather as back then, on that September day, gorgeous heat feathered by the lightest of cool breezes. Why can't things be okay? But Lockyear seems convinced they are. In his pink button-down oxford cloth, with his cuffs buttoned, his shirt tucked into his fresh-pressed khakis, his perennial blue blazer, he is a phenomenon, a pink champagne cocktail of a man, a trivial effervescence in the hallways. Let the others die and disappear. Nothing will happen to him. He's a veteran producer at *The Hour*. He's untouchable.

He turned on his Latin cool jazz, did a step of some kind, as if the world could not be more delightful. Did he raise his fingers in the air and snap? This sandy-haired baby boomer prodigy hasn't aged in a decade. He has a hot plate in his room and makes his own tea. He has the same meal every day, fruit in plain yogurt. He medicates, you say, but I see no sign.

Your disappearance doesn't seem to disturb his equilibrium at all, but any minute now, his correspondent, Austen Trotta, will call, and they will have the unavoidable conversation. Trotta's no fool. He's read the right books, seen the right movies. He knows you won't be fine. He knows you are not undercover. He knows, as I do, you are in trouble. One has intuitions about these things. But Lockyear will resist such negative interpretation. In the phone conversation with Trotta, there will be sub-currents of recrimination, but Lockyear will not acknowledge them. He will abide by the fiction that you are merely tête-à-tête with one of our interview subjects, hammering out a deal.

I wonder what's in his mind, though. Does he know that he's been dis-gracefully negligent? He allowed you too much time to negotiate in Tran-sylvania. By now, you should have phoned and triumphantly told Lockyear that you had a great character and could confidently proceed. A crew should have been booked. Trotta should have received the standard de-briefing. But no word has come, and Ian has died, and Lockyear has expe-rienced the unthinkable—a moment of self-doubt. He has left a dozen messages on your three-phase phone, and you never answer. Once, a man's voice came on the line, babbling Romanian, Lockyear's guess of that language, anyway. He went to Austen and explained that there might be a problem, and Austen has reacted like the governor of a state hit by hurricane. He called in the troops. The American government is involved.

The phone rang. Lockyear snatched it up.

"Absolutely," he answered. "You know I will. Anything I can do."

He hung up. "Here we go," he said, coming by my cubicle. "Her father and her fiancé are in Austen's office. They want a word."

"I should think so."

His bright eyes shrank to a single laserlike point on my person. "Wipe that smile off your face, you little shit. You're coming with me."

Eighteen

E—Lockyear and I walked into Austen's office, and through the plate-glass window, New Jersey looked very close. From my position, in the corner of the room nearest the door, the Hudson River barely registered, and I could see nothing of the Trade Center site below. Do you have any idea what it is like to be a balding, pale, skinny twenty-six-year-old humanoid in a room with four leading men types, each of a different generation. Like a lost child in a wax museum. There was, of course, Lockyear, impeccably turned out in high-end mall clothes. Like Ian, he dresses well; I'm sure that you've noticed. His manner was a calibrated calm, neither indifferent nor panicked. He is slender and feline compared to Austen, who reminds me of the wise old owl in children's books; that's why I call him the Owl. Austen was dressed in one of his pink striped shirts, wearing a red silk tie under a dark blue suit jacket, very sporting. A red silk pocket kerchief poked out of the jacket pocket. Every wrinkle in Austen's face appears to be a matter of careful forethought, as if he deliberated for years before allowing the skin to crack to a rivulet, as if auditions had to be run, permits authorized and references checked. He has the best wrinkles in media, I would say, better than those of Eastwood or even Redford, because these wrinkles exist as a confirmation of character. Austen is the sum total of his wrinkles, one for Berlin in 1956, three for Algeria in 1962, five for Zimbabwe in 1965, and God knows how many for Vietnam. Transylvania may have added one or two more to the masterpiece.

But I would be lying if I said that I cared much about how my over-lords disported themselves. From the moment that I entered the room, I was riveted by the two strangers, your father and your lover, excuse me, your fiancé. First, of course, I saw your face in your father's, and had an uncanny feeling that if I spoke to him, you would hear me. If I said, "Evangeline, come home," his mouth would open, and your laugh would come out, and your voice would say, "But I'm already here, Stimson." After that first glance, the reality of the man reasserted itself. He is stern. You've never said that. He has lightning in his eyes, and a jaw that does not tolerate resistance in this life or the next. I can imagine that jaw in the grave, thrust out like an anvil, never disintegrating. The hair at his temples has gone gray, but the rest of the hair seems to have retained its color. There's nothing round or soft about your father. He didn't convey mercy or easy amiability. He didn't smoke and seemed to take it as a personal insult that Austen did. He kept brushing the shoulders of his Brooks Brothers suit, as if the cigarette ash had sullied the material. He kept his legs crossed the entire time. When he spoke, he stared right at Austen. To him, if you'll excuse my use of your favorite salty expression, Lockyear amounted to pepper on fly shit.

And then, of course, there was your fiancé. What can I say about him? He's gorgeous enough. You like gorgeous men, obviously. As a wildly successful pastry chef, he had to wear the most casual and expensive suit in the room, of course, an Armani T-shirt ensemble, but he didn't comport himself as well as the older men. The outfit had a soiled quality, as if he had slept in it, as if he had not been out of it since your last departure. Robert's his name, I believe. We were all introduced. He is a frightened man, too, inherently frightened. Or maybe that was just the bad news. You told me once that Ian and he had been good friends, that Ian introduced you, perhaps? So maybe he is in double shock—a friend dead, his fiancée vanished. He sat there in a near-catatonic daze, his legs spread wide on the couch, gazing at a particular wrinkle on Austen's face, it seemed to me, as if that wrinkle were the first path on the way to you. His eyes had reddened from lack of sleep or crying. The older man, your father, intimidated him, I think, and it must have been torture to be so distraught in the presence of a future father-in-law.

Your father spoke first, to Austen. "I require a few answers."

"Of course."

"If I get the right answers, there will no longer be any need for us to communicate. I fully intend to take this matter into my own hands. You can call off your own efforts. In fact, I will insist."

"Very well." Austen put a hand on the back of his hip, held the cigarette aloft with the other. "I would be the last person to dissuade you."

Your father gave a nod. "Good."

Your lover gave the appearance of rising up out of the couch to speak. But your father resumed.

"What exactly is she doing over there?"

Austen turned his eye to Lockyear. Lockyear crossed his arms and gave your father a beseeching look of a kind that I have never seen aimed at me. Your father didn't return the look. He kept his eyes on Austen.

"She arranged to meet a gentleman named Ion Torgu. We wanted an interview with him."

"Why?"

"He is reputed to be the leader of organized crime in Eastern Europe."

Your father continued to stare at Austen. "Is that so? You sent my daughter by herself to find this man?"

Austen turned again to Lockyear. Lockyear's arms tightened on his body as if an internal screwdriver had done a complete round on his screws.

"It's standard."

Your father's face went crimson as he directed his next question to Austen. "How much do you pay my daughter, may I ask, to go to Eastern Europe in search of high-ranking mobsters?"

Austen turned again to Lockyear, and Lockyear, without the slightest quiver of shame, turned to me, as if I, the worst-paid member of the entire staff, signed the checks for everyone.

I was keen to oblige. "South of $60,000 a year."

Austen interjected with hints of moral outrage. "Surely not."

Lockyear's eyes widened at Austen's show of incredulity. He rushed to correct my statement. "This man is merely a production associate. He has no idea. It's somewhere close to six figures, I believe."

But your father had done his homework. "It's $55,000 a year, sir." He kept his eyes, as always, on Austen. "For that paltry sum, you may have sent my daughter off to her death in Romania."

Austen cleared his throat and put out the cigarette in a Frosty the Snowman mug on his desk. "Not so fast. I would like to say a word in our defense. We all admire and adore your daughter. If what you say is true, she's woefully underpaid, and we will surely rectify that when she gets back, but for the moment, we need to concentrate on the matter at hand. No?" Austen flicked a glance of raw contempt at Lockyear. "Mr. Harker, you should know that I take personal responsibility for everything that has happened. If necessary, we will go ourselves to Romania. In fact, my colleague here, Mr. Lockyear, will be leaving for Bucharest tonight. Isn't that right, Bill?"

Lockyear nodded, as if he had just stopped in the office on his way to the airport, as if the lie were inexorably true. He used his favorite word. "Absolutely."

This did not mollify your father. "What exactly is her last known location?"

Austen made the now mechanical turn to Lockyear, who was still digesting the ramifications of his new itinerary. He enunciated each word of the reply with a near moral indignation. "A hotel in a city called Brasov. It was a voice mail that she left from her hotel room, which she checked into and out of, very quickly. She wasn't in the hotel for more than an hour. The message said that she would be involved in negotiations for quite a while. She met someone, we don't know who for sure, maybe our mobster, maybe one of his people. And they left together. That's the last time we heard from her. It's been two weeks ago now."

"Did you encourage her to this rash behavior?"

I could see the panic rising in Lockyear. He was being blamed for everything. "We never had a chance to talk, but I would have urged caution—"

Your father interrupted in fury. "I want phone numbers, fax numbers, e-mails for every place she stayed or was planning to stay."

Austen displayed a fuming face, too, as if in sympathy. Lockyear said that he would get them.

"Did you think to ask someone at the hotel to get a personal message to her?!" the pastry chef suddenly cried. The room went silent at this outburst. Tears flowed from his eyes. "I mean, e-mails and telephones. Jesus. One human being to another. That's what has to be done. Did you bribe? Did you threaten? Did you threaten those fuckers within an inch of their lives?"

"Everything," Austen replied with gentle conviction, though I wasn't sure if it was true. "We've tried all of that and more."

"How much money did she have on her?" your father demanded.

I knew. "About a thousand in petty cash, plus a credit card."

Your fiancé blurted out, "And the engagement ring."

Your father glared at your future husband. "Goddamn it. A Romanian would kill her for that alone."

Everything in the room went still, except the tick of the cuckoo clock, a gift to Austen from a German mayor who happened to be the son of a famous World War II tank commander. Outside the glass wall of the office, the personal assistants looked up, like deer surprised by gunshot.

"You're saying I got her killed?" the fiancé asked in a beseeching, horrified voice.

Your father shook his head. "No, sir. I blame these sons of bitches here, and be assured. I will visit tenfold upon their heads whatever has been visited upon her."

"Now, now." Austen waved his cigarette hand in the air, as if to clear more than smoke. "No need for that kind of talk, Mr. Harker. She's an associate producer at *The Hour,* and one of the best. I still have every belief that she has gone undercover to meet with this fellow Ion Torgu and is probably right now making the case for the show. If I know your daughter, if she's anything like her old man, she won't stop till that job is done."

"She's been missing for two weeks," the fiancé replied. "You think it's remotely possible she's still negotiating?"

Austen gave a convincing nod. "I once knew a producer who negotiated for three months with an Afghan warlord."

Your father stood up. "Be that as it may, I'm hiring a team of very rough men to go into Romania, and if they get her out alive, I will demand that she find gainful employment at a place that isn't so chicken shit. I mean, goddamn, boys, if a girl carries your water, pay a wage."

At that moment, an editor, Julia Barnes, appeared at my back. She tapped me on the shoulder, and I leaned forward. She whispered in my ear.

"It's urgent," she said.

Austen noticed her. "What?" he inquired.

Julia gave a compassionate smile to everyone. She gave the impression of knowing exactly what had transpired between us. Maybe she had been eavesdropping. She's one of the best eavesdroppers on the show, in my experience.

"It's Claude Miggison," she said. "He just received word that a case of tapes arrived from Romania."

Dread and relief entered the room. No one could speak for a minute. Your lover jumped off the couch.

Julia saw our condition. "They must be from her, right? No one else is shooting in Romania now."

"But that makes no sense," Lockyear objected, whipping about, defending himself to Austen, to the others. "She didn't take along a camera crew." He whipped back around to face Julia. "Who shot it?"

"Only one name on the shipment, and that is Olestru, which could be the lead camera on the A crew, but we've never used anyone named Olestru before. I checked the bookings file."

Lockyear had gone pale as death. "That's our contact in Romania."

Your father's fist hit Austen's desk. "You boys best get your shit together!"

"Quite right." Austen turned to Lockyear. "You're done, Bill."

Lockyear stared past him at the river, his mouth agape, as if he had walked through Austen's plate-glass window by accident and just realized his mistake. In fact, he had stepped into the free and open air of joblessness.

"Your services will no longer be required." Austen looked down at the floor. "Sadly."

The meeting came to an end.

Nineteen

E—I just vomited into a sink in the men's room. Austen saw, but I don't care. There is no point in continuing this charade. You are not under-cover. You cannot answer. The shipment from Romania confirms my worst fears. I haven't been able to see the tapes, but Julia says there is nothing on them. She said that someone shot ten tapes of a single chair in an empty room. Imagine that. Five hours of dead footage. The audio picks up vague whispery sounds. Miggison thinks it might just be micro-phone fuzz, but he's not sure that the camera crew used a sound engi-neer. There might be a boom mike somewhere. The lighting is not bad, so someone knew their stuff, but the light falls on a wooden chair in a space that tells us nothing. It could be anywhere. This news makes me numb. I am so sorry, E. If there's a heaven, I know you're there with Ian.

Stimson: Are you there? It's me. Evangeline.

E: Oh my God. Where the hell are you? Are you okay?

I'm fine. I gather you all received my voice mail. The negotiations have gone well. Did you get the tapes I sent?

Yes. We got them, but it sounds like something got fucked up techni-cally. No big deal compared to knowing you're safe. We were scared shit-less. Your father was here. Lockyear got fired. Tell me where you are now!

Were the tapes accepted, Stim?

Pardon my French, E, but fuck the tapes! I need coordinates, phone numbers, anything. We're coming to get you.

No. Before we proceed, I must know. These are audition tapes, and everyone must see them before we do this story. Were they accepted?

Yes, Claude Miggison signed for them and logged them, and as far as I know, he gave them to Julia Barnes for safekeeping. That means he accepted them. But Julia says there is nothing on them. Do you read? Nothing but a chair. Give me anything. Give me a location. Tell me that you're okay.

I am fine, Stimson. Please forgive my delayed response. It has been a trying time. Please know that this is the most difficult negotiation that I have ever conducted for the show, that we are dealing here with a criminal mastermind who has demands that are quite labyrinthine in nature, but who has expressed a willingness to tell us his personal story before he turns himself in to American authorities. His own government wants him dead, so our story would be his insurance policy against assassination. He has exclusive information on terrorism, organized crime in Russia and smuggled weapons of the nuclear variety. For this reason, I may be involved in sequestered negotiation for quite a while longer. I have already shared this information with my superiors and am only telling you because you were so sweet as to send me that note expressing your affections, and I wanted to reciprocate with a gesture of trust. You mustn't tell the others that we have communicated.

Reciprocate?

Yes, but not as you wish, perhaps. I have no time for sentiment, but I do need a friend and an ally in this great work I have undertaken. It will be

a story unlike any other ever told, and only the strongest and best may rise to its challenge. This work has already changed me, my dear friend, and I am certain that it will change you, too, if you agree to do everything I say. Are you truly loyal to me? I wonder. And I hope. Your colleague, Evangeline Harker

BO**3**OK

*The Mind of
the Correspondent*

Twenty

The worst part about this therapy journal is the ritual of curtain closing. Every time I want to write, I have to pretend I'm taking a nap and draw the curtains over the plate-glass window. It makes me look so goddamn old. And because it makes me look old, I feel old, and I feel guilty, and I hate to feel guilty for something that I was ordered to do by a very expensive Park Avenue physician. Meanwhile, Peach suspects nefarious activity. She thinks I'm abusing the Percocet and attempts to ration me.

I should make clear my objections to this journal from the start. First and foremost, you have been misinformed. I did not collapse in an interview. The verb collapse wildly overstates the case. I simply stopped speaking, for reasons unbeknownst to me. I became numb. The subject of the interview grew alarmed, and when I saw his unease and got up to reassure him, I tripped and fell on a cord, and this became the collapse. Please make note of my clarification. Collapse implies incapacitation, which implies mania. I am perfectly well in my mind, despite what my company believes. My boss, Bob Rogers, suspects the network is using this notion of my collapse to further erode our authority here at The Hour. Network leaked the matter to the press, after all.

But I'm getting ahead of myself. First, so that this journal will be comprehensible to you, Dr. Bunten, so you may confidently assess whatever impact my workplace may be having on my mental faculties, I feel I must correct a few misperceptions you have about the nature of my contribution to the show. In particular, you once asked me if I was the most powerful man in broadcast news. This question betrays a level of ignorance that may be understandable, given the enduring success of The Hour. *As you noted, we have guillotined our share of unfortunates, helped at least one president into office and contributed to the political demise of another. I have personally been involved in the lifting of a death sentence or two. But the view from outside is misleading as to my share in the fruits of this labor. Furthermore, I fear that, without a proper introduction to the delicate yet viciously Darwinist ecosystem in which I have spent the bulk of my professional life, you will be apt to ascribe my alleged decline to vague and clichéd notions related to the September 11 attacks, a diagnosis that I will categorically and fundamentally reject, should it rear its head. Please take careful note, as I don't want to have to repeat myself.*

As you know, I am a correspondent. In print news, that word is a synonym for reporter. In our business, the broadcast television business, a correspondent means someone who appears on your television screen. I have been one of these light-bathed few for four and a half decades, ever since the early 1960s, ten years as news correspondent for the network, thirty more as one of the familiar faces on a show called The Hour, *which you confessed to me was your favorite program on television. For the sake of absolute clarity, and in case you don't know,* The Hour *is the top-rated news show on American television and has been since it pioneered the magazine format in that ferocious year 1968, when assassination, race riots, overseas war and popular music conspired to overflow the banks of the regular time slot allotted to news. For the last decade or so, there have been five regular correspondents on* The Hour, *five mugs known to millions of viewers: the most notorious being Edward Prince, the nation's ragged hit man, whom you claim to adore; yours truly; Sam Dambles, the national favorite, our cool factor; Nina Vargtimmen, our only woman, mini-skirted at sixty, alas; and Skipper Blant, the most recent addition. Contrary to popular belief, the correspondents at* The Hour *are neither masters of the universe in full control of their destinies nor mere puppets on a string nor can they be considered working journalists in the field.*

To harvest stories, each correspondent depends on a staff of eight, consisting of four teams of two producers each. I'm speaking here about producers, and yet you probably have no idea what the word means in this context. A producer is a person who takes information and transforms it into pictures, a kind of journalist who spends most of his or her waking life concerned with the flow of necessary images. Without images, there can be no news on television. Without images, words perish like squid on the beach, so most producers at The Hour are paid to be good picture people, not real journalists. For that more rigorous work, each producer has a subordinate, known as an associate producer, a younger and less experienced colleague who generates story ideas, pitches those ideas then goes out into the field to investigate the journalistic accuracy and broadcast potential of the ideas. As a rule, the associate producers function as the first gatekeepers of our show. If they smell trouble, no one else ever has to. (As an aside, of indeterminate significance, I should mention another, little-known caste in our business. To help them in their endeavors, these teams of producers rely on the labor of a strata of what we call production associates, young professionals who gather file footage, which is what we call old tape, shot by previous crews, often at other networks. These folk also apply for licenses and permits to use such footage. It is poorly paid drudge work, and as a result, production associates tend to be impoverished, which leads frequently to embitterment and a willingness to leak news about us to the press or to our corporate overseers. Mostly, they are quite young, because the young place no sensible value on their time and can be exploited mercilessly by their desire to be a part of the brand that is The Hour.)

The above information should serve as your key in grasping the importance of the following. Without that key, you will never comprehend the reason why certain circumstances on the twentieth floor forced me to turn to you, Dr. Bunten. My personal trial has come in the effort to be true to myself and to the stories we have told for the last thirty years, against a rising tide of provincialism and vapidity.

How do we make our stories? Once my producers and their camera crews have shot enough footage, we go into an editing room. The Hour has its own staff of editors, the best in the news business, unionized men and women who have been cutting pieces for as long as I have been in this job. In the eyes of many producers, thanks to differences in salaries and therefore social milieu, editors are considered a lower order of being. They reek of blue-collar functionary. To me, in comparison with producers, they are as *angels to humans. And we must beg for our angels. As correspondents, we must go hat in hand to a difficult man named Claude Miggison, who over-sees schedules, and plead for the services of our favorite editors, and if they are free, if another correspondent hasn't absconded with them, we may get our first choice. I don't mind telling you that I will not work with the wrong editor. That's how important it is to secure the allegiances of the right one. A great editor must be plied with kindness, kisses and praise, seduced with wines and chocolates at Christmastime. It is exhausting and despicable, but it is also the truth. Editors must be wooed as if they were fickle women who don't know their own minds. And once wooed, they must be dominated, cos-seted and occasionally slapped hard into submission.*

But I digress. You have asked me before how we take all that tape, hun-dreds of hours, and boil it down to a few minutes. The answer is simple. The editor pulls off a trick, the technological equivalent of the old magic scarf number, whereby the magician produces one red scarf, waves his wand and, lo and behold, that scarf comes out of the hat tied to twenty others. The ed-itor puts each piece of tape into a machine that transforms the analog image into digital files—he or she digitizes the material, as we say—and once this is done, all those separate bits of tape become part of the one big scarf. If I may be more poetic now, in our system, that bewitched scarf of images be-comes a river, spilling, at last, into the great ocean of images available to us in our computers, an ocean encompassing the world, in which we bathe like happy Polynesians.

When we're cutting together a piece, at that magic moment, we Polyne-sians arrange the best moments in a twelve-minute sequence. We bind these moments tightly with cords of words, which we call a script. But script is mis-leading, and I should make one thing clear. The Hour has always been driven by interviews. We do not specialize in fancy camera movements, musical in-terludes, excess verbiage or enormous amounts of archival footage. We live and die by the quality of the people we interview. When my associate produc-ers go into the field, I drum home to them the necessity of finding great "char-acters." Yes, Dr. Bunten, characters, just as in a great short story or novella. And that's how I see my job, as a chronicler of life's little visual novellas. Per-haps that's why I take it all so personally. Perhaps that's why I have been forced, in the end, to seek help from your profession. With the help of the pro-

ducers and the editor, I craft my little novellas, nipping and tucking, polishing
and buffing, till every frame sings, slicing down interviews to their most exquisite moments of human folly and emotion, until we are ready to show our
work to the true overlords of the show, my boss and his associates.

And here is the answer to your absurd question. Am I the most powerful
man in broadcast news? Certainly not, emphatically not, if by power, you
mean the autonomy to do whatever you want, whenever you want, with sufficient financial largesse, and that is the only kind of power worth having.
That honor belongs to a man named Bob Rogers, founder and executive producer of this program for more than three decades. Bob Rogers alone ap-
proves or rejects our story ideas, long before they are shot by camera crews.
Bob Rogers, with advice from his gifted and poisoned lieutenants, reviews
the final product in the screening room, and with a bit more vulgarity than
an ancient Roman emperor, the five good ones anyway, turns his thumb up
or down. I don't care to say how many wonderful pieces have been savagely
destroyed by this man's indigestion, but I must also confess that untold numbers have been improved by his whim. When necessary, in the sanctum sanc-
torum of the screening room, Rogers's lieutenants have fought him and
prevailed, there has been civil war, careers have been destroyed, but out of
this scrap and scrum has come some of our greatest success. Rogers is that
most loathsome of creatures, a deserving recipient of fortune's grace, and I
would be a churl not to credit him with my own modest achievements. Without Rogers, none of us would be here, doctor. And yet he is crazy and devi-
ous beyond your wildest dreams.

A last word before I take another Percocet for the back pain and tumble
into drowsiness. Rogers may be powerful, but he's no Omnipotent. For
thirty years, he has fought our broadcast network to maintain control of
this one little show, which has its offices on the twentieth floor of a downtown office building, and is therefore separate from the bulk of the network's
other operations, which are gathered in a sprawling, unhappy rabbit warren
in the lower reaches of Hudson Street. We call that place the broadcast center, and it is the seat of a malign power eternally directed against us. For
thirty years, the network has tried to bring Rogers down into their primordial swamp, to dictate terms, even to wrest The Hour away and give it a
more youthful appeal, and for that same period, due to his phenomenal

scores in the ratings, Rogers has managed to fend off his enemies. But a great part of my stress, you should know, is my increasing sense that we are beginning, at last, to lose the battle. Rogers is in his eighties, and cannot go on forever. Age creeps up on me, on Prince, even on Dambles. And the network sees, the network knows. When the time comes, it will strike without mercy, with swift and terrible vengeance, and it will take away what we've built and give it to cave dwellers, to the stupid, the greedy and the depraved.

I am now officially depressed, doctor, thanks to you. Out, Trotta

MONDAY, OCTOBER 5, LATER THAT MORNING

Here's what weighs on me this morning: the last conversation with Evangeline Harker before she left for Romania. Had I ever worn a firearm in Vietnam? She really wanted to know. She said that her fiancé had asked the question, and she hadn't known the answer, but I got the feeling that it was more than that. She had some concern about the trip. She feared complications. Normally, I don't talk too much about that era, but she's a sweet kid, and I answered the question. I told her that I only carried a weapon once. It was at Khe Sanh. Someone suggested to me that I should carry a pistol, for self-protection, so I did. This person informed me that certain elements in the U.S. military might try to stage an accident. I never found out the truth, but having the thing scared the shit out of me. I don't know why, maybe because I knew I'd use it. I never carried another. She didn't ask a follow-up. I asked her if she had some more specific concern, and she said she didn't.

Unpleasant business. Had to let Lockyear go. It was the only thing to do. Harker wanted his pound. But we all need change, even the least equipped of us. Lockyear started in radio and can go back. And fresh blood won't do me any harm.

Breakfast break. The cantina smells like bacon grease, and I love the smell, a disgraceful pleasure that grows with the years. I've always been one of those bacon-loving Jews, though I've tried and tried to give it up, and won't eat just any bacon. Despite the lovely aroma, I won't eat that cantina bacon, for instance. It sits there in the tin pans and makes a profound argu-

ment against itself. I order slab-cut from Ottomanelli's. Still, my mother would not care about the quality. Bacon is bacon. She would get the vapors.

This really is a therapy journal. I've already mentioned my mother and pork. If I'm honest, the cantina is the only place on this floor where I truly feel comfortable. No bullshit in there. Everyone's after the same thing. Sustenance.

In the cantina, as it happened, I ran into Rogers. After thirty years on his team, I still feel the weight of his authority, though it's more a mental habit than fear. What the hell can he do to me anymore?

"You heard?"

"Have I heard what?"

Bob shook his head at what he calls my obstinate nature.

"There's going to be an inquiry on this Harker thing. Network's driving it."

"Bullshit. It's none of their business."

Bob nodded his head in agreement, but he wasn't finished. "It gets harder to believe anything they say, doesn't it? But you're saying you heard the rumor, too, and it's bullshit." I hadn't heard the rumor. It scared the hell out of me. Bob didn't pay for his banana. He followed me into the darkness of the corridor.

The twentieth floor has always been unnecessarily shadowy, and I always notice it again after Labor Day, when the golden holidays have receded, and there's no getting over the loss. How happy we were, Sue and I, I recalled, only six weeks ago when the hiatus began, and summer lay fresh and French before me, like a whore I knew in 1968, in Prague. But that whore was someone's informant, and the AP guy in Algeria in 1960 told me later that she moved to the Soviet Union and raised six kids with an East German engineer. She was beautiful. Not really a whore, I'm sure. All of those people are dead and gone, and yet I remember them so well. Her name was Sixtine, and she was a devout Communist.

Bob shook me out of my memory. "Talk to me about Romania, goddamn it."

"My oatmeal's cold."

He shrugged. I shrugged. He's always shrugged. He shrugs and smiles, been doing that as long as I've known him, near half a century, it's his way of signaling a threat. "I gotta tell ya. Every year, I have the same feeling, *that I should have got out the year before. Things like this, they remind me. There's life after broadcast."*

I gave him the look, saying, more or less, we have now crossed the line into totally useless and arbitrary conversation, and it's time for me to go back to my office, where I have more important things to do than breathe undead life into the old lies. No one here will ever willingly leave. No one will ever give up the hiatus. The hiatus is the job. Hiatus. What a word, what a sound. No one else in journalism has it. Six weeks of vacation in the middle of the summer, six weeks of sweet melancholy, six weeks to pretend that you are something else, anything else but a ghost who sits before a camera and smiles like some implied threat at twenty million people every Sunday. We're like some small European country, stranded on a single floor of a single building in Manhattan, with an identity based upon a different sense of time. And we're doomed. I exaggerated when I said twenty million. Network news numbers don't go that high anymore; more like fifteen million, or less, ten million even. Network news is dying, but we're its audible last gasp, still able to pull a decent occasional rating.

Five weeks ago, I sat under a dappled green trellis in a vineyard in the Camargue and ate rillette d'oie on crusts of warm bread. Now I was back in the underworld. We got to my office and I slid into my chair, but Bob stood at the door, one hand in his pocket, another jabbing at me with the banana, which I knew would never be consumed. "Should I be worried, is what I'm asking?"

What could I tell him? Luck was always the unheralded genius of this broadcast, Bob, and for the moment, it's failed us. But I didn't say that.

He opened up again. "I talked to the lawyers, and Ritzman tells me the broadcast could be culpable. Culpable how? For what? You know what the hell he means by that? 'Cause I sure don't."

I had to answer. Otherwise he would never leave. "How the hell do I know, Bob? It's a fucking awful mess, and I don't know what exactly we're into here, but culpable? Lawyers are fearmongers. You know that. Meanwhile, let's not forget that a human being is missing."

This appeal to decency made him indignant. "You sent her over there, you prick."

"May I please eat my breakfast now?"

He shrugged a last time and retreated. The phone kept ringing. Peach called to me, wanting me to pick up. I don't blame her. She doesn't want to be the first line of defense in this situation, but it's her pay grade, not mine. Best to wait. Best to manufacture a calm.

Evangeline's father, this Dub Harker, seems to want a piece of my hide, but he better watch himself. No offense to the girl, but what an affected fraud, that father. Has to try on his John Wayne, but he's no John Wayne; I knew Wayne, and Wayne had nothing like that tiresome swagger. A gentleman, and a gentle man, to boot, except when he got on the topic of communism while drunk, and claimed that Stalin tried to have him killed, and you don't laugh at a man who believes that or you get your lights smacked out. Never laughed at him again, but drank with him a few more times. Maybe Stalin did try to have him killed. Wayne said Los Angeles cops thwarted the hit, and they would have let him finish the Reds off, but he figured J. Edgar would do a fine job and let it go. Didn't even file charges. Wayne had class, even when he was out of his mind.

Harker's a wannabe Wayne, an oilman who raised a beautiful daughter. Dub? No chance it's his real name. Probably Terence or Percy or Sebastian, but couldn't stomach it, couldn't take the taunts, and believe me, we know how that goes, try Austen Trotta at the age of ten, try that on for size, see how fast Trotta becomes pig trotters, takes about five seconds, so he chooses Dub, or more likely the roughnecks in the Midland oil fields give him the nickname and it sticks. Texans think they belong anywhere. Never knew a Texan who didn't feel entitled to walk the earth without fear or supplication, walked into my office without an invitation, takes after his daughter in that respect. But you're messing with the wrong goddamn Jew now. You're dealing with the scion of sham Habsburg royalty now, Jews ennobled in the last waning years of the Emperor Franz Joseph—no meaner, tougher breed, right off the Russian frontier, where they survived Cossacks, plague and Poles. Forget John Wayne. I'll dub you, Harker. Make you the laughing stock of the Dallas Petroleum Club, make you look like the manqué, the poseur, the fraud that you are. Dub Harker, indeed. But you raised a fine girl. You did that, and that's not easy, so we'll call it a Texican standoff. Oatmeal break.

"One more thing you should know."

Goddamn Bob again, back before even five minutes had elapsed. Oatmeal is starting to make me sick. Pain coming on.

"I didn't want to mention it in the cantina."

"What now?"

"I have my suspicions about this Romania situation."

"Oh, Christ."

Bob shut the door behind him. "What if network cooked this up to use it against me."

I'd heard this nightmare silliness before. "Cooked up what? The kidnapping and possible murder of one of their own employees?"

"The stakes are very high, Austen."

"You mean this as a gag, surely."

"I don't know this time."

He shrugged. He didn't mean it as a gag. Lightning blitzed the low of my back. Shells smashed villages on either side of the spine. Time to lie down. Peach has the Percocet.

"Maybe I'm crazy. Hell, I know I am. But the coincidence of this thing strikes me as odd. Just when our numbers take a fall, just when the network starts talking about the aging demographics of the show, just then, a girl vanishes. Course, I doubt it had anything to do with that, but it's sure as shit convenient, and they'll use it against me for damn sure."

Got to land softly on my couch, draw the blinds, sink into oblivion. Peach, please, get the Percocet. Bob backed out. "Jesus, you're in worse shape than me."

"Lumbar."

"We'll talk later."

Time to take a real nap, justify that curtain call. Pain comes down my spine, Hitler through France. This therapy journal does not provide relief.

TUESDAY, OCTOBER 6, 10:15 A.M.

I'm wearing my lucky gabardines. Maybe I'll hear good news today.

Got in late, feeling foggy, and had an irritating message. Julia Barnes wants to talk. It's urgent. Always make time for an editor, I say, but this sounds a bit crazed. When have I ever asked an editor to make an appointment? She doesn't need to make an appointment. She can just walk in. But I wish she wouldn't. She was working with Evangeline on the rodeo clown story before. Maybe she has an insight, a clue. Do I want to hear it? No sleep last night. Time for a Percocet. Come on, lucky gabardines!

TUESDAY, OCTOBER 6, 4 P.M.

The Habsburg fate has finally caught up with me. Wise forefather, you left that world behind; wise, not lucky, as you always said. Bone cancer finally got you, but the Nazis never did. Bone cancer stemming from complications from prostate cancer, but you lived a long life and saved us from history, moved yourself out of the Habsburg Empire in 1912. Two more years, and you would have been conscripted, and our story would have ended like the rest of the Trotta family history, with a bullet between the eyes, instead of here, in this twentieth story aerie, on the airwaves of an America that cares nothing, knows nothing, about the world that you escaped, that was annihilated by the worst calamities of the twentieth century. And now all of that tsuris is exploding up and down my lower back. The older he gets, the more the old Jew must suffer.

Julia Barnes hovered like a specter at my office door right before lunch. She leaned in and knocked.

"Bad time?"

I gestured for her to sit. She shut the door behind her, a thoughtless bit of ostentation. Everyone would pay attention now. In my little world, a closed door goes off like a cannonade. People sit up and take notice.

"What's up, kiddo?"

"Did I ever tell you that my parents were Hungarian?"

As an opener to an urgent conversation, this did intrigue me, I must admit.

"My maiden name is Teleki."

"Nobility!"

She turned her head to one side, hair fell against her lips, and she laughed.

"And in Utica, no less."

I'd had no idea, though now she mentioned it, those eyes of hers betray the infamous Hungarian pessimism.

"Your people come from that part of the world, too, I think."

"Indeed. Polish Jews fom Galicia. Habsburg subjects." I tapped out a cigarette and put my feet up on the desk. "No Telekis, but one of my relatives had a von in front of his name. Is genealogy your concern today?"

"Please don't think I'm crazy." She cleared her throat and lowered her voice, even though the door was closed. "Remschneider is digitizing those tapes that came from Romania."

It seemed none of my business. Was she making a bid to preempt Remschneider in some petty bit of maneuvering for an editing job? And enlisting me in the machination? If so, it wasn't appreciated.

"So what?"

She put an elbow on the desk and lowered her head, as if whispering through a grate in a prison wall. "There's no Romania story. There's not even a budget number for a Romania story. Without a budget number, there can't be an editor. So why's he digitizing?"

I failed to see how this concerned me at all, despite the vague connection to other Romanian matters. But I did feel a twinge of nervousness, as if this information might be relevant in some unfathomable way. "Are you sure there's no budget number? There must be."

She seemed to catch herself at that point. She sat back in the chair and her voice rose a little. She had taken umbrage at my tone, which was all I needed.

"I'm not an idiot, Austen. I'm quite sure. There's no budget number. Anyway, that's not the point."

"May I ask why you care so much?"

Her face reddened, and I was sorry for her. She'd had a sleepless week on the rodeo clown story and needed to go home and rest. In my experience, in this business, loss of sleep is the great unsung destroyer of career.

She appeared to be collecting her thoughts. This was a gifted editor and a good person, but she had her foibles. No one was quicker to make a charge of sexism than Julia Barnes. I don't consider myself a sexist, though I have been accused in the past, and don't want to hand out more rounds of ammunition than are strictly necessary. But her odd fervor begged the question. I fished through papers on the desk for the ashtray and gave her a moment.

She sighed. "Here's why it matters. Those tapes came from Romania, though we weren't expecting them. Our associate producer is missing in Romania. For all we know, she's dead. Okay. This we know. But then, Miggison gives the tapes to me for safekeeping, and the next thing I know, they have been removed from my office and are now in the hands of another editor, who has no business touching them, and that editor is digitizing, as if we need them in the system for a story, though, as we both know, there is no story, and nothing on those tapes is usable for any story that we would ever do. So I put it to you again. Why in hell do we digitize them? Why don't we ship them right to the police?"

She had a fragile point of sorts, though she'd made quite a leap in her logic, connecting two things that might be completely unrelated. For all we know, from what she had told me, those tapes could have been shot by another crew at the network, for Nightly News or the Dawn Hour, and landed by mistake in our bailiwick. I didn't know why another editor here might want to digitize them, but it hardly seemed sinister.

"If what you're saying is there is some connection between Evangeline Harker and these tapes, I would very much like to see some evidence."

She shook her head at me with a slightly patronizing air. Her voice rose a notch. "How about that name—Olestru? Didn't Lockyear say it was the same name as her contact? Doesn't that count? Or am I crazy?"

My temper began to rise, which is bad for my blood pressure. I removed my legs from the top of the desk and sat up. The name troubled me but signified no great proof. The interview was over, as far as I was concerned.

"Anything else, my dear?"

She pushed aside the paper on my desk. "You're not hearing me, Austen. Those tapes originated in Transylvania."

I stared at her in unadorned, unapologetic amazement. This was one of the smartest editors on the floor. This was a rising star, or had been till now. And then, understanding what had happened, I laughed out loud. She had me.

"Oh dear." Tears began to come from my eyes. "Oh Jesus."

She began to laugh, too, thank God. We laughed and laughed. We sobbed. She slapped the top of the desk. We'd been attacked by video vampires. I called Peach into the office, and we told her, and Peach guffawed. I felt better than I had in ages. Laughter is the most profound form of freedom. In their own way, the lucky gabardines had come through. But by the time Julia left the office, Hungarian darkness had returned to her eyes, and I didn't want to know why.

BO OK

The Weather
Under Ground

Twenty-one

Julia Barnes stumbled out of one brightly lit room into the next, out of one conversation with a correspondent into another conversation with a correspondent, thinking as she did that her producer would be back in the editing bay, waiting for her, and wouldn't be interested in the least in the Harker situation, except maybe as gossip, as vital information related to the misfortunes of another team. That would buy some grace, but not much. It didn't help that she had never worked with this particular producer before and had heard terrible rumors about temperament and work habits. But she couldn't walk away from a correspondent. If the man wanted to talk, she would have to talk.

Austen's colleague of decades, Ed Prince, winked her into the room. He gestured for her to shut the door. She reluctantly did so.

Prince shook his head, as if their conversation had already begun. She shook her head, too, thinking it would be the best way to maintain a semblance of collusion without saying anything to compromise herself. He started to laugh, and she laughed, too. His laughter faded, and he beckoned her to sit.

"Look at you," he said.

She shook her head and tried another laugh, but didn't convince him anymore.

"What's so funny, my dear?"

"Oh, the craziness of the situation, I guess."

"What situation?"

146 • JOHN MARKS

His voice accented its meaner tones. She wouldn't play. "Come on, Ed."

"Don't *come on* me. No one around here tells me a goddamn thing. I'm like the crazy uncle."

You are crazier than the uncle, she said in her head.

"I got a producer in my room, Ed. It's a crash."

"Liar."

Prince and Trotta were such different men. A few moments ago, she had been trying to get the latter to see a danger that she herself could hardly name, and he had treated her with indifferent condescension. Unlike most other people on the show, Trotta never gave off an air of neediness, or if he did, it lay veiled beneath layers of withering ambivalence. Prince, on the other hand, despite his national fame, had never found the proper soil for the sense of superiority required to cultivate genuine condescension. He was like one of those old MGM movie stars who never shied away from a photo op, who wanted their love affairs in the public eye, who craved exposure and felt no shame about it. Gripped by this desire, Prince felt underappreciated, underinformed, undernourished and forever tried to compensate, ingratiating himself even with those who couldn't possibly matter. Julia loved that about him, but felt pity, too. How could someone come so far and still want so much more love? Unlike Trotta, who affected a rakish dapperness of yesteryear, unafraid to wear an ascot or put a handkerchief in his coat pocket, Prince launched his assault on fame in the dark blue business suits of Wall Street investment bankers. He didn't smoke and didn't drink and ate without any need for flavor or inspiration. He made his own phone calls on stories and referred to himself in those calls as "Ed Prince, a reporter for *The Hour*." His tan came from months in tennis whites on Cape Cod, where he presided during the hiatus over an interviewless existence that he could barely endure. And all of this effort seemed designed to create an impression of solidity, when, in fact, one always sensed the quicksand with Prince. He might sink at any moment, and who would grab his hand?

She wouldn't. "Why are you asking me, Ed?"

"Because I know you'll tell me."

"Evangeline Harker is missing."

"What else? What were you in there talking to that fey old fart about?"

Trotta was younger than Prince by at least a decade.

"That's between me and him."

"The hell."

She decided to put her neck under the axe. The blade would find her anyway. She would cooperate and get it over with.

"I'm concerned about the fact that tapes from Romania are being digitized when we don't know anything about them. There's not a budget number. There's not a story. And yet an editor has taken it upon himself to put this material into a system that we all share."

Prince moved a step ahead.

"And you think these tapes have something to do with the Harker girl."

Julia nodded. "I do, but I have no proof."

Prince nodded back. He grimaced as if she had just pitched him a really stupid story idea. He picked up his phone and squinted at her. "Why the fuck did I bother?"

She marched out of the room. These old bastards thought they owned her world. They didn't. None of them did. She had a life outside the editing bay. It might be beleaguered at the moment, but it was a life, at least.

She stopped a moment to absorb a sudden burst of beauty. Sunlight had broken through a raft of clouds over the eastern reaches of the Hudson, and that light flooded the offices of the twentieth floor, pouring through the glass walls of the correspondents' gorgeous spaces, sweeping through hanging plants, Venetian blinds, piles of paper and books, and falling like a benediction on the rows of assistants, who so seldom caught such a blaze of glory. Austen's assistant, Peach Carnahan, swam in silver fire. When Julia was a Catholic schoolgirl, she had believed that such natural fireworks revealed the hand of God. Now she knew their true import. They served to underscore the desperate facts of human existence. People who had offices with windows could enjoy sunlight. And those without windows? They could kiss the dappled asses of the demigods.

As soon as she stepped out of Correspondents' Row, out of the light and into the narrow passage leading to the main corridor, her vague uneasiness renewed. The light around her turned from dim white to dark blue. On her left, the cantina glowed and hummed, the happiest place on the floor. She moved away from its solace, down through the darkness, away from Correspondents' Row, and began to formulate a plan. That Romanian tape was contaminated, somehow. Visually, the images reminded her of e-mails containing computer viruses. She could spot those a mile away, the fake appeal to some prurient or financial interest in the subject line, begging to be opened, to spread havoc in the system. She smelled it. The tapes must not be allowed into the computer system. They must not be digitized. She would put a stop to it, and she wouldn't do it by going to network management, where she certainly had friends. She would do it the old-fashioned way, the Weather Underground way, by deceit, sabotage and, if need be, force.

Twenty-two

As Julia entered the editing bay, she paused to look back over her shoulder toward the bathrooms and the elevators, toward the relative cheer of the security desk. She had passed Menard Griffiths, the security guard, and had the usual moment of pleasant chitchat and uplift, as if speaking to a being from another, kinder world. Menard was a warm and decent man, and he always complimented her on a smile that no longer came easily to her face. But he was far away, back there, in the middle of the corridor, beyond the bathrooms and elevators, and she was down here, on the threshold of the windowless and well-soundproofed editing bay. She had been called paranoid all her life. She didn't mind. She stuck her head forward and sniffed. I'm like an animal, she thought, smelling the air. In that scent of long days and interminable nights, of food and stale perfume and cold sweat, she caught something else. The atmosphere back here has changed, she thought. It's all changed, the whole floor. Ian's ghost haunts us, she thought. Or someone else has died. Maybe Lockyear, after hearing he was sacked. Someone reported him dashing out the glass doors of the building, tears streaming from his eyes, dirty words popping off his lips.

She headed for her office where her new producer would be wondering where the hell she was. Trotta's pragmatism had made her impatient with herself. She was a mother with teenage boys. She owned a large apartment in Manhattan and fought traffic every day in a car that belonged in a landfill. She had survived in this job for eighteen years and had no business losing her shit. Let the Lockyears do that. She was tougher, meaner, wiser.

Julia threw open the door to her office, ready with an apology for her producer. A pale man in a blue uniform leapt at her: a corpse-pale Union soldier, caped and holstered, with long blond hair flying in strands beneath a tilted cap. It was like a public broadcasting documentary come to life. Julia thought she heard spectral banjos. She let out a shriek, unable to move from the spot, her heart pounding as the specter wafted forward, within touching distance. The hands rose to her throat. Her shriek acted as an alarm. People poured out of the adjacent editing rooms. Someone switched on the desk lamp beside the door, and Julia saw the truth. The visitor had taken off her cap, revealing shoulder-length chestnut hair and mauvais pearl earrings. The ghost was her new producer.

Twenty-three

A few editors gawked for a moment at the door to the room, watching Julia giggle her way down from a fright. Finally, the producer chased them away. She shut the door and sat beside Julia, introducing herself as Sally Benchborn, a member of Sam Dambles's team.

"Hey, hi Sally," Julia stammered. "Don't let my behavior fool you. I– I'm a fan of your work."

"I guess I should explain." Sally looked even more uncomfortable than Julia felt. "I have a sort of weekend hobby. Civil War reenactment. This last weekend, I was out with my unit, the 27th Massachusetts Irregulars. We took Fort McAllister, and I didn't have time to change. Am I really so scary?"

Julia didn't think so. Her shriek had come from a deeper place. The fear had been growing ever since those tapes arrived from Romania. It had become a physical ailment. This woman had merely triggered it, and Julia felt bad for making such a big deal about the costume, particularly in front of the other editors, who would be merciless about it behind her back.

Julia tried to grin. "Great first impressions, huh?"

Sally dropped the hat onto the top of a file cabinet, next to a clump of South Beach walnuts in a plastic sandwich bag. "I've had some interesting reactions to this uniform, but that's my first total freakout."

"Nah. Not even close. A freakout involves floor time, fetal positions,

paramedics. Trust me. All I saw was this uniform—this old uniform—
and I just—"

"It's actually very authentic—"

"You don't have to convince me."

"You pay for your own kit. I'm not embarrassed to say I paid a sutler seven hundred dollars for this ensemble."

Julia let out a nervous giggle. "Ensemble. I like that. Manolo Blah-
niks, Hermès scarf, Gettysburg. Nice ensemble."

Sally didn't laugh. "It was Fort McAllister, Georgia. A long way from
Gettysburg."

Julia thought Sally might be scared, too. At the least, she was unnerved. Maybe she had sensed the odd currents in the air, the bad vibes.

"What's a sutler?" Julia asked, regaining her composure.

Sally shook her hair, unbuttoned the cape from her collar. "A mail-
order merchant who specializes in this Civil War stuff."

"Does everyone but me know about this?"

"Now they do."

Julia moved from the couch to her chair and checked for Post-it
notes. She swiveled in the chair and grabbed for the bag of walnuts.

"Want one?"

Sally declined. As if preempting an expected line of questioning, she
told Julia that she had always been fascinated by Civil War reenactment
and had once considered making a documentary on the subject of a
particular unit. The documentary folded for lack of financial backing,
but the practice had got into Sally's blood, and now she did it for fun.
Her unit gathered people, mostly men, from around the Northeast,
and everyone had a copy of a schedule and a gun, a bayonet-equipped
Enfield.

"You have it here?" Julia asked.

Sally pursed her lips with a reenactment snob's disapproval. "In the
car. The engagement ended late last night, so I had to stay in a hotel in
Atlanta and fly in this morning. I haven't even seen my kids."

"Can you show it to me sometime?"

"What?"

"The bayonet."

"Sure. Can we talk about the piece now?"

They chatted for a bit about the story, a profile of an English movie star whose movies Julia didn't like. "How the hell did you get that approved?"

Sally raised her eyebrows. "If that's your attitude, I can see we're going to have a great time together."

"No, no, I mean, he's not exactly a household name. I'm just amazed that Bob would let you do it."

"He's probably going to be up for an Academy Award. That's why. Anyway, if you've got reservations, better to hear them now."

Julia felt herself warming to the woman. Sally Benchborn had a straightforward manner. She seemed innocently, honestly determined to make a masterpiece out of her second-rank celebrity, and Julia believed, after the conversation, that if anyone could, it was Sally. They discussed logistics. The main interview was done; film clips were coming in. There would be another interview and a lot of b-roll in the English town of Whitby, where the actor had a second home. Julia would have a fair amount of tape by the end of the week, and she should overtime the digitizing, if need be. Then a silence fell, and Sally Benchborn peered at Julia in the dimness. Cable news played without sound on the television screen in a corner of the room.

"Do you know why I got off the couch when you opened the door?" Sally asked her.

Julia had a walnut at her lips. She ate it.

"I got up because when you opened the door, you looked sick. I thought you were going to faint."

Julia swallowed the walnut. Sally squinted and waited.

"Oh God," Julia said.

She checked the intercom beside the door, making sure that it was turned off and no one could eavesdrop. Her producer crossed a leg, looking bemused. Suddenly, being a Civil War reenactment buff didn't seem so eccentric. Sally radiated trust in her own choices. She conveyed the sense that nothing could be more obvious than her decision to wear this uniform; no pleasure could be more basic than the pursuit of a hobby that combined history, fashion and marksmanship, the occasional weekend theater of bloody combat.

Julia liked that confidence. She trusted it. She told Sally about everything: the disappearance of Evangeline Harker, the arrival of the tapes from Romania, Remschneider digitizing, Trotta's indifference.

Sally's face turned red as she listened. "Where's Remschneider?"

"Why?"

"I'll have a word with him. He's a good egg, but he sometimes needs a talking-to."

Julia put up a hand. She thought she heard a noise outside the door. Sally didn't pay any attention.

"I worked with Fish on my last story. He's quick and smart but he can be juvenile. Actually, I think the exact word for Fish is sophomoric. But he'll listen to me."

Recently, when Julia asked Remschneider how it had been to work with Sally Benchborn, he'd replied, "Freakshow," but that didn't mean anything. Editors and producers operated love-hate; they bit each other's backs with a near-biological urge. Sally called him Fish— because, she explained, he fished shamelessly for compliments. He called her a freakshow. It was a necessity of the profession. Maybe she could talk some sense into Remschneider.

Sally buttoned the top of her muslin shirt, threw on what she called her federal fatigue blouse, a coat that Julia had mistaken for the cape, and put the dark blue Billy Yank cap back on. She followed Julia out the door and down the back corridor of the twentieth floor toward Remschneider, who had a slightly bigger and better room in the second to last corridor. His door was closed, and they could hear nothing within.

"Maybe they went to lunch," suggested Sally.

"Light's on."

"So it is." The producer knocked three times on the door. "Fish!"

Julia put her ear to the door. "I could swear I hear whispering in there."

Sally's cheeks burned a bright red. "Don't fuck with me, Remschneider!"

Julia twisted the knob. "It's not locked, Sally."

Sally seemed about to hurl a tart comment at Julia, but turned the knob instead and stepped dramatically into the room, the federal fatigue blouse unfurling behind her. Julia followed. For a long time, neither of the women spoke. Three men sat in chairs across from three screens: two video monitors and a twenty-three-inch television set. Each man wore a headset, and each headset was plugged into a monitor. Each of the monitors displayed the same image, a wooden chair in an empty room. What the men heard through the headsets was inaudible to the naked ear, but Julia thought later that she had caught the sound of whispers, the last vestiges of sentences leaking into the dry oxygen of the room. What shocked her were the tears. Three men, Remschneider and two others, all in their late thirties to mid forties, all family men, pranksters, music lovers, total pros when it came to cutting together pieces, sat with eyes bloodred, tears streaming down their faces, making crevices in the skin, as if the tears carried acid down the slopes of their cheeks. Their mouths gaped. Their hands clutched their headsets. Like someone stuck knives in their brains, Julia thought.

BO**5**OK

Evangeline from the Maritime

Twenty-four

The birds shout like sailors through the night. I wake every so often and hear them in fights. I get up from my bed, light the candle and try to write down these notes, just as Sister Agathe said I should. She said it's my duty.

When I'm awake, I'm frightened, and the racket of the birds makes the fear easier to bear. It gives me a little peace. I don't know why. I never much cared for birds or the people who own them. They're ridiculous, chattery creatures. But I'm sure these ones are doing me good. I never actually lay eyes on the animals. Every now and then, of course, I have a suspicion I'm hearing things. The burden in my mind has disguised itself with wings and screeches.

It's an odd fact. I've never been to this valley before in my life, but I seem to have a certain kind of knowledge about the whole area. If the sisters here in the cloister could speak my language, they'd be alarmed and amazed at the information I possess. I know, for instance, that there are three mass graves in the valley on the other side of the ridge, and a large one here, just outside the walls of the monastery. I have never laid eyes on the other valley, but I know that one of the graves lies behind an abandoned barracks painted a faded ocher yellow and contains the bodies of twenty-three people, twelve men, eight women and three children, all Jews from a place called Suceava. Maybe that's the name of this place where I am. Another grave lies deep in the woods, where no one goes except hunters, and inside, tangled together like blackberry bushes, are the bodies of three Roma women, each of them raped, mutilated and shot in the back of the head. They are an old woman, her daughter, and the daughter's niece. They died fairly recently, in the last few decades. And then there is the last of the three graves, in the valley adjacent, the oldest, the deep-lying bones of nineteen beheaded Turkish knights. They lie beneath a pond that has only existed for two and a half centuries. The sisters don't even know, I'm sure, and would consider my knowledge the work of demons, but this knowledge occurs to me in the most natural way. Just as I understand that the gathering of clouds holds snow, I know that the curve of the land holds the shards of the massacred.

One bird makes a different noise than the others and seems to call from farther away. It's a softer animal, uninvolved in the other birds' quarrel, and seems to have a distinct mission. It calls me out into the night, asks me to cross back over the mountains and return to the place where I received my burden. One of the sisters told me not to listen to anything that speaks my name. She says I'm to stay in the square within the walls until my burden is lifted. The nightly caller isn't an evil thing, I'm sure. Evangeline, it sings, reminding me of the old song for which my parents named me. I would like to follow. I would like to pursue the trail of knowledge that glows before my eyes. I would like to run along the ground, to find other forgotten souls in this earth, the countless, scattered jewels.

During the day, my mind sits with the stillness of a frog on a lily pad and rests. I have a sunny spot in the middle of the frozen monastery, and the sisters allow me to sit there in bundles of wolfskin blankets while they do their work. I sit and look at the sky. The days pass in iciness, but at night, it gets very warm in my room. One of the sisters comes to tend a fire in a stone hearth. She gives me tea and dark bread. No one speaks good English, but I understand from their gestures that I'm an object of pity, concern and moral shock. I look in a mirror, and I know why. My eyes alone terrify me. I've never seen that woman in my life.

It will be February soon, by the calendar. And then dreadful March, and Easter will come, with its bloody crucifixion. Weeks ago, a person showed up, and I treated him badly. I ordered him away. There were police here, too, and I told them to keep the stranger off the grounds. But he comes back, and they let him. It is my impression that he thinks I might be someone. I had no right to be so unkind, but he told me that he'd be waiting outside the walls for the moment when I would be ready to tell him my name and where I come from, where my home is. But what in the world does that mean?

Home is one of those words that my burden has turned into a riddle, even though in my memory, or the place where a memory should be, I detect an echo of calm and rest and think that must be what the word connotes. I informed my visitor I'm perfectly well, and he started to take notes, which made me angry. I told him I love the feel of snow on my tongue. I love the smell of wood burned at dawn. I love the sound of booted feet cracking through ice, the depth of shadows untouched by electric light. I love the feel of the skin of my knee beneath my hand, the taste of corn porridge at dinner, the promise of a deep sleep that never quite comes. I'm filled with love, but not for people or places or objects. My love overwhelms me. It comes in the form of a long memory of the species, and it has changed me. I love those things that the murdered, insulted, degraded dead love.

My visitor couldn't understand. "You're American, I think. Or Canadian, perhaps? You're lost. You're wandering in your mind, and you need to be home, where your own people can give you care. Please help me, and I will help you." He looks around my little cell with horrified eyes. He is from some government, and we hate governments. He wants to use this unfortunate opportunity to take everything away from me. I wonder what he would say if he saw the sisters give me my evening bath. Sister Agathe comes with another, and they bring a metal pail filled with warm water. I look straight up at the ceiling. I don't want to see my body anymore. But the sisters remove my clothes, and as they apply cloth and sponge, they weep at the sight. I don't want to know what they see, but I do wonder what my father would say, what my mother would do, if they saw. And my lover? Would he still want me home? I look at the ceiling, and I nurture a secret that no living soul knows about me. I long for the taste of human blood.

My visitor is a complete stranger. He rents rooms in a farmhouse nearby. I can see the place from my window at night. There are chickens and a rooster and a dog that never barks. In the gray hours before dawn, the rooster chases off the shouting birds. My visitor comes often, trying to give me an identity. Sometimes he just sits and stares. Other times, he yells at me. He threatens to have me forcibly removed from this place.

I remember one conversation in particular. "You've got one more week," he said. "And then I will do whatever is required by law. I will have you placed in a Romanian institution where our doctors will treat you. I'm going to ask you again. Are you an American? Are you a journalist?"

"I'm afraid for you," I said.

"Don't talk that way."

"What way?"

"Like you know me."

"But I do."

"I'm merely a civil servant, and I do what I have to."

"You'll be gone within the year."

His face turned dark red, and he lost his temper. "I can have you locked away, if I like, and no one will ever learn your name."

"In memory, you will be lost."

He stood up, putting on his coat. "I know who you are," he said, "but I can't prove it, and if I can't prove it, I keep my mouth shut, or I will be held accountable. I won't make a fuss. The local authorities will simply cart you away. Think about it. The women here want you out." He left.

I want to please him. I want everyone to be as happy as I am. I want everyone to feel the love in my heart for existence. My visitor gets an expression on his face when I talk in this way, and I can't bear it. His lips part, and his face becomes moist, and I see how old he's become. When it comes to death, he won't be different than anyone else. He will seep like oil into the ground.

I wake to the sound of the birds and peer out my window across a thawing field to the farmhouse in which my visitor sleeps. In this valley, right there in the depression between me and the farmhouse, there is another grave, new to my mind, lying deep, filled to the brim with prisoners of some great work from an age long past. They are Dacians, executed by Romans, and they whisper to each other, "When do we go home?"

Twenty-five

Dreams about the girl with the golden hair began three nights ago. I've seen her before, no doubt about it. I know her name, but can't get it across my lips. She comes to my door, knocks softly and says let me in. I do, and she kneels at my feet and kisses them. Someone has cut her throat, so this action isn't easy. I ask her if she's one of the people from the grave behind the yellow barracks, and she lifts her head, eyes welling, and asks me if I'm trying to play a joke on her. She asks me to look inside the box of my belongings beneath the bed, but I refuse. I don't want to see.

In the mornings, I tell Sister Agathe about the dreams. She doesn't understand, but she points at my pencil and paper. She wants me to write it down. She insists. So I do.

One night, while I was still awake, that same soft knock from the dream came on my door. The last embers of the fire collapsed into themselves, dark red caverns of flame. I couldn't move. No one usually visited me after the last stoking of the fire, and Sister Agathe had already done that. I should be left alone till dawn.

I wrapped myself in the skins and got out of bed. The flagstones of the floor, so cold, stung my toes. The latch on the door seemed to bite at my fingers, but I slapped it away. When I cracked the door, I saw a pale face that I recognized, but it wasn't the face I expected. It was Sister Agathe. She wanted to learn English from me and had hinted at the possibility that she had another life in mind for herself. We often gestured back and forth while she waited for my fire to rekindle. She longed to travel, I think.

Now she looked at me with terror. She pointed back past the chapel toward the front gate of the complex. She didn't have to say a word. I knew. There was someone waiting for me at the entrance.

"My visitor?" I asked.

She shook her head. She stared at me for a long time, waiting to see if I could explain what she had already seen.

"I'll put on my shoes, Agathe. I can manage. You go back to bed."

"Nee," she replied.

I took her by an arm. "You get to your room and lock your door, Agathe. Yes?"

She agreed, with grateful eyes. I slipped into a pair of thick wool socks and winter boots and went out into the night. Ice-thickened wind hit me. Above the black rim of walls, the stars burned in white, in yellow and red. There were so many I couldn't pick out the few I knew. Everything flared with raw brightness. I could see the band of the Milky Way.

I peered toward the row of cells where Agathe had gone and hoped she had taken my advice to lock her door. I had no real knowledge of my situation, how it had come, who had been its engineer, but it was clear in every way that a terrible thing had occurred, that the sisters suspected my involvement in profound horror, that, despite their kindness, they prayed for my departure. They had no idea where I'd come from. I had no memory of how I came there.

I crossed the snow between my room and the chapel. Not once had I been inside this building. The exterior walls had been painted with hundreds of images of holy events, the stories of saints, the lives of apostles, the rise and fall of the kings of Byzantium, the fate of humanity in the coming ages in heaven and hell. During the day, I read the outer walls, as if they made pages in a book.

My heart beat fast. I leaned against the back wall of the chapel. As soon as I rounded the corner, I would be visible from the gate, and so would my visitor. I thought about sending up my own prayer. These women spent their days in a sustained conversation with God. Surely a prayer would help me to face whatever came. A memory tugged at my brain—this moment reminded me of another one, but it wouldn't rise to the surface.

I rounded the corner of the chapel and marched forward, staring at the snow on the ground. I took solace in the crunch of ice beneath my heels. The sound made me formidable; like a colossus, in the silence, I smashed glaciers. I didn't lift my eyes until I came close to the gate, a stone arch hewn centuries before. The passage had sunk into the ground over the years and made a kind of tunnel to the outside world. After dark, the sisters lowered an iron grate across the exterior entrance. I lowered my head and peered into the well of night gathered between the walls.

"Yes?" I called out. No one answered.

I reproached myself for releasing Sister Agathe. She could have been a help and shown me to the visitor. She could have lit one of the lanterns clanking in the wind against the inner walls of the tunnel.

The wind gusted out of the hills and fought me as I pushed toward the gated tunnel entrance. I reached the metal grate, peered through the crossbars into the gloom between the cloister walls and the woods. My visitor had gone. No one stood there, but it was a beautiful night. Snow muffled the ground. The first flecks of another storm twirled out of the sky, and when I glanced up, the stars appeared to be bursting and plummeting down. Up the hill from the cloister, I made out a figure moving out of the woods through the snow to the walls. At first I considered it an optical illusion created by the movement of snowflakes against the night, but the thing gained in size and shape until it became substantial. The face and body were hidden beneath a cowl made of skins like mine. I had a sudden, lurching premonition. The figure was dressed as me, but it wasn't me. She pulled back the rim of her hood. I pulled back the rim of mine. Snowflakes touched her eyelids and made them open. The eyes were white and shiny as the snow. Blond hair fell into the starlight, tied at the back by a dirty yellow scrunchy.

"Clemmie," I said.

Back in my room, scrawling on these papers for Sister Agathe, I know what happened to me. I know how I came here. And it is bitter.

Twenty-six

I ran for a long time in the forest beneath Torgu's hotel. The trunks of pine trees rose up to stop me. It was cold, and I had no clothes, and I wanted to stop and wrap myself in the curtain I clutched in one hand, but I didn't dare until the woods lay far behind. I held Torgu's knife in my other hand. The struggle had deranged me. It had taken hours to climb down out of the hotel, using the stopped paternoster. My sweats got caught in one particularly tight spot and had to be abandoned, leaving me bare except for my bra by the time I reached ground floor. Torgu, the coward, did not show his face again. I was running down the corridor to the lobby, past the room containing the man's dreadful artifacts, the broken pieces of shattered places, the names of places still whispering in my ears. I hurtled through the lobby, grabbing a curtain on my way out of that terrible place—the word *lobby* seems ludicrous in retrospect. On my way out, I saw for the first time that the hotel was nothing but a deserted wreck. No guest had checked in for years. I thought with pity of Andras, the murdered Norwegian. I hoped he didn't have children. If he did, I prayed they would never know what happened to their father. The curtain sheared away with a single tug. The curtain rod broke and fell. I clasped the material against my nakedness. A shadow moved across the carpet, and I wheeled around. It had been a bird against the sky, its reflection a flicker on the room. I looked around the lobby in the fading sunlight. Pine needles had blown through the front doors and across the soiled carpet to the front desk.

On the counter, I spied my purse. I grabbed it and found the bag of peanuts, the crust of bread and my notes. The passport and cell phone were gone. I hung the strap of the purse over my shoulder. I wadded the curtain. I dashed through the front doors. Broken glass littered the steps and I cut my foot, but that didn't stop me. Nothing but death could.

I sailed out of the long portico leading away from the steps and reached the first trees. I had tried this once before, in the dark, but this time, the light was with me, and I could see the way out. I could see sky through the high branches and a distant slope of green land, falling away. Better than that, through the trees, I saw the car, the oily Porsche, his only means of transportation. I ran to it in a wild flailing of hope, throwing aside the curtain. I jerked at the handle of the door, but it was locked. I went into a rage, smashing my fist against the windshield. I attempted to break inside. I found a branch and brought it down upon the glass. The blood leaking from my cut heel mingled with pine needles and sand, which stopped the bleeding. Tears of fury rolled down my face. But I came to my senses fast, forcing myself to recall the ride from Brasov up to the hotel. Torgu had driven me through that resort where he said the dictator had lived. And after that, I recalled, there had been a meadow with a small building, a kind of chapel. I could reach the chapel by sundown. I could run with everything in my being and get to that place and barricade myself inside. I looked up through the branches. Minutes before, the sun had seemed higher, but it was lowering fast, and I could hear a wind rising, and in the wind were those words, the same words that echoed in my own brain. I dropped the branch. With Torgu's knife, I slashed at the tires of the Porsche. It was hard work, but done fast.

I dashed away again, knife in one hand, curtain in the other, the purse swinging from my shoulder. My foot ached, but I thought of the fate of the Norwegian. I could no longer bear to think of his name. The name would conjure the face, and the face would paralyze me. It was cold in those mountains, and the sharp sting of air gave me an extra burst of energy. My breath came in smoke bursts. But as long as I ran, I stayed warm.

At last, when I had almost given up hope of escaping the forest, the trees thinned, and the grass grew thickly, and I knew I'd reached one end of the meadow containing the chapel. I assumed it was a chapel. Far below and to the right, partially obscured by a swell in the land, I could see the edge of a small white building. I wanted to believe it would be a sanctuary from evil, as in the movies, but my own recent experience had educated me. Torgu wasn't scared of holy places or things. He gathered burnt icons for his collection of bizarre artifacts. He cast a reflection in the mirror. He had lovingly fondled the cross around my neck. What I needed was a strip joint or a brothel. A gush of shame and rage biled up in my throat. I could still hear the voice. Even then, at dusk, on the brink of the meadow, overshadowed by the brows of pine dark cliffs, I felt that I was drowning in a sea of his filthy words.

Gazing across the grass, I recognized a new danger. In the woods, I had been able to hide. Out in the open, an all-but-buck-naked woman would be hard to miss. How many other victims had escaped and come this far? The thought of more workaday rapists, sadists and casual murderers crossed my mind, but I had the knife. I resolved at least to clothe myself. These monsters could take my life, but they would no longer rob me of dignity. Countless women, Christians, Muslims, Jews, Buddhists, had been butchered wearing only their skin. I would not be one of them. I crouched in the grass, using the knife to cut the threadbare red curtain cloth into two long strips. I lowered one strip to my waist and tied it like a skirt at my right hip. I reached the other strip behind my back and stretched it against my shoulder blades, tying it with a double knot in front, hiding the black bra, which hadn't been constructed for the rigors of the Romanian outdoors. I felt better.

I skirted the edge of the meadow, remaining in the shadow of the trees for as long as I could. Finally, there was no more cover. I took a deep breath, put the knife in my purse, curled my forearm up to my shoulder and gripped the strap. I sprinted out across the grass. I had never been so cold. The sun set beyond the western lip of the valley, but its light lingered for a time, a golden flood on the grass. At first, I made for the small white building, but as I ran, I began to have second thoughts. My memory began to fail me. On the ride up, in the dark, I'd received a vague impression. The building had been square, painted white, with a wooden door. Underneath the door shone a light. It could have been anything, a farmhouse or, God forbid, a taverna. Even in my desperate state, it seemed a bad idea to stroll into a rural bar after dark wearing only cheap communist hotel curtains. Below me, I saw an undulation of darkening grass. The valley dipped into a deep shadow, the vicinity of the road, I reckoned. The chapel or whatever it was lay next to the road. Torgu and the Greek brothers would be looking for me along that road. I stopped, catching my breath.

As an associate producer for *The Hour,* you were never allowed to fuck up. If you fucked up, you were out. Your contract offered no protection. In this life, we have a similar contract, though most of us don't know it. At that moment, I read the fine print, and I told myself that the building on the road would be a fuck-up of gigantic proportions and would have to be forsaken. I would have to stay clear of the entire valley along the road. I wiped the tears of disappointment from my eyes. I cinched up the itching, moldy curtain shred, gripped the purse strap and loped westward into the dusk.

I came to the ridgeline and saw below me a vista from a fantastic dream, valleys upon valleys below, land like waterfalls, pink explosions of cloudburst behind mountain jags. The time passed, the stars came out, and I moved for a while as if my muscles were water and air. I traveled in a general northerly direction, but soon lost track. I didn't feel the pain of the effort until it had been dark a couple of hours, and I tripped over a rock and tumbled down the side of a hollow. I wanted to stay there, but I got up again and continued down into the valley, staggering like a blind woman. My foot burned. I'd lost blood from the cut. My eyes shut without my help. They wanted no part of sight. I fell at last in a soft place and crawled like a mole through a tunnel of grass, pure instinct, aiming for something that resembled a bed, found a close approximation and curled up in a ball. Sleep wrapped me in a blanket.

When I woke, some time later, the tintinnabulation of syllables had returned, the awful terrible syllables from those stained lips, *Ashdod, Moab, Treblinka, Gomorrah,* and my eyes flew open. I wasn't alone. I peered through a twist of creepers and saw that I had made exactly the mistake I had wanted to avoid. I had come to the edge of the road, and there was a car, which seemed familiar, but it wasn't Torgu; it wasn't the Porsche. It was a BMW. I could see the symbol on the hood. I had to restrain myself from leaping out of the grass. The automobile had been parked in the middle of the lane; its lights had been left on, its engine left running. I focused on a window, straining to catch sight of an occupant.

Paying attention to every sound, the creak of autumn bugs, the shriek of night birds, the shifting of wild animals in brush, I adjusted my position in the tall grass. My legs began to itch, but I didn't scratch. I reached into my purse and gripped the knife handle and crawled a few inches forward and got a better look. Beyond the car sat the building from my memory, the chapel, and I had an instant of disorientation. I'd recalled the chapel, or whatever it was, as situated on the right-hand side of the road. It shouldn't be where it was. It couldn't be. This was another building altogether, more like an isolated country mausoleum than a chapel. It hardly mattered. I would simply jump in the car, which some happy accident had left on my back doorstep.

I drew the knife from my side and made ready to use it. My foot throbbed with pain, but I willed the pain down. My legs thrust me up out of the grass. I was a Texan. I had survived on the twentieth floor of the nastiest news organization in the history of the broadcast medium. I'd fended off the advances of leprous old men and yelled back at them when they cried for my attentions as if for their milk bottle. I'd been undermined in my intelligence, judgment, looks and taste, treated to sermons about morality, efficiency and trustworthiness by hothouse flowers who lived like pashas on the backs of slaves, and the experience had made me a little intolerant of human indecency, especially of the male variety. Torgu was the final straw, a distillation of every humiliation I'd suffered in the last seven years. I'd had it with them all, these old men and their set ways. I gritted my teeth. I leaped out of the high grass. A figure dashed in front of me, and I grabbed. I raised the knife and shoved the body into the car's headlight beams. It was a woman. She stared at me with terrified eyes. I held the knife to Clementine Spence.

Twenty-seven

In my memory of that moment, several things happened at once. I realized that the familiar BMW was my rental, which raised questions that I had no time to ask. Clemmie gasped as if she'd seen the dead. I didn't know how to explain. What could I have said? I ran past her to the car, dented and mud-spattered from God knows what kind of activity. She, or someone else, had parked the car in the middle of the road, but the engine was running, and the other passenger seemed to be a man, walking a hundred yards from me down the lane of headlight beams toward an object that I couldn't see. I watched him recede into the point where the beams met. I put my hand on the passenger-side door and felt the warm metal. I grabbed the handle and opened.

Clemmie called out a name, "Todd?!" He didn't respond. She cried, "Get back here!"

I got into the car and locked it and saw her turn to look back at me. Her eyes had taken in my near nakedness. She saw her crucifix still hanging from my neck, the long ugly knife in my hand. I had no time for her shock. I still had my own.

I rolled down the window. "We have to get out of here," I said. "Now. Please."

I squinted at the BMW highbeams, followed their trajectory into the shadows, where her companion, Todd, had vanished. She stepped closer to me, peering. "What in the name of God?"

"God?" That one word came in a cold fury. I was hungry, exhausted and in terrible pain. My foot had started bleeding again. The alcohol, the attack, the flight through the countryside, it had all been too much. She saw. She let it go, nodding. She called out that name again, "Todd!" but he didn't come. I checked the ignition and found the keys. I was in no condition to drive, but I would, if she didn't. Clemmie seemed to understand. She came around to the driver's side and got in the car. She shifted gears, gunning the engine, rolling down her window, calling again the name.

"He's a dead man," I said.

"We saw something lying in the road," Clemmie said. "But when we got out of the car, it wasn't there anymore."

"Ambush."

She gave me a look of distrust, as if I was more to be feared than anything outside. "Evangeline?"

"I said your friend's already dead. Get us out of here."

To the left, a few feet back from the road, sat the mausoleum, or whatever it was. Pine woods began a few yards behind the building.

"He's out there," I said. "I can feel him."

"Who? Your guy? The guy from the hotel? Did he do this to you?"

I recalled then that they had met, if that was the word. They had seemed to know each other. She waited for an answer, but I couldn't. I was going to be sick. "Clemmie," I said, my fist tightening around the handle of the knife.

She said, "If that's who you mean, he's not out there. He's gone. I saw him tonight at the hotel in Brasov. A driver took him south toward Bucharest. That's why I'm here."

I turned to her in shock, feeling the import of those words. "Bucharest?" He was going to the international airport.

Before she could answer, I saw shapes flicker out of the pines. One of those terrible arms reached through the window, snatching Clemmie by the hair. "Jesus!" she shrieked.

"Vourkulakis!" I cried out, stabbing at the arm.

Clemmie put the car into gear and shot forward. The hand vanished. We drove fifty yards and almost ran into a man who must have been Todd, who walked into our lights, his hands to his throat, black matter running down the front of his red flannel shirt. He barely seemed to see us. Clemmie slammed on the brakes.

"Oh God," I heard her whisper. "Oh no." She reached a hand for mine.

"It's too late for him," I said. "You have to go now, or we're going to be next."

Clemmie's mouth had fixed like a black hole in her face; after a second, the guttural noise of anguish erupted from her throat. But I'd finished with that. Every muscle in my body went sharp with the will to live. I reached across her body and rolled up the window. Todd's eyes glistened wide in a last surprise, his neck agape; a human sacrifice is never one of those things people aspire to become. Todd was a vehicle for communication with the dead. Torgu's words flashed out of my memory, except he was gone, Clemmie said, so Todd was merely a casualty. The Greek brothers stepped into the light around him. This time, there were three of them. Their dark eyes and long black hair seemed to move in a wind. Their arms gathered around this man as they had gathered around the Norwegian. Clemmie whimpered. A line of blood fell from his lips. One brother pulled him back into the night. The other two gestured to me to get out of the car. I brandished the knife, and they saw, and they smiled. They knew its use. They pulled their own knives, illumined by the car lights. Clemmie came to a decision. She revved the engine. She shifted to neutral, stamped down on the accelerator. The rubber burned in my nose. She was going to run them down. I dug my fingernails into her arm.

"Won't work!"

She screamed, "Get your hands off me!"

The Vourkulakis brothers attacked the car. One landed on the hood. Another banged the handle of the knife against my window, cracking it. Clemmie bore down on a figure of a man, crouching over a darker figure on the ground. Todd.

"In your name," she murmured, "I pray forgiveness," shifting gears again, catching the standing figure midriff, knocking him into darkness. The one on the hood spun away. We heard the sick thump of inanimate weight beneath the tires, the final desecration of her friend. She braked hard, the car brodied, and she reversed hard. She wasn't going to stop.

Another of the Vourkulakis came at our windows, his lips contorted in rage. In our red rearview lights, I saw a third. Three, I thought, and no more. Clemmie smacked the rear fender into the one behind us, and I heard an audible grunt. She threw the car forward, and I caught a movement in the rearview, the dart and dash of all three right behind us, their faces white as the absent moon, their eyes black, their knives stretched out like claws. I thought I heard a communal screech at the stars. The brothers couldn't be killed by a BMW.

Twenty-eight

When we were clear, Clemmie said, "Please tell me what's happening." Tears ran down her face. She was gasping for breath, in a state of rising panic.

"Not yet," I said. "Get us out of here first."

"Were they—are they—?" She couldn't finish, but I knew what she was asking.

"I don't know what they are."

She jerked the steering wheel to the right, to avoid a stand of birch.

"Here," she said, reaching into the backseat and bringing up a rucksack. "Clothes."

I almost wept with gratitude. I reached into the rucksack and pulled out a turtleneck and a pair of jeans. I undressed in front of her, and she eyed me as I stuffed the curtain shreds and bra into her rucksack. "How are we on gas?" I asked.

"Low."

She gunned up a slope through overhanging trees. "Whatever. Get us as far away from here as you can," I said.

She nodded too fast. Her fear seemed to fill the car. She gripped the steering wheel as if it were a branch on a cliff face.

"There should be a ski resort," I said, passing my hands over the jeans, the turtleneck, feeling for the first time a connection between my senses and something resembling the real world. I became even more aware of the extreme state in which she had found me. What in hell must she think?

She nodded. "We'll stop there for the night."

"No. He'll expect that. You get us down out of these mountains."

"I told you. He's gone."

The car had a heater, but I grew cold inside. I wrapped myself in my own arms and felt a sudden onrush of heaviness. I heard myself say, "Please don't stop." I rolled over on my side. "Excuse me."

"You're excused," I heard her say.

I woke. We had stopped, and I saw the eaves of chalet-style buildings. Clemmie was gone. I cried out. Her head popped through the driver's side backseat window.

"Relax. I'm getting directions."

It was very dark. The stars had faded. She left me and walked a few paces to a man in a crumpled hat with a stick in his left hand. He looked like a shepherd, and I couldn't believe he spoke a word of English. I glanced back toward the haunt of woods in the rear dashboard. I could see where we had been, a ragged asphalt road straggling down from the night-enveloped valleys beyond the ski resort. Any minute, the pale brothers might emerge from the stillness. I put a hand to my wrist and felt my pulse. It was triphammering. I remembered that I had peanuts in my purse. The purse lay at my feet, and I almost tore it open in search. I found the bag and ripped it open, scattering nuts everywhere. I plucked them off the floor and shoved them in my mouth, a nauseating hunger.

Clemmie came back to the car and saw. She looked away. "No gas stations open at this hour. We can stay in one of these hotels till morning, when we can fill the tank, or we can chance it in the dark, but we may run out of gas on the road. Your call."

"Chance it."

She waved to the shepherd, and we were on our way. After we had left the ski resort behind, I felt the gradual ease of my own fear, and hers, too.

"Fifteen kilometers down to Brasov," she said. "We might make it."

Awake and alert, my hunger raging, I began to think. "What are you doing up here?" I asked.

"Looking for you."

"How? Why? I don't believe it."

She regarded me with a sidelong glance as she drove, her face full of its own questions. "You have any idea how long you've been missing?"

I shook my head. "A week?"

"Three." She paused, allowing me to absorb this.

"Impossible," I said.

"You've lost track of time. The Romanian police have been combing these hills. There have been FBI and State Department inquiries. You can't imagine what a stink you've made."

I tried to count the days that I knew had come and gone on the mountain. No way could I make it add up to three weeks. But somehow I believed Clemmie. Torgu had trapped time up there, too, it seemed. "How is it possible that you found me, and they didn't?" I asked.

"I knew who, and what, to look for."

I gave her a look of confusion. I didn't understand. She turned her eyes on the gas gauge and the road, which tended down in great easy curves. She could almost have switched off the engine.

"You remember that night in the hotel?" she asked me.

I nodded.

"Right then, I knew you were in trouble. I knew that man—what did you call him—?"

The name came foul in my mouth. "Torgu."

"I knew he was bad news. And he knew that I knew it. Did you see the way that he looked at me?"

I recalled the moment. "So why didn't you warn me?"

A silence followed, and I knew that it was a stupid question. I never would have listened.

"I did, in my own way," she said. And she had. She'd given me the cross. "I regret it. I wish I'd done more."

The car sank down again, another level of mountain. Clemmie continued to explain, guilt in her voice. "I waited outside for you to leave the hotel. When you got into his car, I was in a taxi a block away, and we followed for as long as we could." Her words summoned memories of that night, so long ago, before everything had happened. "I got as far as that ski town. I watched him stop and spit out the window, and then somehow my cabbie lost him. We drove on back roads for hours, but . . . nothing."

"The cabbie probably worked for him," I said.

"Maybe. Yes. It occurred to me later."

As we descended in the car, I had a sensation of flight; not the kind you feel in an airplane, but closer to the sort that comes at the end of a long dream, a soft landing into sleep.

"Anyway," Clemmie continued, "I knew you were up here. And I figured that you would come back to the hotel. I hoped you would. So I waited. And you didn't come."

A well of emotion spilled out. I put my head into my hands and wept. "They must think I'm dead by now," I sobbed. "Everyone."

"I did," she said in a low, pained voice. "Even when you came out of the grass, I wasn't so sure. Even now."

I looked up at Clemmie, and she put her hand tenderly on my knee, and the heaviness swarmed out of the ducts and corners of the car and flooded my senses so that I slept once more. When I woke, it was dawn. The car had stopped. Clemmie stood on the bank of a scenic overlook beside the road. A clean blue light came through the dashboard. I got out and stretched my legs. My left foot hurt terribly. I felt a sharp pain in my head and a jolt in my chest. I lurched over to the retaining wall, vomiting peanuts. Clemmie rushed to my side, lifted my hair with one hand, massaging my shoulder with another. Afterward, in the full light of dawn, we stared across the flatlands of Transylvania.

"Gas pooped out, Evangeline. We'll have to put the car in neutral and coast from here." She massaged the muscles in my neck again until I shrugged my shoulders. "Want me to look at that foot?"

I shook my head. I didn't want to be touched anymore. I just wanted to be left alone.

"Are you ever going to tell me what happened to you?"

I shook my head again. "You still haven't told me everything. When did you see Torgu?"

Clemmie scrutinized me with a benign suspicion. "Fair enough. You look like five kinds of hell, and it's none of my business, and Lord as my witness I'll never tell a word about that get-up I found you in, but sooner or later you're going to have to explain to someone where you've been all this time. You know that, don't you?"

In truth, it hadn't occurred to me. Now that Clemmie mentioned it, I had no clue what to say to her or anyone else. The whole thing seemed unspeakable, and I realized, with a shudder, that I couldn't possibly go back to my loved ones. They would see. They would know. I had changed. My encounter with that thing had changed me in ways that would be visible and obvious. I felt a wave of nausea at the thought of Robert, my fiancé, what he would see on my face, what he would hear in my voice. He would ask about the engagement ring, and I would have to lie and say that I lost it. And he would catch the lie and want to know more, and I would have to tell him. And if he tried to touch me? What then? Would I be the woman he remembered, or some other person, capable of exhibitions he had never imagined? Or would I freeze in horror? And beyond these considerations lay another, the surf of sounds in my brain, ebbing and flowing, like the break of insanity in the distance. It would not be possible to reveal the truth about these sounds without suggesting to everyone that I had lost my mind. I couldn't tell them that the man who had assaulted me had come to live in my mind. I couldn't believe it myself.

She seemed to read me. "Okay. I saw this man, Torgu, yesterday afternoon. To be honest, I had stopped coming to the hotel. With Todd's help—" She stopped and was overcome. She didn't cry, but she put a hand to her mouth and waited it out.

"I'm sorry," I said.

She waved my words away. "He was like me. We'd worked together in Jordan a long time ago. I ran into him in a café. He was running a small mission out of someone's basement, early-church style. I told him about you, and he offered to help."

She went silent for a while longer. It was my turn to give comfort. I put a hand on her shoulder. The sun on the mountainside warmed us.

"So," she finally said, glancing over at the BMW, "this was about a week after you'd left, and it came to me all of a sudden that your rental car must still be parked in the garage of the hotel. The valet remembered that I'd been in the car, and he accepted a gift and gave me the keys, and Todd and I began to drive around in the hills together. He spoke some Romanian, and we gave descriptions of you and the guy, and I got more and more worried. When we mentioned this guy, when we described him, people went silent. They crossed themselves, you know, just like in the movies . . ."

I walked to the precipice and looked down. Below lay the red roofs of an old city. Beyond ran the plain.

"I believe it," I said.

"So this went on for a week or so, and then I began to see all kinds of cars up here, and all kinds of men, and it began to get a little dangerous, I thought, to be driving around in the car that had belonged to a missing woman. Five days ago, your picture turned up on the streets of the city. I parked the Beemer in some woods, and Todd and I took turns at the hotel, him in the morning, me in the afternoon. He was a doll about it."

"Go on."

"So I was sitting in the foyer of the hotel, reading a prospectus that Todd had given me when you know who walked through the door. He looked awful, shriveled, but it was the same guy."

A chill went across my skin. "You're sure."

"Positive." Even the bright morning sun seemed to dim. I heard his voice in my mind, rumbling in deep canyons of feeling. I felt him. I wanted to feel him. "He went to the clerk at the desk and slipped him several bills. I got up. I didn't want him to see me. I walked out the front door of the lobby, and I waited. And it wasn't too long before a car pulled up, a limo, and he came out and got inside. As soon as the car pulled away, I went to the bellhop who had handled the luggage, three or four pieces, and I gave him my last wad of American dollars. I asked him who it was, and he looked at me funny. I said that I was an American, and that I danced in a local bar, and the man had run out on a tab, and I was really upset. He was a nice kid. Maybe he thought I would dance for him. He told me it was some rich guy, headed for Bucharest. And I knew it was my chance."

I shook my head in wonder. It was really happening. "He's going to New York," I said.

"New York?"

She sounded incredulous, and I couldn't blame her. It didn't seem possible that the man would actually try to get into the United States, not now, not with his criminal record. But I couldn't tell Clemmie anything else. I wasn't ready. "I still don't understand," I said. "How did you happen to be on that road last night?"

She looked at me with a certain pride. "It was partly luck, and partly the bellhop. I asked him if he knew where the rich bastard lived, and he gave me a laugh and said he has a hotel up in the mountains. No one goes there anymore, but it's on a road on the other side of the ski valley. Todd and I got in the Beemer, and we drove all over the area." Her face darkened again. "We only stopped because we saw something in the road. Obviously, those men were looking for you."

She bent over and plucked pebbles off the ground. She tossed them into the tree branches beneath us. She implored me with a look.

"I have questions, too, Evangeline."

"I know you do."

She arched an eyebrow at me. "You really want to keep secrets from me? After I found you in the dark wearing nothing but rags?" She scooped up more rocks and hurled them down. "I know what I am. I know what I did. I got Todd killed. But what did you do?" She gave a sigh of impatience. "We have to decide what we're going to do, Evangeline."

She went to the car and plucked out the rucksack. She put it onto her back. We put the car into neutral and rolled it down the hill into some bushes. By unspoken agreement, we deemed that the vehicle had become a liability. The leaves in the trees had begun to change color, but the day was hot. We started to walk.

Twenty-nine

At last, I began to feel the need to talk, if only to tell myself that every-thing had really happened, and Clemmie was content to listen, never asking questions. I told her almost everything, though I left out the part about my final encounter with Torgu. She was a devout Christian, I told myself, and would never understand. Or maybe she would, but I didn't want her to know. If she knew, she would endanger me, said a voice deep inside; I didn't want anyone to know until I understood what was inside me. I contained a great and growing secret. In that se-cret lay a great and growing power. Clemmie listened with avid calm, showing no surprise at even the most inexplicable details. By the time I had finished, we'd reached the outskirts of Brasov.

"Wow," Clemmie said, looking away. "I can see why you're nervous about telling that story."

Still descending, we passed a few restaurants and a grocery store. A photograph of my face was posted on a wall beside the grocery store. The photo had been taken that previous summer, at Newport, and wasn't bad, except for the fact, I thought, that the woman in the picture no longer existed. I wondered if there were photographs of the Norwe-gian. Did anyone back home know that he'd gone missing? Clemmie saw the photo, too, and glanced at me. I didn't break my stride. I was ravenous, but I had left behind every bit of my cash, and she had run out, too. Finally, we came to a crowd of people, foreign tourists climb-ing out of a bus.

"Excuse me," Clemmie said. "Can you tell us if there is an American consulate in this town?"

A Tel Aviv University decal on a bag gave away the identities of the tourists. They turned out to be Israelis on tour. A big man with a gruff manner came forward. He glanced at me and back at Clemmie.

"Can I help you?"

"We ran into some trouble with the locals," Clemmie said. "My friend here is in a bad way."

He didn't need convincing. My appearance told a horror story. He put a hand to my forehead, and I must have been warm.

"Are you a Jew?" he asked me.

"No."

"Hmmm. You look like a Jew. Can you walk? If I offer my arm? There's a hospital close by."

Clemmie stopped him. "Please, sir, that's very kind, but we don't want medical assistance just yet. We just want to keep this quiet until we can speak to some American government officials."

One of the women piped up. "Daniel, it's a smart girl. That one doesn't need to be dealing with Romanian doctors. Give them some money, and let's be off."

"You need money?" He plucked a roll from his pocket and peeled off bills.

"No sir. We'll be fine. We can hitch back to Bucharest."

He forced the cash into her hand. "Don't be ridiculous."

A few minutes later, we were eating pork schnitzel, corn mush, goat cheese and tomato salad.

"You're quite the operator," I said.

She blushed. "Thanks. Comes with the territory. We're always asking for sponsorship."

I wondered which territory she meant; not necessarily the Kingdom of Heaven. It became a matter of some urgency to know. Clemmie had become my lifeline to the rest of the world, and the only human witness to my condition. The coincidence smacked of conspiracy. She must have deeper motives than concern for my well-being, I thought. She hardly knew me. Why should she care?

"What in the world are you up to, Clementine? Really?"

"I told you before." .

I tried to provoke her. "Maybe you're not a Christian at all. Maybe you're just some wild chick who likes to assume different identities. That's what I think."

"Hey," she said, "what happened to your engagement ring?" Her own provocation, but she asked with an edge of real concern. I recalled how she'd stared at it on our first encounter. She had been more interested in the ring than me.

"Lost," I said.

She shook her head in disbelief. Maybe I scared her a little. It wasn't the situation, a missing woman on her hands, a murdered companion, a monstrous tableau. It was something more basic. For lack of a better word, I would call it my being. My changed being gave her an involuntary shudder.

"Was it taken from you?"

"Yes," I lied.

She looked away and told her own lie. "I believe your story. Another person might call it outlandish. She might point out the gaping holes. The omissions. But not me. Why do you think that is?"

"You believe that Jesus rose from the dead. Why shouldn't you believe me?"

Clemmie hooted in derision, and people looked up. She didn't care. "You have a low opinion of my belief. The resurrection of Jesus depends on eyewitness testimony chronicled in no less than four accounts. Your story has a single, potentially unreliable source. Lots of very religious people wouldn't accept for one minute a story about a man who drinks human blood and speaks some creepy language that infects the people who hear it. They'd accuse you of multiple personality disorder. But not me. I know it's all true, cross my heart, hope to die."

She had saved me, yes, but something inside me began to register a vague threat. "If you believe it, Clemmie, it's because you know something." That's why she'd followed Torgu into the mountains. That's why she had given me the crucifix. But her knowledge had limits. She'd been ignorant enough to give me a cross as protection against a creature who collected the damn things. "You're all I have at this moment. If you know something, you better speak up."

Clemmie put a finger to her mouth. We'd attracted attention. The other conversations in the restaurant had gone quiet. People were peering at my face, as if they recognized it. She dropped a bill on the table, and we took a stroll through old Brasov, a medieval town with a scorched black church at its center. Clouds came into the sky, grumbling bowls of blue. The air had an electrical charge. Off to the south, lightning smote the mountains. My foot started to give me serious pain, and I limped.

"Sure you don't want me to take a look at that?" she asked, needling.

"Stop asking." An irrational panic rose in my chest. She wanted to silence the whispers in my mind. She worked against the deepest interests of my heart. I didn't know how, and I didn't know why, but she was in league with my enemies. "Tell me what you know."

Clemmie smiled at me. She liked to be coy. It was part of her Dallas girl way. I knew the nature well enough. I'd had my coy side. But this time, I couldn't play along. My life was at stake; more than my life, I thought. I began to feel a disconnection within myself, as if my body were two steps to my left and moving farther away with every stride. At the edges of my consciousness, too, the voice murmured its alarming rhyme: *Caporetto, Solferino, Borodino, Manzikert.*

"Are you prepared to believe my story just as I was prepared to believe yours?" Clemmie asked.

I nodded through a growing haze in my conciousness. I heard the names and shut my eyes in a vain effort to block them out, but that made it worse. When I shut my eyes, I saw something like a panorama. I saw smoke and the glint of steel and the splay of hacked human forms. They were far away, but I saw them, just as I saw the café umbrellas when I opened my eyes. Both were real. Both remained. A clap of thunder did nothing to dispel the double vision.

"I'm not a missionary," Clemmie confessed.

"You're a change agent. You told me."

"No. I mean I have a different ministry all together."

A few times in my life, I've had the sensation of seeing a person literally change before my eyes, and Clemmie did so, right then. In my imagination, she had been a missionary, even when I'd had my doubts about her honesty. Now I looked at a person whom I didn't know at all, a complete and total enigma. The revelation terrified me.

"It wasn't exactly a lie," she said. "It's just what we tell people who wouldn't understand."

"We?"

The mountain air nipped at the rims of the café umbrellas. Rain would come soon. I wouldn't be able to walk much farther, but I had no idea where to go. I could feel the rise of my own desperation, a resurgence of the fear on the mountain coupled with a dread of what this woman was about to tell me.

"I'm affiliated with an organization called World Ministries Central—WMC. I was hired by them, originally, I should say, and did the usual sort of work in South Asia and Africa. That work included a few exorcisms, though it wasn't our bread and butter. We called them the deliverance. We saw a lot of things, my husband and I."

This confession relieved me, a little, of the fear of insanity. I wasn't the only one who had seen things beyond the pale.

"But a year ago, after my husband left—this was after the incident in Malawi, after we'd moved to Kashmir—I was sent back to London, to base camp, for retraining." She gazed at me a while, taking my measure. I didn't like the sound of the phrase *base camp,* with its military connotations. She sensed my discomfort, I believe, but continued. "I'm attached on a sub-contractual basis to a branch of WMC called the Lower Air Commission, and it's our job to isolate phenomenon that the world body deems to be related to necromancy and other forms of occult activity."

This almost made me laugh. "You think Torgu is Satan?"

She looked at me with very serious eyes. I felt a renewed sense of conspiracy. She had designs. She wanted to know about the voices in my head. She wanted to know what they were telling me. This was the beginning of an interrogation.

"You're the one talking about exorcism," I said.

Clemmie raised her hands as a teacher might, hastening to dispel a false notion. "I'm sorry. It's just that we would never call anyone or any-thing Satan, except as a technical term. Satan is too large a force, too great an infection of the soul or mind. Your man isn't Satan, but if what you're saying is true, he may carry that strain."

I thought about it and shook my head. I rubbed my temples. I sud-denly felt protective of Torgu, and the feeling made me sick. Torgu hadn't had that kind of a virus. He was better than that. "The cross meant nothing to him. He collects artifacts of disaster, and some of them were—are—holy images. He never struck me as unholy. On the contrary. There was something bizarrely spiritual about him."

Clemmie acted as if we'd got off on a tangent, shaking her head. She wanted to get back to her explanation. "I'm an analyst. I'm not sup-posed to do anything but wait and watch in those places, at those times, when there is evidence of a problem. Satan rules this earth. We know this from scripture. It's no secret, and it's not our job to rewire the basic operating system. We only intercede when our own interests are af-fected. In this case, until you disappeared, they weren't."

"Why am I of interest to your commission?"

"You're not. They don't even know you exist. But you're of interest to me. That's what counts."

"So you haven't mentioned me to them?"

"I haven't mentioned anything to them for weeks. They have no idea where I am."

"They don't know you're in Romania?"

She shook her head at me, almost impish. "I was changing planes at Otopeni, on my way from an El Al flight to British Airways, when I saw this beautiful woman and decided to follow her. I had a hunch. That's all, an intimation of trouble. From that moment on, I was AWOL."

The information added a new complexion to things. She had followed me for personal reasons. Did I believe her? And what on earth could it mean? She was vulnerable. The first droplets of rain pelted the café um-brellas, but we continued our walk. Men looked our way, trying to catch our eyes. It was better to keep moving, despite my foot.

"You're basically crazy," I said.

"Crazy like Jesus." She saw that I had perceived a weakness in her

façade. "Meeting you was a divine appointment. I was sent to protect
you, and I have, but there was another reason to be here, if that gives
you any comfort. In London, we heard a rumor that needed checking
out. It's a sort of routine with us. The Germans up here speak of a
thing they call the Ab."

"So it wasn't me, after all."

"It was you, and God and the Ab."

Her voice had a slight tremble. I was afraid, but so was she. "Sounds
made up to me," I said. "All of it."

"Ab, as in abdomen." She caught herself. "But it's pronounced Ob,
short for the German phrase *die Abwesenheit Gottes,* or akin to the Latin,
deus absconditus. The Absence of God, or the Absent God. Or just Absence, might be a better translation."

"And you're saying that is what attacked me?"

She retreated. She was clever and calculating. "I don't know. I was
hoping you could give me more details."

"Absence doesn't sound like this thing. It was exceedingly present."

She gave a significant pause at this remark, which had not been intended to give anything away. I wondered what I had said. My foot began to go numb, and I knew that I wouldn't be able to continue much
farther.

"Anyway," I continued, made nervous by her look of increasing anxiety, as if she had discovered a clue of great significance, "your Ab
sounds more like a condition than a thing."

"Would seem so, but people up here, the remnants of the Saxon im-
migration of the thirteenth century, speak of it as a person. They say
the Ab did this or the Ab did that. It's very intriguing. They say the condition can be spread, like vampirism."

At this, she gave me another anxious look, as if that very condition
had spread to me. Did she think that I was becoming a vampire?

"Do they say what this creature looks like?" I asked.

Another bolt of thunder came, a snap and lash, and rain burst from
the sky. We had to huddle in a stone doorway and were soon drenched.
The ache in my foot had spread to my lower calf. Before long, I would
have to submit to physical necessity, and she, too. She shook in the wet

and cold, but she kept talking, looking at me. Every word out of her mouth had become a question.

"No description exists in the folk mythology, and no mention in the relevant texts suggests one. But I saw the man you met in the hotel, and I knew in that instant that I had found the Ab of the Saxons."

A savage impulse came over me. I wanted to throttle her. The voices beat like blood in my brain. She leaned forward, a drop of water on the tip of her nose. "Isn't there more you can tell me, Evangeline?"

I noticed for the first time that she was wearing that same button-down pink shirt, the preppy one from our first meeting. The water had plastered it to her body. I turned to face her and realized that she was actually taller than me by an inch. Her eyes twinkled with suspicion. My teeth chattered. The cold had got into my bones. On my behalf, she shook her fist at the sky.

"Damn you," she said to God.

"You can't possibly be a Christian."

She arrested me with a dark look. "*Au contraire*. My faith is rooted in deeper places than the virtuous of this earth will ever know." A cruel smile crept up the side of her face. "I'm the Lord's marauder, Evangeline. Beware."

We braced ourselves for one more soaking and ran back into the storm. She took my hand. The waters rushed in rivulets between the ancient stones, licking around our ankles. We came to a wreck of a hotel. Clemmie gave the reception desk clerk a wad of cash and asked for a room. He looked us over and handed us a fat metal key. The room was dank and moldy, with a feel of disuse, but I peeled off my wet things. I was about to get under the blankets when she touched my hip.

"Not so fast. I'm going to have a look at that foot. Lie back."

She had not undressed, and I was ashamed at my nakedness, but I did as she said. She sat at the end of the bed with a tube of Neosporin from her soaked rucksack and lifted my ankle gently in her hand. She cupped one hand at the base of my calf and daubed at the sand and pine needles in the cut with a bit of her wet shirt. I cried out, and she caressed my foot and apologized. I closed my eyes and let her work, slowly. She finished with the cut and began to wipe my legs with the wet shirt, a motion that ebbed and flowed, but never stopped. I let her. I had lost the ability to resist. She rubbed my entire body, turning me over, rolling me back. After she was done, she stopped and put a finger on my abdomen.

"What is this?" she asked, the anxiety back in her voice. I glanced down and saw something like a birthmark, but it couldn't have been. I'd never seen it before. It vaguely recalled the shape of a swastika, and I thought it must be a bruise.

"Don't know," I said.

She examined it more closely, her brow furrowing. She slipped out of her clothes, and I saw her body for the first time, a lanky, skinny affair, but strong, with sinews of the kind I'd never had. She was a straight-haired girl, pure and simple.

She got under the blankets, snuggled next to me, and, as the rain pounded, she continued her interrogation. She wouldn't stop pursuing me. She wanted something precious from me.

"Do you feel better?" she asked.

I looked deep into her eyes. "Did the Saxons ever say how to kill this thing you mentioned?" I asked her.

We were lying on our sides, facing each other, warming each other. She touched my cheek.

"I was hoping you could tell me something about that."

I could feel the blush of panic rising to my cheeks. "If I'd killed it, I would have said so."

The voices beat like bird wings in my mind. She caressed my cheek again, and I brushed her fingers away. The rain smashed at the outside walls.

"You may not have killed it, but you escaped. Can't you tell me how?"

I looked away. She touched my chin, pulled my eyes back to hers.

"Look at you. Turning red? What aren't you saying?"

The rain made her face shine. Her lips were parted with a permanent question. I wanted to shut her up. I wanted to hurt her. I wanted the questions to stop. She could sense my fear. She grazed my belly with the lightest of touches.

"You won't ever tell," I said. "Long as you live."

"Never."

I put my mouth to her ear, damp and cold. Her hands rested on my waist as she listened.

"I knew it," she whispered. Her hands moved from my waist to my abdomen, where she'd discovered the strange bruise. She kissed me on the lips.

Thirty

None of this account is meant to be frivolous. I have attempted, where possible, simply to be honest. My sexuality is a fact of note in this affair, of relevance to the outcome of events. I will say that, in the few weeks of our love affair, I cared for Clemmie very deeply, though never with the sense that our situation would last. In fact, I had premonitions of what would come. Perhaps it was Torgu, even then, whispering our future. I told myself, as we did those things in that bed, that I was not a lover of women in general, but that the experience in the mountain hotel had unhinged a thing or two in me, cut me loose from lines of force and definition that had guided most of my life choices. Those lines are fraudulent anyway. All of us are everything that the species has ever been. I know this now.

In that moment, it would not be wrong to say that I allowed her to put her hands on me for the same reason I exposed myself to Torgu—as a matter of survival. Clemmie wanted more than sex. She wanted answers, and I wouldn't give them. What I could give was another kind of response. I could protect myself by distracting her. If she wanted to enjoy me, in those hours of total fear and confusion, then I would allow myself to be enjoyed. It seemed little enough by way of thanks to let her have what she wanted. I'm far worse than a coward, I now see, but I forgive the fault. I forgive everything. I wanted to live.

The next morning, we ventured out for food, avoiding the sullen look of the reception desk clerk, and Clemmie raised a practical question.

"What now?"

We were running out of money. That night would be our last in the hotel. We could retrieve and sell the rental car. Sooner or later, I had to face the world.

"I can't yet," I said, thinking of Torgu. Every day that passed, I felt more like his follower, and less like his victim. I can't explain the transformation in my sensibilities, but it was as if I was being hunted, and Clemmie, without knowing it, had become one of the hunters. She didn't know yet that she had her prey. "Can we just wander a while? Till I can figure out what to say. You'd like that, wouldn't you?"

"It's no sin, what we did," she snapped back, as if I'd accused her. "Jesus never once mentions it."

"Of course not. I didn't mean it that way. I just meant . . . I would like it . . ."

"Sorry." She had turned red. She gave me another of those anxious looks. "This may not sound very Christian, but why don't you just lie? Say you stumbled across a gangster, that he raped you, beat you and imprisoned you before you escaped. Who will doubt it?"

If it had simply been a matter of my innocence, I thought, I'd have gone to the police that very moment. But it was the other thing that held me back, the generation of a dark, new self. I didn't want to surrender it. I didn't want to lose the power. Complicity must be visible on my face, I thought. The police would see. Clemmie already did, though she didn't know it. She didn't want to believe it yet. But she would, and then I would have to deal with her. So instead of lying to the police, I told a half lie to her.

"I'm no good at deception."

In general, it was true. I've always said what I think, even if my words offend people. I didn't say so to Clemmie, but Robert had once given me a high compliment; he said he knew when he had pleased me in bed, because I didn't make much noise unless something really happened, and that wasn't a frequent occurrence. Now everything had become the opposite. My story grew into a lie. My face and eyes and lips concealed the lie. The truth poured like a river into my mind, filling me up. She might not see it, deceived by her own limited knowledge, but my colleagues at *The Hour,* who knew me, would. They would see every hole in my story before I did. If I'd been beaten, where were the marks? Where had I been held? Who had been my captor—the most famous underworld criminal in Eastern Europe? A man believed by many to be dead? By others to be a myth? And why hadn't I gone right to the police? Why had I meandered around Romania for even an hour with this woman? I couldn't face them without answers of steel.

"When I go to the authorities," I told her, "I'm going to say exactly what happened to me. I'm going to tell them exactly. Otherwise, there's no point."

Her eyes narrowed with doubt. I could see that she'd begun to question my motives, but she was torn, too. I must keep her with me a little while longer, I thought. She said that we should make our way back to Bucharest, but I told her it was too risky. There were too many cops on the road, too much activity in general. And if we went south, we'd have to pass through Torgu's mountains again, and I couldn't do it. I recalled maps I had seen of the country and thought we'd better go north, toward the eastern mountain range. On the other side of the range lay a national highway, and we could take it south to the capital. By then, I told her, I would be ready to turn myself in. She believed me.

October was fading, and the weather grew cold. We bought some gas, retrieved the Beemer and sold it for five hundred dollars to the owner of the hotel where we had escaped in the rain. He didn't ask questions. With that money, Clemmie and I bought used boots, socks and sweaters from an old Roma woman. We needed provisions, too, and outside the city, we came on an apple orchard, heavy with crisp red fruit, and we stuffed the rucksack full. The roads in Transylvania are two-lane and narrow, busy with a traffic spanning several centuries, diesel trucks, horse-drawn wagons, shepherds on foot driving their flocks. We stayed away from motorized vehicles, instead jumping on the backs of hay-hauling wagons. The pace was slow, but the people were kind, offering us onions and dried pork and other simple foods. At night, we slept in barns or hayricks or silos, whatever we could find. The weather got worse, and some days we stayed inside. In one Hungarian village, we spent a week doing chores on a farm, babysitting small children, sweeping floors, shucking corn. We didn't talk much. There was nothing to say. I felt as if I'd wandered from one dream, a nightmare, into another, an idyll, in which things made just as little sense as before.

I saw my first Romanian snowfall. We were bundled up together in a cross-topped barn on the edge of the Carpathians, about to leave behind the plain and climb up into the range. Clemmie held me, and talked about herself. She had a mother in Chicago, but her father had died when she was small. As a young woman, she'd earned a chance to go to West Point, but opted out at the end of her second year. She was too religious for a lot of the other cadets, and military life hadn't suited her. Missionary life had. She found social situations difficult. She loved the edge of things. She liked to live in those places where one culture ended and another began. She'd had boyfriends and girlfriends, had never been comfortable just one way or another. God loved all his creatures. She'd been in love only once, with a woman, another Christian, but they hadn't been able to handle the contradictions. The woman had died of cancer anyway. I wept as I heard, but Clemmie didn't want pity. She asked me to talk more about myself. I couldn't. There was nothing to tell. I was no longer myself. The whispers in my head grew stronger and seemed to point in one direction. Before, on Torgu's mountain, they had seemed malevolent. But slowly, the whispers had become intimate, and when occasionally they seemed to subside, I felt the agony of an unnameable loss. I grew despairing and afraid. The soft insistent lick of those names of places became a song that I wanted to sing, but no matter how hard I tried, I couldn't find the words yet. When Clemmie was out of earshot, I would try to repeat the whispers, to run them over my lips in the same way they slid through my mind, with the same rhythm. At times, I would move to the rhythm of the song, but then I would receive a sharp glance from her, and the impulse would die.

Something even more beguiling began to happen. When I closed my eyes, I began to see the words, really see them, as a panorama of disaster. When I closed my eyes, I began to feel things. I could touch the skin of the words, which were like the skin of the slain. I could stare into the eyes of the dying. I knelt over them on the pavements, in the trenches, in their homes, and held their hands. And then, one night, I came screaming out of a dream that lay within the syllables of the words like a snake in a sack. In the dream, I had been in a house in a valley. The door crashed open, and I heard footsteps in the hall, and men spoke in a language I didn't understand. They entered the room, and a man—Robert—jumped out of bed. They stood him up, forcing his arms behind his back, and they slit his throat. Then they turned to me, and while I screamed, they raped me, and while the last intruder violated me, he slipped a knife between my ribs into my heart. When I opened my eyes the first time, I thought I was waking from a dream of my own death, but it wasn't so. I opened my eyes, and the woman's hair was in my mouth. I had become the last of the rapists. I had Torgu's knife in my hand, and I was pushing between the legs of a woman. Mechanically, I slipped the knife between her ribs into her heart. I woke in screams, and Clemmie held me.

She asked me what was wrong, and I told a small lie. I said that I had been downtown that day in New York during the attacks, which was true, and that I'd had a dream about it, which was false.

"Poor baby," she said, but she didn't look entirely convinced. "Let me have another look at those marks."

I lifted up my shirt, and she traced a swastika, a crescent and a line of cuneiform text with her finger. "There are more," she said. "This is some kind of rash, but it really does look like script, doesn't it?" She looked up at me. "Does it hurt?"

I shook my head. The rash didn't cause me physical pain at all. But I felt the markings as if they had been scrawled onto my mind rather than my body. I didn't tell her so. I didn't tell her that the rash came in my blood with the voices in my head, that they sprang from the same source.

A few days later, as we walked up the road over the Borgo Pass, an arduous climb, she overheard me.

"What's that you said?"

I was startled. I had the awful thought that she could read my mind.

"What are you talking about?"

"Those whispers. Are you praying?"

"I don't pray. That's you."

She stopped walking.

"What the hell's going on, Evangeline?"

I refused to answer. I kept walking.

"Don't you do that. If something's happening, I need to know. We're dealing with serious matters here. Can I trust you?"

I walked on.

"You're muttering biblical place names!" she cried. "Are you aware of that?"

At the top of the pass was a hotel built by the communists to capitalize on tourism related to Western ideas about the vampire. We couldn't afford a room, but the security was lax, and we waited until a bus of tourists showed up. We mixed in with the crowd, mostly Germans and Danes, and split away when they hit the front desk. In more ways than one, Clemmie had a knack for finding overlooked nooks and crannies. We came to a part of the hotel without heat or electricity. It would be freezing, but we had our bodies, our sweaters and blankets.

She was still mad at me, and for a time we kept silent, gnawing on the last of the apples, sharing a can of Coke we'd been saving.

She crumpled the can and said, "Once we get to the other side of this range, you're on your own."

I tossed the core of my apple away. The time had come. "Oh really?"

She wore an expression of distrust. "I don't like the way you look at me anymore," she said.

"Is that so?"

She was sitting with her back to a stripped bed, watching me as if I might bite.

"You like me fine when I undress you," I said.

"You take advantage of the fact."

"You like that."

Her eyes gleamed with fear and desire. I got on my knees, put my hands on her shoulders, pressed her back against the bed and kissed her lips. Her breath came faster.

"You don't mind the way I kiss you."

She pressed me back. "Something's wrong, Evangeline. You're changing before my eyes."

A few days before, her words would have alarmed me. But now I saw her for what she truly was, a frightened religious fanatic face to face with her worst nightmare. She had coupled with an agent of the Enemy, or so she thought. She was precious in her error. I pinned her to the side of the bed and kissed her again. She slapped me. I slapped her back. She tried to slip out of my hands, over the bed and away to the door, but I took her by the legs. I had become strong. I took her by the legs and pulled her back to me. I forced her down on the bed and tore the sweater up over her head and ripped away her T-shirt.

"Get off me," she said.

"Do you remember Todd?" I asked. "Or have I made you forget him completely?"

She was quivering beneath my hands. I took off my sweater. I saw the blue veins at her temples and in her throat and breasts. I cupped her breasts in my hands and put my lips around them and tasted for the first time the pulse of blood beneath the skin. I wanted to eat her alive. And I knew if I did, I would hear loud and clear the song that played on the far horizons of my consciousness, I would finally hear the words between the words, and things would make sense. This was the answer. I would be inside the visions in my mind in a way I never had before. I held her down and took off the rest of her clothes and put my hands inside of her, in every part of her that could be touched, and her insides had the warmth of blood, and I thought every second about how much deeper I might go, how much farther in, and what that would take, and what I would know after she lay spread out in pieces before me, and in the instant before the depths of this new self resolved to tear her limb from limb, I threw myself back from her body, and shrieked at the top of my lungs for the thing in my mind to get out.

Clementine stared at me in terror. I kept on shrieking. I couldn't stop. The thing wouldn't leave my mind unless I shrieked it out. The words would only drown if I annihilated them with my voice.

Clemmie snatched up her clothes. But it was too late. She was already naked, just as they liked, just as they required. I could already hear the thump of feet. They were coming. But it wasn't the police. It was much worse than that. I tried to tell her. We had entered a part of the hotel inaccessible to other human beings. We had entered Torgu's part of the hotel. He thrived in hotels, in their transience. He loved them. They were his only home, and the more decrepit and horrible, the more he loved them. Clemmie grabbed my arm and pinched. For the first time, I saw her real fear.

"A trap, you bitch?"

It was. Heavy blows came against the door. The whispers in my mind grew louder and louder. They became the moans of a man. I had been communicating with him for days, telling him where we were. He knew me. He knew what I wanted. He had given me the gift, too. I heard the words of the dead distinctly now. I heard them as if they were being shouted out of the graves. The hinges of the door gave way. The brothers stood at the threshold. Each of them had knives and a great pail. The pails swung at their sides, caught in a wind of whispers sweeping around the hotel, gusts of a vast storm, the names of the graves of the human race.

I sit here now, pen in hand, and know the truth. I wish that Torgu had come. I wish that the brothers had traversed that distance and taken her with their knives. I wish, I wish. But it's a lie, of course, like so many others. Torgu had left Romania. The brothers were two hundred miles away. Clementine Spence and I were alone in that room. She was my claim to the language of the dead. She was my libation poured into the ground. She was my trench of sacred earth. I straddled her naked body and placed an unyielding hand against her chest. I took the knife from my purse. She pleaded for her life. She begged me. Women who sleep with other women have always been fodder for holy work. And Christians are born to die in violence. Both crimes are punishable. I slit her throat. I drank her blood. I watched her die.

Thirty-one

I looked at Clementine's broken self through the bars of the grate and sobbed. I tried to apologize, over and over, but she didn't seem to care. My sobs echoed in the tunnel of ancient stone and sounded loud enough in my ears to shake the cloister to its foundations, but they died in my chest after a time, and the soft hush of the snow once again resumed its domain. Clemmie waited, as if my emotion represented a formality that must be endured. I had the feeling, wiping my eyes, that she considered the episode embarrassing, though it wasn't any overt response from her; there was nothing overt at all about Clementine anymore. Everything about her lay buried beneath the blanket of death. She was whiter than the snow at her feet, with ash smears closing over her eyes, and slack blue lips, and that horrific throat wound, which didn't bleed or show any signs of trauma beyond the obvious. In her wolf skins, she seemed to have emerged out of an ancient tomb, and this struck me as horribly appropriate. There had always been something primal, archaic, about Clementine Spence.

"Why did you come?" I finally asked.

"There's not much time," she murmured.

"I've been afraid to leave," I said.

"You've nothing to fear. He's gone."

The words should have been a relief. They hung in the iced air like a threat. The shadows of the forest lengthened behind her.

"You're the only one who can destroy him," she said. 'You're the only one who knows."

"What is he, Clemmie? Have you finally learned?"

A sigh came from her lips. She was remarkably patient with me, considering I had murdered her.

"I only know what they say."

"They?"

She gestured at the forest. The shadows of the trees had lengthened again, and then I saw they'd detached themselves completely from the woods. The trees had become like her, wandering toward the entrance to the cloister, toward me.

"Oh, God."

"Don't be afraid."

"I don't understand."

She came a step closer, until her nose stuck through the grate. Her slack blue lips opened. "Blood."

"No."

"You want what he wants. To see the dead. To bring the dead. We know this. We want it, too."

I shook my head. "I don't want that. I don't want any of it. But the voices won't leave my head. And the knowledge. What I know. The graves outside these walls."

Clemmie nodded. "Just the beginning. There are graves that burn with a bright fire, spectacular murders that cry out for acknowledgment, but they are the obvious ones. The Turks, the Dacians, the Jews. The farther you go, the more you see, the greater the immensity. The earth is a massed camp of the dead. A great book of slaughter. We see it, too, but we're in it, so the burden is different."

I heard what she said, but I couldn't grasp its meaning.

"Are you ghosts?"

The snow came in heavier gusts. The shadow army clustered around her, and a wail went through the crowd. I could see indistinct faces now, the cut, the torn, the mangled, the lost visage of a sipahi, one of the beheaded knights, holding his face in his hand.

"There are no ghosts," Clemmie said. "It's something else."

"It's the earth," the sipahi interrupted.

"The earth," Clemmie said, "has a soul, and the soul breathes, and its breath blows up through us, so that we rise like bubbles into the air of this world. That's what some of us say."

"Are you saying you're in hell?"

Her hands clasped the bars of the grate.

"Hell," she sighed, "is where you live." Her fingers tightened on the bars. "No time," she said. "Ask yourself what is happening inside you. Look at the markings on your body. Tell me what you see."

I knew what she meant. It was those birds at night, the dreams and the whispers. It was the weeping when Sister Agathe gave me my bath.

"It's as if the walls between things have grown thin."

"Yes."

"There are different lives that I might have lived, that we all might have lived, other corridors, and they run parallel to us, and all we have to do is reach out and we are in that other corridor, or in the one next to that. We think we are one thing, but one life over, we're murderers."

Her eyes held me. She licked her lips.

I shuddered. "I mean," I said, "it's not some other dimension. It's right here next to me, and I know that I have already walked through one of those walls, and we do it all the time, don't we? I walked through an invisible wall and became your lover. I walked through another one and took your life. But I might not have. It's like street after street after street in a great deserted city."

She whispered, "The city is not deserted."

"What is Torgu? Tell me."

"Two million years of murder in the form of a man."

The shapes behind her had begun to drift back into the woods. I hadn't brought them blood. I had nothing for them, and they would say nothing more to me.

"He brings the blood, and we tell him our secrets."

"Tell me everything, Clementine."

"You know what you have to do before I tell you that. Don't be afraid. You have already done it once."

I saw what she wanted. "But these women took me in."

Her hands let go of the grate. "What is that to me?" She began to recede. "You drink, and through you, I drink, and when I have drunk, I tell you everything. And I am only one. There are so many of us. If you shed the blood of everyone in this valley, it would never be enough."

"You didn't come to help me at all, did you?"

The whispers caught me by surprise, a sudden rush of the words through the stones at my feet, like a howling laugh of derision. *Otumba, Tabasco, Queretaro, Olindo.*

I could barely finish my thought. "You wanted me to drink."

Kosovo, Mycenae, Tannenberg, Iass.

The snow bound the sky to the earth in an endless sorrow. Clementine Spence was gone.

BO 6 OK

A Day in the Life

Addendum to First Half of Text, Found in Personal Papers of James O'Malley, Post Mortem:

Here we have a complete break in the availability of documents. As most readers will know, a fire destroyed the upper floors of the West Street building, and it was only by sheer luck that three boxes of materials relating to these matters were spared, thanks to their proximity to a flooded bathroom. I estimate that at least two more boxes, either stored elsewhere or simply swallowed by the last of the flames, were lost. Readers of this document may choose to elide over this emendation to the text, but I require it to fill in the blank spaces in my own understanding. Rather than forge my own speculative versions of a near three-month lacuna, I hope to bridge the gap through the use of a smattering of research done in the name of evidentiary clarity. The documentary evidence resumes in late January, so I must somehow account for the lost months.

I will describe the world of *The Hour* in that moment before night fell. With the exception of Edward Saxby, most of you will not have experienced the medium of broadcast news in its heyday, long before the loss of audience share and the related advertising revenue, before the string of scandals that demoralized and ultimately extinguished the enterprising spirit of the work. As those with a sense for our history know, there was a time when network news presided over the serious and well-informed American imagination with near-papal authority. And as a former newsman, a veteran of broadcast journalism (and not

208 ◆ JOHN MARKS

coincidentally, a one-time employee of *The Hour,* a producer for none other than Austen Trotta before the termination of my contract on grounds of mutual but unspoken hostility), I witnessed this glorious moment close at hand. For that reason, I am uniquely placed to shed light on the routine reality of the "shop," when *The Hour* still operated as what it was, the greatest machine ever built for the broadcast of televised reality to a prosperous, curious and well-educated public.

I choose a day of some significance to our story, January 16, seventy-two hours before the documentary evidence picks up again. The day I'm going to describe could have been any other in three decades, in terms of routine. I've chosen this specific date on the calendar because, even as *The Hour* went about its business on that January 16, in the midst of record-breaking snowfall, a proximate cause of that day's electrical blackout, the troubles significantly deepened. We know this, in part, due to records kept external to the twentieth floor: air freight manifests, etc. But I confess to some guesswork as well.

You will want to know how things stood by this date, almost three months after the disappearance of Evangeline Harker. On the matter of the vanishing itself, there had been a handful of clues. Witnesses at a hotel in Bucharest recalled that Ms. Harker left in the company of another woman, registered as a guest under the name of Clementine Spence. As it turned out, Ms. Spence had also gone missing, but in the absence of close friends or family, her disappearance had gone unnoticed. At the hotel in Brasov, close questioning revealed that Ms. Harker had left shortly after check-in in the company of an older male, presumably connected to the potential interview subject. Ms. Spence had not checked in as a guest of the hotel in Brasov, and nothing was known of her whereabouts after the departure from Bucharest.

These details comprised the extent of the hard information and didn't advance the cause of the investigation by much. Trips to Romania by a private investigator in the company of Ms. Harker's distraught fiancé, her father and an employee of the Justice Department, doing a special favor for the senior Harker, had led nowhere. Inquiries from the State Department proved futile. No morgue produced a body, no witness reported a crime. In vain, the senior Harker filed suit against the network, the show and the correspondent Austen Trotta for criminal negligence, but there was no real case. It was the job of an associate producer to scout locations, no matter how dangerous.

There had been attempts to broaden the inquiry to include certain odd events on the twentieth floor of the West Street building, but no substantial connection could be established between the disappearance of Evangeline Harker and the arrival of the video and audio tapes from Romania at the offices of *The Hour*. The tapes themselves had been taken out of circulation, and new rules had come into effect about digitizing material of unsound provenance, but such a phenomenon was a very rare occurrence. The editors involved in the first incident were censured, but their physical and mental condition, which had never quite stabilized, seemed punishment enough. All three men complained of insomnia, ghastly dreams and a wasting disease that no doctor had been able to diagnose. Colleagues of these men shook their heads and wondered at the possibility of a scam to obtain medical leave or even more obscure misadventures. The show's founder and executive producer, Bob Rogers, was heard to speculate about a network conspiracy to abort *The Hour* from within by sabotaging technology and frightening employees. To this day, no proof of such a conspiracy has emerged, despite reports in the press to the contrary.

Finally, to be complete in my survey, the entire affair had been investigated by an internal review board at the network level, and in the wake of that inquiry, network executives, with the blessing of corporate shareholders, had determined that the old autonomy of *The Hour* was a perilous anachronism. In the future, overseas stories without clear news pegs were to be placed under special scrutiny. Breaking news and celebrity profiles were to be encouraged. A network transition plan, germinating for months, bloomed in the upper suites, and it was determined, in light of everything, that Rogers himself must bear responsibility for the Harker matter and step down at an undetermined date. Austen Trotta, who, after all, bore an even more immediate responsibility for the disappearance, would be asked, at contract time, to think about retirement. Word of this possibility presumably flittered into the alcoves of the twentieth floor. Untenable rumors certainly reached the ears of competitors. But on the morning of January 16, most of this information lived only as rampant speculation, and the day began as all working weekdays did, with a team of the best producers in the news business scattered around the globe and across the country, finding and shooting stories for household names waiting for their weekly moment to speak with calm majesty and splendid contempt to the nation.

That work began in predawn grayness and snow with the first run of the traffic van out to the airport to retrieve tape sent from overseas. But there I've already made a mistake. Work can't be said to have begun at that hour, because it had never really ended. In distant time zones, between midnight and five A.M. of that same day, producers and crews for *The Hour* had been at four different longitudes and latitudes—on a Vietnamese merchant freighter in the Spratly Islands of the South China Sea, in the great bazaar of Lal Chowk in the Kashmiri city of Srinagar in India, on an Israeli military chopper swooping down the coast of the Dead Sea in Israel before turning landward to check out reports of suicide bomb-making factories in the Judean Wilderness and prowling with hidden cameras the red-light district in Amsterdam, where a young and inexperienced sound man wearing a suspicious baseball cap tried to buy a stinger missile from a Surinamese transvestite who subsequently beat him senseless.

It had been a trying day for everyone. In the South China Sea, producer Raul Trofimovich cursed as he realized he'd spent well over one hundred thousand dollars on a story about islands that did not break the surface of the water. By way of an additional surprise, their only real inhabitants were turtles. Chinese gunships forced him into international waters. In Israel, occasional correspondent Dov Gelder received an angry rebuke from the beautiful pilot of his chopper, a woman who wore a service pistol on her hip and didn't welcome the sexual advances of a man twice her age. In Kashmir, maverick producer Samantha Martin wore an abaya and ate gushtaba, congratulating herself on giving the slip to her obnoxious Indian government minder, a man whom she personally knew to be a spy for the Pakistani Intelligence Services. And in an expensive hotel on the Herrengracht in Amsterdam, the sound man, Jorg-Michael Manks, a German whose father had served as a camera man for the network ever since Vietnam, drank Jägermeister for breakfast and lied to an irritated producer and an appalled correspondent about the details of the encounter with the Surinamese transvestite. No sale of stinger missiles had been made.

Despite these mishaps, par for the course for *Hour* producers, their earlier shipments of tape arrived safely in the air freight district of John F. Kennedy Airport in New York, where the program's courier—we'll call him Bill—arrived to retrieve it, having received word by e-mail that it was on its way.

I met this man at his home in Niagara Falls. He was one of the few network employees willing to step forward and talk candidly about what he had seen. He had nothing to lose: shortly after he played his little part in the drama, Bill went into retirement. But in his own way, on that morning in the snow, he played a critical role. I never told him so, but it's the undeniable truth. And he paid the price. By the time I got to him, he was broken and strange; he heard things in the house at night and had irrational notions about whispers emanating from the Falls nearby.

On his traffic runs, Bill drove a late-model Econoline van, a round and rattling vehicle that handled the accumulation of snow with bouncing indifference. It was an easy job to pick up tape. Bill never picked up more than a few cases at a time. But every now and then, someone would ship back an object of size—crates of caviar or wine, a sculpture, once a monkey dead of plague. For such cargo, the van suited perfectly.

That morning, Bill had waybill numbers for four tape shipments from various points on the compass: a box of eight beta tapes slugged Spratly, shipped via DHL on an Air France flight from Saigon; two more boxes of eight each in a metal case from the Netherlands, slugged Slave Girls, shipped via Sabena Air; and smaller shipments, five each, slugged respectively Kashmir and Bomb Makers, the former shipped Air India, the latter FedExed on El Al from Tel Aviv. It would be a long morning, going from freight shop to freight shop in the snow. Everything would be slower. But Bill didn't mind. Most of the producers were still overseas and not waiting back at the office for their material. He would take his time.

He went to Sabena first and picked up the Dutch load. He had been working with the Sabena operation for years and knew everyone on the morning shift. He got free coffee and cherry pastry. He bitched about the weather and expressed amazement that planes could still land. The white matter swirled thick against the hangars. Sabena freight had received word that the airport would shut down within hours. Bill signed for the shipment and hurried on. The metal cases came in green mesh sacks. Carefully, he loaded the sacks into the back of the van. He reflected, as he often did, that the material in the back of his van had no value whatsoever except to the show, but that value was sacrosanct, and if you screwed up, if you lost or damaged a shipment, there were consequences. Personally, he was afraid of the people on the show and never communicated with them. He let the dispatcher handle that. But he knew of drivers who had been scalded and skinned for nothing more than a briefly misplaced case. Bill prided himself on the fact that he had never attracted the attention of that unforgiving eye.

He continued on his rounds. The Air India people were very polite and extremely concerned that he understand their system. They showed him the computer screen, indicating the cargo and its location. They showed him their paperwork, assured him that the manifest of the plane matched the documents. They wanted to take a look at his waybill, just to make extra sure everyone was on the same page. Everyone was. Bill accepted a cup of chai and went on his way.

The Israel and Saigon shipments went smoothly, too, until he had a chat with the new girl.

"What about this other load?" she asked in a chirpy Queens accent.

"What other load, dear?"

She laughed. "The Motherlode. The big load. The one that ain't sittin' on my hangar a minute longer than it has to."

It was a shuddering moment for Bill, as it would have been for anyone in his position. In the broadcast news business, anomalies mean

trouble. They can instantly cost large amounts of money. He foresaw
the need to begin the construction of his version of events right then
and there. In Bill's experience, people didn't ship large objects without
announcing well in advance their arrival. Tape could come without
much fanfare; people got sloppy. But no one who paid for a large shipment tended to forget they'd done so.

"What are we talking about here?"

The smart-mouthed girl told him three half-ton crates worth, easy.

"Jesus. Do you believe it?"

Shaking her head, she led him out into the hangar, to a wide, blank
space between gigantic, plastic-wrapped turbines destined for a chocolate factory in Pennsylvania, or so she told him, and racks of fur coats.
She pointed at three large wooden crates, stacked side by side. They
were five feet high, at least, and about as wide.

"For you." She had nice fingers, he remembered in our hushed conversation in the condo in Niagara Falls.

"Not according to my people."

"Well, you better get 'em on the goddamn horn and figure it out,
cause they ain't stayin' here."

She gave him a quizzical look, which he hadn't forgotten. She, too,
recognized the extent of the mess.

He radioed the dispatcher and asked if there had been word of another shipment. The dispatcher confirmed his fears. When Bill told the
dispatcher another shipment had come, despite the lack of paperwork,
the pause at the other end of the radio gave him a chill. Everyone understood.

Back in the air freight office, he asked, "There a name on the
shipment?"

She checked. "That there is. Austen Trotta."

"Fuck me," he blurted. "Helluva thing."

"Tell me about it."

He shrugged. The crates looked heavy, and he was alone.

"No idea what's in them?" he inquired.

She checked again. "Says here archeological fragments, whatever
that means."

"And customs cleared it?"

She nodded. "Wouldn't be here otherwise."

Bill went back out to the crates, which were large enough to contain human beings.

"Jesus," he said again.

"Brother, you need a forklift."

Bill tipped the forklift driver fifty dollars that he couldn't afford, but it was worth every dime, just to be able to say that he'd picked up the crates and left them at the broadcast center. He reflected that, if they belonged to Austen Trotta, sooner or later, someone would come for them, and if he left them here and something happened, if even one of the crates disappeared, it would be his head. Archeological fragments sounded like money to him.

"Where from, did you say?" he asked.

She cocked an eyebrow, thinking. She led him back inside. Romania, it turned out, by way of Paris.

By seven, back at the offices of *The Hour,* the first of the inhabitants had shown up, and the night shift security guard had taken his leave. The night before, an editor, Julia Barnes, had stayed until well after midnight, assembling images to match the words of a producer, Sally Benchborn, who also stayed and was helped in making additional last-minute script changes by an associate producer, who sat by her side in her office with its view of the hole where the Twin Towers had been, and watched the ebb and flow of taillights and headlights on the lower reaches of the West Side Highway—a depressing sight, the AP thought, with implications for his own life. The last bits of the script refused to come together. By one A.M., they felt exhausted and defeated by a single line, something that seemed innocuous but had to be both accurate and clear. In the morning, our chosen morning of January 16, their correspondent, Sam Dambles, the show's beloved black correspondent, would read these lines in the sound booth, and there would be no going back. They had snapped at each other, apologized to each other and called it a night, leaving Julia Barnes to finish the pictures by herself in the humming emptiness of the twentieth floor.

Mrs. Barnes got home at one and had a troubled sleep filled with terrible dreams in which she assembled a bomb in the basement of a building and woke up just before it went off in her fingers. She was back in the office by eight. It was still early, but she saw three people, besides the security guard, Menard Griffiths, and was comforted—she no longer liked to be on the floor alone, even if she knew her fears to be ridiculous. Dreadful Miggison was there, scanning expense reports, overseeing the flow of videotape into the vault, monitoring the current of audiotape to the transcription service, sheathed like a knife in his starched shirt, pressed slacks and figgish skin. Miggison handed out editing assignments, and he knew that she was due soon for a screening, which meant, if the screening went well, she would be available soon for another producer.

"Julia!" he called from his office near reception. She had tried to avoid him, but his eyes were keen. She lingered at the door of Miggison's office.

"You got a screening today, right?" He never put his hands on the top of the desk. They remained unpleasantly hidden, she thought.

"It's not official, but probably."

"I'm only asking because Austen's new producer was inquiring about you. Austen wants you for his next story."

She shrugged. "Depends on the screening."

She saw there was more. Miggison had something on his mind. He actually stood and gestured for her to close the door.

"Lemme ask you something," he said. She had never merited or wanted to merit the status of confidante to Claude Miggison. And she had come to despise surprises. But he could hurt her, if he wanted, so she obeyed and closed the door behind her.

"I just got the damndest call from traffic."

The editor experienced a wave of unhappy déjà vu.

"It's really not my business, Claude."

"I'm just askin'. Can you spare me a second? Jesus."

She took a seat on the chair in front of his desk.

"So I get this call from traffic, saying they have three large crates, just picked up from the airport, addressed to Austen Trotta."

She could feel the rise of the old terror.

"Did you call Austen?"

"Hell no, I didn't call Austen. It's not my job to call Austen. I told traffic I didn't know why they were callin' me. Nobody told me a thing about it."

"But if it's tape, Claude."

At those words, his elbows snapped, his arms came up in formation, both raised like soldiers, side by side, his hands balled into fists. "That's the point, Julia. That's the point. It's not tape. Get this. Traffic told me that the manifest lists the stuff as archeological fragments. All together, the crates weigh more than the goddamn staff of the show."

The cold came into her fingers again. That hadn't happened in months. She twined her fingers together, rubbing them.

"Why are you telling me? I don't know anything about it."

Miggison crossed his arms and returned to his seat.

"I'm telling you because you were the one who blew the whistle on the abuse of those tapes a few months back."

She got up. She wouldn't listen to another word. Her therapist had warned her about encounters that might deepen her stress and so shorten her life. She opened the door, despising Miggison for his propensity for bearing bad news. But when it came to it, she couldn't just walk away. She had to know.

"What do the crates have to do with the tapes, Claude? Just out of curiosity."

"Romania."

"What about Romania?"

Miggison grimaced, his default facial expression. "That's what I've been trying to tell you. The goddamn crates came from Romania. Just like the tapes."

"Call the police right now." His jaw dropped in shocked irritation. He regretted saying a word, but she insisted. "Do not allow those crates in this building. I'm telling you, Claude."

"Get outta here."

"Don't get-outta-here me. You asked. I'm telling you. It's completely suspect. There is no way that Austen Trotta knows anything about a ton of archeological fragments shipped here from Romania. You call the police right now. Tell them you have a suspicious delivery."

Miggison shook his head. "All I know is Trotta's an art collector, and nobody told me a goddamn thing about it, as usual, and I'm not doing anything so crazy as calling the cops."

"It's your ass then."

This was an incendiary remark.

"The fuck!"

No one at *The Hour* had a better understanding of the exact perimeter of responsibility than Claude Miggison. He knew to the tiniest fraction of difference what could be expected of him and what could not, and if anyone crossed the line, he immediately fired warning shots. He scattered e-mails to all and sundry and grew choleric, bursting into epithets.

"Fuck it. Maybe I will call Austen."

"Maybe you should."

"Maybe I will."

The editor left him in a state of high alert, his fingers stabbing at the keyboard of the computer, his head entwined with the telephone receiver.

By nine, the twentieth floor reverberated with life. Crews had rolled their equipment into the reception area and begun to set up for an interview in the so-called Universal Room, where the vast majority of *The Hour*'s famed filmed encounters took place, a square, sterile, soundproofed space that could be turned into an infinite variety of locales, mostly offices, with the addition of a few assorted props or backdrops. The best of the camera crews made an art of transforming the universal room into something unique every single time. Others merely tossed the same venerable lamps, paintings, books and vases at the problem until the room in the camera lens behind the subject came to present a reasonably coherent fiction.

It would be wrong not to sing the praises of *The Hour* crews here. They put up with an inhuman amount of pressure and expectation but were never allowed much creative leeway. *The Hour* expected its technical people to grasp with absolute precision the strict dogma of the place. There would be no allowance for fancy lighting or camera moves. There would be a particular kind of framing for the interviews, and a very specific quality of light. If I have to find the right word, I suppose *elegance* might come to mind. There should be elegance without showiness. Bob Rogers despised showiness. He despised a backdrop or a camera move or a bit of scenery that drew too much attention to itself. He wanted the face and the voice of the interview subject to exist at the white-burning heart of every segment, and if a bit of fancy footwork showed up in one of his screenings, he became irate. He'd rant at the producer and insist that the crew who shot the offending moment be given a warning. No one ever made the same mistake twice. Few made it once. Everyone knew the line. The indoctrination slept in the walls, simmered in the soup, so to speak.

On our January morning, Bob came by the universal room and poked his head inside. The elder statesman of the staff crews, Buddy Gomez, nodded to him.

"Mr. Rogers."

"Hey, Buddy. This for the Dambles interview?"

"You got it."

"Great. Can't wait to see that piece."

Gomez gave him an indulgent smile. The two men had known each other for three decades.

"Take care."

"You take care, Bob."

Rogers went on his energetic way, Gomez shook his head. The man was in his eighties. You'd think he'd be bored by the whole affair— Gomez was. But boredom was the least of Gomez's problems. He'd begun hearing things, the names of places in Asia where he had shot footage, the graves, the executions, a ceaseless murmur in the back of his brain, so bad that he had entertained blowing his brains out with a service pistol stolen off a dead GI more than three decades before.

But Rogers would not have understood that, or the boredom. Rogers hadn't constructed a life in which boredom or regret were even possible. Boredom, it may be said, terrified Rogers far more than death, and if death scared him, his fear hinged on the prospect of an eternity without lights, camera and action. That spirit was the engine of all things at the show. Even in his later years, Rogers moved at a tempo that alarmed and amazed the twentysomethings in the halls, who, on their best days, never attained the inherent, generous ferocity of the show's founder. Rogers made the baby boomers look like octogenarians.

On our January 16, covered in snow, Bob Rogers strode onto the twentieth floor of the West Street building at seven A.M., not too long after Claude Miggison. He had walked eighty blocks from his doorman building on the Upper East Side and showed no irritation at the weather. On the contrary, he seemed invigorated. As usual, on those mornings, he liked to chat with miserable old Miggison about what had come in, what was expected, what had failed to arrive. Rogers felt bound to Miggison. Though they could never have been called friends, they'd braced the walls together. They'd seen network heads rise to unvarying decapitation and thump back down into oblivion. They'd seen the ratings soar and slide. The scandals, disasters and sexual harassment suits had washed over them. They'd known the same people, been to the same funerals, though rarely to the same weddings. In sum, Miggison had been with Rogers from the beginning, and so the encounters with him, however trivial, echoed with deep memory.

Those memories did not engender trust. In their conversation that morning, Miggison hid his consternation. Everything's fine, Bob. Everything's great. Right on schedule, right on time, nothing unusual, he responded to each and every question, flavoring each word with a tolerant condescension. He appreciated the bond Rogers had with him, and confidently manipulated it, but he also innately mistrusted the man and knew that if he stepped wrong, Rogers would watch him hurtle into the fire with a lab technician's detachment. This knowledge guided his decision that morning. Miggison knew if he involved Rogers in the crate business, if he uttered a word about Romania or archeological fragments, the thing would take on a life of its own, and he would be in the thick. Before he knew a single detail, Rogers might call Trotta at home and yell at him that Miggison just got a call from traffic about some expensive artwork and what the hell was he doing shipping his personal property on company expense. Trotta would then call Miggison and ream him out for telling tales out of school. It was a hellish existence on the floor, and Miggison dreamed often of boats on golden horizons setting sail for warm, southerly havens. Like Trotta, he considered himself an artist in his soul.

Rogers left Miggison's office none the wiser.

Another caste made its appearance around 9 A.M., the most downtrodden and yet most hopeful and most inspiring, the production assistants, who had no power except their own resilience, ambition and enthusiasm. They didn't have to fetch coffee for people, but their jobs offered similar rewards and satisfactions. They fetched tape. They sniffed out licensing arrangements. They worked weekends. At no point could they deny a request. And, if possible, they should accept their charges with lightness and joy. Gloominess was never appreciated. The producers had glum spouses and children at home. They didn't need attitude from the lower orders. And the PAs mostly accommodated them. If a producer wanted tape in an upbeat minute, the PA had to drop everything and dart. If an associate producer needed research materials from a local bookstore, out scuttled the PA, rain or shine.

Stimson Beevers was the endangered exception. He saw when the producers came to work, around 10 A.M. He registered the fact that associate producers dumped their afterbirth on people like himself. He knew that he was exploited and abused by people who made a lot more money and tried a lot less hard. He knew, and he fumed, and he waited. He had been to the Breadloaf Conference and knew published poets. After college, when he'd lived in Paris, he'd gone to a Robert Aldrich film retrospective in northern France with German intellectuals who knew Quentin Tarantino personally. During the summers, and even on some Christmas breaks, he didn't head for a beach. His friends in the literary world helped him to a spot in a writing colony, or his pals in the theater world got him a job doing extra work in Williamstown. By the time he was fifteen, he personally knew most of the members of the Butthole Surfers. By his own standards, and who is to say he was wrong in such a subjective matter, he was a thousand times cooler than anyone around him, and he deserved whatever recompense he could manufacture.

For half a year, he had been entering the office after Miggison (who was always snooping) but before the other PAs, roughly at 8 A.M. He would buy his coffee on the street, slink onto the floor, nod quickly at the security guard and make his way by circuitous routes, meaning out of sight of Miggison, to his cubicle. At eight in the morning, no one bothered him about tape, and he could have his long conversations with someone whom he presumed to be his friend, Evangeline Harker, who had informed him that her job had been, in fact, a long-term infiltration of the Eastern European mafia, an effort that would lead to one of the biggest stories of the new century. Now it was done, and she was return-ing to New York. He believed her story. He wanted to believe it. Their exchanges proceeded in ecstatic quiet. He told her everything she wanted to know. She wrote imperious responses. He invited her to come to his apartment, though he had a roommate. She was evasive. She told him she wanted to meet him in the office late one night, to avoid the others, to avoid questions about her fiancé. She told him her "evidence" for the story would be arriving first, by air, and he must take care of it. He said he understood. The voice was in his head, whispering, and he wanted it to go deeper, into his heart and guts. He invited her to come to him late at night, in the office, and he would give her every-thing that she desired.

It's impossible to say at what exact moment the rhythms at *The Hour* go from the slightly sleepy to the relentless. That moment of chemical change is elusive, but it's unmistakable. By ten, most mornings, crews have arrived, editors have turned on their computers, producers have leafed through their papers and had their coffee, all but one of the correspondents (and he's the night owl) are either away on a story or have arrived for the day. The executive staff, Bob's deputies, filter into their offices to prepare for screenings. The first of those begins between ten and eleven, and from that moment, another atmosphere prevails on the hall. Producers wait to hear how their colleagues have done, ready with a commiserating story of their own, some of them rejoicing if the news is bad, others truly stricken at another tale of devastation that might soon come their way. Schadenfreude rustles in the corridors. The pages of newspapers flutter and hush, as everyone searches for their next story, grazing like a herd of choice livestock on the printed work of others. There are screams of obscenity, a male voice. Some look up. One of the more theatrical producers is screaming at someone on the other end of a telephone line. "Are you a child? Or are you a child molester? I don't fucking believe this! I won't fucking believe it! We've already sent the crew, and now you change your fucking mind!? If you are a child molester, I will personally see you hounded out of every city in this country! Sure you want to fuck with me?" This was not atypical.

The first screening of the morning belongs to none other than Austen Trotta, in this humble ex-producer's opinion one of the most gifted of the people ever to work in American broadcast, a master of the art of broadcast television news. Trotta's star is on the ascent again, after the screening and airing of a widely acclaimed story, a "classic" about a death row inmate in Texas, a well-known Uighur folk musician accused by China of terrorism, convicted in the United States of murdering two people in a failed bank robbery attempt. A new producer has replaced the old. A new associate producer has replaced Evangeline Harker. The past is receding. Trotta's back problems have improved.

In the screening room, Bob Rogers gets a copy of the script and reads half of it before the lights go down. It's a story about a murdered evangelical Christian lap dancer. Austen Trotta fumes, and when the lights come up, and Rogers suggests a minor change, Trotta explodes. "For fuck's sake, Bob! You didn't even watch the piece!" It's an old bit of melodrama. I saw it myself years ago. Rogers fights a little further for the sake of principle. Trotta waits for the formalities to recede. In his heart, he's overjoyed. This time, he's succeeded. The piece will air. He will hit his number. Trotta's outrage simmers down, and Rogers declares the good news, "I gotta tell you. I never thought this goddamn thing would air, but you guys did a great job. Who knew? Jesus loves strippers?" There is great relief. By lunch, Trotta is dining on sand dabs in grape sauce at a local restaurant, telling amusing stories about how he survived the crusade of the fleshpots, as he calls it. Other screenings come and go and are less sublime.

Despite the weather, there are interviews in the Universal Room with a whistleblower from the Department of Health and Human Services, three cancer patients suing a hospital chain and a lawyer. The crews break down and set up, shift the lights, watch the faces, measure the silences. Room tone rises up to meet them. Along the corridors, the production assistants dart and duck. In their hands, the tape circulates like blood throughout the enterprise. The editors press their buttons, scrubbing, cutting, recutting, the cacophony of their labor rising in bizarre noises from the dark back hallways, the blips, blurts, hisses and jolts of sound that arise when the human voice gets ripped apart by machines, voices transformed from a conversation between two people into a series of mutilated moments that can be twisted, baked and sautéed until the tension pops and the meaning fries. It isn't a matter of falsifying the meanings. It's the skill of falsifying the moments themselves, so that the tedium of Homo sapiens interaction fades away in an act of steady massage and becomes taut as the abdomen of an athlete. It's a thing of beauty, and most fans of The Hour have no idea. The ums and ahs and repetitions fall away, and we become who we want to be. We lose our awkwardness and become decisive. We annihilate our ape past.

But the snow keeps coming, and commuters from New Jersey, Connecticut and Westchester eye the skies. Their families wait at home, hunkering down. Producer, editor, correspondent, assistant—they all want to get away. Lunch is over, but there are two more screenings, and one more interview, and three crates from Romania still to be delivered from across the street. Storms make people a little giddy, but more anxiety than usual is in the air. One of the afflicted editors, Remschneider, has started to tell his neighbors that something bad is coming. It's no joke, he says, thinking of his own nightmares. Julia Barnes hears these words and resolves to get the hell out of the office before the man snaps. She's heard rumors that a fourth editor has fallen ill with the wasting disease. She's on the elevator, pressing a button, when the first of the city's two great blackouts strikes. A relay station in Canada shorts out, overloaded currents ride the networks, the lights in New York City go out, the computers on the twentieth floor die and up and down the halls runs a shiver of dread, as if a guest long expected had finally arrived.

BOOK

The Shipment

Thirty-two

E: Wow. That was scary. Right in the middle of our conversation, my hard drive crashed, or so I thought. Then I heard someone running, and I realized the lights had gone out. The silence was intense. It brought everything back, if you know what I mean, that horrible September day. I was in a state of panic, but you glided from door to door, snatching everyone you knew away from telephone calls, computer screens, video monitors. You issued orders. You moved people into stairwells. You got Ian; you got Julia; you got me. You walked us to the fire exits. Very impressive. Only when we got outside did you seem to realize the nature of the situation. Only then did you put your hands to your face, but then we had to run for it. Do you remember? Anyway, now you and Ian are gone, and when the lights went out, that moment rushed into my head all at once. It was like time travel. But it was only a blackout, thank Hawks. Very quickly, the halls became cold. The building managers tend to keep the heat to a minimum anyway, to save money, so the temperature plunged. The snow was falling beyond the windows, old television static, hiding the Hudson. Light went out everywhere, and your voice, your words, did, too.

"Come on, Stimson."

Someone had noticed me. I stared at the screen a little longer. Let them go, I thought. Let them dissolve like ghosts in the general anarchy. I didn't care to leave you. You had just given me the last details about your boxes of evidence. Before I ran out, which I did, forgive me, I picked up the phone, still working, and called traffic to find out the specifics of delivery. I knew that I should have an answer for you. To tell you the truth, given your new confidence in me, I was a little afraid that I might let you down. But there was nothing to be done. I got out.

In any case, the upshot of this long-winded message is this. The terror of the moment cleared my head a bit, and I do have a few questions for you about the delivery. I have lots of questions, as a matter of fact, and can't believe I haven't put them to you before. So let me know you're okay, you're still with me, and we can discuss. Yours, The Over-Stim

Stimson, I am sorry to hear of your fear in the blackout. That horrible day stays with all of us. It haunts us, moves us. Do not be shy about saying so. I, for myself, do not believe we appreciate the day enough, do not believe we heed the dead enough. I believe we have become immune to their immense power. The time comes, I hope, when I can give you courage in the darkness and whisper comfort into your ears and calm your night terrors. You are doing a wonderful job, of course, and we have discussed everything, and you are full of anticipation, as am I, but you must wait a few hours longer and do a few more things for me, and then it will all be settled, and I will answer every question that you have. But I have to be honest with you about something. When you write to me as you did in that last message, I get the feeling that we've had a misunderstanding. You've made serious promises to me, and as you may recall, I am a woman who expects promises to be kept, and especially now. I will answer your questions, but those questions should never prevent you from meeting your obligations. Are we arrived at a proper understanding? E.

E: You have to understand. I live alone with these questions. Everyone else thinks you're dead. Everyone else puts you in the same category as Ian. They've moved on. The waters have closed over you. Why have I been the exception? What did I do to deserve such grace? Was it really necessary for you to go under such deep cover? Can any story be worth such sacrifice? I do ask myself these questions, but your sense of clear conviction suffices. I am persuaded. And yet doubt gnaws at me. Things have changed since you left. This place was always a blasted heath of horror, a Lovecraftian feast of monstrosities, and yet somehow it's getting worse. Those editors are still sick, for instance, the ones I told you about, and no one, no doctor, seems to be able to diagnose their maladies. Want to hear something even more disturbing? Remschneider, in particular, comes and stares at me for minutes at a time, and I think I hear his voice in my head, and I could swear he knows, E, he knows and is waiting for me to speak the words in my mind aloud. Remschneider stares out of those sunken sockets—and I mean, the guy is CGI awful in appearance—and comes out with non sequiturs about atrocity, Treblinka, Lubyanka, Uitenhage, Wounded Knee, Bad Axe, Mecca, Medina, Masada, not even whole sentences, just names or phrases. It's like that Johnny Cash song where he sings the names of towns, "I been to Reno, Chicago," what's it called, "I've Been Everywhere." What's even more unbearably weird, when Remschneider mutters, I seem to know what he's going to say, like I've had the same thought in my head, waiting for articulation, but not quite ripe enough to suck through my lips. Like the other day, this phrase pops into my brain, a raft of syllables, like Ore-Ida-Door-Sewer-Gland. It could have been gibberish, but it didn't feel that way. So I look up and nearly jump out of my seat. There stands Remschneider, in the shadows, crazy long beard and burning eyes, and out of his soiled mouth come those same syllables: "Ore-Ida-Door-Sewer-Gland." He was like a zombie. He shambled away, and then I tried to Google the words by phonetically spelling them out. The search engine patronized me. Do you mean Ore Ida potatoes? Later, I got it. Oradour sur Glan, World War II, the Germans burned an entire French village in a reprisal. Another atrocity.

There is one other thing, very unfortunate and disturbing, though of no real concern to you. When we returned to the office after the blackout, yesterday, we all had a shock. One of the editors, Clete Varney, an older man who hadn't been sick at all, was found dead in his office, a horrific mess. He'd slit his wrists, but he hadn't left his chair. He was facing the computer screen when Julia Barnes discovered him. I peeked in before the cops came. Someone had spun the chair around. Varney's eyes were wide open, and his blood was everywhere. I thought of Remschneider. Remschneider's office is the next one over. His door was shut.

Anyway, hope you have no doubt. I am yours. You've given me such purpose. Do you know I've lost interest in movies? Now I think only of you. Our project has become the one and only movie, and I'm the one and only spectator, waiting in the darkness of the theater for the screen to blaze. Have we arrived at a proper understanding, as you so bizarrely put it? Your good soldier, the Over-Stim.

Stimson, I am a little anxious that someone who has no knowledge of my assignment might be reading our e-mails. Are you absolutely sure that we have privacy?

E: Nothing is absolute, but I've disguised your tracks pretty well. I had your e-mails sent to my private e-mail account and then forwarded to me, so that it looks like I'm e-mailing myself back and forth. If anyone asks, which they won't, I'll just say that I'm sending documents and streaming video home for work reasons. Sound okay?

Stimson: *C'est parfait.* More favors before we meet? First, please, tell me about the disposition of my evidence. It would put my mind at ease to know these belongings were safe.

E: I meant to tell you. I got your "belongings" from across the street without making an ungodly fuss, as I know you would have wanted. It might not have been the best idea to ship them care of Austen Trotta— that drew attention—but what's done is done, and I managed to make arrangements without Austen's knowledge, and he has no idea that he has received the three crates. Miggison is a little suspicious, but who cares? He's nobody. Not to be immodest, but it was a clever feat. On the morning of the blackout, I overheard Claude Miggison complain to Bob Rogers about some godawful phone call from traffic relating to Austen Trotta, and I knew what it must be, and so I interceded as soon as possi- ble, before Miggison could contact Austen and make a mess of things. You can imagine the craven relief on the man's face. I've always said Miggison was a human silencer, but always in his master's pocket, and if possible, he should be kept there. I told him I knew about the shipment

and would deal with it. The man was grateful. The day after the blackout, I called traffic, and yelled and screamed like I was one of the big bad
bullies, and they assured me it was fine, that the deliveries were quite
large, and they wanted to know when and where the crates should be
handed off. There was even an offer to deliver to Austen's house,
averted, thank God; I played on their own awe at the size of the shipment
and made clear that it was too big to be brought to the twentieth floor
during work hours. Don't laugh, but I suggested the crates must arrive
late at night, under my supervision, so the delicate rhythms of the office
would not be damaged, and traffic bought it. The crates were far too big
for the regular passenger elevators, so around midnight, three burly
guys from the broadcast center hauled them up to the twentieth floor via
the freight elevator. I felt for them. Their eyes bulged with strain and
nerves. They were spooked. One swore that he heard movement inside
the crates. He asked me if Austen collected birds or other animals, and
I made an effort to redirect his suspicions by pointing out that the crates
didn't, in fact, belong to Trotta, but were property of the show for the
purposes of a segment related to a European government's activities in
Africa, classified activities, and therefore knowledge of contents was re-
stricted to a few people. Those guys aren't brain surgeons, so it didn't
take much to convince them, and besides, they wanted to get off the
floor as quickly as possible. There is superstition about our workplace
among the rank and file of the network, it turns out. The men rolled the
crates on dollies to the one place on the floor where they might escape
notice, a kind of dead zone between the producer suites and the editing
bays, that back corridor where the light is dim. You know where I mean?
Gropers Lane, the old-timers call it. And there your crates sit. The corridor is wide, so they don't block the way, in case anyone passes by, but
few people use the passage because it's easier simply to walk through
editing, and nothing else is back there. Your "belongings" are safe. Now,
may I ask, as your completely trustworthy and devoted adjutant, as your
slave addressing his mistress, what exactly are we talking about here?
To be honest, after the broadcast center guys dashed away, I put my ear
to one of the crates and couldn't be sure, but thought I heard something,
a scratching or a gnawing. Is it possible that rats got into the shipment?

Stimson. It is time to meet. I am here, in the city. No more e-mails. How do you like the sound of that?

E: Radiant with joy!

Stimson: Alas, I have one last request, the most difficult and painful of all. After this, we can finally start the real work on our project, but this one last item must be checked off the list.

E: Name it.

Stimson: Invite my intended to come to the twentieth floor.

E: Are you talking about your fiancé, Robert?

Yes.

E: May I ask why?

Stimson: I must see Robert. This may hurt you, and for that, I am sorry. I've never made any secret of the fact that ours is to be a work relationship only. However, if you bring him to me, you may be happily surprised at the outcome.

E: All due respect, but can't you conduct this particular business yourself? If you don't mind my saying so, it strikes me as a violation of the "work" relationship, having me contact the other man in your life.

Stimson: I know this man. He requires personal handling under very distinct circumstances. You must ask him to meet you on the twentieth floor around the same time that you so cleverly arranged the delivery of the crates. Think of Robert as the last of those deliveries. Bring him to the back corridor, where I will be waiting to break the news to him about our future. I ask you this in the full knowledge that I am weak. I am a woman and cannot bear the strain of doing this by myself. I need your help, Stimson. You understand. Before we can proceed, hand in hand, this matter has to be finished.

Jesus, Evangeline. What in the world do I tell him? I'm very uncomfortable.

E: Where'd you go? Please don't stop talking to me. Please don't take away your voice. It's been a day, and nothingness, filling my mind, the sucking void. It's like I've lost my memory, senses, desire. The producers scream at me to find their tape, but I don't know what they mean. What is tape? I freeze at this screen. I sit here through the night. I hear the sounds in the back corridor. I'll do whatever you want.

Stimson: I have taken unspeakable risks. Do you know what it is like to try to enter this country without alerting my own family that I have returned? Do you know what unfathomable routes I have taken? I am ready to open myself up to you, to share the fruits of my labor, and yet you deny me the chance to put my last obligations behind me. Why should I bestow my favors? There are other young men who would be perfectly happy to suffer my burden.

E: It's not good. I called him at work. He freaked out. He threatened me with violence. He said he would call the FBI. I'm scared to death. I had to tell him a huge lie or he would never have complied with such an outlandish request. I had to tell him that there was someone he had to meet, someone who knew about you. I had to tell him that you might be alive. I said the informant came through very discreet channels related to former communist intelligence contacts—dead networks in former Eastern Bloc countries. It sounded so fraudulent, but he's desperate, thank God. And he's a pastry chef. I feel terrible. I don't understand. What a shock to his system this will be. But I understand. You have your ways. It's set for tonight, two A.M., later than the crate delivery, because Menard, the security guard, doesn't go on break till then. I'll be there, too. Are you sure about this? Is this the right way? Is this the decent thing?

Stimson: Calm down. Attend a motion picture. I will see you tonight.

234 • JOHN MARKS

E: Holy shit. Strange and alarming news. Could you clarify? I wouldn't ask if it weren't so extraordinary. There is a rumor, divulged to me just now by Julia Barnes, who heard it straight from Austen Trotta, that you have been found, that you are alive, that you have been recovering from an undisclosed trauma in a monastery in northern Romania. She had her doubts. She was a little giddy with the possibility. The whole affair has taken a great toll. I smiled, of course, knowing it can't be true, knowing it must be someone else. And when Julia said to me, "Jesus, Stim, you look terrible," I realized that she must be playing tricks on me, trying to make me feel like a wretch, I turned my back on her, an exquisite moment of victory, and yet, still, may I ask, is it possible? Are you really coming to me tonight? You wouldn't be so wicked, would you? To lie to me about something like this? About everything? Would you, Evangeline?

BO OK

*The Resurrection
and the Life*

Thirty-three

Word comes from Romania that a girl has been found, a rumor unsubstantiated, but beyond mere gossip. I'm a wreck. I'm smoking. I'm back to a bottle of red wine an evening. My God, if it's true, I don't want to think about her condition. She'll make a religious Jew of me. I would fly to Bucharest tonight, but for Evangeline's father's draconian edict. In communicating the news by e-mail, he reiterated the injunction that no one at The Hour *should be involved and stated bluntly that his daughter will never work for the program again. I wonder how she will feel on the subject.*

If it's true, I should go, despite the father. Or should I stay? Will she want to see me? To have this terrible weight off me, I would give anything, do anything. But I despise the wild hope in my veins, too. Wild hope always dies a horrible death. It's a kind of suicide of the mind. But I shouldn't think that. The hunger for rescue unmans me. Some Romanian government official, working on the case for months, brings Harker Senior the information that a woman fitting a rough description has been found in a clinic attached to a monastery in the Bukovina region in the northern part of the country, one of the famous painted monasteries, he informs us, but she can't remember much about herself and has no identification and won't leave the place under any circumstances. It's anything but a certainty, and if this other news, this terrible coincidence, hadn't come, I would have more composure, but that's not the way life will be for me. There will be no settling back into a long, glorious autumn of retirement. There will be a climb to the lip of the volcano and a long dive. Empedocles in broadcast.

I got the call from Rogers, who first asked me if I knew about some crates in the back corridor, addressed to me; I told him I did not, and he crowed about a network plot. The crates had been placed there, he maintains, by the network, and were, in fact, listening devices wired to the entire floor, though he refuses to have them removed, he says, because he won't foot a dime of his budget on enemy equipment, not even to have it dismantled. He has signaled the network that he knows, and moreover, he adds, as if it were of secondary significance, he is also aware of the plot to kill the fiancé on the twentieth floor, Evangeline's fiancé, who had ostensibly attempted to kill himself by cutting open his own wrists, the second such macabre attempt in a week. This one, thank heaven, did not succeed. Menard Griffiths found him here, on the twentieth floor, in Evangeline's old office, drained of so much blood that he was almost dead. Rogers says it is clearly one more element in the network campaign, though, he concedes, an extreme one.

I'm frankly speechless at the news. I'm squeamish in the extreme, too. In Vietnam, I stayed the hell away from military hospitals. But I must get over it. I must see this boy, as atonement. I must. I almost wish the woman in Romania was a doppelgänger. If it is Evangeline, how in the hell will she manage this new development? Who will console her? If she has any wits left at all, she will blame herself.

What in God's name possessed this boy to try to take his own life at the very moment of reprieve? And why here? It's a lot of trouble and so odd as to be suspicious. But I'm an old, tired, rage-racked human, full of suspicion and indignation. Nothing in this world gives light anymore. Darkness pours down like rain.

FEBRUARY 3

Prince came to bother me. He wanted information. He's a ham-fisted wheedler in person, just as he is onscreen, but I have the advantage of being neither under federal investigation nor impressed by celebrity. Still he managed to goad me.

He put on a cross-examination, as if we had just been having a conversation, which we had not. "What you're not telling me is she's been found. Correct?"

"You're in the midst of a dialogue, I see. Shall I join you?"

He folded his arms over his chest, pouting, and moved closer.

"She has, hasn't she?"

"Who?"

"You know damn well."

"Amelia Earhart."

He blew out a steam of petulance. "Fuck you, you cancerous, withered old fart."

I laughed at him. He didn't leave.

People often ask me whether I like Edward Prince. But I always reply that it's the wrong question. Instead, I say, one should ask if anyone, at all, anywhere, really likes Edward Prince. He's the face of our broadcast for millions, no question, and yet he's a nonsensical being. Why don't people understand? He appears no more frequently on cameras than the rest of us, but he has become more indelible, attracting the spotlight in ways that I could never countenance, exposing his personal traumas, his local failures, to the audience. The man is repugnantly candid, generally speaking, but his candor comes only on camera. It's hard to imagine him confessing a word to the privacy of his mirror or a priest. There's no inducement. His god is out there beyond the screen and needs feeding. Do I like him? Looking at his face as it was a few minutes ago, older than mine, far more tailored and tucked, it's easy to give the expected answer. Christ, no.

After stewing amusingly a few seconds, he redoubled his efforts. "Evangeline Harker, I mean. Has she been found?"

If I tell Prince, I tell the world. It's that simple. The man has no inner life with which to fend off the temptation to publicize. I confronted him. "You'll blab, Ed."

A wounded glee struck his face. This was a precursor to surrender, he knew. "Never."

If I tell Prince, the story will land on the cover of the Post by morning. By next evening, all of broadcast will be onto the story, and if Evangeline doesn't turn up, this whole damn business is revived, just when we'd reached quiet waters, just when people seemed to have forgotten. And that doesn't touch the matter of the fiancé, whom Prince has somehow bypassed.

He became triumphantly sneaky. He leaned on the edge of my desk, and there was a lascivious quality to it. "Tell me what you know, and I'll tell you something big, too."

He triumphed. My weakness lay before him, as always. He got better gossip, always had. Against the last shards of my better judgment, I told him everything. He grinned, ear to ear, and I had that bizarre sensation, common in exchanges with him, that the man had been thinking along far different and more limited lines than I had ever imagined. A soap-bubbly twinkle came into his eye.

"My secret's bigger," he purred.

And there it was, what I have always liked—no loved—about Edward Prince. The man is naïve like a child when it comes to his own pet hopes and fears. He's not a guileful fellow, like so many in our line, and his self-absorption can have the charm of a small child's first interest in his own shadow. He didn't give a rat's ass about the girl. He just wanted to be in the know. It wasn't coldness or indifference. Prince sat next to the only source of light in a great darkness, and leaving this little fire wouldn't just be gratuitous; it would be fatal.

"I will hear your secret," I told him, "but only on one condition."

"Name it."

"You don't breathe a word of this Harker story till we get a confirmation. If this breaks, and the story's false, you know what happens."

He gave me a stern moral look. "A goat-fucking."

"We understand each other. What's your enormous secret? And it better not be a Cloris Leachman profile."

"You wish." His faux somberness lofted into a contrivance of high spirit. "Dear man, I've landed the godfather of Eastern Europe."

It's not often in life that truth blasts fat as a sunrise into your brain. Usually, if I can lay claim to insight, it comes in tablet form, at the end of a long and sleepless night, like the drug that finally puts me out. I'm too set in my ways, too settled in my opinions, a disposition from childhood, when my mother would tell me before school that I would have a good day, and I would *snap back that she had no idea what kind of day I would have. But here I saw it—the grand armature of a design, and it scared the unholy shit out of me.*

"What did you say?"

"You heard me. The godfather of Eastern Europe. That's what we're calling the story."

I knew in that instant that Evangeline Harker had survived. She would be found alive. And, depending on her condition, which must be dire, she would eventually return to this office to discover that the initial object of her trip had been interviewed by the most respected name in broadcast journalism. What did it mean? The blood must have gone out of my face.

"Jealous, you old Jew?"

"Is the man here?" I stammered.

"Who?"

"Your interview."

Prince took a seat on my couch, resting an elbow on a heap of rubbishy overseas newspapers.

"I know what you're thinking, Trotta, and you can forget it. He has nothing to do with your mess, and I can prove it. There's no chance you're going to derail me, much as you'd like to."

There was no time for the usual peevish competition between nothings. "What's his surname, Ed? It wouldn't be Torgu?"

Prince gave a nod of concession. "He contacted me personally." *He paused, staring at the nicotine stains in my carpet.* "Through an intermediary."

"What intermediary?"

Prince shrugged. "Need you know that?"

"All right. How did this intermediary reach you?"

Prince now balked. He knew he was up to no good. He knew everything smelled rotten, but didn't mind. His god had eaten his heart many years ago.

"Answer me, please," *I said.*

"It was a personal contact. Someone here in the office with connections to the former Soviet bloc." *He gave me a defiant chin thrust.* "And I might add that the context of my discussion with this gentleman was disappointment. Grave disappointment."

"What the hell does that mean?"

"I'll tell you what the hell it means. Your girl never showed up. He waited and waited, expecting a producer from The Hour *to arrive when expected. He was offended, if I may be honest."*

"Oh goddamn, Prince, does it ever strike you in the least bit suspicious, all this? The timing of it? The circumstances? Come on. You're a journalist. Or were. Does it strike you as more than a little odd that the so-called godfather of Eastern Europe shows up here and offers to do an interview months after the girl we sent to do the pre-interview vanished? Does it seem plausible at all that you might be the victim of a hoax, perpetrated by someone who knows enough about our situation to make an ass out of you?"

Prince gazed at me in bereavement. He got it. I felt sorry for him, but it needed to be done.

"For Christ's sake. How many godfathers of the underworld do you know who offer themselves up for interviews? If memory serves, these things only happen behind prison bars."

Prince's wave of doubt passed, and he stood up. "I've met the man. He's genuine. He's real." He snapped his fingers. "More real than you."

This confession sent a chill through me. "You met him."

"I did."

"Where?"

"Here."

"He's been to the offices? And you didn't alert anyone?"

Prince shook his head. "What are you raving about? Alert who? Menard Griffiths? Anyone else? I have a terrific story, Austen. Consider yourself alerted."

"When did this meeting take place?"

Prince put hands in his pockets. "After hours."

"You fucking blowhard and idiot—he might know something about Evangeline!"

Prince strolled to the door.

"Of course, you piss all over me. You've been doing it thirty years. Why stop now? But my dear Trotta, you should know that our man has been vetted, and he checks out. He's oil. He's guns. He's poppies and whores. And if you're concerned about his future activities, I predict he will go to prison

in the immediate aftermath of the interview. He wants to. Safest place for him."

This news did not mollify me at all. But I adopted a more solicitous tone. "One more question, if I may."

Prince swiveled away, to hide his wounded sense of triumph.

"Who did the legwork?"

"Which?"

"Who vetted this fellow, I mean?"

Prince acted nonchalant. "Who vetted him?"

"Come on, Ed. Verified his identity and such."

"I believe it was Stimson Beevers."

"That's your insurance policy? That little creep?"

"No, Austen, thank you. Thank you and thank you again for the most vicious response to an announcement of good news that I have ever experienced."

I required one last piece of information. "When will this interview take place?"

His eyes narrowed in rageful defiance. "Not a chance."

Prince is well on his way to ninety years old, but he waltzed away, moving like a parade ground officer at a Habsburg ball. The pain shot down my back, and I reeled backward into my chair, which rolled on its wheels against the bookcase. Peach rushed to me in alarm. I shooed her away and drew the curtains. Now I'm scribbling these notes as fast as I can. This is no longer a therapy journal. It's a war diary.

FEBRUARY 3, END OF THE DAY

There's a DNA match. It's our girl, but she's lost herself. Harker won't relay any more information, so I've got a State Department contact working on my behalf to get news out of the embassy in Bucharest. He says there's no evidence yet that she knows her own name or ever will again. He hints at further knowledge, but won't tell me over the phone. He says that the line might be bugged. I told him I thought those days were over, and he said he thought so, too, but it's something else. I asked him point blank what in hell happened to her, and all he said was, "We don't know."

FEBRUARY 4, 3 A.M.

I had the most awful dream. I need a session with you, Doctor. You say write down dreams so I'll remember them in the morning, but how could I possibly forget? But I'll write. Better than not sleeping for the next six hours. There were three parts to the dream. First, I woke up in a ditch, and it was early morning. I was wet, so I put my hands on my body, and they came away with blood. I realized that I'd been shot. I looked up, and just then, a body fell back on top of me, and everything went dark. Part two, I was the man falling back on the man in the ditch. I could feel objects punching into my shoulder, my leg, my stomach and neck. There was a cloud of smoke in front of me, and I fell back, light as a feather, on top of another man. Last, I was suddenly watching this man tumble backward, right in front of me, and my hands were warm, and there was a reek of gunpowder, and I looked down, I looked down, and there was a machine gun in my hands, and a voice behind me cried, "Nochmal!" And I saw it was the voice of a German officer in a gray uniform whom I recognized and respected, and I turned back as the next line of men filed into my vision, and they were naked Jews, and before I could think, my finger pressed the trigger again, and the Jews flew backward like birds. And then I woke, and when I looked down, I was holding my hard old cock in my hands. God help me. God, and my forefathers, forgive me.

FEBRUARY 4, 5:15 A.M.

I see it now. It's Prince who caused the nightmare. We had an extraordinary conversation shortly after his big interview. I didn't plan to speak with him at all, truth to tell. I ran into him in a back corridor. The whole thing smacks of Fate.

I ran into Prince because I had gone back to the sound booth to do some recording, where I'd had an unsettling experience. One of my older produc-

ers, Radney Plasskin, asked me to track a few lines on the Micronesian meds story. It's not one of Plasskin's great efforts, a solid B-minus, I would say. A few days earlier, we had tracked the main body of the piece, but it needed an additional shot of narrative Tabasco to give it at least the appearance of an investigative story. Plasskin has become a soft, round, hairless man, a dweller in the wide lanes of supersized suburban grocery stores, but there was a time, back when he was first hired, that his investigations sparked congressional hearings. To be fair to him, though, my problem wasn't the story.

Exhaustion came over me in the tracking booth, a swelling wave of lethargy. I had to stop. I put my hands together, closed my eyes and leaned forward on the podium. Plasskin and the sound engineer watched through the glass of the booth, and I could feel their annoyance at this delay. But they needed my voice. They had no choice but to wait. After a few seconds, I finished the lines, checked through the glass to make sure Plasskin had what he required—but his pink-rimmed eyes stared wide at me as if I'd read aloud gibberish. I exited the booth and discovered the reason for his unhelpful expression. The sound engineer had a technical issue. A distortion had begun to affect all the tracks on the floor, including mine, the one I'd just recorded, and though I didn't feel remotely like entering into a discussion about the more arcane aspects of our work, I made the mistake of pursuing the matter. I asked him if I should do it again, and the man shrugged, glanced at Plasskin and said it wouldn't make any damn difference. There had been a problem for at least twenty-four hours, he told me.

"Your track's useless, unless it can be cleaned up in the mix."

"What the hell is it?" I demanded to know, a little irate at being informed of the technicality after I'd gone to the effort of laying down track.

The engineer shrugged and gave me the kind of answer I despise. "In twenty years of broadcast, I've never seen or heard anything like it."

Plasskin rolled his eyes. He'd taken the shuttle back from Washington to hear this obfuscation. I asked the engineer to play the track back for me and he ran his fingers across the great board, and damned if I didn't hear something, and it made me furious. I asked him why he couldn't just wipe it clean, and he gave me attitude.

"So you do hear it? It's not just me."

"Of course I hear it."

"Sounds like someone whispering," Plasskin said, blinking.

"Thank you." The engineer then revealed that the problem was well known right at the top of the ladder. "Bob Rogers tells me it's an act of war. Do you believe it? He says it's network sabotage and to ignore it and work around it as best I can. Network is waiting till he cries uncle, and he won't. Too bad if the show goes down with him, hunh?"

"Do you mean to tell me that Bob wants nothing done about this?" I asked.

"He wants it to become such a huge problem that it embarrasses the network."

"Then he's truly losing it," I told him, "and we're in trouble."

The engineer told me the distortion had been audible on every track made in the last day, and try as he might, he couldn't expunge it from the system. Without Rogers's knowledge, audio fixers from the broadcast center came, and they had been stumped, too.

It wasn't just the obvious problem of airing pieces with contaminated sound. It was the white noise itself. I can't quite get it out of my head. It's almost as if a voice had been buried in the tape, singing a catchy tune just beyond the audible range of frequency. But it can't be a voice. Can't be a recording. Our raw tapes arrive blank. And even if a used batch did show up, the problem would be immediately identified, and the batch scrapped. But the engineer had done that already. He'd tossed out every tape in the original batch, ordered a new one, and found the same problem. It wasn't the tape. It was the system. Something had contaminated the system.

The distortion is in my head right now, and it was in my head in those moments after I left the tracking booth, right before I ran into Prince. And there was something strange about that, too, how I ran into the man. Leaving the sound booth, I intended to turn left to go back to my office and have a nap, but at that moment, at the far end of the main hall, I caught sight of Bob Rogers bounding out of the cantina and heading right for me, as if he had something on his mind. That's all I needed. I darted right instead, heading past the bathrooms, the usual site of a Rogers ambush, and into Gropers Lane, rounding the corner a bit too fast, losing balance and staggering right into Prince. I let out an undignified yelp of surprise, but Prince didn't move. He hardly seemed to notice me, the first unnerving aspect of the encounter.

He stood by himself beside a large wooden crate, his eyes fixed on stenciled words on one side. He might have been asleep, though his eyes were open. I tapped him on the shoulder and said, "Excuse me, chum, I need to get by."

Then he spoke.

"These belong to you." It was an uncharacteristic tone of voice, low and ominous.

And I had no idea what he meant. Prince is a foot taller than me and likes to loom, when he can get close enough. So I wasn't surprised when he crowded me, underlining my smallness. His eyes gazed down into mine, and I experienced dismay. The irises were seamed with wires of red. Christ, I thought, he's either had the greatest interview in his career, or he's just had an encounter that frightened him to death.

"He sent them to you," he said in that same tone of voice, completely unlike him.

"Who did?"

Prince didn't clarify. I noticed the objects to which he referred for the first time then, really noticed them, and they were unremarkable. Someone was constantly stashing detritus back in Gropers Lane. The corridor had an ill repute, like the one deserted street in an otherwise prosperous town, and so it was used as a kind of a bin for items not quite ready for their final disposition. Anything placed there warranted the most intense denial of awareness or responsibility.

"Are you all right, Ed?"

"The bugger made me an offer," he said.

I still hear those words. They become more disturbing by the minute. "What offer?" I ask him, but there was no answer.

It would be an outright lie to suggest that my immediate thought was for his safety. I took a moment to savor a realization. His vaunted interview had obviously crumbled into dust. Justice had prevailed, on several fronts. One never preens about an interview, in my view, but if it's an ingrained habit and can't be suppressed, the habit should be disciplined. It should come only after an interview has been taped and viewed. Only then, on the monitor, do you see what you have and whether it's good. Prince had a different philosophy. He counted his chickens, every time, before they hatched. This time, the fowl had all died in ovo, or so it seemed. The prospect of learning more held me in place. Bob Rogers might be just around the corner, eavesdropping. I touched Prince on the sleeve of his suit jacket, took a step back and peered down the corridor toward the distant cantina. Rogers had vanished. Only the sound engineer was there, leaning against the wall beside the door to the sound room, waiting for the next squadron of audio fixers to arrive. The voices on the tape whispered in my brain.

"What did he say to you, Ed?"

Prince put both of his hands on the top of a crate. "Revelation," he said. This took me aback. It sounded too positive.

"So it went well then?"

"Oh yes."

"So what are you back here moping for?"

"My heart's desire, Trotta. My heart's desire, and I didn't even know it."

It might be said, though only in the most grandiose and distasteful sense, that we are the ones, we interlocutors, who offer heart's desire—we offer it to movie stars who want to take that next step to immortality; we offer it to wrongly convicted criminals on death row, aching for reprieve; we offer it to the husbands of wives dead at the hands of their own doctors, to parents who grieve for children taken by murderers who go free. To the one or two politicians curled up in chrysalis form, we give a chance at a greater destiny. We ourselves are nothing, but we offer everything, and it never, ever, under any circumstances, works the other way. The subjects of our stories give us only a market share of the public. They gain us a rating. Maybe, on the best of days, one of them gives us an answer that will stay with us for the rest of our days. In the rarest of cases, an interview subject will become a friend. But these are oddities, and, in my view, risks of the first order. Our simple deal has been our salvation. We offer everything; we receive nothing in return. Prince had reversed the engines.

"Go home," I told him. "You're not well."

"On the contrary. It's you who are sick to death."

He didn't speak again. I left Prince there for someone else to find.

FEBRUARY 12

Good news makes a real difference. I'm better than I have been in days. We have our Evangeline. She's alive, not so well, but one can't have everything. She is tended by nuns, according to my State Department contact. He says the convent—it's not a monastery, it turns out, and there's no clinic—the convent is remote, three hundred miles from Bucharest by a potholed two-lane highway, and set in a gorgeous mountain valley that seems locked in another time, a depression in the earth on the edge of the eastern range of the Carpathian mountains. It's odd, evidently, because her last known location was a good two hundred miles to the south and east, on the other side of the Carpathians, near a city on the northern slopes of the Transylvanian Alps. No one knows how she got so far, though the sisters in the convent swear that she must have done it on foot, given her condition when she arrived at their gates.

She says nothing, but eats corn porridge every day and has a glass or two of Moldovan wine. The father waits outside the gates of the convent to take her home. He sleeps in a farmhouse just outside the walls. For the first time in months, I feel optimism, a faintly exotic sensation.

FEBRUARY 14

A ghastly Valentine's Day. I went to see Evangeline's fiancé in the Mount Sinai ICU. I quite fancy his pastry, which owes more to the French than the Central European tradition, fruitier, much less cream and sugar, but I do make exceptions for quality. He's recovering slowly, but as soon as he regained consciousness, his family insisted that I pay a visit. They wanted me to be there when they break the news about Evangeline. I hesitated, of course. Evangeline's survival would cheer the boy up in time, but in the short term, in his frazzled state, a near suicide just awaking to the truth of his own desperate act, there was no telling how he might react. Feelings of guilt and horror can take unpredictable turns.

As soon as I entered the room, I knew the moment would be unhappy.

First of all, the boy had become an apparition. His arms had been bandaged up to the shoulder. His skin had gone a bluish white, and the shadows under his eyes accented that wretched quality. The last time I'd seen him, he was movie-star handsome. Since then, he'd shrunk to death's sharp point. It occurred to me that he'd actually died and been brought back to life by unsavory means. The room had that smell of defeated mortality. His family surrounded the bed, tending the drip, adjusting the pillows; they communally chewed fingernails. The boy wasn't yet on solid foods. Something about the scene reminded me of Edward Prince.

The parents looked up from their woefulness when I entered the room. They fumbled at an unnecessary appreciation of my time, and I tried to put them at ease. Never has the incidental fame of my calling mattered less. I went to the bed and put my hand on the edge of the young man's blanket. I expressed my admiration for his cooking and my regret for what had happened.

"Have you told him yet?" I asked.

They shook their heads. The good looks came from the female side, I saw. A determined silver Star of David hung at her throat.

I offered an opinion. "Better to wait, I should think."

"No," the handsome mother said.

"But are we sure he's ready to hear the news?"

The father looked at the mother. She spoke for both. "We're afraid if we don't tell him, he'll slip away." She burst into sobs.

So there was no choice. It had to be done. This thought brought an unwelcome emotion into my chest. These people were bereft. I must be the strong one. Their son had the look of an afflicted knight, wrought in stone in one of those German cathedrals. I could almost picture the sword at his side and see the frogs creeping out of his abdomen.

His mother composed herself and spoke again. "He talked with such fondness about you and the way you treated Evangeline. He said you treated her with respect, unlike some others we could name. You're his favorite correspondent on the show, by the way."

Her voice broke. It became apparent they wanted me to break the news.

"I don't know."

"Please," the father said: a word, at last.

I blanched at the responsibility. What if he took it badly? What if he went into shock?

"Let's have a nurse in the room," I said.

The parents looked at each other and back at me, and I understood. The nurse had advised against it. So had the doctor, probably. I moved to the side of the bed away from the door. His mother pulled a chair for me, and I felt faintly rabbinical. If there had been a flutter of eyelids, at least, I would have felt more confident. Rarely in my life, despite countless snap decisions made in the service of broadcast, have I been called upon to act so quickly and decisively in such a delicate human affair. I'd been spared, I guess, until the last. It was as if the man and woman expected me to raise their son from the dead. I'm a Jew, like you, I wanted to insist. I don't do that number. Lamentation, yes; resurrection, never.

I bent over the boy's neck, leaned my head toward his right ear and whispered, "Robert?"

His lips moved, but no sound came out.

"Robert," I repeated. "I have very big news. I wish we had time to prepare you for it, but your parents are eager that you should know. Are you ready for the news, Robert?"

I reasoned that even a few seconds of preparation might give his brain time to brace for a shock. His lips moved again, and I thought I heard a whispered syllable or two. Nothing cohered.

"She's alive," I said.

The scream came in one long eruption. The parents gaped in alarm. Nurses came tumbling into the room, flailing at tubes.

"What in the name of God?!" his mother cried out.

I beat a quick retreat, practically dashing out of Mount Sinai, down the sidewalk to a Greek coffee shop on Madison, where I am sitting now with trembling hands, having tried to light a cigarette and succeeding till the Turk-murdering bastard who owns the place approached me with a threat of eviction, as if I'm some homeless bum. He didn't recognize me at all. I no longer recognize myself.

FEBRUARY 14, LATER

Okay, Trotta, okay. That's what I've been saying to myself all day. It's okay, and it will be okay.

And now it seems it will be. At home, moments ago, just as I had turned off the television set, the parents phoned. It was the mother, weeping in relief. Her son had made noises, on and off, the entire afternoon, scaring hell out of the other patients until he had to be moved to an empty quarter of the gastrointestinal ward. This information was conveyed with inexplicable joy, and then I found out why. Upon heavy sedation, he became quiet, but his eyes remained open, and he took some soup, and the nurse declared that a corner had been turned. The boy's mother told me his lips had just begun to move, and though she couldn't make out the words, the doctor said they indicated significant brain activity, and that her son's mind was, finally, rebooting. I asked her if she could make any sense of his speech, and she told me that it was mostly nonsensical, but a few times she thought she'd heard place names, and one time for sure, she caught the name of a city. Nanking.

BO OK

The Track Out of Hell

Thirty-four

Julia Barnes and Sally Benchborn noticed the problem right away but had other concerns. It was after midnight. A mood of gloomy irritation hung over their project, the twenty-seventh version of a profile on an overweight, chocolate-pushing health guru whom they had come to despise with every fiber of their being. He was a globular man, thick with platitudes, and the women understood with ice-cold acuity that the first minute of him would be tolerable; anything beyond, an excruciating test. They foresaw a damning silence at the end of the screening. The script would rustle in Bob Rogers's fingers. Julia retained psychic wounds from the failure of the piece about the British actor, and she couldn't go through that again. She wouldn't go down with another ship.

Sally had the usual fourth-quarter philosophical epiphany. Why did every story have to generate this moment of self-disgust before it could become good? Why did she do it to herself? She had a rich husband in Westchester. She could leave the business and live in happiness and peace with her children for the rest of her days. She could become more active in her regiment of reenactors. But the thought of defection made her shudder even more than the health guru.

Julia could sense the turmoil in her producer, and it made her queasy. There was a familiar trap here. In her younger days, Julia had dreamed of revolution. There had been group sex and firearms. She had been one of the original members of the Women's Film Collective, and then a fugitive from the law. She had eluded federal marshals. Her sons didn't know, but her husband did. Julia didn't long for those days again. You couldn't. But every time she got cornered in a room with yet another self-immolating producer, she longed for the animal jubilation of that time. And when the longing became unbearable, as it did in these moments, she forced herself to wake up and face facts: a piece had to be screened for Bob Rogers within the week. The hours of fiddling and tweaking had run out.

So the producer sat on the rickety couch behind Julia and asked to see it all once more, to watch the assembly of moments go sliding past like a visible sigh of despair, a man in a pale green muumuu and rabbinical beard wandering beside a sweating and unhappy Sam Dambles in a garden of dust-powdered lettuces outside of Lordsburg, New Mexico. Sally shook her head. "We're fucking doomed."

The producer's eyes closed in surrender to the inevitable, and at that moment, Julia heard the noise. It glitched up in the very last line of the piece, a burble on the track, but she thought it might be her ears going to pot after fifteen hours in the clenched fist of the editing room. She dismissed the burble and broached the real problem.

"May I be honest, Sally?"

"Oh Christ."

"The real problem here is, why should we listen to a fat guy tell us about our health?"

The final image of the guru had frozen on the monitor. "Look at those cheeks," Sally said. She reached for the pile of scripts beside her on the couch and dumped them into the trash with contempt.

"You're right. Let's go home and try again in the morning." She slipped on her shoes and yawned. "What was that on the last track, by the way?"

Julia cursed her luck. In her mind, she had already been out the door and into her car. "Nothing," she lied.

"Play it back."

Julia gave an inward moan. The producer would get fixated now. The glitch could be erased in the sound mix, but Sally wouldn't want to wait so long. Julia beheld the grim prospect of another hour on the floor. She rolled her chair up to the desk, clicked her mouse and ran the track again. The correspondent's words, written by Sally Benchborn, boomed out of the speakers. *"But that's just fine with Peter Twombly. He says he wouldn't have it any other way."*

"That!" cried Sally, startling Julia.

Julia ran it again. *". . . says he wouldn't have it any other way."*

"Is it me or is the problem getting worse?" Sally said. "Can you get rid of it? It's one of my very few good lines."

". . . any other way."

There it was, barely audible to the human ear, an offensive purling of sound, like a voice murmuring a distant word in an unknowable language. No one in the screening room would ever notice, but the producer had the say, so Julia tinkered. She scrubbed. She lifted the track and put it in a new file, then laid it again over the same image and played it again. But the noise remained. In fact, to Julia's ears, impossibly, the distortion became louder, more distinct.

But that's just fine with Lubyanka. He says he wouldn't have it any other way.

"What the hell?" Sally asked from behind.

"I know, I know. I heard it, too."

"Lubyanka?"

Julia nodded her head. She reran the track by itself, without the picture.

But that's just fine with Lubyanka. He says he wouldn't have it any other way.

The women looked at each other. "Some kind of virus?" the producer asked, her voice growing quiet.

Julia rolled on her chair to the shelf and grabbed the original audio tape. Each tape lay in a case marked by a date and a time. She had played the tape before digitizing it, and the sound had been all right.

"Follow me."

Tape in hand, Julia bustled down the hall past the locked doors of the other editor's suites. After the suicide, she no longer moved slowly on the twentieth floor. She made for the security desk, Sally right behind her. Menard Griffiths sat at his post, watching television, eating a homemade muffuletta. Their presence caught him by surprise. The sandwich gave a twitch, and salami slices popped from the bread.

"Scared me."

Julia calmed herself. She could see that more than her presence had spooked the man. He had seen the body of the dead editor. And he had found Evangeline Harker's fiancé. The twentieth floor had become a really bad job. "Could you unlock some doors for us, Menard?"

"Sure thing."

He stood, wiping his hands. The keys jingled in his fingers, then he looked past them down the corridor from which they had come.

"What's up?" Sally asked.

"Thought I saw something."

"Really?" Julia turned to look back in the direction they had come. The hallway teemed with shadows that could have been bodies. She gasped, and they were gone, only shadows.

Sally crossed her arms. "Can we just do this?"

"Yes, ma'am."

Menard was a big man, six foot five at least, with a kind face and an easy demeanor. He took the lead down the corridor. On their way to the editing bay, as they were passing Gropers Lane, he checked their march and glanced to the right, into the darkness of that hall.

"Hello?" he called.

Julia imagined a face, pale and cruel. It vanished as soon as she saw it. She clutched Menard's coattail. Air rustled through vents. Something ticked, maybe a watch, or maybe it was the scrabble of a small beast across a hard surface. Julia thought of the editor, Clete Varney, seated at his desk, black blood still dripping from his chair. She thought of that hole in the ground next door. In the darkness, she saw the outlines of the three or four enormous crates. She had seen the crates before. They had been sitting there for days. Bob Rogers spread the word that they belonged to network and were listening devices, but no one was to touch them. Julia had never believed this story, but for the first time, she wondered what might actually be inside.

Menard moved on, Julia clinging to his coat, Sally clutching the back of Julia's jacket.

"Did you hear anything just then?" Sally whispered in her ear.

"No."

They came to the first of the editing suites.

"This one?" Julia nodded. Menard inserted the key and unlocked. The door swung in. The women entered. Sally switched on the light. Julia turned on the machines. Neither woman sat down. This was to be done quick. Julia stuck the tape into the beta machine while the computer booted up. She switched on the audio and played the tape, just to hear the line of track again. *"But that's just fine with Peter Twombly. He says he wouldn't have it any other way."*

Sally shook her head. "Who the hell is Lubyanka?"

"It's a Soviet prison, where thousands of people were tortured and murdered."

Once more, Julia digitized the tape. There would be no picture now, only audio. Before she ran the track, Julia turned to Sally.

"If this sounds the same as what we just heard on the undigitized tape, we have one kind of problem. If it sounds different in any way, then we have another kind. Agreed?"

Sally nodded. "Yeah."

"Shall I play it?"

"Play it."

Menard slumped in the doorway, but didn't appear to listen. His ears were tuned elsewhere. Julia clicked the mouse.

Lubyanka wouldn't have it any other way.

Sally whispered, "That line of track is shrinking."

Julia ran it again. "It's not even Sam's voice anymore, is it?"

Sally drew the pashmina tight around her upper body. "Unh-unh."

The security guard had gone away for a moment. He poked his head back in the door and made both women jump.

"Menard, could you open another room, please?" Julia asked.

"Something wrong?"

"We don't know."

He took them to the next room, and the next. They skipped one, the space where the suicide had worked. At the last room on the hall, Menard said, "I ought to be getting back to my post."

"One more," they said in unison. They realized they were standing at Remschneider's suite. Menard opened up. The walls of the room were completely bare, his shelves empty. The place stank faintly. Julia denied a voice inside her that told her to get out of the room immediately.

She performed the ritual one last time, putting the beta tape into the machine, listening to the original line of track, which never varied, *"But that's just fine with Peter Twombly. He says he wouldn't have it any other way."* Then she copied the line digitally and pressed play:

"Lub, Lub, Lub, yanka, yanka, yanka . . ."

Thirty-five

Julia went home. She didn't sleep. She stood under the shower head for an hour, leaning her forehead against the ceramic tile of the stall. She didn't say a word to her husband about what had happened. She climbed into bed beside a snoring man, hoping the racket would drown the horrific word repeating in her mind, a busy signal in the roots of her brain. It did sound like a woman's name, like the plaintive call of a lover for a woman lost centuries before.

The next morning, over coffee in the cantina, before meeting with Bob, Sally informed Julia that she'd had a rough night, too. She'd conjured up the memory of a childhood game to drive the word away. Red Rover, Red Rover, let Lubyanka roll over. It hadn't worked. She hadn't slept a wink. The women resolved to talk to Bob.

Julia had it all mapped out. "You do the talking. You're the producer. He loves you."

"Horse shit."

"Don't try to explain anything. We go back to editing, and we let him hear for himself."

Sally thought about it. "What if the problem is gone? Then we look like idiots."

Julia stared at her. "You want to listen again? Just to make sure?"

Sally shook her head. Someone else entered the cantina, and the women ducked into the corridor.

"And suppose he does believe us? What then?"

Julia shrugged. "Take sick leave. Get an exorcist. It's not our problem."

"You believe in exorcism?"

Julia had no good answer. "I'm Catholic."

"Do all Catholics believe in exorcism?"

Julia didn't like the direction of this conversation. In a few minutes, they would have to walk into the office of the ruler of their existence, and in the most pragmatic fashion possible, they would have to convey a difficult message. Bob Rogers wasn't a man with great depth of imagination. He had stupendous range in broadcast ability; he knew how to maneuver and manipulate people, and how to smell a load of bullshit in a story, how to write lines and find pictures for television. In every aspect of the business of TV journalism, he could be considered a genius, but it was no real preparation for what Julia and Sally had to say to him.

"We can't come off as flakes," Julia warned.

Sally gave her a look of horror. "You're the one who brought up exorcism. I'm having second thoughts now. Maybe we don't say anything. Maybe we let someone else discover the problem and complain."

"Is that responsible, do you think?"

"Is it responsible to risk your job when you have small children? Bob will remember that we're the same two who found Remschneider. You know that, right?"

Julia began to have second thoughts, too. "So what do we say to him when he asks us to explain the nature of this problem and how we found out about it?"

"We say we think it's a virus."

"I don't know, Sally."

"I do. I'm getting a doughnut. You want anything?"

"Three."

For once, Bob didn't get into the office before ten. The women asked his assistant to let them know as soon as he arrived. Julia had just finished her third doughnut when the call came.

"Ready?"

Sally squeezed her arm. They went to Bob. He sat behind his desk, in his corner office, the sky and New Jersey filling the frame of a vast natural television screen. The day had come bright and cheerful over the Hudson, and Julia had an abrupt sensation of regret. They had overreacted to some silly technical problem and could have—should have—mentioned it to tech support, who could have taken it from there. She wanted to laugh at their unenviable position. Bob finished tapping at the keys of his console and turned to them with a giddy smile.

"How's that alternative medicine piece coming? I can't wait to see it. You know, I'm fascinated by all that. And this guy has proof that it really works, right? Echinacea cures colds! Unbelievable!"

"Not exactly, Bob."

"But he's terrific, right?"

"Absolutely."

"I'm going to love him, right?"

"Definitely."

"Great!"

Sally nodded, and a languid smile came over her face. Julia waited for her to change the subject.

"When can we see it?" Bob asked, looking at both of them with a perverse eagerness. He could tell that they thought the piece was shit. He knew. He smelled the fear.

"Whenever you're ready, Bob."

"I'm ready."

"Then let's do it."

Julia was forced to interrupt. She cleared her throat. "There is one little problem, Bob."

A cloud crossed his face, a direct imitation of another cloud passing the sun outside the windows.

"It's really a technical problem, but we think it's serious. Don't we, Sally?"

The producer gave Julia that infuriating smile, as if she'd mentally washed her hands of the whole thing.

Bob Rogers startled them. He laughed in their faces. "I know all about your little problem. It's network trying to fuck with me, and you know what I say?" He lifted his fingers and snapped them. "I say fuck 'em. Ignore it. Move on. I'd love to see the piece in about an hour."

Sally rose, threw the hem of her pashmina shawl over her shoulder and sauntered out. Julia remained behind and said, "You got it."

Bob turned back to his computer screen.

"See you in about an hour, doll."

Julia chased Sally down the corridor outside the cantina. The producer's eyes flared with hostility. "He knew all the time! It was a stupid idea to say anything."

"You just lost your nerve."

Sally's eyes were cast down. "So what? You heard him. He doesn't give a damn. It was bad enough when I had the twins. If I start talking about voices on the tape or whatever the hell it is we heard, it will be one more reason for them to boot me. Bob will tell Sam that I'm hormonal, and that will be that. Why do you think Nina Vargtimmen never had kids?"

They parted ways, one bound for the sunny vistas of the producer suites, the other for the rustling shadows of the editing bays.

Thirty-six

The screening room had been compared to the deck of the Starship *Enterprise* and other fictional command centers, and it certainly had an air of gravity, thanks in large part to the large silver rectangle gleaming against the back wall of the room. That screen gave the space—and the show—its reason for being, and so became the center of all things on the twentieth floor. In front of the screen stretched a chairless wasteland of carpet that ended at the most important piece of furniture in the room, a desk with seats for three, topped by a telephone. The middle seat had belonged to Bob Rogers for thirty-five years. To his right sat Douglas Vass, his deputy, ombudsman and personal intellectual trainer, a keen-eyed journalist who had lived through fifty years of the worst excesses of the broadcast business and picked his fights and won about half. If Bob hated something, Vass alone might challenge his contempt. If Bob fell in love, Vass would be there to destroy an ill-advised romance and dispose of the remains. To Bob's left sat a much younger man whom Julia named the Watcher in the Dark; he rarely spoke in screenings but took copious notes. It was her belief that this Watcher, also known as Crane, functioned as the network trigger man. He retained the memory of who had failed and how and when. Rounding out the judges were two women, gray-haired and formidable, weathered enough to have seen virtually every male on the program do unforgivable things to female subordinates, and clever enough to be unforgiving about it. When the room appeared to welcome opinions, they offered theirs. Both had been heard to say, "Bob, you're wrong," but rarely if Douglas Vass had not said it first. Seated alone in the screening room a few minutes shy of the hour, thinking of the ritual before her, preparing herself for horrors, Julia didn't imagine the room as the deck of a progressively futuristic spaceship. From her vantage at the very back of the room, behind Bob Rogers's desk, directly opposite the wall holding the screen, she understood the screening room as a canny updating of an eighteenth-century star chamber, in which a handful of powerful and influential men and women decided the fates of a caste of slaves, disloyal retainers and desecrated nobility. It was a thumb-up or thumb-down proposition, in which argument could be heard and even sustained, but could never prevail over a determined judgment. If Bob finally decided a thing must be good, then it was. If he refused to back down from a fit of malice, then a thing must be bad.

Julia's fingers perspired onto the tape. She injected it into the machine and cued up the picture. The first image of the health-mad hot-air balloon materialized in the room.

She made sure the sound at the beginning of the piece was okay, checked her volumes, threw a butterscotch candy to the back of her mouth and waited. Before long, the other members of the Dambles team arrived. Sally took a seat against a side wall and refused to look at Julia. She stared instead at the screen. The indispensable pashmina had talismanic status. It hinted at powers of invincibility. Sally's burly associate producer hoisted a copy of the interview transcripts, ready for the defense, and under no delusion that they were about to hit a home run. He gave Julia a thumbs-up and glowed with a mordant smile, which Julia recognized as gallows humor.

Sam Dambles made his usual suave entrance in a turtleneck, suede blazer and black jeans. The Dambles Amble, they called it, a slight lift of the shoes, a soft glide. His coolness alleviated some of Julia's worst fears. It did not seem possible that bizarre computer malfunctions from the netherworld could coexist in the same time-space continuum as this man, who defended his people and his pieces with as few words as possible and whose face, upon hearing an asinine opinion (particularly one directed at the quality of his work), became a plate of steel. It helped, of course, if Dambles believed personally in the merits of the story on the screen. In this case, he had never uttered an enthusiastic word, not even when conducting the interview.

The Watcher in the Dark materialized, asking for a copy of the script, which the associate producer gave him. The women found their seats, two of the three Fates. Douglas Vass was there, too, stooped in suspenders and bow tie, wondering where the hell Bob had got to. Finally, the man himself exploded into the room.

"Can't wait!" he blurted out. He was already flipping through the pages of the script. "You've been working on this so long, I know it's going to knock me out."

"Drop the script," said Dambles. "Watch the screen."

The lights went down. The video came up. It was black magic hour.

The guru did yoga. The guru ate chocolate. He drank wine and scarfed mushrooms. He played music on the rim of an earthen bowl. His digs were fabulous. His medicine raised questions. Traditional doctors excoriated him. He addressed their concerns. Traditional doctors accused him of giving false hope to patients. He begged to differ. It was back to his hometown in Oklahoma. Julia watched with rising blood pressure. Bob could be heard flipping pages, but this was no sign of disaster. He always read the script while watching the piece. He didn't laugh at any of the humorous moments, but didn't seem especially restless. Her nervousness grew with every passing second. The piece ran long at a little over thirteen minutes. The trouble began in the last seconds of the piece. She braced herself to show alarm and surprise. Dambles and the guru wandered through the lettuce patch, having their last conversation. Sunset came over the distant mountains. Mexico lay out there. Julia wished she could leap into the frame.

She'd memorized the line. *"But that's just fine with Peter Twombly. He says he wouldn't have it any other way."*

The fat man knelt in the earth among his lettuces, wielding a trowel. Twilight threatened. Dambles had left the place by then and was already having a massage in a spa outside Socorro. The camera pulled focus into the man's face as he worked on the vegetation. *"But that's just fine with Peter Twombly. He says he wouldn't have it any other way."*

Thank God, she thought, her head dropping forward onto the desk. She expected the lights to come up, but a few seconds passed, and she realized nothing had happened. She looked up. The guru's face had frozen on the screen. The eyes gazed down at the ground, the skin had lost its ruddy hue, the beard had an inadvertent quality, as if it had grown under duress, in a concentration camp. Julia could swear that the image was in black and white. She was sure she'd heard that last line. No one spoke. Bob let go of the script. The judges listened to a kind of white noise emerging from the screen, a hissing, a whine, a wail, as if the wolves of northern Mexico were on the move, howling in their own language . . . *Lubyanka, Kolyma, Kotlas-Vorkuta* . . .

The lights came up. Faces turned to Bob.

"Haunting," he said. "My God."

Everyone in the room applauded.

BO OK

Isle of the Dead

Thirty-seven

My father, the great facilitator, brought me home on the first day of March, through customs at John F. Kennedy Airport in New York City. We had fought constantly on the plane. He wanted me to go home to Texas. He insisted. He demanded. He said that my mother was fragile. He called me by my childhood nickname, Evvy. I hated it. I wanted to scream. He knew nothing. He never would. It wasn't his fault. I hadn't mentioned Torgu or Clemmie or the brothers. A profound and permanent mystery had entered his life. He saw a wild-eyed woman with a bottomless well of rage, his daughter back from hell, and he reacted badly. I can't blame him. He thought if he could get me back to Texas, he could reverse not only the ill effects of Romania; he could erase everything that I had become after college. He could erase New York, Robert, September 11. He had no idea.

I half expected to be questioned about Clemmie Spence as soon as I stepped off the plane, but, of course, nothing of the sort happened. All obstacles to reentry had been removed. I had been issued a temporary new American passport in Bucharest. Customs had been briefed of my situation in advance. The passport was stamped with a compassionate smile. My life was enveloped in a hush of prearranged security. The right people had been told, and no one else cared.

We walked between baggage carousels, my elbow hooked around my father's arm, and I reflected that I was back in a place that I had never expected to see again. I was back in New York City. Before leaving the baggage claim, my father and I had one final conversation about my immediate future. He insisted one last time that I must return to Texas for a recuperative period, but he spoke in a tone of resignation. I told him that I would never leave Manhattan voluntarily. I would go back to my life. I would return to Robert and perhaps even my job. He saw the ferocious look in my eyes. It had been there ever since the night of the dream, when everything had become clear to me. I'd never told my father about that night, of course, but the very next day, I had sent word to the Romanian government official who had visited me that my name was Evangeline Harker, that I was indeed an American, and I was ready to leave the convent. The sisters of Saint Basileus displayed visible relief. As we drove away, they crossed themselves and whispered prayers of thanks to God for their deliverance. They were wise in their gratitude. A few more nights there, and I might have slaughtered them all in their sleep.

I had no luggage, and I looked like a wretch. My father propelled me forward. I felt like a leaf stuck to his coat. He stood in the line for customs and turned my way, putting a hand on my shoulder. I could sense that he wanted to say something. In our time together, we hadn't talked much about the specifics of home. He hadn't said a word about Robert, which came as no surprise. He'd never liked any man in my life. Before the flight, in the Paris airport, where we'd changed planes, I had asked him if people would be meeting us at JFK, and he'd said, "Your mother and sister."

"Robert?"

"He's his own man."

"But does he know?"

My father shrugged. "Your mother's taking care of all that. I have enough to worry about on this end of things."

I told him that I wanted to use his cell phone to call Robert.

"Best to wait," he said, and I'd known that something was wrong. How could it have been otherwise? I'd been gone, presumed dead, for months. My fiancé had found solace elsewhere. I couldn't possibly blame him. I was relieved for him, in fact. How could I possibly have agreed to be his wife without telling him the whole truth? I wept in the customs line, but in truth, I knew that it was for the best. I had dreaded seeing Robert. I'd had dreams in which we began to make love, and he would remove pieces of my clothing one by one, until I was almost naked, and he would see the marks on my body and recoil. Please don't misunderstand me. I wanted him back. I loved my man. But I couldn't bear the thought of that moment, which I knew was inevitable.

We came out of customs on a long slanted hallway, and the first person I saw was Austen Trotta. He stood at the bottom of the ramp, holding a bouquet of crocuses and yellow roses, but he didn't see me. He was gazing off at something else, in the other direction. My father's grip tightened at my elbow. He didn't care for this development, but I felt the emotion of a deep gratitude. Perhaps Ian would be out there, too, and Stim.

Austen saw me, but before I could reach him, my father steered us toward my mother and sister, who threw their arms around us in unrestrained delight and sorrow. They laughed and wept. They'd never imagined that I could look so terrible. My father had grown used to the sight, and perhaps he'd tried to describe my condition, but nothing could have prepared them. My shoulders had become thin. My cheekbones and chin had bony edges. My hair spilled out in luxuriant curls, which reminded me of what they say about dead bodies, how the hair grows even in the grave. I was well beyond pale. I moved like an eighty-year-old, one halting step at a time. But I'll take my time, I thought, and they'll see. I'll rally and be more beautiful than ever. By the time I get back to work, I'll be a person again. Over my mother's shoulder, I searched the room for Robert. Pain stabbed my heart, so that I could barely stand.

Austen interrupted. "My dear," he said, and we embraced.

I saw the toll my disappearance had taken on him. His eyes absorbed my horror. I'd never seen the man cry, but tears touched his eyes, and he looked away. He pressed the flowers into my arms.

"How's Ian?" I asked, quietly disappointed that my best friend from work hadn't come.

Austen pulled me close again, almost crushing the flowers. He shook. And I knew that somehow my lovely Ian was gone, too. Austen didn't even have to say it. Everything destroyed, I thought. Darker, angrier thoughts occurred to me. The tears fell down my cheeks, and my father grew furious.

"Helluva time to tell her," he muttered loud enough to be overheard.

Austen lashed out. "And when would be a good time, in your opinion?"

"How?" I asked, bracing myself to hear the first news of Torgu. "When?"

"Right after you left. It was . . . viral . . . we think." Austen looked away again. My mother thanked Austen for the flowers, and we made our way to the sidewalk, where a car waited. Austen whispered something to my mother. Then he gave one of his characteristic bows, a slight nod of his head, and he walked away.

My mother turned abruptly to me. "I would want to know," she said.

"What?"

"Your father's against it, but I disagree. I would want to know."

"Tell me."

My sister started to cry. My father clenched his fists. "Goddamn it, Marie."

"Your fiancé tried to take his own life."

I felt the flowers leave my fingers and scatter on the ground at my feet.

Thirty-eight

Robert was alive. He was home, waiting. Deep dread gripped me. Fury came, too. None of it was over. My secrets burned like wounds.

In the car, on the way to the apartment, my mother cautiously explained. He had gone to my office and slit his wrists in a fit of despair. The security guard on the twentieth floor, Menard Griffiths, found him in time and saved his life. The convalescence had been brutal, but he had improved enough to leave the hospital. He'd been out for two weeks, moving around on crutches, but he refused to stay in bed. A car service drove him to and from his kitchens, and he had even begun to meet with an architect about blueprints for a new bakery in Brooklyn. He hadn't come to the airport at my mother's behest. She'd been afraid that the sight of him in his bandages and crutches would be too much.

They took me straight to him, as previously planned, and left me there. He opened the door of the apartment, his eyes blazing. I fell into his arms, and he put his lips against my ear. We didn't speak a word. He'd opened a bottle of wine and made a quiche. On the stereo, faintly, I heard Gershwin tunes. We ate and drank as the sirens rose through the windows. I was famished and weak. He cleared the dishes, and we cuddled on the couch, still silent.

At last, he spoke. "I'm sorry."

"Me, too."

"It doesn't seem real, does it? Any of it?"

I longed to tell him everything. I longed to be free of my burden. It was an impossibility. "Let's pretend, for the moment, that none of it happened. That you just proposed, and I just said yes."

He squeezed me, and I heard a slight gasp of pain. One of his bandages showed a spot of blood, and I shrank back from him. I got off the couch.

"What?" he asked me. "It's nothing."

I put my hands to my eyes, trying to stop the tears. He reached out for me, and I shook my head. I ran to the bathroom and threw up the quiche and wine. He called for me to come out, but I wouldn't. The minutes passed. I stared at my ravaged face and spat obscenities into the mirror. "You bitch!" I cried. "You cunt!"

When I came back out, he was on the couch, his face hardening. He had begun to see the truth. I felt his scrutiny in my brain, as loud and clear as the murmur of the names that never ceased. Torgu was there, pulsing like a beacon. Robert doubted me, even though he hardly knew why. He doubted that I had really come back, and he was right. This was pretend. I stayed that night with him, and we kissed briefly, but I became aware right away that he was in no mood for anything more. Nor was I. We slept in our clothes in the bed. He asked me a few delicate questions about what had happened to me and sensed my discomfort. I couldn't answer, and he gave up. In the silence between us, with spring rain against the windows, I heard the ticking of the clock within our love.

The next morning, we had a brief conversation while he made lemon pancakes and stirred a saucer of warm raspberry sauce.

"You can stay with me for a while," he said, at the stove, "if you like."

I nursed my coffee. "Thank you. No."

"I mean it. I, I would like it." He turned away from the stove. "It might do us both good."

"No, Robert."

My words wounded him, and I felt bad. He turned back to the food. "I'm not going to let you slip away from me," he said.

"No, honey. I just mean that it's going to take me a moment."

He nodded, his back turned. "How long is a moment? Do you mean a week, a month, a year? I can tell that something's changed."

"Can you?"

"You're a different woman."

"So why do you want me, if I'm different?"

He stirred the raspberry sauce and flipped the pancakes. "I will not let you slip away from me," he said again, as if talking to himself.

I returned to my apartment. It was like a museum dedicated to a girl who I had once known. The clothing in the drawers smelled like someone else. My mother had put fresh flowers in the room and stocked the refrigerator with healthy snacks. I threw it all out. A week later, my parents and sister left the city, and I was on my own again.

The days passed. I avoided my old friends and haunts. They struck me as paper-thin, burnable trash. I walked the city, looking for signs of Torgu. I became strong again. I went to butchers and bought pounds of raw meat. Austen called me often and inquired after my health. Was I eating? Did I exercise? At first, he didn't raise the matter of work, but as the days went by, he mentioned that everyone on the twentieth floor would be delighted to see me. I didn't believe him.

I called Stim's line at work, but Stim never answered. I lunched with Austen, who never answered my questions about him.

Law enforcement people came to call, and I sat through friendly interrogations. I must have spent most of the month of March in a constant round of talk. They wanted to know if I had really seen Ion Torgu. Had I managed a positive ID? Something official? We went over and over the physical description. I could see the skepticism. Most of them didn't believe that I had actually seen the real Torgu. Their questions indicated a budding theory. I had fallen into the clutches of a garden-variety sadist who had played a convenient role until he had me in his power. Mental health experts affirmed that I had been traumatized. Doctors examined me and concluded rightly that I hadn't been raped. No one believed me when I said that he was here in New York. No one blinked an eye. No one mentioned Clementine Spence. They thought that the whole thing was a strange diversion.

"He had every intention of coming here," I told them.

"So you say."

"Have you made any effort to check?"

"And how exactly would we do that?"

"You have a description. You have a name. Can't you check passenger lists for inbound flights over the last three or four months?"

"Ms. Harker, do you have any idea of the difficulty?"

My dreams got worse. I took sleeping pills, but they didn't help. My nights began to feel like a preparation. I heard the voices, the names of places, as constant as the honk of horns in the street. I walked the West Village till three in the morning sometimes, and no one bothered me. I would stand outside Robert's apartment, just watching, as if to protect him from my own violence. I went to the gym. I jogged in the most terrible weather. I ate like a horse, cheeseburgers and steaks and organ meats.

I went to the New York Public Library and checked out books about vampires. I entered a labyrinth of mysteries, but there were discoveries, too. The most sensible of the books talked about folklore and medical conditions, neither of which concerned me. Other books plumbed the darkness. Crosses and mirrors and running water, bats and wolves and moonlit nights, a mockery of the truth, again and again; Torgu hadn't bitten me. His teeth were crumbling. He used knives and buckets. There was nothing supernatural in his methods. If anything, he worked with crudity, like someone out of the stone age. Weren't vampires supposed to be the most elegant of killers? I watched movies and found more contradictions. Vampires cast no reflection and hated garlic. But I had seen the mirror at Torgu's hotel. Torgu had a reflection and had cooked the chicken with garlic. Or had it been rosemary? Vampires shunned daylight and despised the cross. I never saw Torgu by daylight, but he had a distinct fondness for religious symbols and script. He was very old. He'd told me about his father's funeral, the insult to the dead, and it came to me now that he'd been talking about events millennia in the past. He was descended from peoples I'd never heard of. And what had Clemmie said to me? He was two million years of massacre in the form of a man. What did that mean? Could he be so ancient? My mind rebelled, but some truth lay buried there. And another truth, too, came to mind. Torgu bit with words. His words had fangs. They poured into my ear like poison, poured into my ear, but infected my mind. I had heard the names. Now I wanted blood. So wasn't I a vampire? I didn't mind sunlight. I could control my appetites, though the effort was great. I had been into churches, and nothing happened. Crosses scared Dracula, but only when held by believers. Torgu had erupted at the very mention of the name of Dracula. I had wounded his dignity with that name, a bastardization of real horror, a fundamental lie about the species embodied in a character from a novel. I thought about Dracula all the time. He was a joke.

All was preparation. I turned to history. I wanted to know everything possible about the bloody past of New York City. I craved knowledge of the impromptu cemeteries beneath the stones, the places where whipped slaves and dismembered pirates were buried, where the victims of the battle of Brooklyn had fallen, where they'd been desecrated in death by the British troops. I wanted to know more about the criminals and the gangs, the knife work and the gun play. Robert and I started seeing each other again, and slowly I tried to introduce him to my new self. On our walks downtown, I would guide him down a particular street and tell him a story about something horrible, and he would beg me to stop. He would tell me to stop reading books about gruesome acts. He'd cry.

All was preparation, everything else a distraction. In mid April, we moved in together. It was a concession on my part. I kept my own apartment, with my dad's help, but Robert refused to take no for an answer.

One day, packing things up in my place, I received a knock at the door. When I opened, there was a man in a bad suit and short-cropped hair.

"Sorry to disturb, miss," he said. He was shorter than me and had dark skin and an accent, but he seemed to bear the authority of law enforcement. I hesitated to unlatch the door.

"Do not be concerned," he said.

I let him inside, and he introduced himself as Rene. He worked for Interpol, but he hadn't come in an official capacity. A friend in Paris had asked him to drop by and say hello to me and put a few casual questions about a case that had stalled.

He declined a coffee, and we sat. "You know this woman?" he asked, handing a photograph of Clementine Spence across the coffee table. It was a little blurred, and mountains shimmered in the background. Taken in Kashmir, I thought. The photo trembled a bit in my hand, and my visitor noticed.

"Clemmie Spence," I said.

"Yes."

"We traveled together in Romania. Before . . . everything—"

"I understand. My colleagues have sent me a dossier on your travails. May I?" He pulled a sheaf of documents out of his coat. "A few details will help."

I put the photo on the table. "Have you found her?"

He put his documents on the table and fixed me with his eyes. Without words, he was asking me something.

"Is she in some trouble?"

He cleared his throat. My arms started to shake, as if the room had grown cold. Robert wouldn't want him here. My father would be outraged. I longed to tell him everything, but I didn't know where to begin.

"I've had a very hard time," I said. "I'm sorry if I get emotional."

"I understand, miss, but this woman in the picture is dead. Her body was found beneath a mattress in a Romanian hotel not so very far from where you were discovered. Is it possible that you saw her up there? Again? Somewhere?"

I tried to tell him. I tried to get the words out, but they stuck in my throat, overwhelmed by an emotion that I can't name, a collapse into rage, shame and terror at everything. All is preparation, I wanted to tell him. He became alarmed, realizing that his casual visit on behalf of a friend had turned out to be a strategic error. There would be hell to pay if it got back home that he'd conducted an interrogation off the clock, on someone else's beat. No friend was worth the trouble. Even in my state, I could read his mind. When I looked up again, he was gone. He hadn't even bothered to leave his business card.

Thirty-nine

Robert insisted on a dinner party, and I thought it a reasonable idea. He invited four couples, two of his best friends and their wives, two of my best friends and their boyfriends. I hadn't seen them in months. We put out his mother's Lenox. Three years before, he'd bought wine futures in southern France, but he'd never cracked the bounty, stuff from Bordeaux that particularly tickled his fancy for the expensive and absurd, the bouquet supposedly containing hints of pork fat. He insisted on uncorking three bottles. There were cigars, early spring flower arrangements from Simpsons. He made his signature *tarte aux pommes*.

The friends came. The late-April night pressed cold against our windows, supplying that perfect New York coziness. We sat around the table on the second floor of the West Village apartment and chatted the evening away.

Into the third bottle of wine, one of Robert's friends' wives posed a striking question. She belonged to a book club whose most recent choice had been a biography of the Gotti family. She obviously didn't know the full circumstances surrounding her hosts. No one had told her. She was a little drunk.

"Has anyone here ever known someone who was murdered? Intentionally murdered?" she asked, as if no one possibly could.

Robert glanced over at me. The bandages had just come off his wrists. He pursed his lips, begging my forbearance with his eyes.

"Have you ever heard of the Triangle Shirtwaist Factory fire?" I asked her.

She shook her head.

"It happened not far south of here in 1905. One hundred and twenty-seven people died. I feel I know each of them. I feel as if I watched them burn alive."

"Honey," Robert said.

"Does that count?" I asked the silly bitch.

She blinked, a flake of pastry on her lower lip.

"Another thing that kinda haunts me," I went on, "You know that whole September 11 matter."

"I'm sorry," she pleaded. "I was an idiot—"

"But that's just the tip of the same iceberg that dropped the *Titanic* . . ."

"Evangeline," Robert intercepted. He poured my glass to the dry red rim.

"Right beneath this apartment building, below the foundation, right at the bedrock, lie five Abenaki natives, strangled in their sleep after winning at a card game. They were drunk when they were strangled. They had wives upriver. One of them had secretly accepted Jesus as his lord and savior. But the killers didn't know that. Maybe it would have stopped them. I don't know."

"How do you know any of that?" the bitch asked, her voice quivering. I wanted to rip her throat open.

Forty

Robert's bandages had been off two weeks. We were ready for bed.
The first warm evening of the spring had come. The windows were
open, and breezes fluttered into our bedroom.

Robert had come back from the kitchen of one of the restaurants
and smelled delicious, like roast meat. He sat in bed in his robe, reading
the day's newspapers, as he often did. Without fanfare, I went into the
bottom of the closet and found the Amsterdam box. I wondered if he'd
forgotten about it. A nice Jewish boy, he was simply too polite to ever
speak of the matter again, especially given our new realities. I slipped
into the bathroom and unwrapped the most exotic, the thing made out
of black leather. There were holes in critical places, small tassled curtains of metal that dangled above the holes. I became a house in which
the most important points of ingress hid behind steel curtains.

Now I felt hungry and, as I strapped up, turned on. I liked what
Robert had imagined. I put on a white terrycloth robe.

I called from the bathroom, "Turn out the overhead light and close
the window curtains."

With a beat of startled hesitation, he did those things.

"Close your eyes," I called.

When I walked into the room, his arms were folded across his chest,
and his eyes were closed.

I shed the robe. "Open."

We had a moment of tremendous opportunity. A kind of gratitude spread across his face, as if I had fulfilled a promise that he had long ago reproached himself for extracting. But it didn't last. It died in an instant, and his face became as pale as it had been in those first days of my return. I knew in a heartbeat that I had made a catastrophic error. But I knew something else as well. His face went red. His head shook, almost involuntarily. His fists clenched on the newspapers.

"Get that fucking thing off."

The warm spring air ruffled his hair. The scars on his wrists shimmered in the light from the street. I advanced on him.

Forty-one

All was preparation. I still took my walks, but I no longer moved through Robert's neighborhood. I ranged farther south, coming closer and closer to the hole in the ground. I ate pigeons in the dark. One night, long after dusk, I reached the fence surrounding the spot and pressed my nose against the cold steel of the fence. I couldn't see anything much below, but I sensed the space and what it contained. I had never gone to Ground Zero before. I'd never wanted to. I let the blackness in that hole rise inside me, till it swarmed behind my eyes. I found that it wasn't an empty blackness at all.

Before long, I became aware of another presence. I stood a hundred yards from the corner of the hole, where two streets intersected. Another fence met mine at a perpendicular angle, and over there, a hundred yards or so down the adjacent street, someone else stared down as well. We were kindred spirits, but I was hungry. I was sick of pigeon. He or she stood against the fence, a deepening of shadow, a slight figure of humanity, but I didn't care about the identity. I didn't mind the race, creed or sex. My footsteps quickened. I walked the perimeter of the fence and came to the street corner. I looked at the signs, white sticks in the general dimness. The names of the streets no longer had any meaning. I turned right and looked down the road to where it ended in the West Side Highway. Right there, at the corner, stood my building. Closer to me, still at the fence, stood a human being, a container of flesh and blood. A police car came slowly down the street, in my direction. I had nothing to fear, but I didn't want to be seen there. I stepped back into the shadows just as the headlights reached the other visitor. The illumination crawled up the legs to the head, which was vast.

I almost screamed out his name. The lights revealed the face, the man himself, staring down into the pit, drinking up that blank sight as I had done. Then, as the car passed, his body began to turn in my direction. I staggered back from the street corner. I began to run, south, toward the tip of the island, never looking back until I had reached the restless water at the end of the park. I stayed in Battery Park till dawn, waiting every second for him to come.

BO OK

The Twentieth Floor

Forty-two

Sir—Terror has entered this place. Your terror, I mean, a version of dread that no one here seems to have experienced before. As you well know, I'm used to feeling that the overlords of this place rise above such disreputable bed-wetting sensations. Terror is for serfs. Even on that day, when we had to evacuate, when the sky collapsed on top of us, I don't recall true panic. Now, in your wake, I see these people for what they really are: fear puppets. What a revelation. Seven-figure salaries jump at their own shadows. Their underlings have begun to get sick with what they call "the wasting disease." There has been another "suicide." They tell bad jokes about having audio problems and ask each other in the bathroom whether the vents didn't just say something. And without knowing it, they have begun dropping lines from your song into their sentences the way that American teenagers deploy "like"—as welcome mats for thoughts on the brink of arrival.

I have my own terror, too, which I must manage. That is the cost. When I see that Edward Prince has locked himself in his office, drawn the curtains, I fear that things have reached a dangerous pitch, that outsiders will hear of strange doings at the show and come and wreck our venture. Prince is more than merely a television celebrity. He's an American icon, backed by three generations of corporate dollars, and if word leaked out to the tabloids in this town that he had somehow come down mentally ill or worse and refused treatment and spoke to no one, if such a story were to hit the local press, it would be national and international news in a matter of minutes, and we'd have visitors of a kind that you wouldn't like.

You've thought of another eventuality, I'm certain, and it has come to pass. I will speak bluntly. The woman whom you so artfully imitated in our e-mail exchanges—and with good reason—Evangeline Harker, is returning to work. You recall a few weeks ago my mention of this possibility, though at that point, I had no reliable source for the rumor. Now I do. She told me everything in a series of ever more desperate voice mail messages. I haven't returned them and won't. She's quite desperate for human company. She insists on returning to the twentieth floor, despite best efforts to dissuade her. She was offered an extravagantly generous compensation package, but she wouldn't hear of accepting it. Or rather, she would accept it as a raise but not as a "bribe" to leave. For some reason, she wants her old job back. But Evangeline Harker hated her job. She would have given anything to leave. Right before her departure for Romania, she became engaged and told me she would give notice as soon as she married. The reversal means something.

I can see that Austen Trotta, in particular, is pleased by this news. Maybe he wants to sleep with her. But if I may offer a speculation here, I think that it is something else: more than anyone else, Trotta appears to know that the ground has shifted on the twentieth floor and that the shift is connected with this woman and, frankly, with you. You have never made clear to me the extent of the interaction between you and Evangeline Harker in your homeland. I sense your discomfort on the matter and have resisted the temptation to press it. But if there was ever a time to divulge the truth, this is it, so that I may know, so that I may help.

Trotta spends quite a lot of time on the telephone, hunched in his corner, back turned to the door so that he can't be heard. Who is he talking to, I wonder? Is it her? What's she telling him? Are you absolutely sure that you never actually met this woman in Romania? You did such a brilliant imitation of her, in order to gain my confidence, of course, that I can't help but wonder. Still, if not, tell me again how you gained access to her e-mail account. It's important to know, for instance, on the off chance she lays eyes on you, whether she can make a positive identification. And if she could do so, what sort of ideas would come into her head? Has she heard your voice, for instance? Is she one of us, in some way? I don't mean to be nationalist or ethnic or exclusivist about this, but if I knew she had heard your voice, I would rest easier. Nothing must disturb this last stretch of business. Stimson

Stimson, you have listened without hearing. You have seen without sight. How is this possible? How can I make you understand? You needle me with questions, questions, questions on tiny islands of no import. You keep a ledger of nothings, and every day, you assault me with them. When you speak of my song, do you grasp it? Do you understand who sings? To whom I listen? Let me try to explain as I would to a child, just waking up to the existence of his own dead ancestors. For that is the first answer to the question: I am listening to your ancestors. Do you know who they are? Shall I number a few of them for you, the smallest fraction, so that you recognize their faces when they come for you out of the shadows? Do you know the Roman city of Thessalonika? In the fourth century AD, the Emperor Theodosius massacred seven thousand citizens in the Hippodrome, had them cut to pieces with knife and axe. Eight hundred years later, Sicilian mercenaries killed the same number, and nine hundred years after that, German invaders wiped out almost seven times that number, 45,000 Jews, enslaved, deported, murdered. They tore up the great cemetery of the Jews and made the living beg for the corpses of their loved ones. And I have spoken to all of these people in my time. Do you understand? Do you see? Is that not enough? Do you know of the Panama Canal, that enormous grave, swallower of tens of thousands of Jamaicans, carried on three death trains a day from their shanties to a burial ground called Monkey Hill, twenty of every hundred workers, a third of the army who dug the pit, who carved out their own place in the ground? Do you know their names? Have you seen their faces? Have you heard their stories? I have, and you will. They are coming. I keep them in my heart. I drink, and I hear. Do you know of the eight million dead of the Congo, the million of the Armenian massacre? In the last century, my boy, 187 million people were destroyed by human hands, more than in all the previous centuries of murder, a tenth of the world's population, and in every corner. For you, this is perhaps a staggering number. For me, it is far more. I know their names and faces. I have inherited the gift. They come to me, one by one, in endless succession, and their grief never ceases. Their grief pours over me, and I must listen. And soon, you will listen. You and the others, the entire race, will bear this unbearable burden with me.

If you do not comprehend this, then allow me to respond, as you, with the blunt edge of the sword. I must ask you a last time never to raise this question about the woman with me. If Evangeline Harker comes back here and becomes a problem, the problem will be addressed as others have been. In the meantime, you have one task only, and you know what that is. Do we have the meeting with Von Trotta?

Sir—We do not, as of this time.

This is unacceptable.

Sir—I am trying.

Stimson: You may understand how meaningless that phrase is to me: *I am trying.* I do not care that you have tried. The attempt is nothing. We require Von Trotta. The rest of this assortment of professional layabouts are lost to an understanding that will come too late. This old man alone appears to have guessed a thing that disturbs him to an extent appropriate to the matter at hand. But if we speak, I'm sure his troubled mind will find rest. Once he has heard what you have heard, once he knows the truth about the voices in his head, the visions in his mind, he will be able to bring the others. He will become an advocate. With few exceptions, I have found my voice to be the best means of wooing opinion. Von Trotta, of all people, the wise old Jew, child of wise old Jews, will hear and be swayed. And I know exactly how to introduce the topic to him. It's up to you, however, to open his mind to the idea of a conversation. That I cannot do.

Sir—I had no idea so many people died of human causes in the twentieth century. I am staggered. I do understand. I feel emboldened by what

you've told me. I want to hear what you hear. I want to share the burden.
I will arrange the meeting, as you've asked.

AUSTEN TROTTA'S THERAPY JOURNAL, MAY 20

I can't make decisions anymore. I can hardly put two thoughts together. I have lost that capacity. The minute I close my eyes, unspeakable things begin to appear. I almost kicked my dog to death this morning. Poor thing. She wouldn't stop whining for water, so I walked over and I put my boot into her ribs, again and again, until she became quiet. The maid found me cradling the animal. She called the vet, and the vet just called me and told me that the ASPCA had been called, that it was atrocious what had happened. I could hardly tell them the truth, that I had not been kicking a dog, I had been kicking a Jew. In my mind, I had been kicking a Jew who had been pleading with me for the corpse of his wife. God, god, god. Prince keeps calling me on the phone. He's in the office next door. It makes no sense. He could walk over here, or I could walk over there, but his curtains are drawn, and his door is locked, and if he's not coming out, there must be a reason, and I no longer want to know what it is. Frankly, I'm terrified by the prospect of seeing the man face to face. Something has happened to him, some shock that he can't articulate himself. He won't speak to close friends or even to family, a worrying state for a man who has never been at a loss for words with anyone. He will only talk to me, he says, and only on the phone, but when we talk, it's pure jiggery-pokery, names of places he's been or wanted to go, intermingled with an attempt to warn me of some dire fate. Worse, his gibberish seems to be folding over into my waking nightmare. This morning, he started talking about Salonika, Salonika, Salonika, wouldn't shut up about it, and I didn't say a word over the phone, but that is the very place where I kicked the old Jew, the cemetery in Salonika. Don't ask me how I know this, but it's as clear to me as the sight of the Hudson out my window, as the fact of that damned crater beside our building. And speaking of the crater, it has occurred to me, though I haven't told a soul, that the September disaster lies at the root of this entire thing, that we here on the twentieth floor have begun to experience a delayed collective hallucination related to the trauma of that day. After all, our building was almost destroyed beneath the south tower. Everyone made it out alive, but there were mere minutes to spare. We were close when the collapses occurred. We heard the airplane strike the side of the first building. We saw the remains of people when we ran outside. After our evacuation, we didn't return to this place for two years. We stayed happily in the bunker of the broadcast center on Hudson Street, and I never wanted to come back here, and I told corporate so, and I wasn't alone. But Bob Rogers and Edward Prince insisted. Bob Rogers and Edward Prince wouldn't be cowed by terrorists. They wouldn't be chased away. It was Rogers and Prince, the bastards, who wanted to come back here, even though the place was a hulking, scorched, terra-cotta wreck, even though a woman had died in the collapse, even though corpses had landed on top of the mansard roof. The madmen! Is it any wonder that Prince has lost his mind? The disease probably began as soon as we moved back into this place. Now I see it. Everything went wrong after we moved back. Young Ian died. Evangeline had her troubles. The technology went sour. We are haunted by that horrendous morning, but Prince won't let me explain it to him, and when I threaten to call a doctor, or anyone, for that matter, Prince tells me that he will do something drastic. He means suicide. Shall I believe him? I'm at a loss. He's been in there for several days now, though I suspect he comes out at night, and sometimes I think I hear another voice on the phone, but I couldn't swear by it.

Speculations on September 11 aside, I have a deepening awareness of the more specific nature of his problem. I won't say that I grasp it. That would be a lie. But I have my own set of clues from which to work, and they all point in the direction of this man Ion Torgu, whom Prince claims to have interviewed, who hasn't been seen since, and who, according to State Department records, never entered the country, or at least not legally. That makes sense. If he is an underworld figure, he wouldn't cross the country's border with a legal passport. But I still can't figure out how Prince managed to make this interview happen. I've had discreet conversations with each of his producers, and none of them knew about the interview. On the contrary, they were appalled that their correspondent hadn't brought the story to one of them. When I mentioned Stimson Beevers as his helpmate, they laughed or cursed.

And yet I cannot lay the blame wholly on the interview. That happened months ago, and while I then observed odd behavior in Prince, it passed away for a time. He traveled to Russia for an interview and met with a celebrity or two on the West Coast. The next time I laid eyes on him, which must have been in March, he looked weary, and it occurred to me that his state of mind had quietly deteriorated on the road. This life can wear on a man, and I believe it has worn Prince out. But no one, myself included, wants to tell him that this condition is terminal—this condition of human life. No one wants to break the bad news that even beloved television person-alities must face a time beyond cameras.

And yet, here I go again, swinging wildly in my judgment, waiting for another of those frightening, whispered phone calls, thinking that it's noth-ing to do with his age or his mental health.

Christ, there's the phone again.

MAY 20, LATER THAT DAY

I have tried to transcribe the conversation, which was manic, but here is my best effort.

"Austen?"

"Yes, Edward."

"Thank God you're still here."

"Where would I have gone?"

Long silence follows.

"Is someone there in the room with you?"

"No one."

"Thank God. We mustn't be overheard."

Another silence ensues.

"Why won't you come out, Ed?"

"It's out of the question. Out of the question."

"Just for a few minutes . . ."

"Goddamn it, Trotta, are you with him now?"

"With whom?"

"You old Jew fuck. I knew it."

"Who, Ed? For Christ's sake."

Another silence brewed, though not for long.

"Did I tell you that I saw eighteen men blown to pieces by a 150-millimeter gun at Guadalcanal?"

"You weren't at Guadalcanal, Ed."

"Says you. I can see their faces. I can hear their voices right this very minute."

Here I stopped for an instant, struck by intuition.

"Can you literally hear and see them?"

He didn't answer.

"This is very important, Ed, because you told me that you were stationed in Hanford, Washington, for the entirety of your war duty, working as an engineer on the Manhattan Project."

"I was a marine."

"You never were, Ed. The faces you see, the voices you hear, are lies. Someone is making you see those things."

He coughed in a funny way, as if trying to suppress a much more explosive outburst.

"You'll tell me next that I didn't survive the wreck of the Indianapolis."

"You didn't, Ed."

He slammed down the phone.

As I think back on this conversation, I have a feeling of certainty in the pit of my stomach, in my gut. It's that encounter with the criminal. He told me back then that the man had made him an offer, though he never said what. I've spent every waking night since that day asking myself what that offer could be. I admit I'm not just intrigued on Prince's behalf. I wonder for my own sake. What could this man possibly have to offer Edward Prince? And more important, did Prince accept? I believe in my heart that he did, though it's purest speculation, and therefore bad journalism, and therefore moral disgrace. And yet I believe that Prince accepted and has paid ever since.

But what did he accept? I ask and ask, but he never answers. He ignores the question. There's the phone again.

MAY 21, 9 A.M.

It's early morning, and the schedule for the day looks busy, a good thing. I've become too distracted by these bizarre local phenomena. Out my window, the sun slides bright down the Hudson. Unseasonably hot weather has come, taxing the city's millions of air-conditioning units. It's oppressive. The sky feels too close. Our offices are cool, though, for which I'm thankful, and they're deep in shade, like the bottom of a nice rock. The season is winding down; only two more shows for the year, and half of the segments on those shows are repeats, a lovely time in the cycle, especially when I've done my quota and my producers have already started to shoot the pieces for next season. I can leave for the holidays with full knowledge that, come August, when we return, I can dip back into the work year as if into a wading pool, without the slightest sense of unease or discomfort. And even better, I will be starting this season with an unexpected pleasure. Our Miss Harker will return today, or so I'm told, and resume her duties. She's already booked a trip for Montana in early June, to speak with a couple of potential characters for the "Neo-Nazis in Prison" story, her first as a full producer. To general consternation, I have given her William Lockyear's job and fired his temporary replacement.

If I leave aside Prince, and a few other persistent oddities—the illness that seems to have spread among editors, the suicides, the technological problems that no amount of network money have yet been able to fix—I can honestly say that I feel better than I have in a year. The return of the girl has renewed me. Even my back pain has improved. In a month, I'll be in the south of France, and this entire miserable year will appear in hindsight as one of those anni horribili that come along every so often.

One more irritation. The Beevers boy has imposed on Peach to impose on me a conversation. I'm sure he wants to speak about an associate producer job, working beside Evangeline, but he's simply not my cup of tea. First of all, I always find that women make the best associate producers. And secondly, there is a dank air of the cinema about this young man. I get the feeling that he's watched far more celluloid in the dark than is right and proper *for a human being. Nevertheless, in the spirit of this bright new day, I will hear him out.*

MAY 21, 2 P.M.

How quickly shadow engulfs sunlight. I wish I'd never let that creature into my office. And shortly after his departure, of course, the phone rang, and it was Prince again, stammering in a more overheated way than usual that I was going to betray him, that I must not betray him, that the offer had been made to him alone, and that if I accepted, he, Prince, would take it as a personal affront. This time, I hung up on him.

I wish that Evangeline would arrive. One sight of her would restore my sense of equilibrium. It never fails. We had lunch one day, not too long after her return from Romania, and she had a chastened, melancholy aspect that I hadn't remembered, but there she was in front of me, proof that miracles can occur. Even in light of her fiancé's illness, she had managed to bear up, and as we sat in the Café Sabarsky and ate our lox, sour cream and capers, she informed me with a hint of the old girlishness that the wedding would indeed take place, though a date hadn't then been set. I almost wept at the news. Fate had rescued two young lives from annihilation, and I experienced a rush of hope, a sense of the renewal of all things in the breath of spring, visible in the riot of greenery in the park across Fifth Avenue.

Since that lunch, I've seen Evangeline twice, and both times, her nearness has had a salutary effect. If I didn't know better, I would name this feeling love; perhaps it is akin to the sort a father has for a daughter. But today she's been delayed for some reason, and I have had to deal with the pestilential brat Beevers by myself. But I mustn't be peevish. All things happen for a reason now. We are caught in a scheme of catastrophe, designed by someone who wishes us ill. Bob Rogers thinks it's all the network, but he's mistaken. We are well beyond network shenanigans. Such is my conviction. Prince's rantings aren't just disturbing. They represent the advance of our enemy's scheme and must contain a clue to the nature of what's occurring. The same holds true for the conversation I just had with Beevers. And in reconstruction, I can already see the first outlines of a thing that has been nagging at me ever since Evan-

geline's fiancé tried to kill himself. I may not like this Beevers, but I owe him a debt nevertheless for illuminating one corner of my unease. It's the names. The disease is traveling through the names. But I'm getting ahead of myself.

He showed up right on time, eleven A.M. I looked up in exasperation, and the visitor was there in the doorway, where he had not been seconds before. At that very moment, Peach informed me that Evangeline Harker would be late. She had to attend a sudden doctor's appointment related to her future husband. I mention this because the news sparked a transformation in my visitor. Beevers quickened. That's the only word for it. His usual posture of intellectually mannered sloth, belly protruding beneath the T-shirt, knees practically knocking together in his trademark shamble, suddenly produced the undeniable effect of a human skeleton. The slug contained bone, after all.

"What can I do for you, young man?"

He sat on my couch; he could have stood in front of my desk with hands folded together, but instead he chose to cross his legs, as if planning to stay for a while. This decision, coupled with my sudden sense of an ulterior motive beyond employment, raised new feelings of antipathy against him. He brought up Evangeline.

"We were good friends, you know."

"I find that very unlikely."

"Oh, the best. She and Ian and me were inseparable. Ian, of course, is no longer with us."

I declined his banter as I would send back a bottle of skunked wine—without comment.

He was visibly uncomfortable. I waited. I would not ease his suffering. Finally, he mustered his courage to ask a very odd question. "Do you know, Mr. Trotta, the number of human beings murdered by other human beings in the last century alone?"

"I do not follow."

"I think you do."

It wasn't a question at all, but a threat, delivered by the criminal via his man.

"In the tens of millions, I would presume. Why do you ask?"

"One hundred eighty-seven millions, to be exact."

"You're a student of history."

"Soon."

"Is this what you wanted to talk about?"

"Touches on it." He unfolded his legs. "Someone wants to meet you," the production associate said, rising and closing the door to my office. At her desk, Peach watched with a grave expression of doubt, as if Stimson Beevers might explode like a grenade and tear us all apart.

"Is that so?"

"I don't need to speak his name. Your colleague has told you. Perhaps Evangeline Harker has told you as well."

"I have no idea what you're talking about."

His smile alarmed me in ways that can't be put into words. There were physical clues to the unthinkable. He had always been pale, like the reflection of the moon in a puddle at the trash dump; he was bald at too young an age, with eyes that struck me as fishlike, moonish, ill-equipped for natural light. But these remained the normal human attributes of an unfortunate genetic heritage. What struck me in our conversation was much more unusual. In fact, on the surface, his features had improved. He looked more robust, more alert, less afflicted, but when I peered closely, I saw the changes. For one, the veins in his temples bulged in a way I hadn't remembered. They had ridges and edges. They made plateaus. His eyes, once bulbous, had receded into bloodshot, as if they hadn't closed in weeks. And most heinous of all, least explicable, his teeth had started to go dark. I thought at first of lead poisoning. I once did a story on a Maryland town with water contamination problems, and the children of the inhabitants had streaked teeth. But this was much worse. The ivory in his mouth had started to turn a grayish shade of blue.

"I won't take up your time," he said, "but I will take a few minutes to explain the situation. My superior is asking for the one and only time . . ."

"Bob Rogers."

He gave a wretched gray grin. "No, sir."

"Who then? Tell me his name."

Those slit eyes narrowed even more. "It's not his name that matters. It's the other ones, the names that he speaks, the names you've heard."

This was brazen—and revelatory. "Go on."

"Your colleague next door has met my friend and reaped rewards that you can scarcely imagine."

I laughed at him. *"You mean the insanity, I presume. But he received that reward at birth."*

"I loved your wry humor in the seventies and eighties, when the show still had real audience numbers, but I can see in your eyes that you've heard the real news. You've heard the voice. It's been whispering here on our floor for months now. You've heard it, and you want to hear more. And I know the man who can make that happen. I'm his agent."

I recalled an archaic gesture, once a feature of my father's behavior. He spat at the mention of certain people; Senator Burton K. Wheeler comes to mind. I wanted to spit, but the emotion would be read like an entrail, so I disciplined myself against the gesture.

"Not interested," I said.

Stimson Beevers got up from the couch. *"Everything is being readied. In a few days now, you will realize that you have made a choice today. You had a chance to be either a beneficiary or a vehicle. To be a beneficiary is to see the world for the first time as it is. But you've made another choice, to be a vehicle, and to be a vehicle is . . . well . . . to become merely functional to our vision."*

At last, he had begun to give me what I needed. He had begun to spill information about the man's intentions.

"Your boss," I said, *"is quite a confident man. To have done what he has done."*

"You have no idea."

"I do, as a matter of fact, have some idea." I watched the boy's composure begin to break. *"He's so confident that he will send the least credible person on this floor to my office as his emissary, that he will embolden that emissary to issue threats and insults in his name without even allowing his name to be used. That's quite a remarkable set of balls, wouldn't you say? Or is he just the dumbest human being who has ever walked the earth? One of those sad gigolos from Eastern Europe, all bouffant and bad suit? Frankly, I'm inclined to call the police and have you arrested."*

A sheen of alarm glistened in the ashen eyes.

"What would you tell them, Mr. Trotta? You're hearing things? You sus-

pect the presence of a criminal, but have no proof of his existence? There's no there there. Is there?"

I snatched the phone off the receiver. "Let's find out." I dialed a number, glancing back at him.

"Stop, please."

I lowered the receiver. "Quickly now."

"Mr. Trotta, I've already botched it. What I meant to say is this. Mr. Torgu is a powerful international criminal who wants to turn himself in to the authorities. He came here to tell his story because several governments in Eastern Europe have sent their people to terminate him. Because he knows too much. He tried to tell this to Edward Prince and much more. He tried to explain that he had worked as a double agent for our side during the Cold War and that's why the intelligence services of those old Warsaw Pact countries wanted him dead. But he's scared to come to the American government because of his long history of illegal activities. This interview would have been his means of reaching out. But Prince is ill, clearly, and unable to complete the assignment. So my friend wants to finish it with you. All he asks is that you take a meeting."

I hung up the phone. Elements of this tale had the ring of remote plausibility.

"And what about all that other nonsense? Beneficiaries and vehicles?"

He swallowed. "I've been working too long with this frightening, unreasonable man, and it's taken a toll."

I gave him a long scrutiny. "How did you come to know him?"

He reached for the knob of the door. "Connections."

"One more lie, and I'll dial, and your new friend may take issue with the consequences. He may not like you as much as he does now. Or have I misjudged the warm nature of your relationship?"

At that moment, for the first time in the brief history of our acquaintance, I saw something I pitied in this boy: that he was only a boy, that he was frightened, that he'd got himself in deep with a thing he barely understood.

"Believe it or not," he told me, "I got in this for love, and then it was too late to turn back. That's all I can tell you."

I didn't pretend to understand, but it sounded closer to a version of the truth of his involvement. It wasn't a blatant lie, at any rate.

"Shall I tell him that we have a meeting. After hours?"

I shook my head. "We meet this time tomorrow. In broad daylight."

Having achieved his goal, he recovered his arrogance. "He's not afraid of the light. You're making an understandable but obvious mistake. A lot of people do, and it annoys him no end."

As I finish my version of this account, I understand that every seemingly plausible word from the mouth of the odious cineaste harbors an untruth. He's concealing the most important information by giving me a cover story about post-Soviet criminality. But I'm not dealing with an ordinary or even an extraordinary criminal. The truth of this matter lies elsewhere, in regions that he managed, by accident, to divulge even as he attempted to conceal them. This entire matter has something to do with place names. What exactly did he call it? The voice. And the voice is whispering place names. And I know the names. The vermin mentioned names. I've been hearing the names for months now without having the discernment to do the obvious: write them down.

MAY 21, LATER

Here is a partial list. I don't know what they mean. I don't know if I believe it myself. But my gut tells me this unhinged mobster is using place names to bring some kind of hurt on our workplace. If I had to guess, I'd say it's the remnant of some debased, depreciated Cold War code, a dead signal belonging to a far-flung, now-deceased intelligence service, revivified for purposes obscure. The whole thing reminds me of that old gag about subliminal messages, words obviously dropped into regular language and meant to persuade the hearer. Yes, it has the feel of a sloppy, hilariously overdone parlor trick of ex–Iron Bloc tradecraft, and yet something about it works to unman and unsettle. Is this terrorism? If I close my eyes and listen closely to every passing syllable, I come up with a string of vowels and consonants that cannot, on the surface, possibly be related, but may serve as the markers for a discreet code. A few are obvious place names, if I am correct, and others are more obscure, but sound vaguely familiar, and they go roughly like this: Persepolis, Nicopolis, Atlantis, Carthago, Chicago, Mecca, Masada, Hiroshima,

Atlanta, Chickamauga, Shiloh, Lepanto, Constanta, Constantinople, Kulikovo, Martwa Droga, Poltava, Varna, Mazamuri, Luapula, Salonika, Balaklava, Nagasaki, Hue, Somme, Marne, Tyre, Caporetto, Tuol Sleng, Shenyang, Gaoyao, Congo, Manchuria, Lhasa, Medina, Rumbala, Nitra, Shanghai, Nanking, Nineveh, Gallipoli, Gomorrah, Treblinka, Lubyanka, Kotlas-Vorkuta, Cayamarca, Khe-Sanh, Antietam, Blenheim, Dien Bien Phu. *Some of these are places of infamy. Some are guesses. But why? It's the thirty-eighth in the comprehensible series, Nanking, that provides the first possible hint at the code's meaning. Evangeline's fiancé must have heard some of this sequence, too. He must have come to the twentieth floor and seen or heard something, and they tried to kill him, and he tried to tell someone, but none could understand. He tried to tell his mother. She told me so. He woke from sleep and said one word, and it was Nanking, though he had never been there in his life. Prince must know, too, the poor bastard, but they've scared him to death. And now I'm scared. And I'm clueless how to proceed. The pestilential brat is right. What would I tell the police? In the absence of law enforcement, I have no idea how to respond to this threat, though it might be a good idea to absent myself for a few days. Go upstate. Shutter myself in the country house. It's end of the season. I could call in sick. Under no circumstances should I take this meeting with the criminal. Under no circumstances should I face this person until I have more information. Through the glass window of my office, I see an editor, Remschneider, sleep-walking, lumbering past, one of the sick ones. He's heard the voice, I've no doubt. It's in his mind, just as it is in mine, but he's succumbed, as Prince has succumbed, and now I remember something, a conversation I had last fall with one of the other editors, Julia Barnes, and suddenly a notion is coming back, that odd conversation about ethnic heritage and Transylvania last fall. She tried to tell me something, and I made a joke of it, and then those editors got sick. Julia Barnes knows. It's my gut. She knows. Or she knew. If she hasn't been infected, she's an ally.*

P.S. Upheaval is the order of the day. The network has now decided to move on the show, maybe sensing our vulnerability. Bob Rogers has called a meeting for next Monday. All producers and correspondents, everywhere in the world, must return to New York for a debriefing about the future of The Hour. *It is the end of the season, and if I'm not mistaken, the end of the line.*

BOOK

The Alliance

Forty-three

Julia Barnes had been keeping to herself, which was just about possible in the waning days of the on-air season, thanks to an absent producer and a difficult overseas story. The days lengthened outside her bedroom window. She sometimes walked the several dozen blocks from her Chelsea apartment down the length of the shining Hudson, past the hole in the ground to the building on West Street. She got to spend more time with her boys and see a movie or two. The relaxation of her schedule nourished her mind and soul and made her feel, as she always did this time of year, that a life existed outside the walls of the job. Her husband, a passing good cook, made seasonal dishes. They saw old friends. Yes, she thought every morning, as she made her way along the walking path beside the river, I can survive another year.

But something was coming. When she stepped into the lobby of the building, flashed her security badge and hit the elevator bank, she could feel the darkness anew, and she fought back. The darkness gave her a sense of impending doom, but that was the least of it—it was bad for her blood pressure, hard on her digestive system and bitter hell on her nerves. Headaches came storming into her mind as never before. This was pure stress, because physically she had aged well. Yes, she could stand to lose weight. Of course, she could eat more fish, and get more exercise. Amass those omega threes, and tot up that good cholesterol. Of course, and again of course. Her doctor had told her so. But these were the normal preoccupations of a menopausal woman. There were no real physical symptoms of a decline, and yet in the building she sensed the presence of one, the fact of an advancing deterioration that had already taken hold of others.

She liked to get away as often as possible. It was a boon that she could leave the building for lunch and have a Greek salad and bask in the sun beside the vast construction site where the neighboring buildings had once stood. Proximity to that horrific wound in the cement bothered her much less than the atmosphere on the twentieth floor. Thoughts of mortality and time, terrorism and security, politics and faith, ceased to be heavy topics; on the contrary, by comparison, they seemed like reasonable and healthy material for contemplation.

On the day she got the news about the big meeting, called by Bob Rogers to announce his retirement, and therefore a change in leadership for the first time in the show's thirty-five-year history (this was the rumor), she spent an especially long time on the pier at Battery Park. She had forsaken the Greek salad and ordered a cheeseburger and fries instead and was enjoying them immensely. Her ability to linger on the pier was a function of timing. She couldn't start on her next piece until her producer, Sally, returned from Japan, and that wouldn't happen till next week. Sally had been called back prematurely for the big meeting. She still had footage to shoot, but it didn't matter. She and Sam Dambles would have to return to Japan later. The meeting would be an historic occasion. The future of TV's greatest news show was at stake. In the meantime, the summer heat rose to a new barbarity, above ninety degrees. Downtown, the clothes were coming off. The air-conditioning units rattled like old bicycles in the windows.

Julia took off her shoes and dangled her feet over the water. Skaters boogied past. The laughter of small children gave her pleasure. She tossed a French fry to a squirrel. As much as she tried to dismiss the things in her imagination, she could not. It was a fact that editors had stopped coming to work in large numbers. She no longer stayed in the building after sundown, but when the dusk hour drew close, she sensed the presence of her colleagues on all sides, each one a version of Remschneider, their eyes as dead as ice, their bodies weighted down, their minds filled with an unbearable audio transmission, the whispery noises of the tapes. At first, she had resisted knocking on closed doors. She didn't want to find another fresh corpse. But the silence got to her. Earlier in the month, she had knocked down the corridor, but no one answered. When she complained to the shop boss, he shook his head and said with an utter lack of conviction, "Time of year. Half of them are on vacation." His eyes were dead, too, or dying. She no longer knocked on doors. She waited for the knock to come on hers. Her husband called it an odd resurgence of her old Weather Underground paranoia. The feds would come in the night, bearing warrants. Her boys just laughed and said mom had lost her shit.

But she hadn't. The absence of editors wasn't the only evidence. The producers stayed away, too. They knew that something had gone bad on the twentieth floor. They knew that the technology had soured, making it necessary to farm out their footage to subcontractors until the network could fix the problem, and far worse, that the editors appeared to be sickening, like fruit on afflicted trees. The producers knew they would be next, so they did the next best thing to what any sane person would do: instead of polishing their resumes and looking elsewhere for work, unthinkable because there was nowhere else in broadcast, they made sure that their stories kept them on the road.

Julia reflected on the luxury, and luck, of mobility. In their work, producers could travel. They could move. They were free. Editors were fixed in chairs, in shadows, in rooms. They were slaves.

"May I join you?"

It was Austen Trotta, dressed in a khaki vest and checkered short-sleeve shirt. He held a Greek salad in his hands, but she knew instantly that he hadn't come on a social call. He'd come to talk to her about the troubles. His wrinkled face struck her in that moment as eternally kind, like that of God to a five-year-old. God had not turned his back.

He opened the plastic container to his lunch and gazed mournfully at soggy bricks of feta cheese and slivers of anchovy.

"I'll swap with you."

She laughed. "No thanks."

She saw that it would be hard for him to sit on the pier, so she joined him on a nearby bench.

"I want to apologize," he said.

"Whatever for?"

"Last fall, you tried to tell me something about those Romania tapes, and I wouldn't listen."

She'd forgotten about it. So much had happened since.

"You bring it up after all this time?" she asked.

Sitting there with him, she felt less alone than she had in months. His eyes told her that he, too, had seen and heard strange things and had no one to tell.

"Something bad has come to the twentieth floor. Something terrible."

She nodded. "Yes."

He told her everything. Some of it she knew. She had heard, like everyone else, of the imminent return of Evangeline Harker. She knew, too, that Edward Prince had been behaving strangely, that he was holed up in his office, but hadn't attributed the fact to the developments in the editing bays. But as Trotta spoke of the encounter with Stimson Beevers, a chill came over her, a deeper fear than she had yet known.

"Has anyone besides Prince laid eyes on this underworld figure Torgu?" she asked.

"There must be others. Presumably Beevers. The question is whether I should."

She registered the lack of resolve in Trotta. He hadn't approached her merely to commiserate. He wanted to know what to do. She told him everything that she had seen and heard since the autumn, the noises in the machines, the absence of producers and editors in the corridors, the words in the screenings, the spread of the rot.

"I have to know something," he said.

She caught a gleam of suspicion in his eyes. She had her own.

"Okay."

"Do you know what I mean when I talk about the voice?"

She did. "The names."

"Who else knows? Anyone?"

"Bob Rogers thinks he knows. I told him long ago that we had a problem, but he said that it was the network, and the only thing for it was to hunker down and resist in silence, like Martin Luther King. He actually said that. I went to network, to be honest, but they didn't give a crap. These problems worked to their advantage, in terms of getting rid of Rogers. I was told not to worry. There would be a full internal review. In the meantime, they hired outside editors to cut our pieces at the broadcast center."

She could see that this news about the network interested Austen deeply. He had his own suspicions. "How long was that full review expected to take?"

"Indefinite."

"Long enough for us to dig our own graves." He hadn't touched his salad. "We're on our own."

Julia saw no choice. "You have to meet this guy, Austen. Meet him on your terms. Get a better sense of the threat. Then bring it up at the big meeting next week. Let's clear the air, see what else everyone knows. Strength in numbers. Do you know what I mean?"

He gave her a quizzical look. "Strength in numbers? Against this? You really think so?"

"I do. You go to the police now, by yourself, what have you got? Not even the network would back you. But if we go as a unit, the most respected journalists in broadcast, we'll get a hearing. And in the meantime, I'll see if I can manufacture some means of smoking the old boy out. If he's hanging around the floor, it shouldn't be too hard. We need this prick under lock and key. As long as he's at large, we have no way of knowing what we're really dealing with here."

He stammered, "May I pose a ludicrous question? Completely in confidence?"

She nodded.

"You once implied that we were dealing with something—I can't even get the word out. Something not quite normal. Do you get my meaning?"

Julia reassured him. "I was wrong. This isn't a ghost story, Austen. For the first time, I see it. Maybe Rogers isn't so far off. Maybe we're dealing with someone who really wants to hurt the show. Maybe not network, but someone with their own sick agenda. A lot of people hate us, Austen. You know that. And if they have access to the right technology, anything's possible. You know what I mean?"

Trotta didn't seem convinced.

Julia tried another tack. "All right. Say I'm wrong. Do *you* believe we're up against the supernatural here?"

He shook his head, distracted by an unspoken thought. "I suppose not."

She changed the subject. "Who else can we trust?"

He gave a furtive look. "No one," he said. "I won't be made a fool."

Julia thought of Sally Benchborn, but couldn't be sure. After the screening of the health guru story, Sally had begun to keep her distance.

"What about Evangeline Harker?"

Trotta vigorously dismissed this idea. "Leave her out of this."

Julia caught the note of emotion. He knew more than he was telling.

"She's part of it, though, isn't she? She and her fiancé? You told me so."

Trotta turned his gaze to the water. The heat had become stifling, even with the breeze.

"Is there any chance that Evangeline Harker knows what we're dealing with here?"

Trotta got up from the bench. She had another epiphany, and she followed it. "This man whom Prince interviewed must have something to do with Romania. Right? We've got to bring her in, Austen."

"No."

Julia didn't quite believe him. "Do you mind if I ask?"

"I almost got her killed once, when I asked her to go to Romania. I won't risk her life a second time. I am asking a favor. Do not say a word. I implore you."

He got up and gave a bow of sorts, walking away into the shade of the buildings around Battery Park. Austen Trotta was old world. He used a word like *implore*. He knew how to implore. But she refused to abide by his sense of chivalry. For the first time, she began to see the possibility of a cure to the ailment on the floor. Trotta did, too, but his conscience wouldn't allow him to pursue it. She had no such scruple. She would find Evangeline Harker. She would discover the truth of the matter. Evangeline Harker was the key to everything.

The next day, Julia almost ran to the office. Evangeline was due back that morning, or so she'd heard. There were other things to discuss with Austen. They hadn't talked about the details of the plan. In fact, as she reflected, she realized that Austen hadn't agreed to anything. She went to Peach, who informed her that Austen wouldn't arrive till mid morning.

"Evangeline Harker?" Julia asked.

"She's around."

"You saw her?"

"Of course," Peach replied, as if the woman had never been missing.

Peach glanced at her computer screen and popped half an apple fritter between her lips. She answered to no one but Austen. "Check her office."

Evangeline Harker was not in her office. Julia accosted anyone she could find. No one had seen her. Miggison looked outraged. No one had told him. "She's alive?"

Julia returned to Peach. "You actually laid eyes on her?"

Peach wiped sugar off fingers with a tissue.

"I laid eyes on her. She looks good. Rested. Not so sure about the hair. Did you try the ladies' room?"

Julia went to the ladies' room. Evangeline Harker had been there just moments before, a voice confided from behind the door of a stall. Julia followed the invisible trail. She came to the end of one of the central corridors, to the intersection of an editing bay entrance and Gropers Lane. She peered into the shadows around the crates. She saw something.

"Evangeline?"

A strange beauty emerged. Julia wasn't sure, at first. This woman seemed taller, more remote, more serious than Evangeline. She saw what Peach had meant about the hair. Evangeline's hair had always been slick and straight, and now it was curly. And it didn't look like any perm of this world. The curls slung down her shoulders, headed for her waist. Her eyes had deepened. Where once there had been a willed cheerfulness, as if anything else would reveal vulnerability, the deep brown irises held a violent sorrow. Her eyes dared you to look away. Her fashion sense had changed dramatically. She wore blue jeans, unthinkable before, and a yellow T-shirt that revealed her breasts in such a frank way that Julia wondered if Evangeline wanted to show them off. Had they been lifted? Many a New York woman, under duress, might turn to her plastic surgeon, but Evangeline never seemed the type. Her cheeks were a bright, unrouged red. She said, in a voice low and charged, "He's on the floor."

BO OK

Ghost

Forty-four

First day back on the job, and I sit with my back to the vista, the window where the World Trade Center used to rise, and I think how the world changes when you change and not a moment before. I fight him with all my strength, but I'm losing.

Nine months ago, the window framed a void. The other side of the glass held only sky. Now the sky boils with rage. I feel the fullness out there, behind my back, over my shoulder. If I turn and look, I will see the violence of their eyes. I don't have to turn, though. I know. Stare into Torgu's eyes just once, and the dead stare back at you. Torgu says he will open the door to them, and they will open our minds, pour themselves into us, and it will be terrifying and beautiful. It makes me shudder to my bones, but there's also the thrill, which I can't deny. I have seen for myself.

One summer, I went to Catholic summer camp, and a nun told me that God puts His finger on a person when He wants them to wake up and see Him. So do the dead. Their countless fingers touch me. But I resisted until now.

After the attacks, *The Hour* moved temporarily to the broadcast center on Hudson. When we moved back into this building, I put in for an office without a window. But a lot of producers made that demand, and I was outranked, so I got stuck back in the renovated space and had to contend with a massive pane of translucent, treated glass, which overlooked the hole. Fair enough, I thought, I will simply work around the problem. Maintenance hung blinds, and the back wall became a dead white space. My television and my computer screen sat in front of me, as did the bookshelves, the couch, the lamps. Behind me was nothing. Other people whispered about being freaked out, about the macabre new quality of an office once taken for granted as stuffy and old-fashioned. I abhorred such conversation. I had done the day. I didn't need the rehash.

But I think now about that September morning and understand something with absolute clarity. That day marked my introduction to Transylvania. On that day, the whispers in my head really began.

Before it happened, I was happy. My ill-advised and damaging affair with my boss at Omni Media, Mr. O'Malley, had come to an end, thanks to my resolve. Robert and I had met in the bar of the Maritime and were getting very friendly. I had walked the twenty blocks from his apartment in the West Village to work. Six months before, with Mr. O'Malley's guilty help, I had landed the job with Austen Trotta. I had lost ten pounds on Atkins and looked truly fabulous, the best since college.

One hour after I got to work, that blessed girl was dead forever. I see that now. I heard the first explosion and figured a terrorist attack, though never an airplane. None of us knew that. But an uncle of mine had been at the World Trade Center during the first attack in 1993 and had vividly described the descent through smoke down eighty flights of stairs. I fetched my friends and made them shut off their computers and hang up their phones. I was not a designated fire marshal, but I steered them away from elevators and herded them into the fire exits. I walked us outside. It was me who did those things. I was calm as a Texas pond. When we got outside, we started to move more quickly, down Liberty Street toward Church. Everything in the external world was chaos, cops dashing, no one knowing anything, the north tower hidden from our eyes by the south tower, which seemed its usual untroubled and shiny blue. Up ahead, we could see smoke, and we knew it would be terrible; we were journalists, and such things belong in our lives. But then came the end of the south tower, and I wasn't prepared. Ian shouted, "Don't look!" But I work in television. We always look, and I did, and I was flooded with something. They were jumping. Some of them lay on the plaza already, amid the fires. I gazed up, that girl who had started the day, on the brink of her last moment. I could feel myself inside her body, her fear, her sorrow, her confusion, her memory and disbelief. I think, at that instant, my interior, whatever you want to call it, began to collapse. But that wasn't enough. For the sin of looking, I had to be shown more. As I stood there, beholding the shape of my new life, the second plane struck the south tower.

Ian helped me away—dear Ian. He guided me, with Stimson and a few others, and we ran across Church Street, through the financial district, all the way to the Brooklyn Bridge.

We trudged onto the span, holding hands with each other, trying to reach our people on cell phones, looking back. It was there, I was there, on the span, when the first tower went down in a storm of dust. The buildings reiterated what had already occurred inside of me. I never needed the spooky talk, didn't need the analysis of our traumatized state, didn't need to chew on anything related to the matter, not even on our first day back in those offices, when I walked out onto Liberty Street and made my way to the newly reopened subway. I went about my business. Lockyear did me the favor of never pitching stories related to the attacks. I went about my business, and I built my reputation at *The Hour,* and I got engaged.

This was my little house of grace.

I sit at my desk and write these pitiful notes, letting the waves of yearning roll through me. I want to be somewhere else. I yearn to be *someone* else. This sensation is a relief from the deepening of my sickness, a lessening of the energy behind my back. I can check the blood lust. But the images won't leave me. I am that girl, I am a thousand girls, I can feel the heat of them. I am trapped in them. I am on the floor of one of those towers, and the floor is buckling. I am Clemmie, and she is at the window, the temperature rising. The tangible world, it seems, is fading. The noise of the underworld deafens. In Romania, I felt the presence of murders, fifty, a hundred, two thousand years old, as if those murders had happened yesterday. They glowed with a somber life. Here, in this place, I hear the roar of a gray sea.

No wonder Torgu looks as he does. The sheer weight of his knowledge would destroy most people. Knowing is a physical corrosion that can only be released by bloodshed. People aren't meant to know like this. I'm not. I steady myself and regard my office. The view centers me for a moment. The rainbow-ribbed Kate Spade bag hanging on the doorknob seems to have come from a country where no one has ever wept. I bought it on my last workday before Romania. I spent an entire week's wage, but I never used it, until now.

On the file cabinet, my cacti have perished. While I was gone, other people used my space but didn't water the plants. They've withered into broken thumbs. There is a photograph of me with Robert, taken a month or two before we got engaged. I look haughtily happy. It's a kind of me; that's all I can think. It's the me that dwindled away. There must be others. My mother always told me I was a completely different person at the age of six. I see the long dark hair, hiding its curls like a caterpillar hides its butterfly. I see the same outfit I would have worn before, the dark blue pants suit and blouse. I see the chocolate-brown eyes, but behind them now is the ghost. Robert used to kiss my lips. Now he takes my hands and kisses their knuckles. Where has his darling gone?

I feel Torgu on the floor. I haven't seen him again, but the crates give it away. He's brought his museum along, that bric-a-brac of smashed worlds. What did he call it? His avenue of eternal peace? His strength, he also said. He can't conjure without those objects. Or maybe it's just a matter of comfort level. I ventured into that corridor, drawn instinctively to his possessions, wanting to learn more, pulled along by the aural tumult in my brain. The dead have followed him onto the floor. Or were they here already, drawing him across the water? He could not resist the call of so many murdered at once. Is he aware that I am here, too? I think yes. We are on the cusp of a great communion, he and I. He will need to drink from a deep cup.

I stood in front of the crates and placed my hands on the cold wood. The objects started to hum, I thought, to speak to me, and I understood their significance. These things contain their own songs, their own voices; they are like batteries. Before they could whisper their secrets to me, someone intruded: Julia Barnes.

I said something unfortunate. She seemed to have an inkling of my meaning. She wanted to talk to me, but I tried to get away. How can I possibly tell her what is in my mind? I'm a murderer. Even if she thinks she knows, she can't possibly grasp the implications.

Then she startled me. "Is Torgu his real name?" she asked, when I stepped out of that corridor.

"I don't know what you mean."

She stood in my way. "You can tell me." Her words ran too quickly out of her mouth. She was scared. "Maybe I can tell you things you don't know. Maybe we could help each other."

I forced myself to walk slowly. If I dashed away, she would become suspicious, but suspicious of what? She followed me into the editing bay until we almost ran into a racing Bob Rogers. He didn't look at us, didn't appear to notice that I had returned, dropped a hurried, "Hello, ladies," and vanished into the darkness behind us.

"We're under attack here," Julia Barnes muttered, lowering her voice so no one would hear. "We need your help."

I shook her off.

I longed for Ian. If Ian were alive, he'd understand. Ian would be appalled at my carnality and my violence, but in a good way. He would find the humor in this sickest of jokes. What could have happened? What stupid darkness? I went by his office, which had passed into the hands of another producer, and for a long time, I lingered there, thinking about my friend, about the last time we had seen each other. Stim was there. Ian had already been sick.

I checked right and left. There was no one else around. The twentieth floor brimmed with late-spring emptiness, vivid with invisible life. Yesterday, Austen called me at home and told me about the Bob Rogers meeting, that the staff of *The Hour* would return over the next few days from various missions and adventures around the globe to get big news, but at that moment, silence pressed down on every corner. I could hear the air wriggling in the vents, battling against the great blank heat that smothered a decent May in New York City.

Ian and I met on my first day on the job as Lockyear's associate producer. I had not yet grasped the nature of the difficult man who would be my boss, and I was in my office, feeling joyful and proud, unpacking a few things, when Ian swaggered in, uninvited and unannounced. He wore his usual finery, a dark suit, polished black shoes of Italian leather, a scarlet power tie. I found him ludicrously overdressed. He made himself comfortable on my couch and said, "I truly pity you."

The memory gave me a rare smile. "Do I know you?" I asked him.

"Think of me as a UN human rights observer. If there are violations of your person, I'm the go-to guy. I can't actually help you or rescue you, but I may be able to drop packages of food. And I will definitely broadcast your pain and suffering to the rest of the office."

I had plenty of occasion to recall these words later, but at the time, he spoke them with a smirk on his face, and I could only laugh at their overstatement.

"Ian," he said, sticking out his hand, which I didn't take.

"The UN has no jurisdiction here," I told him. "And it's corrupt."

"God love the corrupt. Without them, we might as well be sharks or wolves, who eat other animals but don't generally screw them first. If you want my help, you'll do exactly as I say. You'll let me buy you drinks and ply you with questions about your boss and his boss. That's how it works. In exchange, I will work in your interests to undermine your persecutors. It's basically a page from the mafia handbook."

"It may sound naïve to you, but I feel I'm just lucky to have a job here."

He shook his head and gave a kind smile. "Work makes us free? That's your motto?"

"If you say so."

"I do."

"Why pick on me, if I may ask?"

"Two reasons. One, actually. You're quite good looking."

I was charmed enough to entertain his company a while longer. I asked him what he did on the show, and he informed me he was technically a wingman for one of Skipper Blant's producers, but Blant had given him a chance to produce, and he'd knocked it out of the park—his very words—and had high hopes of becoming a full-fledged producer with real pay as soon as a new position opened up, ergo as soon as one Blant's current producers got fired or quit in frustration.

"I just want you to know," he said in conclusion, "where you've landed. It's not an office. It's a country. Under the UN charter, it's known as Fangland, and to receive a passport, you need only one thing: the capacity to suffer in vain all things. Congratulations. It sounds to me like you'll be very happy here."

Our conversation ended as it had begun. He got off the couch, offered me once more a chance to rat out Lockyear over drinks and swaggered out. He became a producer, and we became friends.

His office sat at an intersection of light and dark, still awash in the natural glow of sun off the river, but close to the place where one of the cavernous central corridors began. The office had a window overlooking the water. From there, the Trade Center site couldn't be seen, so I liked it. After we moved back onto the twentieth floor, I spent more and more time there. It would be the most natural thing to walk inside and find him alive. Our offices had vacated about the same time. A selfish notion came to me; he'd left his own life to go looking for mine. Lovely Ian. He should have run *The Hour*. He was its best essence. I lifted my hand to knock. I hesitated. Left and right, the sunlight poured through the glass of the other offices and gave the floor a luminous quality, as if it floated within a bright and shining cloud.

I knocked. No one answered, but the door gave a crack. I put my ear close and heard nothing but the wash of a white noise machine. The voices in my mind seemed to recede for a moment, or I noticed them less. Entering this office might hurt. It might hurt worse than I imagined. What if there was no trace of the man I had known and loved? Another producer had been in his chair for months. I listened to the rhythm of the white noise machine. Ian never owned a white noise machine. He thought they were ridiculous.

I pushed open the door. A man sat at the desk, facing the computer screen.

"I'm so sorry," I stammered. "I, I didn't think anyone was in here."

He got up and turned. "Line!"

My shock rooted me to the spot. He was dressed as ever, in a starched white shirt, red power tie, a blue blazer and suspenders. His dark brown hair flared out, brushed superbly back. What a joy of a man he was. He made everyone smile, just to look at him, a benevolent rooster. His vanity had no cruelty. That was the thing. His dimpled chin didn't certify some false sense of rectitude. It mocked itself. I had teased him that it was a botched plastic surgery, and he had teased back that my big eyes could only be the result of an alien insemination in a government laboratory in Nevada.

And there he was, his blazer flying back.

"Oh, Ian," I said.

"Bear hug me, Line."

Only Ian ever called me that. I had some silly notion that my arms would go through him, as if he were air, but I hugged him, and he was substantial, and such a bliss went through me. He led me to the couch and sat me down.

"You've grown curly," he said. "I'm not saying it's a bad thing, but it is striking. You were always the least curly person in the room. Your lack of curliness was almost bizarre."

"You're so queer, but thank you."

"You're welcome. God it's great to see you. The Thin Blue Line!"

"Call me by my real name, for once."

He grimaced. "Christ, no. Your totally agnostic parents should be shot for naming you that. And it's not even how the name is pronounced in that song, except for one time!" He sang, as he had so many times before. "'Evangeline from the Maritime is slowly goin' insane!'"

We had been over this on many a drunken night in downtown bars. "What's done is done, Ian."

"Is that what you said after you murdered your friend?"

I felt those words go right through me. I wanted to answer. I stuttered. "You, you know—"

"Indeed. But we're getting off track. This new curliness of yours. It's very attractive. Very sexy. Does the fry cook dig it?"

His question wasn't glib. It sounded glib, but it wasn't. The minute I grew serious, he would change, too. That was his way.

"He's not so good, Ian."

There came a sigh, like the air through the vents. He put a hand on my shoulder.

"I saw," he said. "I saw what they did to him. I was here."

"They?" He offended me deeply, this fatuous figment of my imagination. "He tried to take his own life. Stop being mean."

He let me know with a look that I was wrong. "They are like you. They bled him, Line. But they didn't kill him."

My mind went black.

"Who?"

"Your friends," Ian said.

I stared at him for a long time, this ghost, and I said, "You know about what happened to me, Ian?"

"I've heard," he said. "He calls you the Whore of Babylon, like he was an old-time preacher."

"You know what I did?"

His face grew sad. Relief touched my rage. Someone else knew, even if only in my mind.

He touched his chest with a finger. "Breaks my heart."

"I wish you weren't gone."

He gave a soft smile. "I'm not."

I bent over and put my hands to my eyes. I sobbed in his arms. He rubbed my neck. He spoke in a quiet voice, for once.

"When people talked about escaping from their lives, I never really understood. I wanted to go deeper. I never wanted out. Never for a minute. It's a colossal scandal that I should be dead."

The pain burst out of me.

"But you've changed, too, Line. You've died, too."

"Have I?"

"Definitely. More than once."

"Am I a ghost then?"

"Something worse."

"What?" I cried. I really wanted to know.

326 • JOHN MARKS

"You're what they used to call a goddess, in the scariest sense."

Those words sank into me. They calmed me. They were so Ian. I had no reason to believe them. But I allowed myself to believe that he existed and had a special wisdom. I sat up, and he gave me a cuff of his shirt to wipe my eyes.

"There's something I have to ask you, Ian."

He nodded, as if the point of the entire conversation had come.

"They're waiting for me, aren't they?"

He nodded. "They're like cats. Once you feed them, they never go away. They're always here." He pointed to his chest. "They will be here till the last hour of the last day. Didn't you know? The twentieth floor is their natural home."

"Torgu's kingdom."

"He's using their desires, as he uses the desires of all those who have been destroyed. He's using their desire to be heard. All of the dead want to speak. He knows this. He knows their terror of silence."

"I know how to destroy him, Ian."

"I know you do."

"But I want something else."

"I know."

"Is it wrong?"

"It's horrific."

"But is that wrong, if that's what I am?"

"You're a murderer now. What do you care?"

"Answer me."

"It's a choice. Become like him, or leave the dead to their own sorrows."

I thought of Clemmie, another ghost with whom I'd had a conversation, though ghost seemed a rude and useless term. I understood why she had come to me. I was her lover and killer. She had grievances. Why was Ian talking? I hadn't drunk blood. Maybe other laws governed the dead. I said, "I once told a friend that the walls between things had grown very thin, that I could stick out my hand and I'd be inside a new reality. And that's what I've done, isn't it? I've walked out of one reality and into another in which you're still alive. I have walked through a wall."

"Through several."

I comprehended that the voice in my head, the images in my brain, had ceased. The effect made me suspicious. "How come you're talking to me? Are you one of Torgu's?"

"On this floor, everything is moving from one corridor to the next. The walls have vanished. The dead walk beside the living, and the living feel it, hear it, sense it, absorb it, but can't yet see it. But they will. Everything is merging. That's how come you're here so easily, Line. It's a fundamental breakdown. This is your opportunity. Destroy Torgu, and you release the dead to themselves. You are released. Follow him, and you lose yourself completely. You'll become him. You'll be worse. Queen of the Damned."

He ran a hand through his hair, the first sign of anxiety. "He came here on their account. Death is drawn to death. That was the original impulse. But you drew him, too. You goaded him, I might say. I've heard the story. He tells it to the dead as if it were a bedtime tale for children. He says that you used your living flesh to commit an obscenity against his dignity, and this cannot be forgiven. Scares the shit out of the listeners, that story. He's gone a little insane from centuries of loneliness, of slim pickings there on his mountaintop. He's a real complainer. I hear him at night, when the office is empty. The mountains had become depopulated. He was tired of waiting. So he's come here, with your help, he has come to a place where he can feel truly comfortable, a place beside a great hole in the ground where thousands died. It's a place rich in death already, and he wants to use it to bring his armies into the world. He wants to sing their histories into existence. It might be simpler to think of him as the most bizarre aspiring celebrity in the world. Romania was too small a market, a niche market, in the end, so he relocated, and now he's just hustling to get as much exposure here as possible. And when he does, the dead will inhabit us, so that we might know their violence. Among themselves, there is an old saying: Beyond the last word, comes the storm. It's time now for the last word."

"But what does it mean, Ian, if they come? Will it be so bad?"

He fixed me with a gaze of terrible warning, the first time I had ever seen him truly angry with me. "If they come, the race is finished. We lose the one blessed thing we have, our animal capacity to forget. Those who live for the dead, no matter what they tell you, become the dead. The last two survivors, steeped in the memory of blood, will tear each other limb from limb."

An unexpected objection rose out of me. "God help me, Ian, but isn't there something utterly beautiful in that?"

He smiled without pleasure. "The exquisite moral beauty of buildings on fire."

I was waking, or he was getting ready to depart. He held out a hand to me, indicating I should rise.

"Which people can I trust?" I was losing him, like a voice fading in cell phone fuzz.

"No one can help you. Austen Trotta has done some smart pieces over the years, but he's out of his depth here. Even if you tell him what you know, what you are, he won't believe you. Do you understand me?"

"Stim?"

Ian's eyes were sad and exasperated at the same time.

"He's like you."

My grief understood the truth. Fury overwhelmed me. "He attacked Robert."

"Torgu's going to murder everyone on this floor. He's going to cut every throat. And then he's going to open the door and bring the dead. Time to break out the resolve. Time to suit up. You hear me?" Ian opened the door to leave. I stayed, as if some danger lurked outside.

"I won't do that again, Ian. I won't dance for him."

He diminished into sunlight. I was alone in the office.

Sir—I've had an alarming encounter, and you'd better know. It happened half an hour ago. After I arranged the meeting with Trotta, I bent myself to the task of doing my usual chores, logging tapes, dealing with archives, nailing down licenses, though it must be said that the latter end of May tends to be slow, and even the most diligent production associates see a lag in activity. Nevertheless, I had one or two items on my list for next year, so I moved forward. I lugged a VCR machine to my desk and began to watch footage from the 1972 Olympic games in Munich. That's when she showed up. I mean to say, Evangeline Harker. It was an attack. She slapped the tapes right and left; she swatted the material like flies and made a terrible commotion. No one came to my rescue. The halls were empty. She stood there, staring at me, eyes incandescent. She's still very beautiful. I told her to be careful with the tape, that if she had damaged a reel I couldn't be held accountable. This remark detonated something. She reached down to the VCR machine, pressed the eject button, jerked the tape out of the machine, and hurled the machine against the wall. I mean, she bodily wrenched the machine out of the conveyor, lifted it over her head and slammed it full force against the opposite wall. It was my turn to become incensed. "What's your problem?!" I shouted, hoping to stir up enough noise to bring an immediate end to this encounter, but as I've told you, most of the staff don't return till tomorrow, and not a soul mustered on my behalf. I'm going to quote her. She said, "Why?"

I never for a moment believed in my obligation to respond, but she refused to go. Having destroyed the video player, she turned to the television. She hoisted it up and dropped it to the floor with a crunch. Hairline cracks split the screen. She snatched tapes off my desk and flicked them at my head. I have never seen her like this. The vestiges of my old sense of responsibility reasserted themselves, I'm ashamed to say, and I became emotional.

I'd like to stop here and defend myself a bit. I'm telling you everything because I know you'll get it out of me anyway but also to remind you of my absolute sense of loyalty to you. I don't have to say a thing. I could make you work to get it out of me, but that's not what's happening. I'm volunteering information. She slapped me, and I broke into tears. "Look at your teeth, Stim. Have you seen them? They're turning his color." I shot back the obvious. "And you, Evangeline? What about you?" She stopped her mayhem. "What are you talking about?" I wiped my eyes. I didn't answer. If I'd had my knife, things would have gone very differently. But I didn't. "You never got my e-mail, did you?" I asked. She clasped her hands at her chest and closed her eyes. She looked more beautiful than I have ever seen her. "God, Stim," she said. I saw my opening, and you will be proud of me. "He's not so bad, though, is he? Our man. I mean, he's pretty fascinating, wouldn't you say?" She reached for my face, put a finger on my chin as if I were a small child, and said, "He's a bloody massacre, and you know it."

I put my cards on the table. "I loved you and would do anything for you. That's what my e-mail said. If you had received it, you might understand how I came to this pass."

She is cruel. "I would have deleted it, Stim." I was too hurt by her honesty to reply. She would have deleted it. You warned me. I dropped my head to the top of the desk and cried in humiliation. I cried until tears covered the desk. I doubt anyone at *The Hour* has ever cried as long or hard as I cried. Why would she have deleted my e-mail? Why? I told her to go away, but she began to goad me. "You need to tell me where he is, Stimson. You need to tell me everything you know."

A last time, I want to account here for my moment of weakness. I had a choice. I could have told her to go to hell. But I didn't. She still holds some sway over my heart. Tell me what I need to do, and I will do it. Command me, and it's done. Want her dead? Say the word. But in that instant, I caved. I collapsed. I told what I knew. But what is that exactly? Do you see? I don't know all that much. "Where does he hide?" she asked. "No idea," I honestly replied, "but he's always in the central corridors after midnight. He strolls and sings and unpacks his things." I did tell her that much, and I rue it, yes, I do. "What is he doing here? Has he told you that?" This was a lucky moment for me. It's one thing to have questions. It's quite another to know the right questions to ask, and she didn't. "He's doing what he always does. He's listening. He's singing." Her next query hit closer to home. "But where does he get the blood, Stim? They don't come to him unless he drinks the blood. So?" I didn't say a word. There were no specifics in my face. But she comprehended enough. "You murdered for him, you wretch." I did nod. I nodded, and she shivered in outrage, and I was about to say how proud I was when she took me by the head and slammed it down hard on the desk, breaking a tooth. "That's for Robert," she said to me. "If I thought it mattered,

I'd kill you myself. But that's his job. In the end, he will slit your throat from ear to ear. He can't help himself. You better run." As a final humiliation, she came very close and committed an act of infamy that would have repulsed the old Evangeline. She stuck her warm tongue in my ear and rasped a lascivious message, "Tell him something he already knows. Tell him the dance of life is more powerful than the song of death. Tell him that." Herewith, I pass that laughable message on to you, along with this plea. Understand my confusion. You told me that you'd never met her. It's a bourgeois convention, and I say this with all due respect, but it would appear that you lied to me, and as this e-mail attests, I'm not guilty of the same vice. You lied for reasons of your own, no doubt, and I'm educated now in the protocol and see that certain decisions have to be taken outside of conventional boundaries, but this strikes me as breaking trust, and inasmuch as I have always considered us friends, I would ask that you take my hurt feelings into account when judging this case. Yours in truth, Stimson

Stimson: This, alas, is our final communication. Take the concubine's advice. Run from this place. If I ever find you, there will be no apologies proffered, and none at all accepted. I

To hell with Evangeline Harker, Julia Barnes decided. It's time to get serious. Time to call a man about a dog. It had been thirty-five years, at least, since she had thought of her old ordnance supplier Flerkis. Back in those days, she'd had a semi-regular business tab with the man, and he'd never once given her name to the authorities, or even come up on the federal radar, far as she knew. That was how low to the ground he worked. And there had existed an entire society of Americans in his style and fashion. They had formed a true underground world, an alternate universe of banks, shops, bakeries, bed and breakfasts for people whose idealism had led them to oppose the U.S. government. Looking back, it seemed a preposterous way to live a life, but Julia had done it for three years, sitting in a forgotten corner of a rust belt city or two—Jersey City, Utica, Bethlehem—waiting for the phone call to go to some

other city, less scarred by capitalism, where an action would be undertaken, a bomb in a building after hours, some such thing. No one had
ever been killed, but a lot of office space had been reduced. In those
days, she had moved in circles that her colleagues at *The Hour* would
now either scorn with a depthless contempt or find quaintly amusing,
a life as trivial as bell bottoms. Either that, or they were too young to
know—was the Weather Underground a Web site related to weather?
She didn't mind. She looked back on that era with, at best, mixed feelings. But she'd never felt so strongly, in three decades, the need to activate one piece of that past for her own personal ends.

Flerkis had lived in a flat off the Grand Concourse in the Bronx and
spent his days as a bus driver for the New York City schools. He never
associated with Panthers or radicals or their hangers on, and in that day,
there had been a wide assortment in the South Bronx, acupuncturists
who loved Ho Chi Minh, preachers who carried shotguns, Vietnam
vets who practiced Buddhism—Julia's old chums, but anathema to
Flerkis, who drove his bus by day and ran a side operation in the
evening related to the order and purchase of explosives and firearms.
He had four children with a Jamaican girl named Daisy and had to support them somehow. Julia had regarded him simply as "real," an unavoidable chunk of human reality that the dark powers wanted to
ignore or avoid, and one of the key reasons, in addition to her knowledge of film editing, why she had been so valued by the heavies in the
movement. "Got to see the brother man about a dog," they would say
to her, when it was time. Flerkis was the nom de guerre, obviously
fraudulent, of a black man of African descent.

But on that late morning in May, playing hooky from work under
the grill of the furious sun, air-conditioning units in broken housing
stock sputtering and dripping in shock, she could find no trace of her
old supplier. She asked around. A couple of ladies remembered the
African gentleman and his wife, Daisy, though the name Flerkis meant
nothing to them. It hadn't been real, of course, any more than hers had
been; aka Flerkis would have looked in vain for aka Susan Kittenplan.

The day was waning. Her sons would be getting home from activities. Her husband would wonder about dinner and company. She

ceive a difficult impression of me, a lasting and final impression, and it will make them unhappy for a time. They will be left with the apprehension of dawning deliria, and the thought rankles. My body has debilitated, but never my mind, and I loathe the idea of a legacy based in fraudulence and misinformation. It would be easier to burn this entire journal and leave the rest to silence, but that tack would be a violation of my decades of journalistic probity. So my loved ones will have to suffer. But if I'm honest, this last account of my state of mind before the meeting with that freak—I have decided to go forward with the Julia Barnes scheme—is not meant for my family. Nor is it for the mass of viewers who have watched me on television for the last four decades, one on network news, three on The Hour; it is for the handful of friends and confidantes who have constituted my social circle in this city and life. And maybe it will be of benefit to a smattering of others, this town's snobs and cranks, who have never been very fond of me, who already hold a low opinion, thanks to my chosen medium, though I have never yielded to their automatic derision of a form that served me and the populace well enough. Reading this, they will have every bit of ammunition needed to bury my reputation, the very memory of my work, beneath a pile of critical rubble. But I defy them to do it. I spit in the collective face of that mob of big-city provincials.

Here is what I wish to have known for the record. In the late summer and early fall of the previous year, one of my associate producers, Ms. Evangeline Harker, went missing in the country of Romania, in a region of the eastern Transylvanian Alps. I have every reason to believe that she was kidnapped and somehow molested by an underworld figure known as Ion Torgu. Torgu, who claims to have privileged information about Cold War governments and who also claims to be on the run from assassins tied to former Eastern Bloc intelligence agencies, appears to have access to chemical and/or biological and psychological weaponry of a sort that I have never encountered before. He also appears to bear some animus against our program, the nature of which I will try to ascertain momentarily. We gave Evangeline Harker up for dead. To our delighted surprise, she resurfaced half a year later, very much alive, though she has never been able to speak about the period of her disappearance. My speculation about her encounter with Torgu is based on a hunch, and nothing more, but it is an overwhelm-

ing hunch. *Roughly around the time of her disappearance, the network received a shipment of tapes from an unknown origin in Romania. Those
tapes contained little or no visual information and had come unsolicited.
They were not shot by network crews and were part of no known segment of
The Hour. No producer has ever stepped forward to claim them. Nevertheless, for reasons I still fail to understand, an editor digitized those tapes,
thereby bringing this foreign material into the technological pool shared by
the entire office and contaminating by as yet unknown means the entirety of
our editing and recording system with some form of audio virus. The tapes
appear to have had an odd side effect on those who viewed them as well, a
degenerative lethargy that has spread like a sickness among the editors and
a few other employees of the twentieth floor. There is also cause to believe
that the tapes engender violence. I myself have experienced several episodes
of blind rage in myself, one resulting in the near death of my dog, and have
been made aware of the "suicide" of at least one employee under mysterious
circumstances. Unknown persons staged a near-fatal attack on the fiancé of
Evangeline Harker. To my shame and frustration, no doctor has ever been
able to diagnose this collective illness, and our wonderful, indispensable
people have been left to defend themselves against a force beyond comprehen-
sion. It is my earnest belief that these men and women have been progressively poisoned by a chemical and/or biological weapon disseminated via
the tapes. At the time of my writing, according to Julia Barnes, at least a
dozen editors have failed to show up for work.*

*These allegations would be sinister enough, but there is far worse. In the
early part of this year, not long after the winter storm blackout, my esteemed
colleague Edward Prince came to me with news of an exclusive interview
with none other than Ion Torgu. At the time, the name alarmed me, but
Prince gave assurances that his interview would put the man behind bars
forever. Rather than call the police and scuttle his opportunity to break a big
news story, I ignored my better judgment and waited for results. As it happened, Prince's interview with Torgu turned out quite differently than my
colleague had expected. Prince is now a virtual prisoner in his office and a
raving lunatic to boot, and both of these conditions pertain to Torgu, who
has now, through a loathsome intermediary, requested an interview with
me. For that reason, I've recounted my suspicions. I have no hope of emerg-*

ing from that interview in my right mind. For the record, I have never contacted the law, because I never had any hope that legal authorities would believe my story. Journalist that I am, I know the difference between a credible
and plausible complaint and an unproven conspiracy theory. Having said
that, I remain convinced that we are under attack and that our assailant
means to obliterate us and carry out some further plan of which I am currently ignorant. One way or another, I take full responsibility for the decision to confront this man, and for any consequences arising therefrom. May
the God of my fathers forgive me if I fail in this effort; no one else will.

Julia came home and made the beloved Shake 'n Bake chicken for her
sons. She had been home by five, through the door and into the
kitchen. After preparing the chicken and popping it into the oven, she
went down to the basement, where she regarded the cardboard box on
the stone floor of her building with a horrid eagerness. She had loved
bombs as a young woman. She had to admit it. Other kids loved
sparklers; she'd loved the bigger stuff. In the box were six foot-long bars
of C-4, wrapped in olive drab paper. In a sack beside the box lay an assortment of ten crude fuses.

Flerkis had hooked her up with a younger man, a nephew, who happened to have a kit ready to go, a kilo of C-4 rendered available by last-
minute circumstances. It wasn't custom made for her, which Julia
didn't like, but it would have to do. Julia had gone through her wow
phase with C-4. All the Nam vets she'd known had adored it and used it
for everything: warming dinner, knocking down trees, blowing up
mines. For this stunt at work, which had only half formed in her mind,
she'd place one bar, maybe two, light the fuse and run. She told the
Flerkis nephew nothing about her plans, and he liked it that way. Same
old game. He wouldn't guarantee anything, but offered a hopeful
smile. Julia offered half price; he wanted it out of the house. The question of storage arose. She didn't want to deposit it in the same apartment building with her children. The park across the street might do,
unless a homeless interloper came across the explosives and made

them disappear or detonate. None of her ex–radical friends would help. The old underground networks had long since ceased to operate.

After the remarkable conversation with Evangeline in the corridor, there hadn't been much else to say. The girl had obviously been raped by their mutual enemy and traumatized into silence. It wouldn't do to let a woman in her state hide explosives.

Julia would have to deposit them in the office. She gloved her hands and placed the package at the bottom of a shopping bag. She threw on a loose-fitting orange T-shirt and a pair of slacks, an urban mom heading into work to pull some overtime. At the last minute, she placed the bag in the foyer of the building, under the watchful eyes of the doorman, and raced back upstairs to turn off the oven. She came back down, hoisted her bag, flipped on a pair of shades bought circa 1975 and stepped out into the blaze of the dying day.

BO OK

History Lesson

Forty-five

Medical personnel have come and gone. Doors and windows are locked. I'm still alive. I've had too much red wine.

But I must calm down and order my thoughts. I have met the man.

The hour came. A heavy quiet lay on the twentieth floor. I had given Peach the morning off and sent the other front office assistants on various errands. Most of the overseas producers and correspondents hadn't yet returned for the big meeting. The rest, increasingly repelled by the atmosphere on the floor and sensing the approach of bad news from network, stayed away. Frankly, I had underestimated the degree of the malaise. I had expected more people to be around.

Five minutes after eleven, the door to Prince's office creaked open. I heard the hiss of a long breath and expected to see my old friend finally come to his senses. But it wasn't Edward Prince. It was another man, the strangest I have ever seen. What made him so strange? Before I approach that question, I should make clear that his profound ugliness was the least of his objectionable qualities. His ugliness made him human. He had teeth as black as coal, small ones, like pebbles on a lava beach I had seen once in Catania, lodged in a maw of visibly swollen, plaster gray gums. Imagine that black lava beach strewn with a litter of dead fish, and you will have the overall effect. His head bulged thick—I mean, rather, dense. It was the largest head on the smallest body. But the head wasn't fat or chubby or bloated. It was massive, and it sat on a trunk that tapered to nothing. His eyes were red, but so what? Mine are, too. His outfit puzzled me, a dated white leisure suit of sorts, too small at the cuffs and hems, over a dark blue shirt, a non sequitur wardrobe, clothing stripped from the body of another human being. He had a wispy blond curl of hair at the top of that rock of a skull and a pair of dark blue socks at his ankles.

When he entered my office, I experienced a wave of personal sorrow that near brought me to my knees. I struggle to comprehend the nature of this effect, but I can describe it with precision. There was no mistaking the outline. He walked in an atmosphere of my own worst history; he walked, how can I put this, in a nimbus of torture and murder that felt immediately accessible, completely tangible, as if I could reach out and stroke it, as if he wore an expensive coat made of the living skin of humans under interrogation. And when he opened his mouth, I knew it would become worse. I cut him off with a sharp question.

"Where's Edward Prince? What have you done with him?"

I leaned forward on my desk, unsure whether I could handle whatever he might tell me. He shuddered, as if his heart had twitched, sought the support of my wall and pointed back at the door to my office. "See for yourself."

Alarmed, I hastened out of my chair and around him, moved out the door and to my neighbor, but I was stopped in my tracks by a sight so nightmarish that it gave Torgu a measure of rational substance. Prince wasn't dead. At least, he wasn't immobile. I wished he had been. The man was very much alive, but he was naked, and he kneeled on the floor in front of three video monitors on carts, fumbling in wild agitation with dials and switches. I couldn't see the images on the screens, but the room was otherwise completely dark, and I could see a random flickering, as of static, across Edward Prince's naked back. A beard had grown long on his face. His withered and sagging skin glowed the shade of the screens. When he saw me, he barely displayed recognition, but he did speak.

"Oh Christ, the motherfucker, the betrayal, the dirty shitting asshole of the universe betrayal of our arrangement . . . look at this . . . for God's sake . . . for the love of God . . . will you look?"

This last word held a particular emphasis. It wasn't gibberish. Prince did, in fact, want me to see the images on the video monitors, and though I have never wished more to turn my back and walk away—I have never believed that we are truly our brothers' keepers—I stepped forward into the darkness, making my way, inch by inch, wary of a lunge or attack from a person who had clearly lost his mind. I came to a point where the angle allowed me to behold, from the side, one of the three monitors. He ran his fingers across those screens, and I saw the thing that caused such demoniac raving in him. I had no further doubt about his mental health. Edward Prince, my rival and fair-weather friend, had gone missing in his dreams and would never return. On the screen was a standard moment in the Universal Room, two chairs, unoccupied, two water bottles beneath them, no cameras visible, the facsimile of a library in the background. There was no audio, or he had turned it down, and I had no intention of asking for volume. I watched for a while. Finally, I put a question to Prince.

"What is it, Ed? What's so terrible?"

His head spun round at me, his mouth gaping. His teeth, too, had gone blue, like those of Stimson Beevers. I winced, trying to expunge the implications from my brain. "What's so terrible?!" he shrieked. "What's so fucking terrible?! There's no me, you withered old viper!"

I didn't understand, and I'd had enough, and I backed away, but as I did, I witnessed on the screen a thing that I refuse to believe to this moment. I tell myself that the phenomenon was suggested by Prince himself, and made to seem real by Torgu's uncanny behavior, but I am attempting here to report everything as I experienced it. In short, I saw on the screen the movement of a water bottle, from the floor of the Universal Room, into the air, and back down again. Someone drank from the bottle. That person could not be seen by the lens of the camera. That person, I believe—I know—was Edward Prince. I flung myself out of the room, my hands over my eyes, and back into my own office, where Torgu had occupied the sofa.

"Life is a disappointment," he murmured. "Death is no different."

I had an impulse to beat him, but I lost my nerve. I was afraid he would begin to speak again, and in my weakness, I couldn't bear the voice. Moreover, the man's head appeared to grow before my eyes, like a plant fed on blood. I don't know why. I can't explain the effect, unless it was truly happening, unless his coming performance required an extension of the physical boundaries of the already enormous skull.

"What have you done?"

"I did nothing. He's upset by the terms of an agreement that he himself made." I stood five feet away, and the foul breath assaulted me. I could feel, increasingly, another effect of his presence. It seemed to me, with little visible evidence of the fact, that we were no longer alone in that office. If you've ever been in a room on a warm windy day, with windows open, your papers flying around in rampant breezes, then you may know what prompted this thought. We were on the twentieth floor. My window, a twelve-foot pane of plexiglass, could not be opened. Neither wind nor rain could enter, and yet something had. He sat at its vortex, on my couch. I noticed then that he had brought a bucket with him, a pail of metal, and out of it jutted the handle of some instrument. The bucket sat at his feet.

I stumbled to the desk, gripped it, as if it might help me. "What agreement?"

"I told him he would live forever if he drank the blood that is my gift, and he understood a very different meaning of immortality and imagined himself on screen for all time. I couldn't imagine a less edifying, less worthwhile form of immortality, so I didn't bother to tell him about the side effect."

I will confess that I began to grasp his meaning, and I believed his explanation. I look back now and see the absurdity, the ridiculousness, of the proposition, but I set it down here for the sake of journalistic accuracy.

"The side effect." I repeated his words as encouragement.

"Those of us who gather the histories cannot be seen by any technology known to man."

In a drawer, on the right-hand side, I keep a letter opener. I could no longer bear to let him live.

"By camera, you mean."

"Never again," Torgu whispered. "For him, that is finished. For you, too. You are about to begin reporting on a much greater story than you have ever undertaken. Did you know that Stalin had thirteen thousand of his own soldiers shot in Stalingrad during the siege of that great city? They will be made available. I trust you will handle this responsibility with greater dignity than your colleague."

My legs began to shake. I believed him, I confess. The idea of doing those interviews actually appealed to me. I fumbled with the drawer. He must not open his mouth again. If he did, I recognized, it would be the death of me. I had the letter opener, a spike of steel. But I was too late. He spoke. What he said froze my hands.

"By the way, I have had words with your great-aunt."

"Who?"

"Esther, Herr Von Trotta. I have seen Esther."

The letter opener turned to ice, stinging my fingers, dropping to the top of my desk, knocking over a foam cup of coffee, spilling coffee across papers. I looked back through the window of my office for Peach, for Bob Rogers, for anyone else to verify that this was really happening. Esther, my great-aunt Esther, had been dead more than sixty years, since July 1942, to be exact, when she and her four children, including the infant, had been executed by members of the German Reserve Police Battalion 101, First Company. My sister had obtained the files of that battalion from a historian, an old friend of the family, and we had read with searing amazement the first-person accounts of participants in the slaughter. Of course, we didn't know for sure how Esther met her end. Her name was never mentioned. But she and her family had been some of the eighteen hundred Jews who lived in the village, and no one had ever seen another document bearing her name. Her husband, my great-uncle Jozef, died in the Belzec concentration camp. This we knew, and nothing else.

What follows is an offense to reason. I confess it now. But there would be no honesty in this report if I lied on the score. The man in my office began to fill in the gaps in the story, and I will swear to my dying day, he did so in the voice of a woman I have never met.

I tried to prevent it. "You are a blackguard," I said, though clenched teeth.

"It would be wrong not to tell you what she told me . . ."

"Shut your mouth—"

"It's not my mouth," he murmured, "but hers, and you are the only living member of her family with whom she has ever had a chance to converse."

My arms hung at my sides as I listened to the testimony, though I'm afraid my emotion and my respect for the dead will not allow me to deliver even snatches of what he said in a long unbroken obliterating stream. Here my duty to the journalistic record must stop. I can say only that it was the authentic account of the extermination of a mother who had watched each of her children die before her. I can say only that. Such accounts come to us in massive volume. They ride in files or flicker across screens. She begged for their lives in German. She begged for her own in German. She was allowed to live long enough to watch the death throes of her eldest daughter. Someone ran out of ammunition. This came in a voice in my ear, and the voice struck two contradictory notes; on the one hand, it craved my reception; on the other, so caught up in its own horror, it did not heed me at all. This is what the monster brings. This is the nature of the chemical and biological attack, a form of knowledge more devastating than any dose of sarin. My aunt believed, at the last, she was dreaming.

I don't know how long before the sacrilege concluded. The worst of it was, I desired the testimony. I wanted to hear. I wanted to know. He expected me, perhaps, to fall at his feet and beg for mercy. I was sick, it's true, and I understood my blood pressure had risen, and my back had returned to its old agony. I would die in that office, as I had sworn many a time, but not as I had imagined. I would perish from the shock of my own unbearable family history. So be it. But my rage precluded incapacitation. No matter my state, the theft of my aunt's death filled me with a cold determination to finish him. I clutched the handle of the letter opener and waited for him to come into range.

"There are others," he said, now rising, "but you will hear them after, hear them for yourself. It's no longer my sole job to convey this information, thank the heavens. We are going to change the world."

The air blew with remarkable force. Papers burst off my desk, as if making way for him. His head hovered above the tempest. His pupils appeared to shrink, the orbs to beam a bright white. Despite his immense power, the man appeared to be seriously ill, and I don't mean in the way that monstrous personalities can often appear to suffer from disease. No, Torgu had a feverish, unstable quality that I associate with people who either need bed rest or have just arisen from a ravaging illness; moreover, the material of his suit had been spattered and smudged by God knows what horrific practices and conveyed a state of degenerative sloth, as if he was no longer capable of taking care of himself. He suffered from a plague that he was about to give to the rest of the species. He turned the corner of my desk, a mesmerist, holding the bucket containing the instrument, which I knew to be a knife. He was sick, but he was engorging. He was inflating with the energy of his constituency. He faced me, an incipient giant, or was I shrinking? He came within a yard. I plunged the letter opener into the gob of his throat. He spoke again, the steel in his windpipe.

"You will bear the violence well, I am sure," he rasped. "I, on the other hand, require a moment. No matter how many ages have passed, I never become used to that sort of thing." The dark teeth floated on the foam of gray gum. The lips broke in a wan grin. Horrific pain seized my lower back, and I crumpled back into my chair. He slid the letter opener out of his throat. Blood gouted down. His knife clanked restless in its bucket. He came forward a pace, raised the letter opener, and brought it down through the flesh of my outer thigh, into the chair.

He put one hand over my mouth and began to prepare his slaughter. He placed the bucket on the floor. He knelt with some effort in front of me. Outside this building, I knew the sun baked the Hudson. I knew the buildings glittered. I knew the girls wore short skirts, the traffic helicopters whirled, the barges churned. But in my office, the last arrangements were made for slaughter.

He took me by the collar. "Treblinka," he murmured. "Vorkuta. Gomorrah. These are words from the endless poem. Medina. Masada. Balaklava. If you know anything about me, you will know my integrity when it comes to the gift endowed to me by the curse of a father, enduring through untold centuries of grief. You will know how little I tolerate disrespect. You will know what a mighty defender of the offended dead I am."

He saw I wanted to speak and lifted his hand off my mouth. "Do you think," I rasped, "this world really needs your monstrous history lesson?"

"A history lesson," he replied. "You do see my intent."

"But it's a lie."

"The names don't lie. They cannot."

I found the energy to oppose him with my own words, powerless though they were to save me. "The deepest memories of the race do not require names. We saw the stars before we knew what they were called. One human being touched another before we knew a syllable. Women bore children with moans that predate language. The names are like your bucket. They carry only blood."

I was about to be gutted, and my lousy pig death had made me insolent. I was inordinately pleased with myself, it would have made a good lecture, *but the feeling passed. The pain of my back assaulted me. His breath defoliated. He subdued me with a horrible moment, a memory, one of my very own. We had stumbled across a rubber tree plantation in Vietnam, and the corpses were everywhere, VC and South Vietnamese regulars, dead for days and left to rot. They were like hacked vegetables, left in a field. We didn't shoot those faces. I asked my crew to leave them be, out of respect, but they had endured in my head, or Torgu had brought them into the room. I was losing strength. The presences in the air gained strength. He began to chant two things at once; his mouth offered two separate and completely different conversations. In one voice, he spoke the names of the places, and I could begin to see those words, fire-rimmed, dripping, emanating and within them, images of the most varied atrocity. I could not defend myself against Esther, the Vietnamese, or that other field in Algeria, the death strip in Berlin. How much death I'd seen. It surprised me somehow. I hadn't realized. At the same time, his mouth offered a proposition. He wasn't going to cut my throat, he said. He was going to cut his wrist, and I would drink from him. He wanted my allegiance. Torgu's eyes closed. "I ask your blessing on this."*

I reached for the letter opener in my thigh and wrenched it out. He took that as a refusal and jabbed at my head with his knife, caught my ear. I lifted my unhurt leg and kicked him back to the floor, and with the last of my physical strength, I hobbled bleeding out the door. He came howling behind.

I almost ran into Peach, who dropped a box of pizza and shrieked. Torgu had me by the coat when Evangeline Harker appeared before us like a vision in a dream. I felt the floor fall away beneath me. I heard a tumult of cries, up and away. Everything went black.

When I awoke, I was here, in my bedroom at home. I refused to go to the hospital. A nurse tried to keep the bottle out of my hands, and I sent her away. I must sleep now.

For an instant, I saw him again, face to face, and he saw me. *Evangeline,* I heard his whisper in my brain.

He had deteriorated horribly. His body had shrunk, his head had grown, like a tick too long on the back of a dog. It was only a matter of seconds, but the world seemed to stop, and I saw deep into those eyes, into the weariness, the hunger, the fear. It was nothing like before. He couldn't bear it. He burst past me, past a shrieking Peach Carnahan, his entourage following in a great wind. Austen staggered to the carpet, awash in his own blood. My Transylvanian instincts kicked in. I ripped away a piece of my T-shirt and tied it as a tourniquet around Austen's leg. I heard a fading roar of outrage. I ordered Peach to call the show's private ambulance service. For an instant, on my knees beside Austen, I peered through the open door of Edward Prince's office and glimpsed something inexplicable, a shadow that scuttled between three bright screens, but the door slammed before I could register it. I had no time to plumb the mystery. Austen had lost conciousness. Torgu was gone.

MAY 23

The nurse gave me a new bottle of Percocet. I use too much. I need something stronger. I am resisting the bottle. The weekend is here. I stagger around on crutches. Outside, the day has dawned in beastly heat. Record highs broke last night in the darkness. Con Ed is warning of overload and asking good citizens to conserve energy wherever possible. If I weren't a rational man, I'd say Torgu uses the sun against us. I have gone to the street to get the newspaper. I will not go outside again.

Sir—A deep breath on this molten Saturday. I know you're not speaking to me. I know you wish me a horrible fate. I know, too, that you plan to exact vengeance for my perceived lapse. My remorse cannot be over-stated. But I refuse to give up on you. I refuse to accept this judgment, and here is my first expression of penitence. You must be made aware of what's happening the day after tomorrow. Every single producer and correspondent of this show has returned from near and far to pay re-spects to their leader, Bob Rogers, the founder of the program, who will step down after more than three decades as executive producer. It's a historic moment in the annals of broadcast television. There has never been a show like *The Hour,* and never an executive producer like Bob Rogers. But what should concern you are numbers. It is rare for the entire staff of the show to be assembled under one roof. It is unheard of, except on the most serious occasions. For you, it represents an opportunity that will not come again. In a mere forty-eight hours, you will have at your disposal almost one hundred bodies, some old and decrepit, others supple and strong. Between the youngest and the oldest employees of this shop lie five decades, half a century. Think of it. They would be the very people to deliver the kind of information in which you specialize to a broad mass of Americans. The rest will do as vehicles, of course.

Here's the schedule. People arrive around ten. There will be a breakfast buffet in the screening room at eleven, and these are usually quite nice, with lox and bagels from Zabars, fresh boiled shrimp and a kind of micro-pig in blanket that I have yet to encounter elsewhere. Trotta thought he was being clever by planning to tell everyone about you at the meeting. He thought that the existence of a meeting with large numbers of people would influence your ability to speak your mind. He thought to intimidate you with this maneuver. But I have heard the glorious news. He has experienced your wonder. He knows better now. For my part, I will attend the Monday meeting and take notes. It's possible that you'll welcome this information. It's possible that you'll forgive me, if I bring one hundred talented, arrogant, pliant souls to our party. Godspeed. Stimson

My period came, the first in months. I sat on the floor of the bathroom in my apartment and watched the blood stream between my legs. I touched the blood with the tip of my fingers. I raised the fingers to my eyes. What is this stuff really? It was as if I'd never seen it before.

I know what I've done. I see her face every waking minute. I have no idea what I'm becoming.

Austen has called me. He wants me to come to his home. He wants to discuss the Monday meeting. He has no idea, I think, how close he came. If Torgu hadn't been surprised by my presence, he would be dead now. But the bastard fled, and I was able to get Austen out of the building and into the ambulance service. Peach helped. We managed, by miracle, to keep the police out of it.

After we got Austen home, after the doctors came, I went to Robert. It was past midnight, and we hadn't talked all day. I walked from the East Side down to the West Village and let myself into the apartment with my own key. He was asleep. I made myself a cup of coffee, went into the bedroom and watched his chest rise and fall beneath the blankets. There was one last thing to be done. He's tried so hard to recover from his trauma. He's been so patient. We've been intimate only once, that time when I slipped on the Amsterdam exotica and almost devoured him, but he says the wedding will go ahead. He's back at work and eager to move on with his life.

I unbuttoned my sweat-stained white cotton blouse with the bows on the shoulders and removed my khaki slacks and walking sneakers. It was a bit late in the day for ultimatums, but we can't always choose the hour of decision. Robert has pulled a lot of favors and thinks he can still get our church and our favorite restaurant and a country-western band for me by Labor Day. I'm letting him make the wedding cake, as he always wanted. He's in a rush, a little manic, and I can't blame him. He's also cross with me for showing less enthusiasm than I once did for our wedding plans. I tell him I plan to make full producer now. I tell him I might even run the show someday, and he chalks it up to the unknown horrors I must have endured in Romania, and I don't discourage this line of thinking, though it's dishonest.

I straddled his body, thinking against my will of Clemmie, and waited. I looked down at his face, anxious to see what he would do when his eyes fluttered wide. I didn't bother with another Amsterdam outfit. He needed to see my nakedness. He needed to understand what was happening. I wore only the black bra that had saved my life. He wasn't entirely awake, but I checked beneath the sheet and found that necessary part of him in a state of insurgency. I composed the words in my head, explaining myself in brief. The minutes passed, and every explanation fell deeper and deeper into error. The heat crept in beneath the air-conditioning. My hands moved on his body. He must see me as I had become. He must see me, and then I would tell him, and everything would be fine.

He began to moan beneath my hands, but his eyes wouldn't open.

"It's time, my love," I said.

I noticed with an alarming rush of hunger the circuitry of blood in his neck and forearms. Nurses never had a problem finding the right vein in Robert. My veins are small and cause problems for needles. I could feel his veins in my hand, too, thick and pumping. He would not look at me. The waking world no longer accorded with our best wishes for each other.

I took off the bra. "Open your eyes, Robert," I said.

And he did, and they saw. His lips parted, and he gazed at my pale belly and my breasts that he had loved so well and across them those signs that had been growing every day since I had escaped Transylvania, like little freckles, at first, like scratches from a rash, so small I had refused at first to believe them, or what they meant. But his eyes told me everything I needed to know. He had seen them before, hadn't he? But that hadn't been enough for me. I hadn't wanted to believe. I hadn't beheld myself in a mirror in months. Now I beheld myself in the mirror of his eyes, which gazed upon hundreds of tiny incisions in my flesh, a dread kind of flaw that no amount of tummy-tucking would ever destroy, a Milky Way of swastikas, hammers and sickles, crosses, crescents, stars, stripes, the flags of the nations of the world since the dawn of time sweeping in uproar across my skin, around my nipples, up my neck, I had become the paper upon which the dead drew their designs. I let go of his flesh. Had I dreamed it all? I longed to believe so. I longed to believe that Ion Torgu, a brutal criminal, had raped me over a period of days, and in my imprisonment, I had given birth to a wild version of events in which I emerged victorious. It was a fairy tale. A creature of deep time had come among us. It drank human blood and drew the murdered dead like flies to sugar. The lost souls spoke to this creature, touched it, infected it, and the creature in turn passed the infection further, the weight of millions upon millions of savage little histories fed into the minds of human beings wholly unprepared to accept the burden. I knew this for fact, and my colleagues did not. I grant them that. But they had seen signs. They had evidence of a wider, stranger reality, which they denied. So did Robert. He despised the transformation in my limbs. He despised me, in fact, though he could never bring himself to say so, though he didn't even know why this deep repulsion had come over him. I knew. I haunted him at the cellular level. My mind, my skin, my scars took me farther away from his ken with every passing day.

I crept off the bed. I sat beside the sweetness of that still form. His eyes stared ahead, as if I remained there on top of him. I kissed his mouth. Maybe in that other reality, where Ian walked and talked, we had married, and I was pregnant and happy. I hoped so. But in this life, we were finished. I put on my clothes and left the apartment.

Julia despised being in the office on a Sunday afternoon. She always had. If you came to the office on a Sunday, it meant one kind of a calamity or another. It meant that your piece needed last-minute surgery. Or it meant that a disaster of some magnitude had occurred in the world, and you were required to forge out of that disaster a few minutes of narrative, gun to your head.

On this particular Sunday, an even less appealing kind of calamity drew her to the twentieth floor. She got off the elevator. Straight ahead, grinning, surprised to see her, sat Menard Griffiths.

"Pulling a little overtime," she said, before he could ask.

He nodded. "You heard the news I'm sure. Everyone's coming back tomorrow. Some of them back now."

"Really? On the floor?" Julia kept walking.

"You bet. Whoa there. Got to look in the bag."

"You're shitting me."

"I wish I was, but, you know, all the strange doings, the whole show coming, so they want maximum security. Every bag to be checked. Hoist her up here."

This was bad luck. Menard had never checked her bags before. She had piled a late lunch and a change of clothes on top of a box of matches and a knife for cutting fuses. She had already smuggled the C-4 onto the floor, thank God, or there would have been real trouble. She might still have to answer his questions about the matches and knife, but she could handle those. The lunch attracted his interest.

"Uh-oh. What's in there?"

She didn't answer, at first. She was looking at Menard and thinking it would be better for him if he discovered her plans. It would be better for him and for her. If the worst happened, and someone got hurt by the explosion, this kind man might somehow take the blame for negligence afterward. Security guards could always be held accountable, and he had done nothing to deserve it, and she was a peace-loving woman who had long ago renounced violence as a course of political action. He picked up the lunch and gave it a disappointed sniff. "Southwestern chicken salad."

He set it aside with disdain and reached back into the bag, through the clothes, and stopped. He lifted the matches and the knife from the bag. He looked at her.

"You use these, Julia?" he asked, perplexed by the objects. "In your work?"

"I do, Menard."

He didn't care. He didn't think for a moment that she might be the problem. "Okay. Just checking."

He put the objects back in the bag. She watched with a sudden exhaustion. She wished that tomorrow would come, and the fight would be over. Menard seemed to sense her dismay. He insisted on coming around the desk and giving her a hug. Before she could say no or slip away, he'd embraced her. Squeezing her shoulders, he peered down into the bag.

"See you," she said.

"Ribs," he said. "Bring me ribs next time."

"Can't eat them."

"A nice lobster roll, then, or . . ."

He was still musing when she passed out of earshot. Back in her office, she locked the door behind her, removed the lunch and the clothes and placed the bag under her sofa, next to the box of ordnance. She took the box out, pried off the lid and had another peek. There they were, six bars wrapped in olive paper. Her idea was simple. She wanted to blow shit up. No, that wasn't it. She believed that Austen would need some help convincing the others of his story. She unwrapped one bar, and it was soft and cool to the touch, a pale creamy foot of explosive. She thought she heard a footstep outside her door. She froze. There might be other people around. Menard had said that some of the overseas staff were already back on the floor. Sally Benchborn had returned from Japan. She'd left a couple of messages on Julia's voice mail, asking about progress on file footage, but Julia hadn't returned the calls. Was Sally lurking outside the door? The moment of alarm passed. Julia wrapped the C-4 again and returned it to the box. She focused again on her plan, going over the details. To her mind, a small explosion in Gropers Lane, timed to go off during the meeting, might helpfully underscore the reality of the threat. It would be a small lie, she told herself, to bolster a larger truth. If the explosion happened to destroy those mysterious crates, so much the better. Julia knew that the crates were part of the danger. She'd seen how Evangeline Harker looked at them. She recalled very well the night when she had seen something back there in the hallway. She half expected their nemesis to be asleep in one of them. The thought gave her a chill, and she banished it from her mind, closing the lid on the box.

A rapid knock came on the door. Sally was relentless. It was Sunday, for God's sake. The knob jiggled. Julia was glad she'd locked the door. The producer would have seen the box and wanted to know the contents. Nothing was ever lost on Sally Benchborn. There came a long pause and another, less urgent knock. Whoever it was wouldn't go away. Julia slid the box back under the couch. She said, "Just a second," straightening her slacks, preparing to tell the truth about the amount of work she'd done on the Japan story, which was zilch. She unlocked the door and opened wide.

Remschneider, six feet, two hundred pounds, glared at her. His lips were slack and wet and dark. He had a knife.

Sir—Still no word from you. Fair enough. It's Sunday, and, to my surprise, the producers have begun to show on the hall. Sally Benchborn is here, bitching and moaning, carrying something in a long case, probably her precious tapes. I've heard conversations. They already guess the time has come for the old guard to resign. Doug Vass and the women will go, too. They express surface anger and profound curiosity. They vilify management and speculate on motive. They lay odds on the wording of the speech and predict job cuts and worse. The ratings will drop. The quality will decline. But maybe it's for the best, they secretly whisper. They're blind as only successful journalists can be. The big story for them, for everything they have ever been or ever will be, is right here in their midst, and yet they believe all that's at stake is a professional reorganization. This is how empires fall. So give me orders. I crave orders. In the meantime, unless I hear otherwise, I remain determined to sit in the front corner of the screening room, right beside Bob Rogers, taking notes on my laptop. Stimson

Julia punched Remschneider in the nose with her balled fist, but he bore down with his size and managed to get through the door, a blind lurching stack of flesh. She backed into a corner and flung tape at his head. When he stumbled a moment, she raked his cheeks with fingernails and tried to get around him, threw her body, missing, tumbling to the floor at his feet. The box of explosives sat at eye level beneath the couch. She fumbled for it, reaching inside, grabbing for a bar. Before she could do anything with it, Remschneider had her by the neck. He lifted her up, his hand around her throat. He moved her away from the door and shoved her against the back wall. The man reeked of every foul excretion. He'd been murdering his colleagues. His lips were moving. He was speaking, low and whispery. Ritual, she thought. He's going to cut my throat. She heard *Lubyanka, Vorkuta,* the rest of it. She struggled, pushing him back. She tried to get the knife. He tightened his grip on her throat. He was too big. She felt herself fading, the air rushing out of her lungs. He shuddered a moment, uncomprehending. His eyes went wide. The knife flew out of his hand. His grip around her throat loosened, and he fell forward, as if in an attempt to hold her down with his body. He gasped for air, saliva bursting, his mouth yawning in an abrupt rictus of surprise. He spat blood. Sally Benchborn appeared in the frame of the door, wearing the pink pashmina, cradling her authentic Civil War–era Enfield, topped by its blood-tipped bayonet.

MAY 24, LATE EVENING

Evangeline came to my door at eight, flushed with some passion. Her brow had furrowed. I had wanted to speak with her about tomorrow's meeting. I had intended to seek her counsel. But no more. She has been damaged far beyond anything I had imagined.

"I have to tell you something right now," she said. "It can't wait another minute."

She had evidently marched eighty blocks uptown. I protested she was still too weak for that kind of effort. She gave me quite the unfriendly glare. In retrospect, I see why. She may be unhinged, but she is anything but frail.

I told her we should wait for Julia Barnes, who was also invited, and I poured a medicinal Irish whiskey, which she eyed with a distinctly unpleasant humor. She downed the glass in a swallow and requested another. She refused to take off her coat.

"How is Robert?"

She shrugged, an unsettling response. Julia Barnes arrived. With her was Sally Benchborn, whom I have never known well. Something had happened, I could tell. A significant silence moved between them. I asked Julia if everything was fine, and she nodded. I gave them both an Irish whiskey.

Evangeline snapped at us. "Are we ready now?"

The women hadn't had time to take a seat. "What's going on?" Julia asked, evidently surprised to find the Harker girl in my home. Then she caught sight of my crutches and bandages. She hadn't heard. I explained briefly that I had met our enemy, and that my condition was the outcome. I promised to reveal more, but deferred to Evangeline's urgency.

I gestured at Evangeline, and she asked us to sit. She began to talk. An hour later, Julia, Sally and I were still seated, staring at the Russian icon over my fireplace. We had polished off most of the whiskey, and I rummaged about for a bottle of port. Something gentle was needed. I had experienced

the fall of an irrevocable axe. My hopes were dashed. Time would not heal
this girl. There would be no making good. Julia Barnes and Sally Benchborn
gazed at the Andrei Rublev, as if imploring it. They had expected perhaps a
discussion of tactics, not a revelation of murder and sexual violation that
exceeded their worst nightmares. I didn't believe a word of the girl's story, a
literal word, I mean, but I could guess at the unspeakable acts she must have
endured, in order to concoct such a vile fantasy.

The same thought seemed to go through the others' heads. We were
speechless. We couldn't look at her.

"You don't believe me at all, do you? Ian said that you wouldn't be worth
a damn to me."

"It's not that, dear," I began.

"I'm not dear!" she cried. "I'm this!" She tore open her shirt and revealed her naked chest and stomach. I didn't know what to say. I've never
seen anything like it. There were hundreds, thousands, of nicks and scratches
across her flesh, and they seemed to form some kind of pattern. She had been
tortured. I put my hand over my mouth and slumped in my chair.

"He did this to you—" Julia's mouth trembled in a rage. The Benchborn
woman would not look.

I glanced at the editor again and raised my hand. There would be no further use in the discussion. We had both heard her mention her dead friend as
if the two had spoken recently.

"Ian?" I asked her, hoping she would see the position she had put us in.
"You don't mean our Ian, dear?"

Things got ugly then. She paced back and forth, shouting at us about the
stupidity of trying to outwit this imagined creature, this manticore that she
had tackled firsthand in Romania. I confess a total loss. I had seen the man.
I recognized a monster. She didn't have to convince me of his horrors. But
she made no sense. On the one hand, she protested that she had become like
him, that she has murdered someone and desecrated the body. On the other,
she apparently intends to destroy him with some undisclosed act of seduction. I didn't investigate the contradictions. There were so many. In the end,
she fell on her knees on the rug at my feet and said that she would do whatever I wanted, with clear erotic connotations, if I would only listen to her. I

tried to pull her off the rug. Julia attempted a womanly intervention. But it all ended with an unfortunate row, as Evangeline stormed out of my house and into the night. I couldn't stop her, and frankly didn't want to.

She can be of no use to us, I'm afraid. It's a genuine ethical question whether I can conscionably repeat in this journal the details of what she has told us about her interaction with Torgu. If, as I've made clear, pages here are to be understood as a last will and testament, then her revelations would become a part of that body of documents. It's my judgment they should not. What she has to say belongs in the realm of the deepest confidentiality. I am sure she's falsified her account, and I hold the strongest possible intuition that what she claims to have volunteered freely as a weapon was taken by brute force. Does her fiancé know?

Julia Barnes, Sally Benchborn and I stand as the last redoubt.

BO**15**OK

A Gathering of Eagles

Forty-six

Monday morning has come, and I'm putting together the last of these notes. I don't know why, but I'm certain that they will have to be completed by someone else. If, at some future date, the story of *The Hour* is finally told, I can only hope that my jottings provide an insight into the truth. My handwriting is generally legible, but it's the least of my concerns. I want to be believed, and it will take a special sort of interpreter to avoid the pitfalls of the ostensible, the obvious, the mundane. I tell myself that such an interpreter exists, and that he or she will rescue me at some unknown future date, but I know quite well that it's irrelevant to my immediate circumstance. I have greater concerns.

I'm placing these notes on top of my bed. They cover everything from my first night in Romania to the present moment. If I have a chance, at work, I will write a quick addendum. If not, if no such chance presents itself, perhaps my eventual savior will.

After my conversation with Austen, Julia and Sally, my options became clear. One, I could simply walk away. From the moment I first arrived back in New York, my father has wanted me to leave the city. He would be happy to grubstake my move to greener pastures. I could start over, far from this mess, trusting that Torgu is no more than an outsized if repugnant criminal of no real concern to me. If this were really an option, however, I would long ago have taken it. Unfortunately, the truth of the matter lies in my blood, on my skin, beneath my conscious mind. I can't cut and run from myself, unless, of course, I

364 • JOHN MARKS

take my own life, which has occurred to me more than once as the log-ical solution, if anything about my predicament were logical. I would take my own life except that I know what awaits. The violent act would be the precursor to an eternity of blood hunger, among billions of oth-ers. Truly, if I want to become Ion Torgu's slave and servant, the quick-est way would be suicide. But I'd sooner become the mistress of his house.

And so I come to my only real choice. Despite Austen's wishes, I must go to the meeting. I don't give a damn about the fate of Bob Rogers. He should have retired years ago. Before I vanished, he barely knew that I existed. But the meeting has little or nothing to do with him. Its real purpose, unintentionally achieved, is to facilitate slaughter. I saw Torgu's eyes. He had set himself the task of slitting Austen's throat. He could practically taste the drink. But he was denied, and now he's in the mood for a feeding frenzy. Somewhere on the floor, overdue for his moment, he waits for the staff to assemble, like cattle herded into the holding pens of an abattoir. And beyond him, around him, mass the drinkers, waiting to be heard. He will come. And he will act.

I'm out the door.

Julia and Sally used their security keys to enter the building. Before dawn, before Miggison, they entered the twentieth floor and saw with relief that they had timed it right; Menard had left the desk to unlock office doors up and down the corridors. They slipped by his post and headed for the editing bays. Julia felt the dread almost as soon as they reached Gropers Lane and was glad that Sally had brought her Enfield. As it turned out, after the health guru screening incident, Sally had never once come to work without it.

They passed the vault, where the newly shot tape was kept, and Ju-lia glanced at the door with anxiety. After Remschneider's attack, they'd relocated the explosives to the top of a shelf at the far back of the vault, where no one would be liable to look for it. There had been no alterna-tive. Julia hadn't wanted to risk taking the C-4 back out of the building. She hadn't wanted to risk another encounter with Menard. The vault had been the least unsafe hiding place, but it came with significant disadvantages, foremost of which was Claude Miggison. The room wouldn't open until Miggison turned up. He had the sole key. They went to Julia's office.

Sally paused at the door, regret on her face. "I hated to do that to Fish," she said. "He won an Emmy for me. He was a good editor. A really good editor. But I'd say he crossed the line."

"You think?"

Julia put her hand on the knob. The women stared at each other. Sally raised the tip of the bayonet. "You said you wanted to see my gun," she said. "How do you like it?"

"Fucking A," Julia said. "I only wish that we'd taken Fish to an incinerator. Just to be sure."

Sally's face shivered in repulsion. It was a horrible thing to say. Julia's own words filled her with disgust. She was still a mother. She still had a heart for the poor and the homeless.

Julia inserted the key and opened her office. The body was gone. She slammed the door shut. Had someone moved the body? Had it somehow moved itself? Could he still be alive? And if so, where was he? These thoughts crackled in the air between the two women. Neither said a word. They looked at each other, peered at the closed office doors on either side. Where were the other editors? Sally walked point, and they crept back down the corridor to the vault. They chewed gum and waited for Miggison to show. Sally rested against the wall, safety catch off the Enfield.

Miggison materialized, grumpy as ever. He shot the keys out of his cuffs. He eyed the women, craning his head around Sally to absorb the fact of the gun. "Good morning, ladies," he said with a jaunty malevolence. The door to the vault swung open, and Miggison went on his way, casting one last glance at the weapon and sighing, from years of long practice. "Didn't see a thing."

Julia found the box and counted the bars of C-4. They were intact and untouched. She would have another hour or so before the floor began to fill up, before the children of Bob Rogers came for the debriefing. Sally stood guard between the juncture of Gropers Lane and the editing bay. Against the wall, in the shadows, she could see movement in either direction. Julia had told her the plan of attack, and she had no objections. She'd seen and heard enough. She hid the gun beneath her pashmina. Julia crouched just inside the entry to Gropers Lane and got down to business.

She worked from memory and a manual. She kneaded one bar of explosive until it was as thin as a rope. She kneaded a second bar and attached it to the first, making a single long loop. Two bars didn't satisfy her requirements. She kneaded a third and attached that, too. She strung the loop around the circumference of two of the crates. Three bars would be sufficient to cause a ruckus. No one would be hurt. They would all be at the meeting on the other side of the office. She could stand in a suite of adjacent offices and keep watch. If anyone turned up, she could wait until they moved on. Only then, after the meeting had begun, when the coast was clear, would she light the fuse.

When she finished making the explosive lasso, she turned to Sally. "Go on now. Take the gun. At the meeting, tell them everything. If Austen speaks out, back him up. I'll be all right."

"Sure?"

"Go."

"You be safe."

"You, too."

Sally strode away, still concealing most of the Enfield beneath her shawl. Julia was glad. Solitude enhanced her concentration. The main thing was not to forget something. Back in the day, she had been supremely focused. But that was before kids and work and life. She constantly reminded herself to pay attention. Here are the fuses; here the matches; here the box containing the rest of the explosives. Here is my purse. It wasn't so much to remember. She would watch the thing blow and then head on home. Call it her resignation speech.

The rest of the C-4 could be handed over to the NYPD to allay fears about further bombing activity. If need be, she would do it herself, confessing everything. The thought stopped her for a moment. She hadn't given that aspect much consideration. If the police held her, even for a very brief moment, until the facts became clear, she would be labeled a terrorist. Her police record would come up. She could go to prison. She fought a rush of panic. Her boys would never understand. They would not know this woman, their own mother, a bomber. Her husband, an old radical, would be horrified. But we renounced violence! he would roar. Still, she was impelled. The threat against the show gave her no choice. She repeated the formula: the threat against the show, the threat against the show. It was a lie. She wanted to kill someone. That feeling overrode everything else. Sally Benchborn had it, too. Remschneider whetted their appetites. It was time to take some more fucking life. Julia snapped off latex gloves and peered over her shoulder. She felt observed, but couldn't locate the source of the anxiety. No security cameras operated in the vicinity. There were no people. There might be another one of those zombified editors around. Remschneider might have recovered from his wound, though it seemed unlikely. She checked her watch again. The meeting would begin in two hours. She attached a fuse to one end of the explosive loop and ran the fuse behind the crates against the back wall. She wouldn't leave the material unattended. It would be too risky. Suppose someone came along and saw the stuff. Enough people on the floor knew from explosives, and then what would she say? She would have to sit for a while, let the day get under way. Like a guard, she thought, on a watchtower.

MAY 25

As if matters haven't become difficult enough, who should show up at 8 A.M., before anyone else? Bob Rogers, of course.

I had just begun to quietly sip my coffee and read the Times *when he darted through the door. He didn't sit. He just stood there, hands in his pockets, bobbing on his back heels, waiting for me to look up from my paper. I didn't want to oblige. He didn't comment on my crutches and bandages. He didn't want to know.*

"Can we speak frankly?" he asked. "About everything?"

I folded the paper. He appeared less subdued than I might have expected, under the circumstances. He wore a light blue shirt, unbuttoned at the neck, beneath a light summer jacket. He was smiling. I had seen him sulk for weeks and weeks during other, more successful battles with corporate and had anticipated a much more profound bout of this melancholy in the hours before his forced resignation. On the contrary, he seemed jubilant.

"How long have we worked together, Austen?"

Other conversations had begun this way. They were long ones. "We don't have to do this, Bob. It is what it is."

He shook his finger. "No. That's precisely the thing. It's not."

"Do tell."

"I am not too old for this job. Neither are you. That's a fiction promoted by people who want our jobs. But we both know the truth. Once we're gone, there will never be another show like this one."

He had a point, and I conceded it. "No. There never will be."

"Aren't you sad to see it go?"

"But what good will it do if I am, Bob? My sadness is my own."

"I understand. And I respect and admire you. Of the people here, you are the one whom I trust the most. You would never milk your emotions or play false with our legacy."

"I never have."

"No, you haven't."

"So?"

He came around to my side of the desk, an irritating but time-honored habit, leaned one brown hand down on the desk and said, "I've made a very important decision, and I want an assurance that you will support me in that decision."

Bob was Bob. No one could expect otherwise. If they were shoving him out the window, he had every right to be himself as he flailed through the air. "That depends. What's the decision?"

"You can probably guess, but I can't tell you, or it will look like a conspiracy. I am asking you for a blank check, Austen."

"Never wrote one in my life. Wouldn't know how."

"Horse shit."

I glanced at a clock. Before long, Bob would be standing before his people, announcing his news. There was no time to ferret out his meaning. Moreover, I needed his help. When the time came, I might need him to rally behind me. I tried to broach a difficult subject.

"Did it ever occur to you that this, this trouble we've been having, these technical problems and so on, that they might have nothing to do with the network? That we might be under attack from a completely different quarter?"

"Such as?"

He waited. It was a question that I couldn't answer, not without sounding an utter fool in his eyes.

"No, Austen. I won't be fooled again. Network would love me to believe that they are innocent. Network would love me to expend my energy chasing shadows. But I'm Bob Rogers, don't forget. I may not be the brightest kid on the block, but not so goddamn stupid either. For a year now, those pricks have been waging a war on this shop, upping the ante every time, seeing how much I could take, thinking I would throw my hands in the air and walk away. Now they think they've won. They think I'm about to surrender." His eyes were twinkling. "What sound does a dynamite stick make when it explodes up a horse's ass?"

It was no use. He believed in his struggle more than he did in the show, or himself. The struggle was everything.

"They're not getting me out of here without a fight. Okay? I plan to die on horseback." He lowered his voice. "Die with me?"

"Whatever you want, Bob."

He placed his hand on my head, bent down and kissed me on the cheek, a first.

"That's how much I think of you, Austen Trotta," he said, and he rushed out the door.

"Evangeline!" someone cried.

I strode into the screening room, past the astonished faces of correspondents, producers, camera crews, and production associates. Applause went up. "Check out the hair!" someone shouted with genuine enthusiasm. I thought fondly of Ian. I went to my usual spot in a comfortable chair close to the giant video monitor and waited while a startled Skipper Blant jumped out of his seat. He wrestled with the thought of human contact. I scared him a little. He threw his arms around me. The others gathered, too, and not just the living ones. The gray sea flowed into the room like a tide, though no one else saw. "What a great omen!" Skipper blurted out, betraying his anxieties. I seemed to see him for the first time. He was not a bully and a sadist, as I'd thought back when he'd treated Ian so poorly. At least, he wasn't only those things. In his red-rimmed eyes, I saw stark self-loathing. I saw a refugee from terrors rivaling Torgu.

"You shouldn't be here," Sally Benchborn whispered into my ear, as if my condition were delicate. I signaled that we would talk at the earliest possible opportunity. God knew what Julia or Austen would say to me. I searched for them in the crowd. Where could they possibly be? The moment drew near. As Sally slipped away, I glimpsed the butt of a rifle jutting out the back of her pashmina.

Sam Dambles, ever courtly, came over and offered condolences for my travails and asked me to come by his office and chat. The men and women of The Hour lined up like wedding guests. They hugged and kissed me and asked about Robert. They complimented my looks. Everyone wanted to take me to lunch.

I saw Stimson. His lip was swollen, his mouth shut. He had a computer in his lap, and he stared down at the keys of his laptop, avoiding my gaze. He hadn't taken my advice. He hadn't run. I looked around and counted people. Most of the staff, minus the editors, had come. How many of the people in the room belonged to Torgu? As if reading my mind, a producer called out, "What is Remschneider on? Did anyone else see him this morning?"

Bob Rogers entered the room, and a cheer went up. The screening room grew close with so many people. I smelled the steam rising from sausages, the aroma of cold, boiled shrimp. Someone popped a champagne cork. The heat of the day pressed down upon the walls of the building, but the twentieth floor stayed cool. The vents pulsed with presence. The gray voices crashed and thundered, calling for Torgu. Rogers raised his hands to silence the crowd. He had something to say.

Sir—I transcribe verbatim. The meeting begins right on time. Bob Rogers says the following. "You guys are terrific. You've made me what I am today, so it's me who should be applauding. Here's to you." He claps. Applause follows from the crowd, which I will describe as the truly eclectic face of the show, the best face, a collection of veterans and newcomers, men and women, black and white, but beyond that, a wonder cabinet of disparate personalities gathered over the decades by Rogers to bring him his weekly show, cameramen who'd shot with Trotta and Dambles in Vietnam, editors who'd cut pieces fresh off rioting streets, women who had broken the sex barriers in international reporting, heiresses and radicals, gourmets and sex addicts, nervous wrecks, alcoholics and cowboys, a collection of real human life in all its glorious vanity, the elect of the broadcast news profession, given the chance to globe-trot to find the great, weird, burning news stories of the day, who had bribed and fucked and lied and nearly died in the effort to bring to Bob Rogers his feast of breaking craziness, his beloved images. But I'm getting away from myself. Rogers says, "Quickly now. I've made an important decision. I'm not asking you to support me, and I won't be disappointed if you don't. I'm not a child." You can hear the proverbial pin drop. In that moment of silence, I can hear you. I can hear your song. It's coming, as you promised. But there is another tension in the air, too. "So here it is." He claps his hands once. "Fuck these bastards, I ain't leavin'!" A gasp of astonishment before a wild cry of approval goes up. "I created this show, with your help. I dragged it through three decades, with your help. And they ain't gettin' it out of my hands unless those hands are ice fucking cold!" People are yelling. He is lifted off his feet. "I'm with you, Bob!" shouts Sam Dambles. "Up the Revolution!" Skipper Blant leaps up. "Mutiny!" cries Nina Vargtimmen, in her miniskirt and high heels, and gives Bob a big smack on his lips, and everyone sings "For He's a Jolly Good Fellow," and it seems to me a new golden age is dawning for all of us who care about *The Hour*. I hear a high fine note of glorious possibility: no more pandering to the lower intelligences, the more vulgar angels of our being, no more stories about celebrities who have made three decent movies, no more shit-eating from shareholders, the unspoken villains in our tragedy, the despicable shareholders who have only ever encouraged us to debase ourselves. And in this moment of joy, I am one of their number. The past is erased. I have not tasted blood. I am weeping, sir, with happiness. Suddenly, I catch a concerned expression on Rogers's face. He asks to be put down. He points at Sally Benchborn. "What's with the gun, sweetheart?" She isn't feeling my bliss. She isn't happy or clapping. Good God. Rogers is right. She's holding a rifle fixed with a bayonet, and she says, "Why don't you cut the crap and tell us what's really going on, Bob?" At that moment, the door to the screening room slams open, and there's a shriek. Austen Trotta staggers in, covered head to toe in blood.

Austen staggered over to me, his body pierced with wounds. "Evangeline," he said. His eyes implored me. He fell against my body, all but finished.

A hush fell over the room, of the same kind, but far more terrifying, as the hush that always follows the screening of a terrible piece of broadcast journalism. Normally, in that very room, such a hush would be followed by the sound of Bob Rogers's voice, saying, "This piece of crap will never air on my show." But Rogers was speechless, too. In his eyes, thoughts worked themselves out. He seemed to be putting together an idea. Austen and I stood in the middle of the room, where he had been. People began to murmur to each other.

"Tell us, Bob!" Sally cried out again. She stepped forward from the mass of people standing, leaning or sitting at the four walls. "Or don't you know?"

"He doesn't," I said. Everyone looked at me now. "He doesn't know anything."

"Listen to her," Austen said in a weakening voice. "For God's sake, there isn't much time."

As soon as he spoke, a change came over the room, as if more people had entered. They had, in fact. There were two doors into the screening room, leading from two separate corridors, and through these doors came a line of ashen gray editors, led by Remschneider, who looked deceased. They pushed through the assembled crowd to the center of the room and stood in a cluster, eyes on the carpet. At the end of the last line, completely naked, gray-bearded and mumbling, was Edward Prince.

"What the fuck?" someone said. "Is that Ed?"

Sally fired her gun in the air. Plaster burst from the ceiling, the smell of gunpowder spreading with the smoke. Panic entered the room, a tautening of every muscle in every body in that space. "People!" she cried. "We're under attack! Ask Evangeline! She knows! She's the only one who really knows!" Our colleagues looked at Sally; they looked at me. Trotta leaned forward, his face haggard. "Torgu is out there," he said, more to me than anyone else. "Forgive me. I should have listened."

He put his hand on my shoulder, and I had a moment of professional and personal sadness, a peculiar grief that I had never felt before. I was losing my correspondent.

"Sally Benchborn is right," Austen called out in that failing, beloved voice, known to me since childhood, a friendly spirit arisen from the television set in my parents' den, long ago.

He collapsed in my arms. It's amazing what such a sight, the savaged body of a well-known man, will do to people. At that moment, in the screening room, the balance of things shifted in my favor, and I felt a first breath of what might be called courage in my lungs. The staff of The Hour, lovely, impossible, vain people, grew quiet with understanding. It had been coming for months. Now it was here, the object of their hidden terrors, the source of their bad dreams. They could see it. Or so I supposed for an instant. But they couldn't help themselves. Their instincts outweighed their reason. I was still just an associate producer making less than six figures a year. They turned to Bob once again, as if he could help them.

"Austen?" Rogers alone seemed to grasp his own ignorance. "What is this—?" He looked at me, beseeching, as if I could revive him. Everyone

374 • JOHN MARKS

In the screening room looked at Bob. "Is this what the hell I think it is?
They've finally done what I always suspected they would."

Austen was faltering and couldn't speak. I didn't know what Rogers
was talking about. Neither did anyone else. But Rogers did. He came to
Austen, who measured his breaths one at a time and seemed grateful
for them.

Bob turned to the rest of us. He seemed to be discovering the truth
as he uttered it. "They did this."

"They?" I looked at the lines of semi-comatose editors. I looked at
Edward Prince.

"The goddamn suits."

Austen groaned out of his stupor. "Oh Christ, no, Bob, you're missing it—"

"They're going to take us all out."

For one instant, I think, a few believed. Most were too good at their
jobs. One look at their colleagues, at Prince, and they knew that we
were way beyond office politics. And the dead, whom none consulted,
knew everything. On all sides of me, their presences had grown, and
the lines between things diminished, just as Ian had predicted. Maybe it
was the haze of gunpowder from Sally's gun. Maybe it was my imagination. But the four walls of the screening room, beyond the minions
of Bob Rogers, dimmed before my eyes, as if they had been nothing
more than fogbanks. The spaces beyond those walls began to recess
into infinite distances. We might have been perched on the edge of a
battle plain where the nations had massed. I saw Clementine Spence.
She stood in an encampment, one shadow upon a million, a molecule
in a cloud, but visible to me. The voices of the nations boomed. The
memory of the race arose. The dead sang. They raised their arms like
shields in defiance and supplication. They had come for Torgu, for me,
for all of us. They were hungry. They sorrowed. I became hungry. I sorrowed. They watched me with their pale faces. I began to see. They
wanted something, in particular, from me. They knew what I hungered
for. They knew about the bucket and the knife. They knew about my
body, too; they knew I had the marks of power.

No one else saw. The staff of *The Hour* watched Bob Rogers. Buddy

Gomez, who always brought his camera along, hoisted his camera onto a shoulder. "Fuck it," he said. "My job is to shoot pictures. No way I'm not getting this."

"Bullshit!" Sally Benchborn cried. "You put that thing down until we get this straightened out or I'll run you through."

"I'd like to see you try, bitch!"

She threw a flap of the pashmina over her shoulder and drew down on the camera man. "Give me a reason, *pendejo*."

Stimson Beevers jumped between them. Sally cocked the rifle. Stim was smiling.

"Wake up, you two! Wake up, everyone!" His voice held the exuberance of a revival preacher. No one there had ever seen him so animated. "You're all about to die, and there's nothing to be done about it."

"You're part of this, you little mall rat?" Sally poked him with the bayonet.

"You don't understand. It's beautiful. It's knowledge. It's wisdom. You're about to be *inducted*. I was afraid, too. I doubted. But I've come to my senses. And now he's here." Stim paused, raising a hand, gesturing at one of the entrances to the screening room. "And it's going to be fine!"

Torgu came. Enraged, brutish, he stomped out of the darkness, his head immense, his long knife an ax, clanking in its bucket. He stepped into our midst, and the struts in the walls shook. Bob Rogers saw only one enemy, a demon from the pit of the broadcast center on Hudson Street. His mouth twisted into a snarl. He pointed a finger.

"Network!" he cried.

Stim laughed. Sally Benchborn lowered her bayonet. The others made a scrum behind her. I sank to my knees with Austen. The dead hordes sang their coming triumph. Stimson Beevers stepped in front of Sally Benchborn's bayonet, still amused. Did he mean to defend Torgu? She rammed the bayonet into his gut. There was a moment of still shock. Sally let go of the weapon, and Stim shambled back from her, amazed. Torgu went to him with a calm majesty, a great and merciful king of the dead. The bucket clanked. The king's arm rose high over his head, the blade of the knife spun down, catching Stim between shoulder and neck, carrying away his balding head, hurling it into the tumult of the blood-starved. Torgu flung away the knife, took Stim's body by its shoulders and put his mouth where the head had been. The dead finally came to life, their song bursting forward like a full cathedral choir. The editors raised their heads and beheld their colleagues. Edward Prince cackled.

Beside me, Austen's eyes fluttered open.

"Do it," he whispered to me.

"I can't."

"Show yourself."

Close by, Torgu heard us. He allowed Stim's torso to drop, a horrid final lapse of the affiliation between master and slave. Human juice ran down his chin. He saw me, and his eyes grew round with an emotion of great ferocity. He knew my secret. He knew the dead had fallen in love with me, that they had turned on him. Around us, the living registered the overwhelming force of a malign power and succumbed, dropping, one by one, to their knees. I could see the Civil War dead devouring Sally Benchborn's mind with exquisite relish, her pashmina shawl fluttering like the flag of a routed army. She fell on her own bayonet. Sam Dambles participated in his own lynching. His legs shook at the end of a rope, his hands fixed the noose. Nina Vargtimmen burned witches and screeched in Salem drag in the flames. Skipper Blant sat on the floor, calm and cold as a Buddha, and pulled out his own fingernails, never once uttering a scream. The rest were lost, too, each in a private miasma of death.

Torgu no longer cared about them. He approached me with his desolate gaze, but his will had weakened. He issued no command. On the contrary, he sought something from me. He was speaking. The truth unfolded without a word between us. These people, my colleagues, weren't for him. They were gifts. He was giving them to me. I nodded. He nodded. The exchange sent a ripple of pleasure through the massed armies of the dead. Torgu wanted to give me his burden. But he couldn't do it willingly. It would have to be taken from him.

I left Austen on the ground and stood. Torgu took my hand. There was a moment of true and pure connection. The walls rumbled, the floor heaved, a wave of power shocked through me, knocking me to the ground.

Julia Barnes had lit the eighth fuse of the morning. She had watched it flare and fizzle away. The Flerkis nephew had sold her a box of lemons. And if the fuses were bad, the explosive would be, too. What a fool. Years ago, she would never have made such a mistake. She returned to the crate, poked a finger at the lasso of C-4 wound around the two crates. She took out the last two fuses. Might as well, she thought. No one could accuse her of quitting. Afterward, though, that's exactly what she would do. She'd quit. Why had it taken so long to wise up? She would leave the show for good. Ten years at the place, and here she was, lighting fuses. The job had gone sour. *The Hour* had met its maker. Three and a half decades was as long as anyone got in the media business. It was over.

She attached two fuses to the C-4, ran them back across the carpet to her spot in the suites across the hall. She didn't care anymore about results. She was already thinking about picking up steaks for her boys. The things wouldn't light. She poked the side of the matchbox, took out two sticks, struck them on her zipper and lowered them to the fuses. Both flared, one died. The other hissed on its way. How about that? She watched with surprised pride as the sparks snaked out of her room, around the corner of the door, across the carpet toward the crates. There was movement among the crates. Oh Christ, there was someone in there.

"Get the hell out!" she cried. "It's a bomb!"

Instinctively, she grabbed her purse. She located the container for the fuses, reached for the box holding the other bars of C-4. It was nowhere to be found. She scoured the carpet on every side of her body, as if hunting for a contact lens that had popped out of her eye. "Oh crap," she heard herself say. The other bars sat in the box beside the crate, where she'd left them by accident. Her teenage sons would roll their eyes. Typical mom. At the last second, she rolled herself in a ball.

She prayed for the safety, happiness and health of her loved ones. The explosion enveloped her like a holy visitation, a final bright gasp of the glory of her youth.

After a moment of silence, people cried out, shocked from their torments. I lay face to face with Torgu, who had fallen, too. He had lost his focus. A terror played across his mind, and it wasn't fear of me. I could see in his eyes his panic at the prospect of an unexpected betrayal.

He hissed through the darkness like a surprised cat. "Evangeline!"

He leaped off the floor and darted away, leaving me in the wreckage of his vast mess, in the aftermath. Austen groaned. In the dimness, the dead blinked their lost eyes. They waited and watched. They knew my intention, and in their hearts, impatience grew. I would follow and finish Torgu, but first came responsibilities to my colleagues. The smell of cordite rode the halls. The force of an explosion had taken down the far wall of the screening room, and the carpet burned. Smoke filled the halls. People hacked their lungs out. They crawled along the carpets, scrambling away from the fires. On the intact side of the room, the load-bearing structures remained intact, and people were calling out, gathering their collective will to evacuate. Austen would not go far. The pain was too great. He'd lost too much blood. He asked to be taken back to his office. I hoisted the old man in my arms and carried his form back to the correspondent suites, where the nude body of Edward Prince lay in mournful coolness across the desk of his assistant. He'd made his way as far as his office, and no farther. On his face, I saw a lasting peace. I lay Austen on his couch and fetched his diary. With papers from his desk, I wiped blood off his face, and I left him there, dear old fellow, and returned to the carnage in the screening room.

Postscript

Evangeline Harker, before she went about her business, was good enough to locate this document, allowing me to complete the last critical entry before my strength gives way. It must be a disclaimer. As a safety precaution, I am going to place it in the vault beneath my desk. Should any harm come to me or this office, it will stand as a record of my suspicions and no more. Let me be clear about that. Appearances to the contrary, I continue to maintain we're dealing with a terrorist with access to biological and chemical weapons. He is also good with a knife, which suggests some military training or perhaps natural ability. They say Chechens are especially handy with blades, so maybe he is one of them. Everything else is an act of psychological warfare conducted by a very sophisticated enemy. For a moment, he managed to gull me, but I am clear-eyed at the end. Semper fidelis, Austen Trotta, May 24

Sam Dambles, freed from his persecutors, helped people off the floor, urging them to leave the building. Most were paralyzed with fear, unable to get off the ground. I made my way past them, and they watched my movement in a mixture of bereavement, horror and disbelief. I found Torgu's knife and bucket, not far from the crumpled body of Sally Benchborn, still impaled on her bayonet. I closed her eyes and went about my work. It was a sign of Torgu's disarray that he'd left the objects. I claimed them for my own and followed the trail. I knew where Torgu would be. He had one last place to flee. The corridors of the twentieth floor popped with flame. The sprinklers kicked in, too late. The lights had shorted out. The smoke thickened, searing my lungs, doubling me over. I went on. The elevators were useless, their systems shut down. Windows had been smashed by the explosion. Air flooded in, stoking the heat. The fire would burn fast. There would be little time to escape. Who had done this? Had we, Torgu and I, when we clasped hands? I didn't believe it.

I found Torgu on the brink of Gropers Lane, sobbing, waiting for me, at the place where his crates had been.

"You did not do this," he said.

"No."

"Another woman," he said.

"Julia Barnes."

"She was a fool. She blew up my precious things."

"She stopped you."

He shook his head, glancing over at me, grinning. "But not you."

"She blew up your things," I said, "but why so much damage? I don't understand."

He shrugged, wiping his eyes. "If you place dynamite beneath the living dead, you must expect the worst."

I saw. His things were not merely objects. They had been vessels. The gray hordes had lived in those vessels, in his stones, shards, pipes, the graveyard remains, but they could never go back, they could never renew their vows to Torgu. Julia had seen to that. The C-4 had ignited their energies. The destruction of the twentieth floor had been centuries in the making. Torgu mourned. No trace of conquest remained. He stared at me in longing, chin dripping with Stim's blood. He made his noises, as if they still had power to seduce. He spoke the names: *Vorkuta, Treblinka, Gomorrah.* His lips murmured, but the words no longer echoed. With one hand, I held the bucket, knife clanking within. With the other, I took him by the lapels of his jacket and drew him down the flaming hall. My muscles had grown. My hips were strong. My veins ran hot. I was the fire itself. He would go down in my heat, as he desired. I required a space of sufficient intimacy to conduct the rite of elimination. I led him, and the dead followed. There was no need to insist. I moved down the corridor, removing my clothing with every step. I kicked off a shoe, I peeled off what was left of my pants. The fire wouldn't touch me. I burned brighter. I was protected. Here and there, the ceiling sprinklers cooled me. He beheld the glistening engine of his destruction, and he whimpered, but there was no reason for gloom. I watched with pity as he came along, afraid, an old ghoul of the earth mortified and redeemed by the unendurable spectacle of the human flesh. He whimpered at the perfect design of it, at the membranous pink truth. The knife clanked in its bucket.

We stood in the hallway beside my office. I didn't know what would happen when he died, when his privilege became mine. I didn't know if it would be painful or sweet, but I knew this spot on the earth would never be clean of sorrow. No spot ever is. His greatest secret, now mine, was evident. There is only one list. The names spoken by the dead are the names of every place on earth. There were no towns, no cities, no hollows or hills, where the race had not left its slaughtered ghosts. My knowledge, once gained, would never leave me. I would not ascend to heaven. There would be no host of angels. Clementine had called Torgu the Ab, the Absence of God, but I could do nothing with that notion. It didn't help me. God had not helped me. My goal was the darkness.

Should I dance again for him? It had been nearly impossible to perform the last time, when I was desperate with fear and didn't grasp for sure its effect, when every move meant the difference between life and death. This time, I would be sure and soft; mine would be the work of an unruffled mistress. I would be easy. I would coax him until he crawled into the enclosure of my office, which would be his tomb. The door was gone. The blast had blown out my windows, and the wind thrashed surfaces. My dead cactii had flown into the void, along with the Kate Spade bag. The fire vaulted high in the empty spaces made visible by collapsed walls and floors. The conflagration would take everything. We would all die. Out the window, I saw the glints of offices on the far side of the hole. Time had passed outside. Night had come. I heard the sirens blaring up the island. They were coming for us, as they had before.

At my feet was Torgu. I stood there a long time, allowing him to regard my body with his eyes, to count the symbols on the rim of my waist, inside my thigh, this new skin he'd given me, the written account of terror on my body. The tears rolled down his face. He bubbled with desire. But I wouldn't dance for him. I decided then and there. It was his turn to go naked. I put down the bucket and knife.

His clothes had caught fire. I tore them away from his body, and it was like ripping away flaps of human skin. He howled in stunned humiliation. This was his reward? But he knew what I had in mind, and he tried to crawl away, a ludicrous failure. I pulled away the last stitch of fabric, and I saw one more horrific secret of this creature's existence. Physically, he resembled nothing more than the compacted, violated, sum total of his collection of destroyed objects, his shoulders chunks of scorched masonry, his ribs a stack of painted, smashed cradles, his legs pipes, his skin layer upon layer of inscription and symbol, a host of linguistic paramecia tattooed into his flesh. He gasped. He sat before me, like me. One day, I thought, this will be me.

The dead waited. For a while, I didn't move. He reached for me, licking, writhing, trying to bring me down to his mouth. But I backed away and picked up the bucket and knife. The moment of transformation had come. I felt a religious awe. I could see back through time in ways unimaginable, our history a rocking ocean of blood, the ocean burning like the building.

I knelt in front of Torgu, gazing at him, putting the bucket down. I placed a hand on his shoulder to comfort him, and I whispered the truth, "This is an act of mercy."

Beyond Torgu, I watched the lights of Manhattan snuff out, the blackout come down at last, and I lifted the knife out of the bucket, feeling its cruelty. He had wanted to see me raise my arms over my head, lift my long dark curls of hair, snake my hips until I could smell the creature's obliteration smoking out of his own pores. This is how Torgu had envisioned his own demise, and the loss of this dream was insupportable. Tears flowed off the wretched face and down the scars of the body. If he'd known my intention, he would have killed me.

I take one of his ears in my fist and point the knife at his throat. We are close now, like lovers. He is very old. I am very young. Hisses of gratitude merge with the noise of sirens, the din of explosion. The flesh of his limbs has sunk to the bone. The dead have lost patience. They are poised to fly from him to me. My hand is trembling, and in that instant of indecision, he sees, and I see what is in his mind. And I comprehend my true desire. I am lured by the gray hordes. They're my future home and husband. I want to know everything about them. I want that power inside me. But I want other things, too. I want a life that was stolen. I want what is truly and only mine.

I drop the knife. I take Torgu's defaced monument of a head in my hands, and I kiss him as hard as I can. I pour my saliva into that maw, a form of kiss that no one else will ever understand. At the last, before the final trace of his horrid lips hushes into dust, as my kiss subsides into tremor, and my hands become empty, I hear a whisper of names, the names of the places of the dead flitting like butterflies, ascending to a heaven of smoke and dream. Before they abandon us, before Torgu departs utterly from this world, as a parting gift, I crouch over flame, naked as the very first girl, lay my hand flat and let the flesh burn a farewell on the monstrous historian's funeral pyre.

"Adios," I say to him, to all of them.

But he, and they, have gone. And I am left alone with the memory of Clementine Spence.

Mea Culpa, Post Mortem

A last word remains necessary. Throughout this document I have attempted to stay true to the extant source
materials, but the final hours in the existence of the
broadcast presented a terrible challenge to my efforts. What we know for certain is this: fifty-four
people perished in the blaze on West Street, among them
some of the most famous names in the history of television news, including Austen Trotta, Edward Prince,
Skipper Blant, Nina Vargtimmen and Bob Rogers. Sam
Dambles alone survived, though horribly burned and
unwilling, to this day, to speak of these matters. Various producers and editors also met their end, as well
as numerous support staff. Another number, greater
than the count of the dead, are simply missing, chief
among them Evangeline Harker. The coroner's report
bears me out: No trace of this remarkable young woman
has ever been found.

However, I would be lying if I said that my version of
the last moments of *The Hour* represents a mere act of the
imagination. Before committing these final thoughts to
paper, I spent a sleepless night standing on my back
porch in Connecticut, absorbing the noise of crickets,

observing the stars, listening to the heartbeats of my wife and children through the narrow walls of their bodies. In that darkness, Evangeline Harker came to me and revealed herself—whether because our bond has endured beyond loss and disaster, or because of my own affected state of mind, I do not know. Whatever the case, her testimony in this memorandum should be viewed as the transcription of a final conversation. Any failings there may be in rendering this account are entirely mine. The medium is imperfect, the message faint, and I follow the whispers into the shadows.

Acknowledgments

For his great enthusiasm, friendship, assistance and support, thanks to my editor Scott Moyers and to Ann Godoff for backing him up. Thanks as well to Laura Stickney for her invaluable help. Also, many thanks to Jason Arthur for his contributions. From the very first pages, Joe Regal believed in this strange book, and I will be eternally grateful to him, and to everyone at Regal Literary—in particular, Lauren Pearson and Bess Reed, who gave me good, tough, much needed advice. Thanks to Rich Green as well, and to Jonny Geller. As always, endless gratitude to Debra and Joe for putting up with me as I fought the vampire, to Debra for her love, laughter, advice and book smarts, to Joe for his high spirits and hugs and kisses. I owe a profound debt to my friend James Hynes, the unsung master of the modern horror novel. Without the guiding light of his masterpieces, *The Lecturer's Tale* and *The Kings of Infinite Space*, I doubt that I would have had the nerve to write this book. I owe Jeff Cooperman for his persistent advice about the broadcast business—and for getting me to take a big step. Finally, a special debt of thanks to the folks at Don Hewitt's 60 *Minutes*, or as I like to think of it, the CBS News Writer in Residence Program. It was my privilege to be a part of that now vanished place, and I never in my life worked with a finer, crazier, funnier, meaner bunch of people.